BOUND BY SCARS & SECRETS

REALMS OF MAGIC BOOK 1

SIENNA ARCHER

MYSTIC COVE
PRESS

Cover design by Seventhstar Art

ISBNs: 978-1-961598-01-0 (paperback), 978-1-961598-02-7 (hardcover), 978-1-961598-00-3 (ebook)

For my sisters by birth and ring.
I would go anywhere for you.

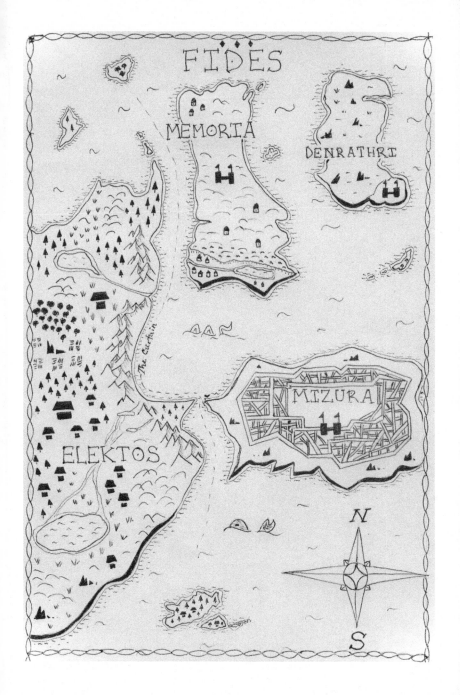

A NOTE TO THE READER

Dear reader,

Please note this coming-of-age story includes violence, themes of abandonment, and very brief mentions of self-harm and torture (neither on the page), as well as family member death.

It also includes adventure, romance, magic, and plenty of heart, so I very much hope you enjoy reading this book as much as I enjoyed writing it!

All my best,

Sienna

CHAPTER 1

I scrape my finger through the groove of the newly carved letter. The curved crook makes almost a whole truth carved without a single misplaced strike.

If she saw these perfect letters, Mama would kiss my forehead and whisper, *Alathea, my sweet truth-lover.*

Unlike Mama, Mother wouldn't care.

Outside the village's assembly house where I carve, a summer afternoon storm rumbles. Our fields of precious wheat will welcome the rain, and the dark forest will drip with pine.

Perhaps my mothers will find shelter, wherever they hide.

Beyond the fields and forest and cowardly mothers, I have no inkling how our enemies across the Scorched Mountains will receive the storm.

Likely they swallow the raindrops to cool the destructive magic in their veins.

Trembling, I align my chisel's bevel on the stone.

Ten more letters, and this one-hundred-and-seventh truth of Elektos, my most perfect carving yet, will be complete. *Thou shall not speak of our enemies, nor of their magic, nor of monsters long vanquished.*

Tap-tap-tap.

Today, I have no time to consider Elektos's enemies, nor where my mothers hide.

Today, there is a truth-hater sneaking this very hallway, determined to land us both in chains.

A door shushes and the truth-hater herself crouches at my side, breeches coated in a fine layer of dust. No more than twelve, dark hair tied with a yellow string, Tenion could almost pass for my younger sister four years ago. In the few days since she's been assigned to help me carve, Tenion has parroted more than one of my sister's treasonous claims.

The girl replaces the smallest chisel she stole from my tools. "The key wasn't in that room, either."

Treasonous claims, and too much nonsense.

"I already told you"—at least ten times this morning—"the Sancta holds all the keys."

"Then help me." The girl shifts her attention to the far end of the gray hallway, to where the leader of Elektos resides. "Soli said the Sancta favors you."

Of course my sister would say that, despite what the Sancta does for us. Without the extra food she's awarded us, we would have starved since our mothers left. "The Sancta favors me because I believe the truths she gifts me to carve."

"It won't matter what you believe, if the rumors are true," Tenion says.

But I only shake my head, even as the chisel wobbles in my hand. For days, rumors have flown from tongue to tongue even in the assembly house that monsters with claws and massive jaws are circling Elektos.

From the window, a chill breeze spears and thunder rolls.

"Can't you feel it?" Tenion says. "Across the mountains—the magic is shifting."

My mallet hits my chisel at a wrong angle, a missing sliver in the stone where it shouldn't be. I stare at that mark. At the wrongness of it.

"I think we feel the shift, because the magic is in trouble," Tenion whispers. "They might need our help."

And beneath my stone-dusted blouse, in that hollow in my chest, a buzz flares to life.

Hard and writhing and destructive.

Tenion whispers, "You *do* feel it, don't you?"

I meet her gaze, and I shove the buzz back into a notch in my chest. "Our enemies across the mountain deserve death, not our help."

"They aren't our enemies. If we can find a way across, we can help, too. Then we might have a chance of dreaming again. Can you imagine, friend? We might have *hope*."

"You're mistaken." I strike my mallet to the chisel, hard. No one dreams in Elektos. "I don't have any friends."

And what use is hope?

Down the hallway, a door creaks open. A man with sharp cheekbones and winter-white hair frowns our way. He wears wool the color of clay and black leather boots. I don't need to glance at the rope at his waist to know what he carries. Chains, a knife, a metal baton.

All the watchmen carry the same.

Tenion hands me a medium-sized chisel that I don't need, her focus suddenly on the limestone, as if she's finally about to assist me like she was assigned here to do.

The door thuds shut, the watchman gone, and Tenion picks up a chisel again, scurrying to a new door. "I have to keep looking. Mama said the key was here."

From a hollow deep in my chest, an old echo of a scream and a sob rise, propelling me to my feet and after Tenion. I dig my fingers into her blouse and tug her back toward the new carving, but she shrugs me off, as slippery as a pine marten.

"You need to be *quiet*," I say. "Stay out of sight, and don't let anyone notice you. That's what you *have* to do. You—"

"Girls." A watchman's voice booms from the end of the hallway, in front of the Sancta's door. "What's this?"

With a jolt, the buzz escapes from my chest. It gathers in my limbs, whirling like a collection of autumn leaves, a faint whiff of wood smoke.

A woman with three blue stars stitched on her sleeve steps from behind the watchman. "I am certain our head truth-carver would not be engaged in improper behavior."

The smoldering buzz in me shatters into dust.

The Sancta marches for us. Her clay-dyed wool is starched stiff, the stitches fine and fitted to her broad, tall frame. She halts two steps from us, the watchman at her back. Shadowed green eyes examine me from a square face, silver hair flat on the crown of her head. "Answer the watchman, carver. What is happening here?"

I glance at Tenion, willing her to keep quiet, to not say a single word. *Quiet, quiet, quiet.*

But Tenion lifts her chin in a gesture I know well. Just like my sister. The girl opens her mouth—

"She was speaking lies," I say, pulse racing.

Before Tenion can even argue, the Sancta nods, and the watchman drags her to the stairs. I strain for the sound of a door —a creak of metal will mean she's gone to the cages beneath the assembly house. A clap of wood will mean she's bound for the wagon that circles Elektos lane by lane, searching for truth-breakers.

Wood slaps, and I push my boots to the floor to keep from jumping.

The Sancta watches me, green eyes bright. "You are right to protect what you hold dear, Alathea." Striding to my unfinished carving, she wipes a finger across the two stray lines. "Even a rock can crumble, if struck in the wrong place."

I pin my gaze to the chipped stone, to how close I just came to being dragged to that wagon myself and abandoning my sister to a life alone. "I understand."

"Good. Then I will have an extra food box sent to your door tonight. Ensure you and your sister are both there to receive it," the Sancta says. "See that this doesn't happen again."

As she marches away, I change out my heaviest chisel for the smallest one, the one Tenion dropped as she was dragged away, her key unfound. I raise the bevel to the wall, the gray of my blouse blending in once more with the stone.

Precise, confident, quick, I *tap* and *tap* and *tap*, until that flare of a buzz in my veins is no more than a false memory, and there is not a single scratch out of place on my newest truth.

CHAPTER 2

*R*ain has transformed the lanes between the cramped log homes of Elektos to mud by the time I depart the assembly house. Ducking beneath mold-coated overhangs to avoid the downpour, a few other villagers scurry to their homes. As usual, no one notices as I slide toward mine from shadowed corner to rain barrel to a berry bush picked dry. In summer, even the hoarder squirrels gorge while they can.

Far above, a flock of wide-winged birds caws, a V heading west to the forests that cloak Elektos all the way to the sea. As swift as winter wrens, they must be night-raptors migrating earlier than usual. The storm nearly swallows their cries, but a second V soars behind them, faster and larger, gray wisps trailing in their wake. The thrum of massive wings beats even through the rain.

The magic is shifting.

I shiver and creep from the corner of a log home. Obviously, the girl is wrong. The only thing shifting is this storm, now nearly as thick as a curtain.

Today, I should head straight home. No doubt my sister is lost in her own world, forgetting to strike the hearth's flame yet again. If it wasn't for me, I'm not certain that she'd eat at all.

There is no reason for me to go anywhere but straight home. No reason to check the dark, abandoned home across the lane.

And yet...

A flicker of movement catches my eye and drags my attention across the mud. I stretch again for that movement, for any sign of red hair, for the sweep of a well-fitted cloak.

What if she's returned?

Heart thundering with the storm, I splash across the lane and duck into the doorframe. Quick, unseen, I extract a sliver of a chisel from the leather pouch at my waist and press it into the door's lock as I've done one hundred and fifty-seven times before.

Click.

I crack the wooden door open, peering into the dark—

"I knew you stole from the assembly house."

I whirl to find my sister smirking under the home's overhang.

Hair unbound, Soli's amber eyes and warm beige skin are the only feature we share. Where my hair runs black and wavy, hers is the brown-blond of fresh-cut wood. Even without the scars across the warm beige of her collarbone and cheek, her muscled frame shouts *fighter.*

For once, at least, she's wearing a gray cloak, blending in nearly as much as I do.

"I didn't steal." I shut the door and re-lock it, tucking the borrowed chisel into my pouch. I'll store the tool under my pillow at home, no one the wiser. "It needs sharpening."

"In that door?" Soli folds her arms. "You could use your talents for a cause that actually helps our people, dearest sister."

I ignore the first part. "I can't be the dearest if I'm your only sister."

"That is exactly why you're the dearest—my dearest storm cloud of a sister."

7

Despite myself, my lips curl upward. "You know I only love you some of the time."

Fast as a sunbreak, Soli plants a kiss on my cheek, smiling, too. "I know." She nods at the abandoned home. "Does that mean you're going to tell me who you hope to see, when you sneak in this door?"

Into the mud I trip, away from my nosy sister and toward our home. "No one."

"You haven't gotten any better at lying." Soli splashes after me. "What girl or boy lives there?"

"No one." Faster, I head for the next rain-veiled home.

"Protesting *and* lying. Alathea, have you been hiding a lover?"

I shake a finger at her. "You're too young to know about lovers."

"Sixteen is barely younger than you. I never imagined *you'd* be one to break that rule."

Truth Sixteen. When you desire a match, the Sancta will gift you one.

"I haven't. I didn't. I don't desire a match. Not yet." I stomp the mud hard to resist glancing back at that abandoned home. "I swear. There is no one."

"I wonder if our mothers ever said the same, before they were matched."

I swallow past a sudden rock in my throat. "We should add it to the list."

"On it goes, right after 'everything.'"

Everything. Over the years, our list of questions for our mothers has grown long, starting with: *Why did they abandon us?*

A heavy creak cuts through the patter of rain. Before us, a set of oxen heaves into the lane. Behind the beasts, two watchmen ride the open bench of a hide-covered wagon.

"Abomination." Soli spits into the mud. "If I had magic, I would destroy every one of the death wagons."

In that hollow in my chest, leaves stir. Smoke ignites.

Magic.

The memory of the first wagon I ever saw hooks into me, dragging me down, deep and piercing.

Nilo and I bury our short fingers into the dirt for worms. At my side, my three-year-old sister Soli pats mud on her bare legs, humming a silly song about bams and sprites. Since I'm her older sister, I can ignore her as long as I keep her safe, like Mother told me to.

"I found one!" Nilo holds a wriggling worm in his pudgy palm—and drops it on Soli's legs.

Soli shrieks, and I push Nilo.

"Don't do that to my sister," I say.

"She's just a stupid baby," Nilo says, pushing me back.

"She's not stupid." I help my sister up, and my skin itches, like I'm covered in the poison ivy Mama warns against. "Don't call her that."

Nilo's face reddens. He marches to Soli and shoves her into the dirt.

The wiggling in my skin gathers and rises as the air coils around me, building, collecting sticks and mud and smoke until I'm surrounded by a cone of swirling earth. "Don't!" I say, and the sticks and mud and wind hurl for Nilo. For my sister.

Soli cries out and they're gone—the wind, the smoke, everything.

For a moment, Soli and Nilo stare at me.

"Ala?" Soli touches her collarbone...where a bloody gash has appeared.

I hurt her.

Nilo whispers, "Magic." His round face pales, and he backs farther away. "Magic!"

From behind us, a door slams open and Mother rushes toward us. With a single move, she smears mud over my cheeks, as if I've rolled on the ground. "What have you done?"

This time, Nilo screams, "Magic!"

"Hush, child," Mother says. "Hush."

But Nilo screams again, "Magic! Magic! Magic!"

His own father rushes from his front door, eyes wide.

From down the mud lane, wooden wheels creak.

An enormous pair of animals with smoke-colored horns drag forward. Mother tucks me behind one of her legs, Soli behind the other. The beasts snort, their hooves bigger than my head.

A man in a shirt and breeches the color of clay talks to our parents. "What happened here?"

I reach for Soli, but she jerks away, eyes wide and watery.

"I didn't mean to," I whisper to my sister.

Mother reaches for my arm and squeezes, so hard it hurts.

"She made magic," Nilo says.

Mother pushes me farther behind her legs. "Keep your truth-breaker away from my children."

She shoves me and Soli ahead, toward our home, but the man in clay-colored clothes blocks our path. "That child accuses yours of magic."

Mother raises our two arms in her tight fists, her elbow blocking the gash at the base of Soli's neck from the man's sight. "As you can see, the only thing my girls have talents for is rolling in the mud like wartpigs."

"She has magic," Nilo says. "I saw it. Blue and silver and it hurt Soli!"

The watchman looks at me, at Soli. "Let me see them. Let me ask them myself."

Mother leans closer to the man. "It wouldn't take the Sancta to see that child knows the word because he hears it at home."

"Talia." Nilo's father gasps. "How could you?"

For a moment, his brows drawn to the top of his nose, the watchman glares between Mother and Nilo's father.

Mother steps up to the watchman, dragging Soli and me behind her, until we're so close I can see the stitches on the side of his breeches. Mother leans to his ear, and whispers, "I can always call the Sancta herself, if that would help you reach the clarity you need."

The watchman's nose flares like an ox, and he steps away from us, fast. Raising a hand, he points to Nilo's father. "Into the wagon."

"No." Nilo's father lifts his son. "No. You can't. It's not my son. It's not—"

I tug at Mother's hand. "Mother, it wasn't—"

She wraps her arm around my head, snapping my jaw shut, as Nilo screams. As his father shouts, and they're dragged toward the wagon.

At my side, Soli trembles, crying. We watch the wagon rumble away.

Mother crouches at my side as it starts to rain. "Listen to me, Ala. Sometimes, when we become angry, we can do things that seem impossible—but that's exactly when you hurt those you love most. Did you mean to hurt your sister?"

"No." My lips wobbles. "I was trying to watch her. To be good."

"Did you want to hurt your friend?"

"No."

Mother holds my face in her palms, amber eyes bright. "But you did. You did both of those things."

My skin itches all over again. "I didn't mean to."

"Then tell me how you'll make sure this never, ever happens again."

"I won't do it again."

"And?"

"I won't tell anyone." I sniff. "I'll hide."

Mother presses a kiss to my head. "That's right. No matter what just came from inside you, you must hide it. You must hide, and hide, and hide, until it no longer exists. Until you are no more than Ala, my good, careful, obedient daughter. Understood?"

I nod as the wagon trudges away, as my friend and his father's cries follow me, long after the wagon disappears.

* * *

THE SNORT of the oxen returns me to the mud and rain of Elektos, to my sister, no longer three, but sixteen and bouncing at my side. A watchman leaps from the bench of the wagon. He knocks on a wooden door five homes down.

We both know what comes next.

"Who do you think is in there today?" Soli whispers, eyes not on the door but the wagon.

I stiffen. Her friend. I open my mouth to tell Soli—and close it. If she knew, my sister would charge ahead and no doubt find herself in that wagon, too.

The mud sucks downward on my boots, but I yank my feet free and tug my sister. "Come on. We're almost home."

We advance through more rows of wooden homes and shacks, past closed shutters and drenched patches of vegetables guarded by shards of glass.

On the edge of our mud lane, Soli halts. "I have to make one more stop."

"No, you don't." I tug her again. "You should—"

With a hard splash, two oxen round the corner, close enough the punch of mist from their nostrils drums my skin. I draw us back, flat against the logs.

Behind the oxen, four watchmen flank an uncovered wagon. On the wooden platform rests a long silver-black shaft of iron, angled halfway to the sky. From the top of the beam an arched half-circle of iron wings outward, its open ends linked by a taut strip of leather.

"I heard they place a massive arrow onto the beam and light its tip on fire," Soli whispers.

The oxen and watchmen ramble past us with their precious cargo—from the weapons shed behind the assembly house, no doubt. I've never been inside, but the sprawling shed is impossible to miss from the windows in the assembly house.

"See?" Soli says after the wagon and watchmen disappear behind a row of shacks. "Even the watchmen can tell something is different. That must be what they're calling the monster-killer. I can't wait to see what happens when the baya—"

This time, I do grab my sister, and drag her into the rain-shadow of the nearest home. "Do you *want* to be in that wagon?"

A baya. To even mention the three monstrous beings that reign over the enemy realms across the mountain is forbidden—and with good reason. Truth Four. *Magic is death.* Death, which anyone unfortunate enough to encounter the monsters would find either at the baya's claws, or at the hands of the murderous mage and sorceress at each of their sides.

"Ala, something is changing. Something in the air, on the rain. Can't you feel it?"

Not for the first time, I wonder if my sister feels the itch of fallen leaves in her veins, like I do in mine. If she recalls what happened, that day we first saw the watchmen's wagon.

When I first learned how dangerous I was.

"I feel nothing."

"If Mama was here," Soli says, "she'd remind you the truths say don't lie. And if Tal—"

"Don't." I slap my hand over her lips. "You promised. We don't belong to her anymore. Don't give her name that power."

"Perhaps not saying her name gives her *more* power over us, dearest sister."

I cross my arms, this time refusing to play, and Soli sighs.

"Fine," my sister says. "If the person who birthed us was here, she'd say—"

"Nothing at all, because you'd talk too much for her to get a word in elsewise." I hook a finger in the loop at her waist and pull her across the rainy, empty lane. "Just stop, Soli. Let's go home."

"You can't hide forever, Ala." My sister digs her heels into the mud. "I've let you ignore the real truth for so many years, but now—now you *need* to listen to me. You *have* to. I have one stop to make, and then I'll be home, and you're going to listen to me. *Promise* me you're going to listen."

"I listen to the sound of the watchmen's wagons every day outside the assembly house. Don't make me listen for the one that's carrying you." When our mothers first left, Soli listened to me. But lately, the closer I try to hold her, the further my sister slips away. "Come home and wait for the food reward I earned today—the Sancta said you have to be there. They'll check that we are home, both of us."

"Whatever twisted reason she has for treating you like her pet, it will end one day, and you will be no more favored than any other person in Elektos."

I ignore the dig and tug her forward, toward home. "She's helping us both, Soli. Just come home."

"I will—after I make this stop." With a glance toward the Scorched Mountains, she slips from my grasp. "When I get home, you're going to listen to me, even if you don't like what I have to say. Even if it forces you to yank your head from the mud and actually be noticed by someone besides your little sister."

"Soli!" I grab for her wrist, but she's already dashed away into the rain. A single man in the muddy lane stares after her, and I shrink into the shadow of the nearest shack. If I chase, I'll only bring more attention her way, so instead, I slide toward our home.

Soli is wrong, just as her friend was. Nothing is changing. Nothing is shifting.

The only thing I have to worry about is that one of these days, my sister is bound to be caught.

CHAPTER 3

*B*y the time I face my sister in our log home, the rain has stopped. The light of our two moons gleams through our cracked window to a feather-soft wishing flower in my palm. The stalk is delicate and sticky.

Such a fragile apology gift.

"You promised one stop."

"It was." Soli watches from a moonslit corner of our home. "It was just a long one."

I wish I could cradle the dandelion long into the fate-starred night. I wish I could retain the warmth of Soli's crushing squeeze from when she burst in the door and pressed the flower into my palm. She found me kneeling, the hiding stone from the hearth at my feet, holding our secret sketch within a wooden frame.

Years ago, in that sliver between summer and winter, Mother surprised us with a picnic beneath burgundy maples. Her friend sketched us while we ate tart red apples. The creator captured my tight-knuckled grip on the linen purse around my neck, a gift from Mama that same day, even as I worried about us being found with the forbidden fabrics.

"Try to enjoy this day," Mother had said. "I promise, it's far better than the alternative, Alathea Thymisius."

"Don't use that name," Mama had snapped, a tone she only ever used with Mother. On Mama's wrist, the circlet of pumpkin seeds I'd pieced together from our garden clinked. "We all only belong to Emon now."

Emon, who founded Elektos as a safe haven from our enemies. Alongside the Sancta, Emon protects us—as long as we adhere to the truths.

Setting the framed sketch aside, I stare at Soli's flower-gift. The floor creaks as she shifts toward a corner of our one room, where the candlelight almost doesn't reach.

Almost.

The last of the warmth skitters from my bones as Soli widens her stance. This time, I catch a glimpse of woven burlap behind her.

A burlap sack, just like the one our mother held the night she left two years ago.

"What's inside the bag?" I bite my lip to keep the real question inside. The one that I can't bear: *Where are you going?*

"My friends said the baya has called me."

I reach for the wool curtain that separates our room in two. Once, years ago, Mother jumped out and surprised Mama from behind this threadbare fabric. I never heard Mother laugh like that again, nor Mama swear so colorfully.

I wish I could wrap myself in the wool now and make Soli's words disappear. "Don't. Please. Just—don't."

"Don't what? Don't go? Or don't tell you, like usual? You *promised* you'd listen this time."

"I didn't expect *treason* to be a part of what you'd want to say." Treason, planted by Mother, with her whispers of before. Before, when magic thrummed in the air of Elektos and dreams were plentiful and our two moons throbbed silver-blue.

Even as, to me, Mother whispered, *Hide*.

"Ala, *stop*. Can't you at least *try* to be less afraid?" Soli hefts the sack to her side and slides toward the front door. "Whether you want to believe or not, the beings in the other realms—the magic isles—they are *good*."

I cup my palms over my ears, but she continues with the wish-filled manure I've ignored a thousand times.

"Memory, and Dreams, and Nightmares. Just there, across the Scorched Mountains and over the sea. Their magic is in danger. They need me." Two steps from the front door, she pauses. "I know you don't want to hear this, but they need *us*. It's time to stop hiding and *do* something."

I slide between her and the front door. "You and I have *nothing* to do with *anything* across those mountains. With our *enemies*. Don't you know how dangerous they are?" The candlelight flickers on the scar at her collarbone. *Don't you remember how dangerous I am, to you?*

Soli blinks from the shadows. "Some days, I'm not certain we were raised by the same parents."

"Some days, I'm certain you'll come home with worse than a cut cheek or a burned wrist."

The corner of Soli's mouth tips upward, soft, as she raises her palm to the more recent scar on her cheek. Only I know that she made that slash herself, that I stitched it as best I could with trembling fingers, that somehow it healed straight as an arrow. "My friend thinks it's daring. In fact, he wrote a song about it just a few days ago. Shall I sing it for you?" Dropping the burlap, she flourishes a neat half bow, and releases a high hum. *"There once was a girl born with a blade, her skin like honey and her scar homemade."*

"Stop it." I wrap my arms around my chest. "It's not funny."

Soli's lashes flutter like a butterfly in the breeze. "It's a *little* funny, Ala. Admit it."

I bite my lip to keep the twitch of a smile inside.

Not from the awful song, but because nothing can contain my

sister. Just last week, she returned home singing about a girl with raven hair who held a flame in her hand and jewels in her skin. She sang until I begged, half-laughing, half-desperate, for her to stop—or to at least sing some other tall tale.

Soli peers closer, searching me for the hint of a smile even now.

"I have more sense than your latest flirtation," I say.

Her grin fades, sinking, the sun gone. "I doubt that, sister." She glances toward the back of our home, to where our shed hovers at the edge of a ravine, toward the Scorched Mountains beyond. "I very much doubt that."

"Then tonight, let's just leave it be. Let's leave it and I'll pour crow stew and we'll look for holes in the moons."

"I can't, Ala. Not this time." She steps toward me and gently chucks my chin, just like Mother used to do. "I'm trying to make our world better."

"Better is no more scars. Better is following the truths."

"Have you forgotten it's their truths that put us in that cage two years ago? The watchman who did this?" She grabs my right hand, forcing my wrist into the moonslight through our broken window. In the gray beam, the grooves shine fine, delicate, as if a bracelet has been carved into my skin.

"I haven't forgotten." How could I ever forget the searing pain of the watchman's branding iron that night our mothers left? In my nightmares, I often see him still, the watchman with one blue star on his clay-colored sleeve, my sister's screams filling us both as he holds my wrist in the cages beneath the assembly house. Even now, the memory of it speeds my pulse, the thought of ever seeing him again rolling my stomach.

But I'm not there. I'm here, in my home. Safe. With my sister, who always forgets the watchmen let us go when they realized we didn't know where our mothers had fled.

"You saw how they were rounding villagers into the wagon

today," I remind her now. "If you're not here when they arrive with our reward, they will find you, and they will punish you."

"Let them try. Let them take me to wherever they actually take all of Elektos to, when they cart our people away." Soli's eyes spark as she lifts the burlap onto her shoulder. "Who knows, maybe I'll even find the bones of our mothers at the end of the wagon ride."

My chest burns, and I widen my arms across the front door, blocking her exit. The wishing seeds crunch beneath my boot. "This isn't a joke. Where are you going that could be worth that risk?"

Soli raises a single hand and points toward the back door. "Across the—"

I capture her wrist, quick as a snake in the summer grass.

She tries to wrench away, but I squeeze hard enough that her fist unfolds.

Within her palm, a shade lighter than her unmarked skin, is a wicked scar. A circle slashed by a single line, beveled, like someone took a newly sharpened edge and chiseled into her skin.

I drop her hand and press a fist to my ribs as the leaves crunch inside my veins. They twist and rise, smoky and crackling and loud enough I'm certain my sister can hear. I force a deep breath. Deeper. To keep it in. To keep everything in. "What have you *done*?"

Soli folds her arms, chin higher than ever. Daring me to say it. To say what this scar cannot be. Because if it is—

I dive for the sack and snatch it from her hand. I punch through the wool curtain, past our straw beds, out the back door. Into the slick mud, between our vegetable rows, through the night.

Soli chases. "Give it back!"

At our brittle shed, heart in my throat, I thrust the door open and hurl the bag inward. It plows into the dirt, lodged among garden spades and spiderwebs.

I spin to block the doorframe, but Soli dives past me, unafraid of the dark. She scoops the dirty bag into her hand and twists to face me—

As I heave the door shut and smash the bolt in place.

"Ala!" Soli rams into the other side of the door, but the bolt holds. "Stop being so stubborn! Let me out!"

From somewhere in the night, the splash of oxen and the faint creak of the watchmen's wheels wind through Elektos.

"I can't." Fingers shaking, head spinning, I touch my forehead to the night-cooled wood, quick and brief, before backing away. "It's just until they arrive. Just until the watchmen deliver our reward."

She slams against the door again, the small frame shaking, and I back toward our house, hoping the families nearby can't hear. That they won't report any strange shouts. That the buzz in my veins will stay hidden, even as it fades now, like a storm released and over, with Soli tucked safely away.

I sink onto a wooden bench at our table, watching the shed tremble through the window. My legs bounce as I glance between the front door and that shaking shed. The crushed wishing seeds on the floor draw my gaze.

No matter how many truths I carve for Elektos, one will always be first.

To keep Soli safe, I will do anything.

I scrape the seeds from our wooden floor, tuck them into the hidden purse around my neck, and await our reward.

CHAPTER 4

$\mathcal{T}$he muted grunt of an ox startles me awake next to the smoldering hearth. The watchmen. Their wagon awaits outside in the dark.

Their death wagon. Soli's poisoned whisper slogs through my sleep-webbed mind.

Soli.

I scramble up and sprint out the back door, through the drizzle falling on our patch of Elektos. By some small mercy, all is quiet from the shed. Soli will be covered in dirt and cobwebs, so we'll say she was working the garden. A small lie, but she won't have any trouble uttering it.

Frowning, I slide back the rusty bolt. When did she stop pounding?

"Soli?"

I tug the door open.

To an empty shed.

No. More than empty.

Half destroyed.

Opening straight into the wooded ravine, a Soli-sized hole

has been carved out. Beyond it looms a direct view to the Scorched Mountains.

Gone. Just like our parents.

I whip my palm to the cool wood, and the deep grooves on my wrist burn.

Whispers from the carvers' tool room in the assembly house slink past my ear, rumors passed like a flask of sleeping poison.

They carved out her tongue.

They lashed his palms with chains.

They broke his neck.

This time, I do know something. I know that my wild, reckless sister is planning to run to our enemies.

Across the mountains. They need us.

Behind the shed, between the maples, a figure separates from the trunks.

A watchman.

I slide into the shadows inside the shed. Spiderwebs lick at my neck and hair.

The figure steps closer.

"You don't look much like her." A stranger's voice, amused and curious and male. Gray eyes appear beneath night-shaded leaves. "I was certain you would be taller."

I flounder for the shed's shovel, curling my fingers around the wooden handle. He knows my sister. Does he have her already?

"But with that instinct to beat me into the ground, I have no doubt." A slice of moonslight cuts across his face. Short black curls fade to smooth, chiseled cheekbones and warm brown skin.

A watchman no older than me—he must have circled my home wide from the wagon. How deeply do they already suspect us?

Rose-colored lips tip upward as he nods at the shovel in my hand. "Has she been training you? She's only beaten me once, no matter what she claims."

I swallow a grim smile. I didn't realize my sister was still challenging watchmen to fight—and clearly still beating them raw enough to sting. "Where have you taken her?"

"Taken? Soliana? Last time I attempted to make her do anything, she nearly snapped my leg in two."

I grip the shovel harder. "But...you are here with our reward. With the food that the Sancta promised us. The food reward."

"I'm not much of a cook." His laugh is soft, like the brush of cotton on stone. "I've been known to bring a lady breakfast, but usually we spend time in bed first. As for the Sancta, I take no orders from her."

A watchman who ignores the Sancta's command? I peer closer at the young man through the cut hole of the shed's wall. A dark linen shirt hugs his chest, fitted unlike any watchman's, unlike any in all of Elektos. His arms are thicker than the boys of his age, too. "Why is your wool not clay-colored? Why is it so tight?"

White teeth gleam in the dark. "How else would you appreciate this beautiful body?"

"You— I— What? No. I am not interested in your *body*."

"Don't worry." The boy winks. *Winks.* "My mind is just as attractive."

This is no watchman. Perhaps he is here looking to tumble my sister, or one of her treasonous friends. Either way, he is the last person I need with the watchmen at my door and my sister missing.

From the front of my home, three sharp knocks ricochet.

Next to the boy, a silver light flares. It hovers midair, illuminating what was hidden.

Ink curls along his neck, intricate whorls of black and blue. The fabric of his shirt—not just *not clay*, but blacker than deep night.

And in his hand...

A spear, honed by an expert's chisel to a deadly teardrop. In any other moment, I would have paused to admire the artistry of that teardrop, its beveled curves.

But this teardrop of a spear glows.

In my own veins, the rustle shivers, flutters, flares. Wind floods my blood as the word drops from my lips. "Magic."

Not a watchman. Not a boy.

Magic.

A *mage*.

A murderous mage.

My back slams into the wood of the shed, the flimsy structure shaking.

Magic is death.

My *enemy*. The wind in me dies as fast as it rose.

The mage glances behind him, to the Scorched Mountains. "The brighter it glows, the closer the threat. Come, Alathea."

I flinch. "How do you know my name?"

"How would I *not* know your name? Your sister speaks of you every time I see her."

Every time. "You lie."

The boy lays a hand to his chest. "You wound me. Come now. Has she truly not told you anything? We passed a warning to her just in time. The shield of Dreams has died, and your sister accepted the shield's power. She stepped through the grounded gate a single breath before the power found her."

"Impossible." All of it. Every word from this boy is impossible, even as Tenion's warning at the assembly house echoes.

The magic is shifting.

"That's why I'm here." The mage extends a hand toward me, through the back of the shed. "To take you before Orkayha's first wave of monsters do."

Truth One Hundred and Seven. *Thou shall not speak of our enemies, nor of their magic, nor of monsters long vanquished.*

I grip the shovel's handle hard enough to crack. "If there were any monsters left—which there aren't—the watchmen would protect us. They have the gift of monster-slaying from Emon."

The boy snorts, and leaves rustle at his side. "Your watchmen have been gifted no more than fire and idiocy. They couldn't stand against Orkayha's underlings. No one here could, on this side of the silver curtain."

I wish for the curtain inside my home. "Then for whatever madness you're here—you have exceptionally poor timing and must *leave*."

"*We* have to leave, together." The boy frowns. "Now, before her monsters get any closer."

Another of Tenion's whispers from the assembly house find me. *It won't matter what you believe, if the rumors are true.*

"Even if this were true, even if there are"—I choke on the concession—"monsters, I would not follow my enemy anywhere." And certainly not to the monstrous ruler this mage serves.

"Did your sister truly tell you nothing?" At my silence, he swears, soft as a spider's web. "The monsters hunt magic. They are hunting *you*."

Mother's whisper curls upward from that hollow in my chest. *Hide*.

Again, the boy reaches for me.

This time, I throw the spade at him, using the single beat of his distraction to dig into the pouch at my waist and rip a sliver of a chisel free.

The boy squints at the chisel now pointed at his chest. "Is that a pine needle? Are you threatening to prick me?"

"More than prick, if you come one step farther."

From the front of my home, an insistent pounding thunders.

"Why are you behaving like a frightened bird?" Up, the mage swings an armored plate, knocking my sliver of a chisel to the dirt. He tucks the broad plate on his back. "Come now and we will avoid your watchmen. I prefer their company even less than Orkayha's creatures."

"Truth Four."

"All right, you've got me. What is Truth Four?"

Hide. "Magic is death."

"Death, you say?" The mage presses two fingertips into the hollow below his square jaw. "My heart beats well enough." He ducks inside the shed toward me, through the Soli-sized hole. "Would you like to check yourself?"

I flail backward, out the front of the shed, the tiny structure suddenly much too small. "I told you, not a step closer."

This time, the pounding knock shudders the frame of my home.

"While I'm happy to debate the finer points of your truth, as you call it, we have to go. The baya sent me for you. I saw monster tracks not half a day's walk to the east. By now, we should both be far from here." The mage ducks through the front of the shed, toward me, and I wish I could collapse the walls upon him. "In truth, I thought Soliana joked when she said you believe the swill on this side of the curtain."

My jaw clenches, but he pays no mind.

"Magic is not death," the mage says, "nor destruction, nor any of the many so-called truths you've been fed here. You're in far more danger in Elektos than you will be across the mountains."

"Stop lying."

"Why do you think I'm the one lying?"

"Because I was born knowing that's what creatures across the mountains do."

From the front of my home, another roof-shuddering knock.

The mage thrusts his free hand to me, palm up. "Ala, you will be the next sorceress of the Realm of Dreams, and the baya calls you from hiding. The baya of Mizura is hunting you. If her monsters find you, they will drag you to her realm and throw you in a pit and you will live what you fear most over and over until you no longer *remember* your sister. Your so-called friends are about to knock down that shack of a home behind you, and I'm in no mood to spill watchman blood. We must go *now*."

My heart stops. Because alongside his treasonous, impossible words, in the center of that broad, open palm, rests a mark.

A circle, pierced by a single line.

I stagger backward.

"You were right. I'm not like my sister." Backward, I splash through the mud, toward my home, away from the mage. "I don't trust our enemies."

Behind me, a boom rocks my home.

CHAPTER 5

$\mathcal{I}$ sprint for the back door of my home, the notched logs shuddering from the boom. *Sorceress of the Realm of Dreams*. Madness.

I rip the door open. "Help!"

Hands close around my throat, and I slam into a wood beam, my braid grinding into the back of my head. I gasp, choking.

A watchman with flat brown eyes and a single star on his sleeve sneers into my face—the watchman I last saw pressing a burning iron to my sister's wrist. "Where were you? Why didn't you answer?"

I dig my fingers into the wood. *Hide. Hide and hide and hide—*

Harder, the watchman presses. "Where. Were. You."

"Watchman Minteph." For the second time today, the Sancta's three stars appear in the corner of my vision. "She cannot answer if you squeeze the voice from her."

Minteph releases my neck and rubs his fingers clean.

I sag against the wall. For whatever reason the Sancta is here, she's my best chance. "Lady Jayton." Her green eyes flicker at the name that she told me once, long ago in the ravine behind my house, when she found me and sent me homeward. "I need help."

With a crook of her finger, the Sancta tilts my face upward, the wreckage of the boom clear behind her. Our front door is gone, two shards of blackened wood in its place.

"We help those who are deserving, Alathea. Are you still deserving? Where is your sister?"

Could the Sancta possibly know where she's gone? Is that why she's come with the watchman? "I don't know."

"Sancta." From Minteph's fingers hangs a small, wooden frame. "This was lying in the hearth's ashes."

Panic skitters down my chest, right to my feet. The sketch of our mothers—I'd forgotten to stash it behind the hiding stone.

The Sancta releases me and takes the frame between short nails like it might contain venom. "In my chamber, truth-carver, I have a green bird in a cage. Are you familiar with it?"

I nod, eyes wide. Every day, I hear the bird when I near the Sancta's door to retrieve my chisel and mallet from the room where the carving tools are kept safe. I hear the bird's squawk, its constant chatter: *Pretty. Quiet. Danger.*

"You have also known a cage before, girl, correct?"

Again, I nod, the grooves on my wrist pulsing.

"Then answer me well. Your parents were deserters, were they not?"

"They were."

"Yet you kept this." She releases the frame to the floor.

The frame splinters, and a shard of wood nicks my shin through the thin fabric of my breeches, but I press my lips tight. I've thought of destroying that sketch myself every night, ever since our mothers left us.

The Sancta stoops to pick up the sketch, and turns it over.

My stomach follows.

Even in the thin light of Minteph's candled lantern, the mark on the back of the fabric is clear.

A faded circle, a single line slashed through the middle.

The same as Soli's scar.

And the mage's palm.

Minteph's voice worms across my home. "This mark—what is this?"

"I don't know."

"Truth Five. No lies." With two quick strides, Minteph's arm arcs. I duck before I can even consider what I'm doing. Soli's love for grappling in the woods when we were young remains ingrained in my bones.

His eyes flame. "You dare avoid a punishment?"

Trembling, I slide toward the back door. The Sancta responds first. "She's mine to punish either way, watchman."

"*This* is why I brought you here, Sancta. The younger girl was sighted far from her assigned route today. With the threat rising across the mountains, we cannot bear any risks. It's clear the sister has deserted. Just like their parents."

The accusation punches low, hard, even as the mage's words ring in my head. *The duty has fallen to her. She's crossed the mountains.*

The Sancta halts my retreat. "This is your chance, Alathea. What was your sister doing?" She lowers her voice, until only I can hear. "Tell me something, and I will let you go. Anything."

"Please." My gaze darts toward that back door again. Toward the shed, where my sister was safe, until that mage took her away. "I—I saw someone who has magic. Just outside. A boy."

This time Minteph's palm connects with my cheek. I tumble to the floor, my palms ripping into the wood, splinters digging into my nails.

"Minteph." The Sancta's voice is a lash. "If more of our enemy's monsters have already arrived, I would hear what the girl saw. We will need to take steps."

"She wasted her chance." Minteph hauls me upward, and cold metal chains smash onto my wrists, pinching the skin so tight that I can't contain my cry. "I'm glad you carve the truths, girl. You know which ones you have foresworn."

He drags me out, across my destroyed door.

Toward a hide-covered wagon.

"I saw magic." I dig my heels into the mud. I spoke the truth. The watchman should be *helping* me. "I swear it. Just let me explain—"

"Minteph." The Sancta's voice slices from the shadow of my doorless home. "Bring her back here. I want to interrogate the girl. We need to know if she saw one of their mages, or worse. That's an order."

But Minteph ignores her, hauling me away.

"Watchman!" The Sancta's voice snaps like a whip. "You cannot disobey me. I remain the leader of this village, not you."

"Take it up with them, and we'll see." He unrolls the latched hide of the wagon. I gag as a hollow of sweat and fear leaks outward.

"Please." I reach for the Sancta, around Minteph's torso. "Please, don't send me away."

"I will set this right." For a breath, the Sancta shoves the watchman aside, her mouth at my ear. "I will come for you. I promise."

But then I'm ripped up and away, feet lifting from the mud, the wagon looming.

"*You* help *us*," Minteph says at my back. "There is no other way."

And he heaves me into the dark.

* * *

I'm uncertain how many shifts of the fate-stars have passed since I was thrown in the wagon, but with no light slipping through the thick canvas, it must still be night. Certainly enough time has passed to make my backside ache from the wooden bench and my wrists chafe from the iron chains.

From the sweaty heat on either side of me, my bench holds

three villagers. Across, on the opposite bench, are three more. One of them is unchained—another watchman.

From his corner of the wagon, the watchman snores loudly, the jolt of the wagon interrupting the awful sound for a blessed moment before it restarts again. I've lived in fear of Soli drawing their attention every day, but until now, I've never drawn their ire. I never imagined they'd refuse to listen, especially with the Sancta ordering otherwise.

The watchmen are supposed to help us. To keep us safe.

My neck throbs where Minteph pressed.

I can't chance asking for help again, not with where this landed me. Not with my sister missing.

Soli may be unpredictable, but she would never intentionally put my life in danger. Could the mage have bewitched her? Fed her the exact lies she's longed to believe her whole life, and that's what caused her to risk crossing the mountains?

The shield of Dreams has died, and your sister accepted the shield's power. You will be the next sorceress of the Realm of Dreams.

No matter how many times I try to carve the words from my aching head, I cannot shape them into anything that fits with what I know to be true.

I curl further into the wooden bench, into the dark.

Keep quiet. Escape, and find Soli. That's my only option.

At the bench, a soft tap moves against my chained wrists. I twist to find a young girl with a yellow string in her dark hair and bright blue eyes.

Tenion, who I had thrown into this very wagon to save my sister.

Key? Tenion mouths, silent now, unlike this morning in the assembly house.

I glance toward the watchman in the opposite corner. His snores continue.

"No key," I whisper. I roll my shaking palms upward, toward her. "I'm sorry."

Light as a marten over snow, her fingers remove the wooden splinters from my hands. "So they finally saw you, too."

"I did nothing wrong."

"*Everything* we do is wrong." Tenion leans closer. "Do they have your sister in a wagon, too?"

I shake my head.

"Thank the Fates," Tenion whispers.

From the other side of the girl, a woman shifts forward, deep lines flowing from her eyes and black coils framing her face. "Was she called? Was it the magic?"

The shield of Dreams has died, and your sister accepted the shield's power.

"My sister is not that." I bite my lip at the word I cannot utter, not here, with a watchman across the wagon's interior. *Magic.*

A thump from the front halts the wagon, and the watchman in the corner jolts upward, awake. The canvas at the back of the wagon furls from outside. Bright gray light filters in.

The watchman prods his striking rod at Tenion's shin. "You first." Roughly, he grabs her arm and hauls her out.

I strain against the iron at my wrist. "Where are you taking her?"

"Piss break, girl," says a white-haired man on the bench opposite from me, his voice like mud. "They take us out one at a time so they don't have an insurrection on their hands. To make sure we arrive safe and sane and in one piece." His lips spread in a toothy, maniacal grin. "It's when we arrive—that's when they tear us apart, unless we tear them in two first. Right, Hook?"

"Hush," says the woman with the deep lines and black coils. Hook, then. "We don't know if we can trust this one."

Goose bumps creep across my arms. Why does she sound more worried about trusting me than the old man's warning of where we're heading? What am I missing?

Before I can piece it together, the watchman tosses Tenion inside. I'm unchained and dragged outside.

Legs nearly buckling, I take the first step in what must be more than a half-night, blinking at the bright light of the moons. The three fate-stars shine between them, the rest of the sky empty of all but the deepest black.

The watchman releases my arm and paces away as I crouch. Marking east and west, the two full moons illuminate glassy dark water that lurks on either side of the wagon. In the still reflections, the moons' glow is more silver than their usual gray.

Silver, not unlike the mage's spear.

I shudder and consider the water. If it's any more than ankle-deep, I can't escape through the water. Soli always hounded me to learn to swim, but I'd resisted yet another idea that would only draw attention our way.

If she could see me now, she would gloat.

Gloat...and then she would find a way to tear off these chains and destroy that wagon. Perhaps if I crept toward the front—

"Hurry up, girl."

I re-tie my breeches and turn. Far ahead is a low, constant roar. Beyond, a black mountain rises. Different from the Scorched Mountains, this range rises sheer obsidian, dark and unforgiving. These aren't the mountains Soli crossed. They couldn't be. It almost looks like...a wall.

"Where are we going?" Around us, there are no settlements of Elektos, no soft night sounds of our people. Only trickling water and forest and silence.

"You won't be going anywhere if you open your mouth again." The watchman points with his rod. "Back in the wagon."

My boots squelch as I trudge toward the open canvas. From the corner of my eye, in the expanse of black water at the forest's edge, a flash flutters.

A flash of glowing silver.

"Faster." The watchman's rod digs into my spine. I climb into the wagon, thunking onto the bench, chains refastened.

I lean for the opening of the flap, for that flash of silver again.

It was no more than the shimmering reflection of the sky. Perhaps even the flicker of the fate-stars.

Certainly no more than that.

A woman with flame-red hair stumbles out of the wagon, wagging her tongue at me. The flap shuts.

Tenion slides her smallest finger around mine. For a beat, I recall Soli at twelve, already strong and so rarely afraid, her slight body shielding mine from a rabid dog in our lane, waving a stick until it ran away.

Shield of Dreams. Sorceress.

What has my little sister gotten herself into? Gotten *us* into?

Tenion tugs at my sleeve. "Don't worry. We'll escape once we're in the magic realms. You'll see."

"Why would you want to enter our enemy's land?" I ask.

"Because that's where my father lives," Tenion says.

"Teni..." Hook's tone is soft. "They are taking us to Nightmares. If your father is there, if he's been in the pits, he will not recognize you."

"If he's there, I'll find him. My mama said there's a song he used to sing to me when I was little. If he hears it, he'll know it's me." Light and bouncing, Tenion's voice rises and falls. *"In spite of the sprite's spurious songs, go* bam! *your little baby bones. Just light the baya's eyes with the love of the skies..."*

This time, my pulse skipping toward the opening of the canvas, it's me who shushes the girl. "That song is nonsense."

Hook pulls against her chains. "The only nonsense is you, spouting their disgusting lies."

"The *truths* are important."

"So is that song. How would a truth-licker like you know those lyrics anyway?"

I clamp my lips tight.

"Papa said it wards against nightmares," Tenion says. "I like singing it."

"Truth Seven," I say. "Nightmares aren't real."

"And yet here we are," Hook says, "in this death wagon, real as any—"

The watchman returns, re-chaining a truth-breaker and removing Hook.

"Nightmares are real, girl," the old man says, once they are gone. "The real monsters can create them with just a flick of their claws. But I recall the time before, when we had dreams. When we had hope. Unlike you, I'm old enough to know the difference." He nods at the empty seat where Hook sat. "You should listen to her. Hook knows what she's talking about. Plenty of creatures lurk out there, in our world. In the forests at night, in the shadows of the day. Across the mountains. Here." He leans across the bench, his half-toothed mouth gaping. "Some would even say...monsters."

I slouch into the back of the bench, and Hook returns, a young boy taken out. To my right, the red-headed woman stretches her neck, curving her forehead toward the canvas ceiling. "See this?" Across her neck is a patchwork of deep scars.

"A mon-monster did that?" Returned, the young boy stutters, eyes as round as plates. "Mother said the baya is the one who shreds your skin."

"This is nothing compared to what they'll do to you," the redhead says. "Broken feet and broken hands and broken necks. The more broken the better. They break you into a thousand bones and stitch you back together for the next night when they break you all over again." The boy's eyes widen to the size of summer beetles as the woman continues. "I heard about a brat like you, years ago. A snot-nosed truth-breaker, babbling about a *magic girl* as they carted him through the village. You should see what they did to him."

Deep in my bones, the leaves rustle. The smoke gathers. Heat and wind rise. Tenion's gaze slides to my hands.

"Broken feet and broken hands and broken—"

"*Stop* it," I say. "Stop scaring them."

Mother never told me what happened to Nilo, my friend who cried magic, after she sent him to the wagon in what should have been my place.

"Maybe Red is warning us, did you consider that?" Hook says, and then glares at the old man. "*This* is why we're not trusting her."

But the old man looks at me instead, grave. "You should be afraid. We're heading for the very belly of the beast."

"The watchmen wouldn't let monsters into Elektos," I say.

Even I can hear the quiver in my voice. The quiver that hasn't left my bones since I asked for help, and Minteph answered by throwing me into this wagon.

I'll come for you, the Sancta said.

I believe her, because she's always found me. The Sancta has always watched over me, ever since she found me wandering in the forest six years ago. Mama had sent me to locate a hiding place for one of Mother's trinkets, and as I searched for a spot Mother would never find, I ran into a watchman. I expected a scolding for how far I'd wandered, to the very edge of our village's fields.

Instead, the watchman had asked, "Do you remember me?"

I could not distinguish her clay-colored garb from any other watchman's, and said as much. With a soft smile, she told me to call her Lady Jayton. "Your mother comes to this place some-times," she said.

I had no idea. Even then, Mother was gone more often than not. "Where would my mother never go?"

"What an odd question for a daughter to ask," Lady Jayton said. But she pointed me to a hidden place Mother would never trod, and warned me there were worse things than monsters prowling our village. She nudged me toward home.

Not a year later, I was gifted the role of truth-carver on her hallway in the assembly house. Every day from the second-floor windows, Lady Jayton has watched me arrive. Every day, she pauses in the hall with a nod and praise. Always, she watches me cross the stone square for home.

I'll come for you.

I don't care if that makes me her pet. At least I know she'll come for me.

And yet…why didn't Minteph listen to the Sancta?

I twist in my seat and yank harder at the chains on my wrists. "Truth Ten. Elektos cares for us."

"That sort of care?" the old man says, eyeing my scarred wrist. "Or the breed of care you'll find at the re-education square?"

Soli's furious whisper surfaces in my ear. *A pretty name for a torture cell. No one escapes without skin flayed the length of their torso from the clawed creatures, their mind splintered.*

Could my sister have been right? Is that why no one ever returns when they're taken by the wagon? Could our mothers' bones truly be there? These last two years, I've tried not to imagine where they went. I've never truly believed they were dead, that *that* was the reason they hadn't returned.

I hunch my shoulders forward, and Tenion curls in closer to my side.

"You look heartsick, girl," the old man says. "Didn't get a goodbye to your lover, eh? Don't worry. They'll find you someone new where we're heading—they might just have a few more rows of teeth than you were expecting. They'll have one special for you and her and me. For all of us, in the bloody battle they want."

The watchman is back, the last truth-breaker chained into place. The canvas slaps shut, locking out the moons' glow as he climbs in with us.

But it's not enough to block the last words from the old man.

The bloody battle they want.

You're in far more danger in Elektos than you will be across the mountains, the mage said.

The wagon rocks into motion. Foul breath flows over me, Red at my side, sliding closer. "They are real, you know."

I gag, gaze darting to the watchman, willing him to not hear over the clattering of the wooden wheels.

Keep quiet. Arrive. Escape.

I *can* do it.

Red wheezes, closer, tongue out, wagging—

Across the wagon, the old man growls, "Now."

With a grunt, Hook kicks the watchman's knee. A crunch of bone, a high shriek.

A tongue drags up my neck.

I shout and lurch away, off balance. The watchman swings wildly across the bench, right for Tenion.

"No!" I jerk toward Tenion—

And a single sharp current rips from my skin, downward, straight through the wooden bench.

The wagon jolts. Rocks. Heaves to the right, hard, at an impossible angle.

The watchman falls to his corner, gaze locked on me. "What have you done?"

The wooden floor cracks in half.

We tilt forward.

For a breath, I am suspended, my body lifted, bound only at my wrists to the bench.

Bound, and tilting upward.

Up, up, up—

We smash down, head on into a wall.

The wagon heaves flat and rents in two.

And lowers.

Lowers and lowers and—*sinking*.

Not a wall.

Water.

CHAPTER 6

*B*lack liquid rushes into the wagon and steals my breath. I scramble to draw my feet onto the bench, tugging hard at my trapped wrists. All at once, the chained truth-breakers in the wagon are shouting orders, at each other, at the watchman who is smashed against the sinking canvas.

Water gushes inward, unstoppable.

I wrench against the chains, my skin splitting as the water licks my fingers.

"Unchain us," the old man yells to the watchman. "Elektos needs us."

As if the demand finally unfreezes his shock, the watchman's wild eyes jerk to the white-haired prisoner. Rising, he drags his injured leg toward the closed flap.

The old man slams his foot into the watchman's leg, and the watchman crumples with a splash.

"Unchain us!"

Sputtering, swearing, the watchman gains purchase and stands, chest heaving. Rod gripped hard in his fist, he whirls and swings, fast and vicious.

Crack.

Blood spatters across the canvas, across us all.

A sob breaks from my chest, and I yank harder. *Harder.*

The water rises.

"Again!" Tenion shouts at my side, tugging at my hand.

"It wasn't me!" But I have no breath in my lungs for more than that. No heat in my veins. Water claws to my chest, to my chin. Higher and higher, enclosing my jaw, my cheeks, my head, in a suffocating, icy blindness. Down, it presses me, like frozen stones.

I sink and sink and—

Soli. I yank the chains again, hard, lungs bursting.

From somewhere above, the water booms, followed by a rip through the canvas.

Something solid brushes my wrists, rough, urgent. A bright light flares in front of my closed eyes.

My chains snap free, and I'm pushed upward.

Breaching the surface, I suck in air, greedy, spitting water. My lips tingle with the burst of air. Bubbles glug from the death wagon as it struggles to escape, just like me.

Gray eyes burn a breath from mine.

The mage.

"Swim to shore! I'll get the others." He shoves me away, through the frigid water, toward the far-off shore—and I sink again.

An arm wraps around my chest from behind, dragging me upward. We crest the surface and I gulp in air. "I'm guessing that's a *No, Daesen. Thank you for saving me, Daesen. In fact, I can't swim, Daesen.*"

I scratch at that band of an arm, but my movements are sluggish, my fingers ice. Rapidly, he plows me toward the shore, and dumps me in the shallows with a splash.

"Don't move." The mage plunges back into the icy water for the wagon.

Shaking, I scramble from the shallows into tall reeds at the

41

water's edge, putting more distance between us even as my gaze remains on the mage. *Daesen.* I need to see Tenion's yellow string above the black water. Under, Daesen dives, a head popping to the surface. Under again, another head, over and over.

From all around the shoreline, splashes and shouts ring.

From fifty paces to my right, ahead of a clump of thick reeds, a flare of silver draws my attention. A watchman digs through the water and mud. "I've lost my spike!" he shouts.

But behind him...my heart stutters. Behind him, there, emerging from the reeds, by the light of the silver moons, is a nightmare come to life. Long black hair slices the night and a bandolier of daggers stretches across the chest of the fiercest, most beautiful girl I've ever seen.

She pounces on the watchman.

The man cries as her arms clamp around him, as if he's no more than a fly.

The watchman thrashes. "Let go, or I will fill this lake with your blood."

"The only thing you will do, you piece of rot, is die." Her voice, sharp as a chisel and hard as a hammer, slices across the water.

With one hand to the watchman's cheek, she holds him tight at the juncture of his shoulder and neck.

"Witch." The watchman spits, dark and red.

"You have no idea, human."

A loud crack, and the man crumples into the water.

Broken feet and broken hands and broken necks.

A shudder rakes my spine as the girl searches the lake for the next threat. At her forehead, a band of silver glows.

Human. Unlike her. And if the boy is a mage, that means...

Sorceress.

Monsters are real.

"Lidja!" Daesen breaks the surface of the water, a small figure in his arms, a yellow string bright in the dark.

"Where is she?" the sorceress calls. "You said you would haul her out. Where did you dump her?"

The reeds quiver. Her. *Me*. That deadly witch, that liar of a mage—they want *me*.

You will be the next sorceress of the Realm of Dreams.

Daesen rubs the nape of his neck, gaze surveying where he dumped me, twenty paces from where I now hide. I hold as still as a doe in a thicket. "I left her right here. I told her to not move."

"Oh, you told her to stay put? Brilliant, you overgrown bam. Brilliant."

They both stare at the shore, and I sink lower still.

This pair trailed our wagon, hunted me here. They'll find me in these reeds in two breaths. I have to move now or they'll find me and I'll never escape to find my sister.

So I creep through the reeds to solid ground and leave the magic pair in the freezing water. Silent, hidden, I plunge into the forest, alone.

CHAPTER 7

*B*ranches scratch at my water-logged limbs as I sprint under the maple and hemlock canopy. Luckily, it's only midsummer, when being wet outside at night isn't deadly. If it was after harvest, when snow envelops our world in white...

Even so, with the constant full moons, darkness is never complete, especially as dawn marches closer. I won't be difficult for my enemies to spot. Soon, I'll need to exit the forest to find a path toward the Scorched Mountains. Until now, I never imagined that unfamiliar terrain would require so much attention. I slow, wishing I had my chisel in hand, a door to pick open and hide behind if only to sleep, to awake refreshed and determine where I am.

One day, you'll regret never exploring beyond the village fields, Soli often said.

I hate when she's right.

"You're going the wrong way."

Every muscle in my body locks as Daesen steps from beneath a pine not fifteen paces ahead.

He tosses a red apple in the air, his tattooed neck flexing with the motion. Catches it. Again. His lips tug up at one corner, and a single black slash of an eyebrow rises as if he doesn't have a care in the world.

As if he's not preparing his next lies to me, like he did with my sister.

I step backward and my boot catches on a root. My breath whooshes as I land hard, back flat on the leaves.

"Baby oxsails are quieter than you."

I cringe into the leaf-coated dirt as the sorceress's face slides over mine. Even more beautiful up close, her hair shines like deepest night. Full lips grace an oval face, two streaks of mud across warm beige-brown cheeks. Black breeches and a matching blouse hug her from knee to long, graceful neck. She can't be much older than me.

But unlike me, she is deadly. At her brow rests a silver weave of razor-edged blades, like she's crowned by death itself. Her bandolier is complete—no doubt some of the knives newly red. An axe dangles from one of her hands, a foot from my face.

"W-witch," I breathe, frozen.

Her lips press tight as she stares at me, deep brown eyes unreadable, perfect eyebrows drawn in a severe line. "The Fates would *not* be so cruel."

She wheels away, and I scramble to my feet. This is it, my chance.

Run.

But Daesen blocks my path. "The Fates like to play, Lid. You know that well."

With a grunt and snap of her wrist, the sorceress drops the axe and hurls a dagger from her bandolier into a pine not five paces from my chest.

Another.

And another.

I blanch, bracing for the death blow. For her to turn, for the slice of her blade.

I lurch to the right, but the mage shifts easily and grabs my wrist, a grip as firm as the watchmen's chains. "As much as they love to play, I am certain the Fates did not bring us together for a racing contest."

"No one brought us together," I say. "You're the one hunting me." Worse things than monsters *do* roam now—and this mage is one of them. I dig my heels into the dirt as the sky begins to shift from black to deep blue. "Release me, mage."

The sorceress huffs loudly, and paces the forest floor gesturing wildly, no doubt conjuring evil.

"As much as I love the title, I am not a mage. As for her"— Daesen points to the young woman, a sly grin spreading on his lips—"when she is in this mood, I agree. I would not hesitate to call her a witch."

A hiss slithers through the pines. "The next dagger will slice your tongue," the sorceress says.

The mage's smile only grows as he winks at me. "Feeling threatened by the next power to rise in Fides, Lid? Perhaps we should set the two of you to a contest."

The sorceress says, "Absolutely not."

I yank my wrist free from the mage's grasp. "This is not a *game*."

"Unfortunately, I agree. Although I would greatly prefer one." The not-mage knocks his chest with a fist. "Daesen, shield of Memoria. Although Soli says you call it Memory, on your side of the curtain. Like you call the Realm of Denrathri *Dreams*, out of pure laziness."

"We are *not* lazy."

"The worthless bam only says that because he's lazier."

"And that"—Daesen grins toward the young woman—"is Lidja, sorceress of Memoria." He tips his chin toward me. "Sorceress, like you."

Lidja hurls another dagger, the blade missing Daesen's neck by a hands-breadth. "*High* sorceress, bam."

Daesen's dimples flash.

Sorceress. Like me. "But you fight."

"Of course I fight. I've known since I was five that the baya of Mizura will hunt me and drag me into a pit until I beg for death. It would be the height of idiocy to not know how to fight." She eyes me from head to toe. "Can *you* fight?"

"I can hold my own." I avoided Minteph's swing. "I escape."

The blades on her forehead catch the waning moonslight as Lidja steps toward me. "And how is that working out for you?"

I fight the instinct to utter Mama's favorite curse words, and instead pin my gaze to the trees behind her.

"Running will only get you so far against Orkayha's monsters," the sorceress continues. "You'll need to stand and fight, too, if you want to survive. Perhaps the bam is right. Perhaps we should test how you fight now, before we go to the trouble of crossing the grounded gate."

Muted, far away, a watchman's horn bellows. Which means in addition to the mage and sorceress hunting me, watchmen have found the crashed wagon and their dead fellows.

"Lid." Daesen waves in the direction of the horns. "The gate? The monsters hunting?"

Lidja shakes her axe at the mage-warrior. "As I said—lazy." With a final glare in my direction, she stalks into the forest.

Perhaps she'll fall in one of the many ravines in our forests. Then I'll only have Daesen to escape. "Does she have far to search for this gate?" I aim for casual.

Daesen quells a twitch of his lips. "We'd best hope not, or we'll have a journey of a week ahead rather than moments. The grounded gate is a shortcut to our realm, and there are watchmen camped around the Scorched Mountain's base that we'd prefer to avoid. We arrived through another grounded gate near a camp, and trust me, Lidja was *not* happy with how dirty her blade became."

I shudder. So her blades were bloodied even before the lake.

A loud crunch comes from the mage, drawing my attention

back to him and away from the forest where the murderous sorceress wanders.

"Hungry?" Daesen asks, red apple in hand.

"No." I brush aside the sudden tightness in my stomach. "You're heading across the Scorched Mountains?"

"Not just me. *We.*" Daesen reaches behind his shoulder, and I tense, but he simply extends a second apple. "Are you certain?"

This time, my stomach growls.

He tosses the apple high, and on instinct, I catch it. My mouth waters, the tang of tart fruit in the air and the weight of it in my palm nearly making me sway.

Eyelids hooded, he watches. Watches...like it's a game.

As hungry as I am, this boy is magic. And magic, as pretty as it may be in this package before me, is dangerous.

"We learn about your kind from birth." I toss the unbitten apple back at him. "I know better."

Quick as a night bird, he snatches the fruit as it arcs downward. "What exactly do you think our kind are, Alathea?"

The sky lightens, and I slip farther into the shadow of the maple. "Enemies."

An enemy...but one with a way to reach my sister, if he's telling the truth. If Soli truly is across the mountains.

"We have only one enemy, Ala. Maybe two, if you count Lidja when she's at her worst. But aside from Lidja's sour moods, the baya of Nightmares is it. Orkayha. Since the Fates birthed our worlds and Orkayha believed a lie of her sister's, Orkayha has hunted the triads of the magic realms. She is *our* enemy. Yours and mine and Lidja's." Daesen tosses the core of his apple and advances toward me. "And unless you have your sister's fighting skills, you had best prepare."

"You know nothing of my sister. Or of me."

From somewhere in the pines, a horn blares, and Daesen halts, the toes of his boots nearly touching mine. Sage and salt curl around me as he inhales deeply. "I know you smell like thyme." Again, he inhales, deeper. "And lavender." He grins. "Do your watchmen allow such frivolity?"

"Do you smell all of your attempted captives?"

"Only the prettiest ones."

Dried leaves crunch, and Lidja slips next to us. "Enough, Dae. Playtime is over."

"What's crawled up your backside, sweetcakes?"

"Your vocabulary remains atrocious. Sorry, was that too big of a word?" She flutters long lashes. "It means you're an ass."

"And you're being an awfully big—"

"Finish that sentence and you'll be a dead ass."

Hands up, Daesen shrugs, both dimples out now. What kind of twisted relationship does this pair keep?

Lidja lets her axe drop and nods to the east. "The gate is that way. The damned arch grows between two maples like it's meant for a union ceremony."

"Then lead the way, my lady. I've never said no to a party." Daesen waves a palm forward with a half bow...a bow just like my sister's last night. "High sorceresses first."

But I don't move. Instead, I stare between the two. Could I possibly trust my enemies to lead me to my sister? Should I? "How do I know you're not lying? Why isn't my sister with you, if you know each other so well?"

"I'm in no mood for questions, oxsail." Lidja glares at Daesen. "Tie her up, Dae. The sooner we are home, the sooner I can go back to ignoring you."

I tense, readying to run—

Again, Daesen slides between me and escape. "I warned you about her moods." Gray eyes shine in the dark of the forest. "Your sister sent us to fetch you, Ala. That remains true. When the shield of Denrathri died, all of his magic flowed to your sister. Soli accepted his power, like the gift it is. She waits for you now, in our home."

Another horn blasts, closer.

Lidja hitches her axe into the sheath at her waist. "Unless you want to be comatose on the ground as your watchmen circle, we need to move now. To return to Memoria before Orkayha slays the high sorceress in Denrathri and her power flows to *you*."

"I don't want it." Whatever that magic is, it would be no gift.

"Are you certain *she* is Soliana's sister?"

Ignoring Lidja, Daesen says, "I swear it, Ala. If Orkayha's underling monsters find you, if they throw you into one of the pits in Nightmares, you will die there, exactly like every sorceress before you has. But by the fortune of the Fates, we found you before they did. For the first time in five hundred years, we have a plan to stop Orkayha's hunt. But that chance only begins *if* you accept the power of the high sorceress of Dreams when it flows to you. *If* you and your sister open the gate to the Realm of Dreams, so that all of Fides can dream again." Daesen extends his palm farther to me, the circle and slash etched into his skin. "Without dreams, Ala, there is no hope."

But I keep staring at that scar in his palm, the twin to Soli's—both just like the line and circle on the back of Mother's sketch. "Prove it. Prove you know my sister."

Lidja swears, but Daesen says, "We know she wasn't at her assigned role yesterday. She wasn't delivering grain like she was supposed to."

"Which only means you've been following her." Has my sister been in danger, and I didn't realize?

Daesen's eyes narrow. "I cut her out of the shed with this." He taps the teardrop spear tucked on his back.

Something carved away that siding. "Maybe you spelled her."

Lidja says, "I re-made your filth stitching after Soliana cut her own face two years ago."

My gaze flings to the sorceress.

Impossible.

And yet...how else? No one, absolutely *no one* else knows the truth of that scar on Soli's cheek but my sister and me, that she cut her cheek herself to escape her assigned work in Elektos. That it wasn't a random accident, like we told the watchmen, but her own hand. I'd always wondered how the stitches—jagged from my trembling hand when she'd come home bleeding—had ended so fine and straight.

But if that's true, if this sorceress mended Soli's cheek...

"She's told us all kinds of stories about the two of you, Ala. Your sister trusts us," Daesen says. "You should, too."

Willing my pulse to slow, I draw air deep into my lungs. Because, for all the improbable, impossible ways this shouldn't be happening...I believe him. I believe that Soli has gone across the mountains, that she's taking some ill-advised, dangerous role of magic. That she thinks I have a role to serve, too.

As wild as my sister is, as wrong as she can be, I believe she would do this. She's always wanted a grand life, something beyond what we were born to in Elektos.

But none of that changes the truth.

Soli is not the one who hurts everyone who draws near. She is not who nearly drowned a wagon full of people. Who cut her mother's wrist and sent our parents running in fear.

She is not the one who made her own sister bleed.

"I can't." And I almost, *almost*, want to say more—that I wish this could different. That *I* was different. Again, I step deeper into the shadows of the trees.

The watchmen's horn blasts, long and unending.

"Ala," Daesen says, as Lidja's hand tightens on her axe. "Don't go that way."

"I have to find my sister." Another step, and this time, they both freeze, still as statues. Are they finally listening?

"Alathea, *do not go that way.*"

I retreat farther.

A breath curls from Lidja. "Oxsail..."

Again, I step, my chest filling with hope—

And halt. A shiver rakes up my spine and sinks into my bones.

The horn stops.

All around us, in the sudden silence, the very air ripples, pulses.

A rotten stench floods the forest.

Goose bumps zip along my skin.

Slowly, Daesen reaches for the weapons at his back, his muscles cording. He draws the spear and thick rounded plate of armor to his chest, the weapons glowing silver-blue. His tattoo shimmers, and Lidja shifts the axe to her left hand.

"Do not move," Daesen whispers to me, knuckles tightening on his spear.

Run, Lidja mouths. *Hide*.

Daesen's gaze pins behind me. "Go back, underling."

A low growl swells, and through the trees comes a voice of sludge and torture and death. "Try to stop me, dog."

"With pleasure." Daesen hurls his spear.

A sharp shove digs into my side, and I roll into a maple. Lidja blocks my view as I scramble. I crawl around the trunk, wincing, staring at what heaves between maple and hemlock.

A monster.

CHAPTER 8

*B*eneath the brightening forest canopy, eight arms of exposed muscle each end in a deadly spear-tip of a claw. The monster's torso of raw scales shimmers, and within its snouted head, glacial, clear eyes scan the forest floor. Thick trunks of legs with peeling yellow talons root into the undergrowth only paces from the sorceress and the mage.

A real, living monster.

Black spots prick my vision as I flatten further into the trunk of the maple.

Run. Hide. Lidja's silent command slams through my bones.

But with the monster between me and the Scorched Mountains, and my sister beyond them…I need a weapon.

From closer still, a horn bellows.

The watchmen. The watchmen that protect Elektos from monsters like this one. Monsters that are *real*.

The monster punches a clawed arm downward, and Daesen blocks the strike with a clang on his armored plate. Lidja launches at the creature with her axe. Its roar shakes the trees as she rips a slab of pink flesh from the monster's shoulder.

The monster retreats, stumbling over a rock, and Lidja

pursues, swinging her axe again. A slice of stone cleaves from the rock—a jagged, sharp piece that would fit perfectly in my palm.

Quickly, silently, I slide from behind my tree closer to the rock.

"Servants of the weak one, your magic reeks." That awful rasp of a voice. "Have you forgotten how you bleed on this side of the curtain?"

"Not as well as you." Daesen lunges for the monster.

I slip forward another step. Two more, and that rock will be in reach.

The monster whips its claws, and Lidja and Daesen fight, a clash of metal and heaves and flat thuds. The fight leads them away, farther into the forest. Farther from me.

I edge closer. One step left.

"What are you protecting?" the monster says. "What is hiding in this rotten wood?"

"Nothing, you piece of mash." With a grunt, Daesen smashes his armored plate into the beast.

I slide forward, reaching for the jagged piece of stone—

The monster halts, its snout snapping up.

I freeze.

Its razor teeth bare. "I see it." The monster slams its arms into Daesen and Lidja, hurling them through the trees.

I snatch the rock from the ground and run.

The ground thunders behind me. *"I see it I see it I see it."*

Ahead, the forest gives way to a steep ravine, at least five paces wide.

"Head east!" Lidja shouts as I rush for that gap. "Jump!"

But my heart stutters at that too-wide gap, and I fling myself downward instead, half falling, half scraping my way down the side of the ravine until I'm deep in a cluster of pricking bramble at its base.

Above, at the top of the ravine, branches snap and the ground shudders, but the monster pauses.

"Come out, little mystery," it rasps. "Come out and greet me. My lady desires to know what lingers."

I curl as small as I can and sneak forward. Metal and shouts ring from above, Lidja and Daesen no doubt fighting the monster. Faster, forward, I creep along the base of the ravine, ignoring the tear of my sleeves and breeches, the scrape of thorns. Faster—

Until black boots and clay-colored breeches stop me.

Up, I look, pulse racing, to find a single star on a sleeve.

Minteph.

"Little troublemaker, far from home. When I found that wagon, I had a feeling it was you." Minteph hauls me up from the bramble, sneering in my face. "And I am always right. I found her!"

Behind Minteph, the ravine opens outward to the forest floor, and I brace for a row of watchmen, for the slap of chains.

Leaves crunch.

The very ground trembles.

And through the trees, that horrible rasp says, "Hold it."

I writhe against Minteph's hold. "We have to run. Use your power from Emon. Call for the weapon they're preparing in Elektos, the monster-killer."

"Ignorant child." Minteph doesn't move. "What you saw was no monster-killer. That weapon is to keep your treasonous friends in line."

"We have to run run *run*—"

From the pines, the monster emerges, bleeding pink ooze, inhaling deeply through its massive snout. "What is it? What have you found for me, watchman?"

"A new addition to your pits," Minteph says. "Tell your baya I expect the reward she promised."

A reward. From the baya of Nightmares...to this watchman, who is not fighting, not running. The watchmen and monsters... they are on the same side.

The same side, against me.

Under my skin, the leaves rustle. Smoke unfurls. Wind rises.

The monster sniffs. "Magic."

I kick, hard. I scrape and scratch and shout.

"This thing?" Minteph says. "She is nothing more than a girl who thinks she can flout the truths."

I wish desperately for my chisel. I'd stab it right through the hand that holds me. I kick harder.

The monster clacks its snout. "It is something. It smells of home. Hand it to me."

Minteph shoves me away, himself between me and the monster. "Reward first, then girl."

"Unwise watchman." One of the monster's claw-hands plunge forward.

I brace for the puncture of the claw—

Minteph shrieks, and I drop to the ground. I scramble to my hands and knees, away from them both.

"You filthy creature, you—" Skin slaps, and Minteph falls silent.

I push to my feet to run, and a monster arm plunges down ahead of me, behind me, trapping me with limbs and rank breath. "What. Is. It."

I open my mouth to deny I'm anything at all, but a bright line of flickering lights appears from the east, deep among the pines. Bright enough that all of us pause, watchman and monster and me.

As if lightning flashes in the forest, the lights advance in a single streaming line. Closer, it comes until the light curves and streams toward us—not a single line, but thousands of twinkling lights.

Toward us, the lights fly.

Toward *me*.

I raise my hands to block the strange lights from pelting into me, and instead, the lights halt right over my head, pinning in the air above me like a towering headdress.

Minteph's bleeding arm leaks across his clay shirt. "Magic. You're *magic*."

"The magic of Denrathri," the monster says. "I have been searching for it."

The line of light pulses, bright, once.

I dive through a gap in the monster's arms and sprint.

The twinkling lights follow as my legs pump, my feet slip. My lungs burn. I run and run and—

Two massive maples emerge ahead, on the other side of a brief clearing. Between them, an interlocking bridge of branches creates a clear arch.

The gate.

From behind the maple, Lidja emerges, limping, to face the monsters at my back.

"Where is Daesen?" I pant, searching the brightening forest for the mage-warrior, but only the monster and Minteph stalk closer.

"Bleeding his thick head out from that mawlyr's attack." Wincing, her black blouse wet with blood, Lidja narrows her eyes at the flowing line of lights. "It's happened, then. The high sorceress of Denrathri is dead." She shifts her gaze to the monster behind me. "Stay behind me, oxsail. Daesen and I will not open the gate until these filth-rakers are dead."

The monster slams a claw into the ground. "In six days, no gate will keep your realm safe, sorceress."

"*High* sorceress, carrion." Lidja lunges forward, fighting once again. Her axe swings for the monster, but it's nothing like the rapid strikes of earlier.

I search again for a sharp stone, for a stick, for any weapon. I need Lidja to open this gate, to get to my sister.

A blood-coated hand clamps over my arm. "This time, I'll drag you to the Realm of Nightmares myself," Minteph says. "Once I see you there, at the bottom of a dark pit, screaming for mercy once more, I will find your sister and throw her into the next one."

I buck against him even as the flickering lights above me begin to buzz. "If you come near my sister, *I* will hurt *you*."

Paces away, Lidja slows further, as the monster's claws slip through her attacks and slice her skin.

"In six days, all of Fides will be Orkayha's—it doesn't matter what havoc you conjure to wreak upon us." Minteph points at the flickering lights that circle me still. "Elektos has fallen, Denrathri has fallen, Memoria will fall, and you will be deep in a pit, where no scrap of light can reach you."

The monster lifts one of its claws high for Lidja as she raises her axe, slowly.

Too slowly.

Lidja, who stitched my sister's cheek, while this very watchman burned iron into Soli's wrists. The watchman who was supposed to protect her, protect *us*, when all they've been is *friends* with monsters. When all they've done is hurt her, hurt *me*, and lied and lied and lied.

Magic has hurt me, hurt my sister. But so has this watchman, over and over.

Brighter, the lights pulse above me, stronger. No longer like a headdress, but an ever-expanding ball of light. Of *power*. *Magic is death*...but a magic mage saved me from drowning today. A sorceress helped my sister.

And if Soli trusts this sorceress, this mage...

Maybe it's not always death.

Maybe magic can help me, too.

I rip from Minteph's grasp and reach upward for the pulsing lights—

Magic explodes from within me, sudden and bright, as lightning splits the woods.

CHAPTER 9

*L*eaves crunch as I gasp upward, sudden, head whirling. Not five paces away, rammed through with a spear, the monster's head lies on the ground. At its side, Minteph is unmoving, Daesen and Lidja hovering over the bodies.

Shouts ring from close by—more watchmen are coming. It wasn't only Minteph after all.

Lidja sways, her face streaked with dirt and blood and ooze. She presses a hand to her still-bleeding side. A deep cut mars her cheek.

"You're hurt," I croak.

"I've had worse." Lidja sinks to my side, skin paling.

Daesen crouches next to her, a thick red streak leaking from his own temple. "If that wound was in my side, I'd be unconscious."

"I know," Lidja says. "Barely a scratch, and you're no better than a baby. What a weakling."

"A moment ago, I was a bam."

"I was in a good mood." Lidja slumps harder, gaze flicking toward me. "You accepted the high sorceress's magic."

Magic. The word, the *thing* inside me buzzes and rattles, but my gaze returns to Minteph. "It was the only way to stop him. Is he dead, too?"

"Stunned," Daesen says. "As likely the Fates themselves are, from the size of that flare." He tucks his armored plate against his back, alongside his spear. "Imagine what you'll be able to do when you find the word that fully unlocks your power."

Fates, words, power.

I know I should ask, but only one truth circles me now: *Minteph saw.*

He saw that I used magic—right after he called the monster to him.

Now they will know the secret I've been hiding. They know what I can do.

Magic is death. Those are the only words that matter.

The shouts of watchmen grow closer in the forest.

"We need the healing power in Memoria, Ala," Daesen says, as Lidja's eyes flutter closed. He points to the arch between the twined maple trees a few paces away. "And you need to learn how to wield the power of a sorceress."

"High sorceress," I say, my gaze on Lidja, on the band of now-dull blades at her brow. Her lips curl upward at my correction. "I don't know how to be one."

Tucking an arm beneath Lidja's shoulders, Daesen hauls her upward. "Lucky for you, you'll have the world's worst instructor to help you learn."

"Better than a silver-tongued bam," Lidja says, head flopping to Daesen's shoulder. "You're basically a big beetle, you know."

"Mixing up your names for me—you really are in pain." With quick steps, Daesen helps her toward the arched maples.

"She has to promise, Dae," Lidja says, her speech slow and slurred and loud enough for me to hear from a step behind. "*Make* her promise."

"No," I say. "I would never be fool enough to make promises to strangers."

Daesen's gray eyes find mine. "Then welcome to your first time. If you want to see your sister through on the other side of that grounded gate, Lidja and I need to open it. And my high sorceress says before we do that, you have to make her a promise, so a promise it is."

A morning breeze rustles the leaves of the arched tree. "You're lying."

"Oxsail is right," Daesen mutters. With a growl, he helps Lidja forward until they stand next to one of the trees. The two each press a single hand to the bark, their bodies connected where Daesen supports Lidja's weight. Silver-blue unfolds across the joined branches, and a transparent veil unravels from the arch to the ground.

My feet jerk forward, as if by their own accord, called toward the hum beyond that gate.

Shouts ring again, close enough I can make out the threats.

Daesen extends his scarred palm to me across the sorceress. "Make us this Fates-damned promise so we can get out of here." He crooks a finger when I don't move. "*Now*. The words must be bound by a sorceress."

Still, I hesitate—

"Your sister is with the baya," Lidja whispers.

Soli. With a monster that shreds minds. I slap my hand onto Daesen's.

Lidja flops a bloodied hand over ours. Long, chilled fingers spread across the back of my hand. "Say it, Dae."

"Alathea, do you promise to bind yourself as the sorceress—"

"*High* sorceress, bam."

"—high sorceress of Denrathri to restore your realm to its fated glory, until the last breath leaves your body?"

I swallow at the gravity of question. "Why Soli? Why me?"

"Because they named you as their successor," Daesen says. "As for why they did, that Fates-forsaken reason has passed with them."

61

"That's what the bam thinks," Lidja says, barely more than a whisper. "I think it's because you were born unlucky, just like the rest of us."

"But what of the monsters with claws?" The blood from Lidja's wound sticks to my skin, metallic and bitter. "What if *I* hurt someone?"

"There are no beings with claws in our realm, Ala." A dimple flashes, fast and deep. "The only monsters you'll find in my home are Lidja and your sister."

Lidja brushes a palm against Daesen's chest, a failed slap. "He means you won't hurt anyone, not now that you've accepted your power. Not if you use it as the Fates intended. But if you two keep jabbering, I might find death less painful."

Death. That's what waits for me here, if the watchmen find me with a monster and an unconscious Minteph. The shouts escalate, and boots shuffle through the leaves, so close now—

"Swear you will take me to my sister. As soon as we cross, you will bring me to her. You will ensure that she and I are safe. Together. Swear that, and I will promise what you ask of me."

"I swear it," Daesen says. "I will not stop until you are at your sister's side, and you are both safe, together."

"Then I swear it, too." I place my palm to Daesen's. It can't be that different, after all, across the mountains. "I will become the high sorceress you need. I promise."

Lidja fingers dig into our bound hands. "So be it."

At Lidja's brow, the band of blades pulses rose-gold. Heat jolts through my veins, piercing and jagged and raw, like a thousand pins dragged along my skin straight to my hand, to the point where our skin connects.

A branding.

My palm burns as Daesen and Lidja press their hands around mine. As wind and summer storms and wild clover gallop through my blood. The rustling in my veins awakens. Roils.

Rose-gold light pulses around us, my chest full and light and—and—

Magic.

Magic thrums and throbs through my veins with the force of a summer tornado that flattens a home to the earth.

Lidja slips her hand from mine, and the thrum drops.

The sorceress melts into Daesen, and he sweeps her into his arms. He plants a kiss to her forehead, and the sorceress's brow-blades dull once more.

"Remember. You're the weak one." And her head falls, unconscious.

I stare at the scar seared into my palm. A circle and a slash, bright pink and puckered.

What have I done?

A shout rings out, "I found them!"

Daesen tilts his chin to the silver-blue arch, an unconscious Lidja in his arms, and shoulders back, I launch forward, through the shimmering gate, for Soli.

CHAPTER 10

*H*eat presses into my skin, saturated and heavy. Insects clamor and clack in a lush forest all around Daesen, Lidja, and me, where we've stepped through the shimmering gate. Early morning sky stretches through fans of green. The ground is dark with overgrown plants that have long, reed-like leaves. Steps ahead, an ivory dome looms, propped by braided columns.

This is *nothing* like home.

The buzz of insects grows.

No, not insects. The buzz is inside my head. Layered voices, low and high and all speaking, all at once, much too loud.

Loud, until a single scraping voice cuts through. *"I can quiet the new memories if you request it, Alathea of Elektos."*

Between the columns, a creature sways. Towering and thin, the color of ash, the predator's eyes shine gold with a horizontal slash of black. A deep burgundy robe gapes as the being raises a bony limb.

That voice was *inside* my head.

"We save our voices for only when they are needed most."

"Then save it. Don't speak to me. Not like that."

The creature lifts and lets fall a bony shoulder. *"As you wish."*

What I wish is for my chisel, or a knife from Lidja's bandolier.

The wraith's gaze flies to my hands.

"Lucius." Daesen draws the creature's attention from me, and I nearly slump against the tree behind me in relief. "A mawlyr found us on the other side."

The creature sinks down the steps, placing a skeletal hand on Lidja's limp shoulder where she lies in Daesen's arms. With a gasp, the sorceress jerks awake. Her slashed skin closes piece by piece, the blood slowing.

The creature reaches his other hand for me.

I jolt back, but the creature—*Lucius*, Daesen called him—only watches, silent and steady. He reaches again, fast, and I squeeze my eyes shut, ready for the blow that must be coming.

"I can help you."

"I don't need your help."

"Lucius is a wraith," Daesen says as Lidja stirs at his chest. "They are gifted with healing magic, which can ease the voices of the memory-power you just accepted. Unless you want to swoon at my feet again, of course."

"I didn't swoon. I—I..." I search for the words for what I did in the woods, when I reached for the line of flickering lights, and they swooped into me in an explosion of golden light. Exhaustion laces through me. "How do I make the voices stop?"

Daesen's gaze shifts to understanding. "When we accept our power, the memories from every being who held our role before comes with it. I may be eighteen, but I know every one of the centuries that our world has existed. Most of the memories fade rapidly, there if you need them, but otherwise they are a part of your bones already. Their knowledge, yours. Every fight, every loss, every victory." His dimple flashes. "Every caress."

Even as he speaks, the voices in my head quiet to no more than a dull murmur.

"You can ask Lucius for help, Ala. You can trust him. He

answers only to the baya."

I stiffen. Does he really think that will make me trust this creature? "The baya is a *monster*."

"Only when he's hungry." Lid presses against Daesen's chest, and he releases her to the ground. "I've called him worse."

Through the gaping side of her blouse, a thick scar remains.

A monster has my sister.

Lucius's voice rasps inside my head. *"Not all magic is to be feared, Alathea."*

"Then you don't know all magic," I think in return, before I can stop myself. Shoulders squaring, I turn my back to the wraith and face Daesen. "Take me to my sister."

"It's a half-day walk, unless you're ready for a Dae specialty." Daesen flexes his arms with the flash of a dimple. "Trust me, it's the ride of your life."

"No. Absolutely not. Point the way, and I will walk to my sister. Myself."

"Suit yourself." Daesen crooks a grin at Lidja. "What about you, princess? Fancy a round in these arms?"

Lidja snatches a leaf from the nearest tree, and with a flip of her wrist, the leaf shudders, writhes—and shifts into a green snake.

Magic. I recoil into the forest.

"I warned you to not call me that one more time." She opens her palm, and the snake lunges for Daesen. He slams his armored plate upward and the snake drops to the green bushes. Daesen lifts the edge of the shield to bring it down—

A light pops and the snake is gone, Daesen's shield thudding into soft, empty earth.

Blood runs from a new strip of cut skin at Lidja's temple. She swipes a finger through the red and wipes it on Daesen's neck. "Worth it," she says.

This is why I don't want magic. Dangerous. Deadly. I need to find my sister, and then lead us somewhere safe.

"This is playing," Lucius says. *"This is no more than small magic. Their realm magic is broad and powerful and bound only by the baya's commands. Daesen holds the magic of weaponry for the shield, and Lidja strategy for the sorceress. With her word, she can aim the shield, and the shield attacks."*

From the ground, Lidja selects a stick, and with a flick of her wrist, an even larger snake appears.

Both his dimples flash, and Daesen unsheathes the teardrop spear.

Lucius says, *"If you care to watch, they've been known to play their games all day."*

"This is not playing," I say.

"Then follow me, and I will bring you to the palace, where your sister rests."

I hurry after the wraith into a thick grove of palm trees, the ground coated in bright green ferns. We pass by a temple with its braided columns that rise from a flat dais to a hollowed dome. To carve marble like that, to make the lines so fine and smooth...for a moment, I want to leave all this and simply study *how* the carver created such curves. Within the temple's shade, fireflies with tiny lights on their backs flicker.

Palms. Temple. Fireflies.

The ferns lick at my dirty breeches. I've never seen any of this in Elektos. Where are the words coming from?

"From the memories of the last high sorceress of Denrathri," Lucius says, as if he heard my silent question. *"You have her power, and her memories of power and place—the memories you need to fill this role, to survive. This is her gift to you, just as yours will pass to the one who follows."*

The fireflies twinkle, the same as that line of lights in the forest before it dove for me. "They're memories."

"They *hold* memories," Daesen says, the ferns shushing as he catches up to me. Gently, he cradles his hands around one of the bleeping insects. His voice drops, expression soft. "On their back, each carries one. These are what we protect in the Realm of Memoria."

"Not we." I stare at the firefly, at the bleating light. "You. What I protect is elsewhere."

But instead of an image of my sister amidst this heavy air and lush palms, a different image swells inside me—one I've never seen before, of swirling columns of sand, of bright pink and pale yellow and soft blue lights that bounce through the air, of a sparkling ocean, and clean, soft air.

The Realm of Dreams. Denrathri.

And if here in Memoria, they protect memories…that means I am the protector of dreams themselves.

In my whole life, I've had only one dream, the night when I turned eleven. I dreamt of a long, unending sunset over crystal waters, of not just the three fate-stars in the sky, but a whole cascade that glitters over the sea like precious gems. I cherished that dream long after it faded. When the long winters dragged onward, when even the shadows of Elektos felt too deep, always, I held onto that bright, single dream.

I raise my gaze to Daesen. "Someone told me that without dreams, there is no hope."

"Then that someone has never visited my chamber." Sparks alight in his gray eyes. "In fact, the last visitor said they were so full of hope, I would be welcome to keep them from sleeping ever again."

I sputter at the outrageous claim, searching for a response—

"Bam!" Lidja emerges from the palms, axe in hand. "Shut it and walk. Soon we'll be no better than her side of the curtain if we dawdle the whole way to the palace."

His amusement flees. "Fates, Lid, don't curse us."

We make our way down a jungle-blanketed hillside, and up another, exhaustion sinking deep into my limbs. Minteph's words from the woods swirl in my mind. *Elektos has fallen.* What could he have meant? "My home isn't so awful, you know."

"How would you know, if you've never left it?" Daesen asks.

That's exactly what my sister would say.

Silent, even slower now, I follow the wraith, my tread like a winter ox, bumbling and heavy. I yearn for the muddy lanes of Elektos, for the shadowed corners I know so well.

Even if we don't have dreams, it is my home.

Clangs and clacks break through the dense palms ahead. Grunts of pain come from too close. Daesen prods my back as Lucius moves faster.

Again, Minteph's voice rises in me. *In six days, all of Fides will be Orkayha's.* Clearly, Minteph has gone mad, but with the sounds of a clash in this jungle…"Is your realm at war?"

"That is our soldiers at practice," Daesen says. "Although soon, the commander's army will have more than practice, if the protective layer over our realm falls."

Before us, a sea of green forest undulates, broken only at the far horizon by sparkling blue. Ivory temples dot the canopy, and everywhere, fireflies flicker. On the highest point, looming over the hills around it, stands a sprawling, bone-white palace, large as the hill it stands upon. Soaring columns hold up a massive domed roof that sweeps upward into cupolas at each of the four corners. Morning light sparkles on the marble, as if fireflies shine within the stone.

The palace of Memoria.

"It never fails to take my breath away," Daesen murmurs at my side.

I glance upward—and find his eyes on me.

My cheeks warm, even as my stomach drops.

Lidja groans. "Don't fall for it, oxsail. This one will flirt with a rock."

Daesen's grin only grows. "Your sister is in the palace. Knowing Soliana, she's working on prying every secret from the baya's tight lips."

The baya is the one who shreds your skin. How could Soli

possibly be safe with a being like that? With a monster?

A wind, hot and weighted, shushes through the palms and ferns. From behind us, more clashing metal splits the hum of insects.

Lidja says, "Bam, do you hear that?"

I hesitate and listen, but I hear no voice, no tread of a monster.

"Yes. I believe I do." Daesen cocks his head, as if listening harder.

I strain for anything other than the palms and insects, but—"I hear nothing."

"That's because he's our baya, not yours," Lidja says. "Without the power of their throne, yours cannot summon you."

Smooth as a breeze, Daesen slips his spear from his back, tip tilted forward. The tip...that begins to glow.

"Danger," Daesen says. "And I have a feeling I know from who."

Soli. She's with the baya—which means she's in danger, too.

Daesen and Lidja burst into a run and I sprint after them, ferns nipping at my breeches. I don't care if the baya is a monster. If he has placed my sister in danger, we'll soon find out just how destructive this magic inside me is.

I spill from the jungle to orange earth and soft green grass, thunder up broad white marble steps, and through massive wooden doors.

A clash of metal rings from ahead, from a massive hall.

"The throne room!" Lidja calls.

I sprint faster, legs burning, right on Lidja's heels.

Turn after turn I run until the clash of metal smashes from within.

I hurl myself inside, farther into this realm, into the palace of Elektos's enemy—

And there is my sister, back on the marble floor, the tip of a sword at her chest.

CHAPTER 11

The magic in my veins roars to life as I take in my sister on the marble floor. A broad-shouldered man holds the tip of a jeweled sword to the center of her rib cage. I barrel forward after Lidja, Daesen just behind me.

With a sharp flick of Lidja's wrist, wooden spikes shoot upward from the floor, blocking my path. "First lesson, oxsail. Do not interrupt Visander's sparring sessions."

Sparring? "He has a blade to my sister's chest." Smoke curls from my skin. "Tell him to stop."

"He's the one giving orders, not us." Lidja narrows her eyes at the rising smoke. "Although *I* am giving you this one—calm your temper. The Fates did not grant us magic for it to be misused."

For a moment, no one moves as my sister remains under that blade, the man towering over her.

Next to me, a smile plays at Daesen's lips. "I knew it. She almost took him down."

The man with the sword speaks, his voice low and smooth. "Do you yield?"

"I absolutely yield," my sister says. "Completely."

Slowly, so slowly I strain against the spikes keeping me in

place, the man removes his sword from Soli's chest. He nods. "Well fought, my—"

Soli smashes her knees to the side and the man leaps to avoid going down to the floor.

My sister pops to her feet as the man swears softly.

"That wasn't yielding," he says.

My sister grins, broad and warm, with a shrug. "I hate losing. I—" Soli's voice dies as she catches sight of me.

With a twist of Lidja's wrist, the wooden spikes disappear and I run to my sister.

We meet halfway across the room, her arms already around me. I squeeze tight and push her back in the same breath, frowning. At her jaw is a new shallow scratch, long and red.

"He hurt you," I say.

Soli shakes her head. "That happened last night as I slept."

"Last night…" A stone sinks in my gut. Me. That was from me. My magic, when I sunk the death wagon. Still, that would be nothing compared to the burst of magic when I accepted the high sorceress's powers. "And this morning? Are you hiding another injury?"

Soli quirks a brow. "I'm not the one who likes hiding, dearest sister."

I release a breath. Lidja was telling the truth, then—as long as I use this magic as the Fates intend, I will not hurt my sister any more.

Who the Fates are, and what they exactly they intend…that's a whole new matter I'll need to understand soon enough.

"Besides," Soli says, drawing my focus back, "Vis wouldn't hurt me, even if I didn't wear the jillbracer."

She taps a fist against the sleeveless leather vest she wears, and it clinks like a layer of metal underpins the fabric. Soli grins. "*I* almost beat *him*. I thought with the shield's power that I *could* beat the baya. Apparently, I was close enough to cause Dae's spear to glow, so that's a near-win for now."

"But..." A second stone clunks in my gut. My sister was fighting the baya of Memoria. The *baya*. "You could have been killed."

"You don't need to protect me here, Ala," Soli says, followed by a scowl. "Although no one other than a watchman would actually consider locking me in a shed to be *protection*."

"I was trying to keep you safe." Always. Especially here, in this dangerous realm—dangerous enough that my sister carries an armored plate and wears a metal vest. "How do you know this place? How *long* have you known this place?"

"Long enough to know what it feels like to be free. To learn to fight without worrying about being thrown in a wagon. To have friends. Real friends, who aren't afraid of their own shadow, or always hiding in someone else's."

"Shadows are safe."

A discreet cough comes from across the hall. Now that he doesn't have a blade at my sister's chest, I take in the baya, even as he observes us with uncanny stillness. A white shirt fits his medium-sized frame, black breeches tucked into knee-high brown boots, the jeweled sword bound to his waist.

"Where are his claws?"

"Ala! Don't embarrass me." Soli drags me farther from the center of the room, toward a long table lined with food. "Those stories are for idiots in Elektos. Use your eyes. Vis is only frightening if you happen to be a bright shiny object; he's worse than a hoarder-squirrel. His chamber is so cluttered, even a new gift would go unnoticed. But he certainly doesn't have anything as terrifying as claws."

Where he stands at the foot of a dais with Lidja and Daesen, Vis holds out his hand, examining his fingers.

Can he *hear* us? All the way over here?

I lower my voice further. "You didn't see what I did, Soli. When those two brought me over, the way they fought the watchman...You don't know what they're capable of." The crack of the watchman's neck in Lidja's bare hands echoes through me.

"I know very well what they're capable of. I'm the one who's been here before, remember?"

"How could I remember, when you never told me?"

"You didn't want to know. You're just like all the others in Elektos. Like the watchmen who keep their heads in the sand. Who did nothing as nightmares have taken over our home. You buried your ears to avoid knowing it, just like Mama."

I reel back, even as a memory from my childhood pricks my skin.

"You can't keep your head in the mud forever, Bex," Mother whispered to Mama on the other side of our wool curtain, when she thought Soli and I were sleeping. "Nightmares find you there, too."

I watch my sister as she assesses the food on the table. "I'm here now."

"What did they say to convince you?" Soli selects a bunch of purple orbs, and lifts them by a thin branch. *Grapes.* "Did Daesen promise you two boxes of reward food?"

"Don't eat it." I snatch the bunch from her hand. "It could be spelled."

"Don't tell me you came here just to continue believing the Sancta's lies."

"I came here to keep you safe."

From the foot of the dais, silver-blue light flares, and a wind bursts forth from where Vis, Daesen, and Lidja hold hands.

I slide in front of my sister, eyeing the door—

"They're the ones keeping us safe, Ala. The triad keeps the Realm of Memoria safe. This realm holds the memories of our whole world, for all of us."

The wind picks up, stronger, tugging at my shins, pushing at my back. The plates of food throw scents of sugar and cream, and Soli's hair lifts. The very skin on my arms lifts into goose bumps.

Magic.

This is the magic I know in my veins. Destructive. Terrifying. Far from the healing magic of the wraith. "We should return home the first chance we have. We'll find our mothers. Wherever they are—that must be safe. We'll stay with them."

"That will be hard, given Vis just reinforced the protective layer around his realm."

The wind dies, and a silver-blue shimmer coats the marble ceiling high above us, spreading like an overflowing river.

"You mean they're locking us in."

Soli raises a brow. "I would have thought you of all people would understand, sister. But no—they're keeping enemies *out*, like most people would bolt a home. Enemies won't be able to enter, but we'll be able to leave through the gate to our realm, when we open it to Denrathri."

The shimmer coats the walls, downward, flowing to the floor, toward us. "What if you stay somewhere safe, while I find this gate?"

"You can't open it without me. As much as I wish it otherwise, sister, we're stuck with each other."

"What if—"

Soli stomps a single booted foot. "I know this realm. You don't. I'm not going anywhere. We belong in the magic realms, you and I both."

"But..." I search the room. The possibly poisoned food, the baya and his shield and sorceress, the silver-blue magic streaming from their hands. My sister, who practically shines with confidence here, while I... "It's dangerous, Soli. It's too dangerous to stay."

Soli takes my free hand and rolls back my sleeve. In the blue shimmer from above, my scarred wrist glows. "This is danger, Ala. This."

Gently, she releases me. "Don't you want to be something other than the Sancta's underling? Don't you want to stop fighting each other and be on the same side for once?"

"I've always been on your side." But I can't look away from the deep grooves in my skin. The grooves carved there by Minteph. Minteph, who the Sancta brought to my home.

Soli holds her wrist to mine, scar matching scar. "Did it ever occur to you, sister, that in our home, where watchmen you work for have been taking our friends for years, *I've* been protecting *you*? That I've brought you here, to keep *you* safe? That I knew they would come for you?"

I *knew* my sister would never leave me behind.

"Here, no one is chasing us. No one will tell us what to do or not do, who to kiss or not kiss." She points to the bunch of grapes still clutched in my hand. "What to eat or not."

The blue shimmer fades, and the baya releases hands with Lidja and Daesen. The three stay close, conversing.

No cuts, no death.

No one pays us the slightest attention.

Safe.

Is my sister right? That here, she's safe? That I'm safe, even with this magic in me?

"No more protecting me, Ala. No more hiding. You have a role to undertake, and that's what you need to do. Not run around thinking you're protecting me."

But I can't promise that. Whatever else I am, I am Soli's sister.

"What if...what if we agree to protect each other? To take on these roles together?" I extend the grapes to her, tentative.

For a moment, Soli eyes the offering.

I hold my breath.

With a nod, she plucks a fruit from the vine. "Fine." My sister smiles and points to the baya. "Go prove it."

CHAPTER 12

*M*y steps barely register in the massive room as I cross the marble floor to the dais. Columns line the walls, interspersed with windows. A warm breeze pushes through the openings even as the bright light of late morning dims. Far off, a muted roll of thunder hums.

The baya—Vis—watches me approach. At his nod, Daesen and Lidja slide away. Up close, a silver streak cuts through his night-black hair and a tattoo of a fanged serpent licks the cool beige skin of his collarbone. The sword that met my sister's chest is sheathed in a belt at his waist. The marble throne looms behind him.

Three steps away, I halt, fighting the urge to keep my eyes on the floor. "My sister calls you friend."

"As I call her." His voice is deep and soft, like night silk. "What shall I call you, Alathea?"

"The end of you, if you so much as bring that sword near her ever again."

"You dare to threaten a baya?"

I glance over my shoulder to find Soli talking with Daesen,

her nervous gaze on me. *Protect each other.* "For my sister, I would more than dare."

"As would I, to keep my realm safe. As did the baya before me, and the baya before him." Vis steps down from the dais, until I'm forced to tilt my chin up to hold his gaze. "Perhaps we will not be friends, Alathea, but we can understand each other. If we're both willing to lie for what we want and kill for what we protect."

I open my mouth to object, but only a squeak comes out.

Kill.

Magic is death. Maybe not all magic, like Lucius's power, but this man, this baya...

"Soli *is* in danger here."

"That is true. Every one of us who holds the power of the triads in Memoria and Dreams is at risk. We may live long lives, but we die like any other being, if a strike is true. Not one of the bayas of Memoria before me have walked this plane even the forty-five years I have. We are all in danger, Alathea."

"Is my sister in danger from you?"

"As you correctly observed—no claws today."

"That's not an answer."

"Your sister is not threatening my realm. So no, right now, today, Soliana is not in danger from me." Outside, thunder rolls again, as Vis continues. "But she is not safe. Orkayha will not cease hunting any of us until she believes she is avenged."

"Daesen said Orkayha believed a lie." At the table of food across the room, Daesen whispers something to my sister, and Soli's laugh bursts forth. "What lie could set anyone on a quest to kill for five centuries?"

Vis follows my gaze. "She believes her sister was wronged. Grievously wronged, by the bayas of Memoria and Denrathri, which I know to be false. But Orkayha knows it as truth, and so that is what matters." Vis cocks his head, searching my expression, nodding. "It's not so difficult to understand, truly, what we would do for those we love—for our own family, if they asked it of us, if they said they were wronged."

I can't hide the understanding on my face. "I will not let my sister fight. She's not made for battle."

"You mean, you do not wish her to be." Vis's gaze fixes on Lidja, where the sorceress examines pastries topped with berries, ignoring Soli and Daesen trading barbs. "My family is not born of the same blood, but the bond between a baya and their shield and sorceress is just as impossible to sever. Even after death I would feel their hearts beside mine. I will lie and cheat and kill to keep Daesen and Lidja safe, too."

For a heartbeat, I wonder if our mothers ever said the same about me. If they ever threatened the moons to keep us safe. "I have only my sister. I feel nothing like that for"—I wave my hand at Vis—"for a being like you."

"You will, once the baya of Denrathri takes their throne. Then you will hear the baya's call and heed their commands. But with the gates to Denrathri closed, all routes in and out of that realm have been lost. Right now, the missing baya carries only a sliver of the power the throne instills, and they do not yet carry the curse it holds."

Mama's colorful curse from years ago rings in my ears. "Is a baya so fragile they can't withstand a salty word?"

Vis's mouth spreads wide, a smile brightening his face. If he wasn't at least twice my age, I might even find him attractive.

"This is not a curse like you know it, Alathea. This curse is what ties the bayas to the throne, to our realms and roles." Vis frowns. "Never before has a baya avoided their destiny, so how painfully this curse will lash the baya once you open the gate, we cannot know. But not knowing cannot stop us." The serpent tattoo at Vis's neck shivers. "Some days I wonder if knowledge of the curse is why the new baya has been hiding. Or perhaps they did not realize the baya themselves feeds dreams into our world.

Whatever the reason, we all have our secrets, our scars that guide our choices and shape who we are."

Over the hilt of his sword, the back of Vis's hand flexes and a sunken ridge of flesh twists, as if an old wound drew in on itself as it healed. Vis nods as I return my gaze to his.

"Scars also allow us to live, and while the baya of Denrathri has remained hidden, they have lived. I'm certain of it. As certain as I am that we must find the baya and bring them to the throne of Dreams before our protective layer falls. If that happens, Orkayha can enter my realm." Bright brown eyes pierce my own. "Which means, Alathea, you must find the gate to Denrathri quickly, and open it. Only then will all routes be reopened into the realm, and the baya can claim their throne."

Again, thunder rolls from outside, and a stronger breeze cuts through the room. I picture the arched maples that Lidja located, the shimmer of silver-blue when she and Daesen had opened that gate. "There can't be that many arched trees in your realm. Why don't you just point me to the gate?"

Vis's brows dip to a V. "Only a high sorceress can sense a key-gate."

Mama said the key was here. Tenion's words in the hallway of the assembly house...was it only yesterday? I feel a decade older than my seventeen years since then. "Your high sorceress made no mention of keys."

As if she heard, Lidja glances up from the table, her gaze upon me as cold as a blade. I *knew* she couldn't be trusted.

"Perhaps you have yet to earn her confidence. Once opened, a key-gate can be used by anyone to travel to and from the realm of the baya that created it. They are among our most treasured secrets." He waits, as if deciding whether to trust me himself.

I cross my arms. "If you want me to find an object, you'll have to give me more than that. What will it look like?"

"I do not know what the Denrathri key-gate will be, Alathea. It could be any object, anywhere, as small as a firefly and as large as an ivory statue. Only a baya can create a key-gate for their own realm, and its true nature is revealed only to a realm's high sorceress." He levels a wry gaze at me. "All I know is that there is one, here. When the last baya of Denrathri visited me twenty-four years ago, she hid a key-gate in this realm. She told me that much, although not where. She didn't expect me to live this long. She didn't want to chance exposing that secret to Orkayha, not when every previous baya has been lost to her pits by the age of twenty-five." He shakes his head, as if throwing a heavy memory from his vision. "Lidja will teach you to find the key-gate."

This time, Lidja's eyes pin mine as she caresses the top of her axe.

"What about—" I will the pitch of my voice downward. "What about Daesen? Can't he show me instead?"

Daesen...who is currently smearing globs of cream on my sister's blouse. Soli screeches and smacks him back with a glob of her own.

A smile plays at the corner of Vis's lips. "Lidja's tongue may be sharp, but when she trusts you, you will find no one more loyal. No one more brilliant regardless of friend or foe. She mastered her word of power long ago, and she will help you find yours so that you can become a high sorceress in action as well as title."

Daesen's laugh echoes through the throne room.

"They both have lessons to teach you, Alathea. You have neither to fear. Much." The mirth disappears from his expression as quickly as it arrived. "We all have a role to serve. And right now, mine is to find the missing baya. After all these years, I believe I have found their hiding place. Two days' travel there and two days' return, and I will have your baya of Dreams here, ready to proceed through your gate. You and your sister must have the gate open at sunset on the fourth day."

Four days. Four days is what this man—this baya—is giving my sister and me to open a gate. With magic. The hills we walked through simply to arrive here stretch through my mind. "I'm not certain four days is enough."

"It will have to be. Our protective layer of magic has kept Orkayha's creatures from our shores for twenty-four years, but every day, it weakens. Even with it in place, there are weaknesses to be found, if one knows where to look. If it falls, our last defense is gone."

I shudder, the mawlyr that found us in Elektos a creature I hope to never, ever see again. "I won't let those monsters anywhere near my sister."

A firefly flits by Vis, the sudden flare reflected in the baya's eyes. "Then find the gate to Denrathri, Alathea. Opening the gate to Dreams, with the triads of Denrathri and Memoria intact, is our best chance to capture Orkayha. Only then can I carve the memory of the lie from her, and we will end her hunt."

The bloody battle they all want.

I watch my sister push Daesen into the table. Dimples flash, and the warrior-mage winks at my sister.

How could I ever convince Soli to remain away, if a fight is near? "It cannot come to a battle, not even among the few of us."

"Then do what's necessary to find that gate. No matter what it takes. As I will do, to find the baya."

That hollow in my chest quivers.

My sister deserves to be safe. She deserves to eat pastries and push Daesen into that table for the rest of her life, if that's what she wants. And if, to make that happen, I have to find a magic object that's been lost for twenty-odd years…

"Tell me where to start."

CHAPTER 13

The door to the palace's throne room groans shut behind Vis and Lidja, Soli trailing after them, which leaves me alone with Daesen.

Which is where I should start, according to Vis, as we walked slowly toward the food table, carefully peeling more pieces of information from each other.

Daesen wipes a hand across his face, removing pastry cream from his fight with my sister. Gray eyes settle on me as he licks cream from his palm. "Where to, my loveliest high sorceress of Denrathri? I am but your honest, honorable, and handsome guide."

Perhaps the baya wants me to suffer after all. "I notice humble isn't on your list."

"That's why I said 'honest.'" He grins. "Command me, and I am yours."

"Vis said you should take me to the curtain."

The curtain. Here, not a wool hung in a home, but Fates-made magic that keeps the magic realms apart from Elektos. Fates-made by actual god-Fates. Not just the name of the three stars in our sky, but the beings that created Fides, Vis said.

I didn't bother sharing what I was taught in my school room.

"The almighty curtain it is." Daesen extends his palm. "Lucky for you, I know a shortcut."

I narrow my gaze at the twinkle in his eye, tentatively placing my hand in his.

The entire world spins out and around and down.

Stones clack beneath my feet, and I grip Daesen's forearm hard. A vast, undulating blue swirls in front of me, the sun just past midday. Heavy, wet air presses into my skin, each inhale a labor. "You didn't tell me the shortcut would feel like that."

"And spoil the surprise? It only works in a shield's own realm, so I have to show it off where I can."

"I would have preferred not to feel it at all."

"But that's how a shield's quick-portal is, Ala." Daesen flexes his forearm. "Strong and hot."

I yank my hand away and sit hard on the stone shore. The smooth stones jar the nausea out of me. Behind us, the jungle creaks and caws, shushes and sways. A few strides from my booted toes, the sea glitters clear blue in the midday sun. Heat presses upon my skin, more humid than Elektos at this time of year. I squint across the sea, searching for any sign of the mainland, of the Scorched Mountains.

At my side, Daesen flings a stone into the sea. It skips over the surface, light and easy.

"What are you to my sister?"

"I'm her friend. Although she'd probably refer to me more as her punching bag these days."

"Only friends?"

The next stone halts in his hand. "Is that so hard to believe?"

"Perhaps."

"What else would we be?"

The sea laps at the stones, crackling with each wave.

"Ah." Daesen's skipping stone thunks into the water. "You think we're *lovers*? Soliana and *me*?"

I jerk a shoulder up and down. That song she'd sung last week —perhaps she'd been hiding this boy behind it. "You could be."

"Certainly, we *could* be, if she held one drop of interest in me, or me in her. But no, Ala." Dae shakes his head, those awful dimples returning. "She's not my type." His smile widens, and I keep my attention on the sea, even as my cheeks heat. "Would you like to know what my type is?"

"No." I force my breath to calm, like the sea before us. "That's enough for now."

"Is it?" The stones knock, and sage and salt close in. "Don't you know the difference between how friends and lovers look together, Ala? Have you not had a lover?"

I glare at the sea, a flash of red hair at the edge of my memory, of that home in Elektos where Soli caught me waiting.

"Or perhaps you've had no friends."

I hurl a stone at the water, and it plunks downward as I ignore him again.

"I wonder if it would be lonely or dull, to not have any friends," Daesen says, quiet. "Perhaps both."

My knees wobble over the uneven rocks as I stand. "Perhaps you should stop wondering about things that don't concern you and show me how a curtain is supposed to help me locate a gate."

Dae rises next to me. And rises. I didn't realize how much taller he is than me before now, when he's close enough that I could reach and touch his chest. "There is no 'us' in gate finding. That will be you, and Lidja will show you how. But first, to find a gate, you need to know what realm magic feels like. That is why Vis pointed you here."

"I already know what magic feels like." That awful gathering in my veins, the thrumming, invisible current that leaps outward, that I cannot control.

"No, you don't," Daesen says. "You know what the lash of magic feels like when it's wrong. That's not the same. Look up." He points to the eastern moon, tracing a line down to the sea.

Not one hundred paces from shore, the air shimmers. It wavers and glimmers, as if the thinnest, finest cloth hangs from the sky. From the eastern moon, all the way to the western moon, it continues, a nearly invisible sheet.

"A curtain," I breathe.

"*The* curtain. It was woven by the Fates when they birthed our world. It keeps the magic realms safe from what lies beyond."

I stare at the shimmering layer, and a tug yanks low in my gut, echoed in the scar in my palm. "You don't need to be kept safe. Elektos needs to be kept safe from magic. From these realms."

"You *are* these realms, Ala, and you look safe enough. For now." He sends me a wolfish smile, and I barely smother an eye roll.

"My mother..." His voice trails off as he stares at the blue horizon. "My mother told me that many centuries ago, the curtain was not so firm. That the people of the magic realms and Elektos moved freely. But over time, the villagers in Elektos grew to fear what they didn't understand. After the Realm of Denrathri closed their gates, and the last baya died, the throne has sat empty these many years. Dreams have disappeared and fear has grown. Nightmares pull at me when I sleep, just as they pull at you. Fears have worsened on both sides of the silver curtain. These days, that curtain is the only reason your people don't launch an attack on us."

Another lie. Impossible that *they* are afraid of *us*.

Daesen continues. "Unfortunately for us, the silver curtain doesn't keep out the other magic realms. The protective layer we wove earlier will keep the monsters from Mizura at bay, but it's far from foolproof." A trickle of sweat slides down the tattoo on his neck, disappears beneath the black shirt that clings to his chest in the heat. "What do they call the curtain in Elektos?"

"We have nothing like this. Only curtains of wool." Like the one in our home. For a beat, I hear Mother as she jumps out from behind the curtain to surprise Mama, shouting, *I could disappear.*

86

Mama's heart truly would stop if she could see me now, here, with this curtain of magic.

Another tug curls low in my stomach. As far as it is, I reach toward the curtain, as if called by the wavering sheen—

I'm hurled backward, my spine thudding into the trunk of a palm tree.

Daesen crouches to inspect me. "That's going to hurt for a while."

When my voice finally returns, it's hoarse. "That would have been helpful to know beforehand."

"Important note, my sweet pine needle. I *didn't* advise you to reach for the powerful magic object."

This. *This* is why I don't have friends. Because this is how magic works. It's dangerous. It hurts.

For a moment, I ache for Mama, for her soothing salve that most often went to Soli's skinned knees. If I must have magic, that is the kind I want. Not the kind in my veins. "How am I supposed to find the Denrathri key-gate if it's going to rip me in two when I get close?"

"It won't. When you find a gate to the realm you belong to, it won't."

"How do you know?"

"Because that's how magic works."

I wait.

And wait.

"Are you expecting a formal invitation to explain this to me?"

Another damned dimple. "Perhaps. Depends what form this invitation takes."

I pick up a stone, weighing it.

"You see, needle, we could become friends, too."

"Tell me."

"There's the command I was hoping for." Dae salutes. "Realm magic is two things. First, truth-bound. You can only use magic that belongs to the role you are bound to. So, I, your most handsome shield of Memoria, can only use magic that will serve to protect this realm, and the people within it. Namely, weapons. I am very, very good with weapons, of all kinds. Small ones, big ones. Very, very long ones, of just the right...girth. Would you like to see?"

I nearly choke—"*No.*"

His grin grows. "Another time, then."

"And"—*me*—"Lidja? What is a high sorceress's magic?"

"Being brilliant and overly demanding. You'll fit right in."

I fold my arms and wait.

"I don't want her rapping on my door in the night again, threatening to slice off my favorite finger for getting the slightest detail wrong, so you'd best ask her. She's very particular."

"You said two. That was one."

"Fates save me from impatient sorceresses. Two is purpose-bound. Magic must be bound to your role to be successful. The Fates birthed the first triad, and from there, all beings of Fides were bound to their will. If we use our magic in ways they did not intend, it will whiplash." Gray eyes pierce mine. "And I think you've had enough tastes of the Fates' lashes to know where that leads."

To mothers leaving. To hurting my sister. To death wagons.

"Which is why you're fortunate you're here now," Daesen says. "You train with Lidja. You train with me. Maybe I will even let you try my favorite weapon."

I wipe the swamp-heat from my brow. "We have your type in Elektos, too, you know."

"Then you know how well our weapons fire."

"*Honest* my foot." No wonder Soli covered his face in cream. "More like smug, smarmy, and self-absorbed."

"I'm usually called handsome, glorious, or even most beautiful and strong, if you happen to find yourself lucky."

"I wouldn't call anyone those names, let alone you."

The lap of the sea softens, slows. "Did I mention I love challenges, sweet pine needle?"

"Don't call me that."

"Then how about friend, like your sister?" He holds his scarred palm out, the mirror of my own scar.

I stare at his carved skin. "Why should I trust you?"

"Because I don't lie, Ala, not about the threat we face, nor Orkayha, nor her monsters. Not when they ripped my mother from me."

My very breath freezes. I shouldn't have anything in common with this charmer. But here we are, motherless, the both of us. "What happened?"

The play seeps from Daesen, and he turns to the sea. "I couldn't even tell you, precisely. Not anymore. There was a time after she died when I couldn't think, couldn't sleep, couldn't move without hearing her screams. When all I felt was her suffering. Over and over, I saw the monster rip her throat."

I shiver.

"I was only eight when it happened, and every night, for almost a year, that's all I saw. That monster, and my mother's blood. The light in her eyes dimming, the way she whispered my name so her power would flow to me. The stillness of her, when I placed the dagger to her chest for passage across the fields of Ahnaysa.

"So when Vis offered to release the memory's hold over me, I said yes. He released it, and at first, the memory grew and twisted and took over every thought, every piece of me, and it was all I was. I thought I would crumble into the very ground with the pain of it, that it would be the end of me, too, but the memory splintered. Like a crack of light forced its way in and shattered it completely.

"After that, I didn't hear her screams anymore. I couldn't see the attack itself. The sorrow, the grief—that all remained. But there was room for other pieces, other plans, in my heart. For more than just grief and pain. For a way forward. For hope." He rolls a shoulder. "Some days, I'm not certain it was the right path to take, to release that memory. But I couldn't stand the pain, and it was the choice I made. I have lived with it, for better or worse."

That pain and grief…I hear them now, still, in the strain of his voice. I know echoes of them both, deep in my blood, when I look at that scar on my sister's collarbone. I know them in the hollow of my chest in the deepest of night, when I see again Mother turning and running from me. "I can't imagine that kind of loss."

Daesen's eyes glow, and he steps toward me. "None of us want our roles here, Ala. Not truly. I'd prefer an apple orchard and open sky myself. But we do what we must, because keeping the memories of the world matters. Bringing dreams back to Fides matters. That's why you should trust me." Again, he opens that scarred hand. "I will do as I was born to. As your sister will. Will you?"

The promise I made to cross that grounded gate from Elektos burns in my hand, and I wonder…

Perhaps this warrior-mage is not an enemy after all.

Maybe, just maybe, he can be a friend.

Try, Ala. I can almost hear my sister. *Try to be less afraid.*

So I say, "I want to find a weapon of my own."

CHAPTER 14

*D*eep in the palace of Memoria, tall doors open to a room lined with floor-to-ceiling cabinets, locking out the mid-afternoon sun—the weapons room, where I now stand with Lidja.

Alone.

The high sorceress crosses her arms as the door slides shut behind me. "I don't intend to make this easy for you."

"Of course you don't." I cross my arms and radiate my best impression of Soli. I have no doubt this magic being would kill me like she did that watchman if she didn't need me.

Lidja lifts a brow. "Are you missing Dae's honey-tipped tongue already?"

"I am missing my home. I am missing what makes *sense*." Or what used to make sense, anyway, until my sister crossed to this realm. But I won't let Lidja and her forked tongue stop me from acquiring some kind of weapon of my own.

I stalk to the door closest to me and rip it open. Inside the deep, narrow space are panel-to-panel silver spears—and this is only one in a room *full* of cabinets. "Why do you need so many weapons, if this realm is safe?"

"These are from the first battle of Fides that was waged on the seas, with ships and sea horses pulled by fierce commanders who lived under the waves."

"That sounds...awful." And untrue, more like a bedtime tale meant to scare children into behaving than something possible. I turn from the spears and face the sorceress.

This close, she's taller than me by a single handbreadth. The brown of her eyes is crisper, like the burgundy of a maple tree in autumn. Wild clover and citrus itch at my nose.

Her gaze traces the lines of my face. "So you don't trust me."

Either.

I can hear it as clearly as if she said it. "I haven't yet discovered a reason to."

"You don't have much of a choice, if you want to survive." Her gaze dips to my lips. "Truth, oxsail. Why don't *you* trust *me*?"

For a breath, the memory of her over me in that forest flashes. *The Fates wouldn't be so cruel.* The crack of the watchman's neck in her hands follows.

My breath whooshes outward. "Because you hate me."

Surprise flickers in that burgundy-brown, before it shutters. "Hate is such a strong word."

But she doesn't deny it.

Instead, her silence thrums between us. It stretches, taut, until it's as clear as a string near breaking.

Lidja draws the tip of a single finger under my chin and tilts my face up to hers. "Let's try again. What has you so afraid that you believe you need a weapon?"

The way her full lips move over that word—

I rip my chin from her finger and slide to the next cabinet door, one step, three, five away from the sorceress. Unscented air fills my lung. She will not kill me. She needs me just as much as I need her. More, perhaps.

"I'm not afraid." I take another pace away, just in case. "It's just

—if monsters break through the protective layer, I don't want to be helpless again."

"Then here is lesson one. Find your weapon yourself."

I swallow a swear word on her name and reach for the cabinet in front of me. A whiff of clover is the only warning before Lidja smacks my hand away.

Glaring, I rub my hand. "I'm doing as you said."

"You're doing it *wrong*. The magic of a high sorceress is strategy. We create the plans that execute our baya's commands. One day soon, you'll direct your sister's first strike."

Daesen said the same, but hearing it from Lidja, hearing my sister's magic laid bare like that…"My sister isn't a weapon."

"Until you find your word of power, your sister is no more than a talented fighter. Besides, I thought you weren't afraid?"

I pivot on my heel and stomp away, deeper into the room, right to the center of it, and eye the lines of cabinets.

Strategy. My magic is strategy. The wraith Lucius said the same, when I first arrived. If it's true, if I can trust this at least… perhaps it's not so different from a game, like the ones I played with Mama when I was younger.

Slowly, I turn in a circle, assessing the hundreds of closed cabinets for where my best weapon hides. The buzz in my veins rises, and for once, I let it loose. One after another, potential plans unfold in my mind, fast and bright, like a flower's petals in the wind.

Open them one by one. Ask her. Find Daesen and ask him. Locate a list.

Wild clover approaches, breaking my concentration. I sneak a glance at the sorceress, at her hips, to make sure her axe hasn't moved.

"Mother said I was born with it in my hand." Catching my gaze, she strokes the head of her weapon. She cocks a single brow. "What were you born with, besides an overabundance of foolish ideas?"

"Manners."

Lidja barks a laugh, full and round. Her face transforms, her whole body pulsing joy so unlike her usual sharpness that I can do nothing but stare.

The smile fades from her face, and she catches my gaze. Holds it.

My pulse skitters. In the burgundy-brown of her eyes, I could swear a star appears.

"Dae was right," Lidja whispers. "There is something about you." She steps closer, until no more than a breath separates us. "But you're more of a pain in my backside than in my chest."

On instinct, I push against her shoulder and stomp away, for a cabinet, for whatever damned weapon is closest. As long as it's sharp and—

I'm thrust from behind, forward, into the wood of a closed door. I whirl around, already reaching to scratch the sorceress.

She pins my wrist to the cabinet door. "I said *use your magic.*"

I reach for her axe—

She pins my second wrist. "If I were Orkayha's monster of a shield, his magic would have already cut you in two."

For a moment, we simply glare at each other, our puffs of breath hard and mixing. Two lines grace her otherwise perfect cheek, the lines that formed when she crafted the snakes to scare Daesen.

"You want me to use magic, but your own magic cut your face," I say.

"Use your realm magic correctly, and you can keep your pretty face, oxsail. Misuse it, not as the Fates intended, and the Fates will remind you what magic truly is, at its heart. Cruel. It will lash those you love most."

Herself. *Of course* she loves herself most. "You cut yourself *twice.*"

"I happen to believe that if you go through life afraid of a scratch, you will never do anything interesting at all." Lidja smiles again, but this time, there is no trace of joy. "When Dae was six and I was eight, I poisoned my own lips to keep him from trying to kiss me again. Some victories are worth a little pain." She presses my wrists into the wood. "Stop trying to tame what you have, to keep it in a box or a cage or whatever Elektos taught you to do with things that don't fit your precious truths. *Use. Your. Magic.*"

For a single heartbeat, the force of her command freezes my muscles. But...she's not a watchman, nor the Sancta, nor anyone else I have to listen to.

And I don't need my hands to scratch.

I dip my lips toward her neck, teeth opening—

"Don't you dare!" She leaps out of range of my bite, releasing one of my wrists. Quicker than my next breath, she unsheathes her axe with her free hand, and with a flick of that wrist, she whispers, "*Snake.*"

Her axe tremors, shudders.

"I'm not your shield. I'm not afraid of serpents." And as I yank hard at my still-trapped wrist, my own magic flares awake.

"Helpful to know." Lidja flicks her wrist, and the half-axe, half-serpent pauses. Eyes narrowed, she whispers, "*Rabid dog.*"

The axe trembles, shifting once again. Stretching, writhing.

"You don't have to be so awful." Inside my veins, my magic flares and twists, rattles, a storm building. Plans fly through me. *Kick. Scream. Flail.*

"You mean I'm not pouring honey in your ear like the bam." She squeezes my wrist hard, harder. "I'm actually challenging you instead of—"

My wrist.

And just like that, a plan illuminates.

Use your magic.

I flick my free wrist and whisper, "*Doors open.*"

My magic rockets through me like a boom of thunder and the cabinets obey, hurling me forward, Lidja losing her grip on my wrist. Her axe clanks to the floor, the half-formed dog gone, no more than a weapon once again.

"It is amazing how you can make something simple look so hard." She picks the axe from the marble and turns her back to me. "But that wasn't completely awful."

I stick my middle finger at her back and stalk to the center of the room, glancing at the open cabinets as I go. Each is filled with a different type of weapon. Stack upon stack of heavy black balls, swords that gleam, and an entire three cabinets lined with razor-sharp axes like hers.

Lidja as I first saw her flashes in my mind, her hair gleaming in the moonslit lake, death in her hands. For a breath, I imagine what it would be to feel like that.

To be unafraid, like her.

"Go on," Lidja says, eyes hooded from where she watches, several cabinets away. "Try an axe. I dare you."

I sniff and lift my chin. "It's not for me." Onward, I continue, past maces and armored plates and—

I feel it. A tug. Somewhere in this room, a vibration not unlike the silver curtain, but not like it, either. Warmer, closer to the hollow in my chest. As if somewhere in here, there is indeed a weapon of my own.

I stride faster past gleaming arrows and bows, past long poles with double-ended blades. The *tug* increases, warmer, incessant, until—

I halt in front of a cabinet of gleaming silver chisels.

My fingers tremble as I slide one of the pieces from the cabinet. Light and firm in my hand, it's several times longer and wider than my chisels. The tip is narrowed to a single brutal point.

Above the chisels is a shelf of ornate mallets crowned with metal thorns. Tacked to the wall is a line of leather bandoliers.

"A stake and hammer," Lidja murmurs at my shoulder.

"They're weapons," I whisper.

"Did you hit your head? Of course they're weapons."

This time, I ignore the sorceress, because all I can feel in my hand is *my* chisel, *my* mallet. The way I held them every day, the truths I carved. I knew they could be dangerous, of course. I split enough of my own skin with wrong strikes over the years. I threatened Daesen only yesterday with the one in my leather pouch. But to see them laid out here, so clearly, in a weapons room...

How could I have not seen this before?

Truth Three. Elektos needs you. Truth Two. We care for Elektos. Truth One. For Elektos, always.

The truths. That's how.

I whisper, "They taught me to not see this."

"*Truth*-carver," Lidja says, scoffing. "This is the real truth: The words they keep from us and the ones they give us—those are the greatest weapons in all of Fides."

My stomach caves as if smacked by one of the hammers. She's right.

And worse, all along... I've been the one wielding this weapon for the Sancta.

"They used me."

"And now you know it, so you can stop it from happening again. Find your single word of power here, and you will unlock your most powerful magic. That power is more than weapon enough."

"So I can use my sister as a weapon? I won't let her be used either."

"Then figure out what you *do* want, Alathea, because Orkayha is coming for us all either way."

My magic stirs again. "I want to be strong. Stronger than Daesen. Worse than you."

Teeth flash, brutal and fast, across Lidja's face. "Careful, oxsail. If you keep talking like that, perhaps I won't completely hate you after all."

Hands trembling, I reach into the cabinet and unhook a bandolier. I tie it over my shoulder, knot it at my waist, and sheathe a stake into one of the empty bands, and then another. Another and another, I fill each empty space on the bandolier until the weight of the weapons grounds me to the floor, and I meet Lidja's burning eyes once more.

"Perhaps I want to become a weapon myself."

CHAPTER 15

*P*ale dawn stretches across the unending green hills outside the palace. The scent of dewy grass rises, crisp and cool, the bleep of fireflies warm and constant among the trees of the jungle. I lean farther out the window of the bedchamber where I slept last night, and whisper words as they come to me.

"Firefly. Sister. Power."

My magic remains dormant, no larger power unlocked, so I reel myself back inside. A large bed dominates the sleeping chamber, blankets askew from where I collapsed upon them last night, after Soli found and brought me here. When she opened a door and pointed to this bed, I collapsed, only awakening now, with three days left until she and I must open a key-gate I have yet to find.

I pivot back to the window and crook my finger into the strange eyelet of a hook on the windowsill, stretching outward again. I scan for a tug of anything that will make my search for the gate quicker than Daesen quick-portaling me across this entire, massive isle.

Daesen. Not my enemy, like Lidja, but a friend.

I press my cheek to the cool marble at the window's side. My soft, too-big blouse blends in with the marble, the color of day-old cream. I'd found it in the cavernous wardrobe once I'd awoken, the least bright and most likely to fit of the clothes tucked into drawers.

Behind me, a throat clears, and I spin around, pulse jumping—

To find Daesen, lounging in the now-open doorframe.

"So you do find me charming."

"Whatever would lead you to that awful impression?"

"What other impression could you have meant to give by sleeping in my bed?"

My breath halts. *His* room. His *bed*. "Soli showed me here. She told me I should sleep."

"Soli could devise a battalion's worth of tomfoolery, and not a single one of her plans would fail." His eyes stray to the rumpled bed. *His* rumpled bed. "It looks like you found this comfortable enough."

Clearly, my sister isn't the only one who likes to play.

The shield ambles toward me. Close, closer—I hold my ground, lifting my chin, even as the warmth from his body reaches mine. He stops at my side, peering over my shoulder out the window, at the drop below the window. "Much too far to be certain of survival, if you were considering another way out."

"I was considering where the gate to Denrathri hides, and how I'll find it."

"Let's hope it wasn't on the southern shore."

I glance out the window. A plume of gray smoke rises in the distance. "Has the protective layer fallen?"

"No. A rogue guard let several monsters through a grounded gate she should have been protecting. We killed the monsters who broke through this time, and the guard will rot in our cages until Vis returns. But there is always a weakness, Ala, and they found it. Whether it be land or beast or…girl. The challenge is finding it."

His words on the shore yesterday come back to me. *Did I mention I love challenges?*

Daesen sinks onto the bed. Exhaustion lurks in a line at his forehead, in a crease at the corner of his eyes. Both only make him look more rugged, more handsome. If this is how he looks without sleep, how does he look well-rested?

"See anything of interest?"

My cheeks flush. "Not at all."

Quick, soft, Daesen flicks the tip of my nose. "This is why you're the needle."

"I can see why my sister beats you into the ground."

A dimple appears. One, two. He bounces on the bed, on his wrinkled blankets where I slept last night. "This is really made for two, you know. In case you're wondering."

"I was not. Am not. Never."

"Never is a long time, beauty."

"Don't call me that either."

His unmarked palm stretches forward, a scant pace between us.

Too much. I said too much.

"What would you have me call you, high sorceress of Dreams, if one day you do wonder what it would be like to find a place deep in the palms to lie with me? To search the moonlit night for something more than the fate-stars?" Next to my ear, his hand hovers.

"I would say go find your own bed." My voice is breathless, and—that's not what I meant to say. Not at all.

"It's right here. Found. Easy." Lightly, so lightly, he touches a strand of my hair that's escaped my braid and wraps it around his finger. "And although it does not have the fate-stars above, it is spacious." One rotation at a time, he wraps that stray strand.

Around and around, until his knuckle warms the nape of my neck, not quite touching. "Plenty of room for all sorts of games."

"You're very forward."

"Too forward?"

"Yes. Definitely."

"Yet you haven't run. Why waste time when you know what you want? I know what I want. The real question is—" He takes in my cream-colored clothes. "Do you?"

I jerk to the side, to the window, gulping in fresh, non-sage-scented air, and flatten my palms against the marble, against my racing pulse. Only earlier this year, I was content to meet my lover in our secret room, to savor stolen moments. But here, in the dawn of Memoria...

Behind me, Daesen shifts on the bed, and sage washes over me again.

I clutch the bottom of the too-big blouse in my hand, staring at the soft fabric, at the way it blends into the marble floor, as if doesn't exist.

As if *I* don't exist.

I've spent so much time blending in, I don't know what I want at all.

"I've heard stories about how Elektos has changed on the other side of the curtain," Daesen says, "but I keep forgetting how very different it must be. How different my own realm will be, if Orkayha finds our weakness and a way in."

Smoke curls in the south. Three days. I need to find that gate. And as much as I don't want to face her again, for that, I need Lidja. "Where is the high sorceress?"

Dae points to the hallway. "Lucky for you, she's in her very best of moods this morning."

"Why do I think that means the opposite?"

"Because you're getting to know me, friend. Perhaps even like me a little." Grinning, he offers his arms to me. "I'll show you to her. Care for a spin?"

"I'm walking. *Only* walking."

"You're certain?" Daesen flexes his muscular arms, front and back, brows waggling.

I bite back a smile.

And as I follow Daesen into the hallway, I wonder if perhaps *friends* isn't quite right either.

* * *

DAESEN LEADS me through the wide main hallway of the palace. Marble columns extend to the arched ceiling. Everywhere, fire-flies twinkle.

"Last I saw her, Lidja was lurking in this corridor." Daesen turns left into a narrower hallway. I follow, right on his heels.

And nearly crash into the armored plate on his back.

A woman, bald and built of thick muscle fills the passageway ahead, as if she is a mountain that ends the hallway altogether. Black whorls stain her biceps and neck. A phalanx of deadly weapons shines from her back, and a set of silver keys jangles from the rope around her waist.

Daesen widens his stance. "Rexar."

"Commander Rexar to you, boy."

"Not boy, *Rexar*. Shield of the baya." Daesen leans in, no trace of his usual buoyancy in the lines of his face. "Commander myself, if I ever decide Vis's offer is worth the trouble."

The mountain snarls. "Best you not forget who the baya left in charge."

She steps toward us, and I flatten against the wall.

Dae holds his ground, blocking her path.

"Is this the day you've finally chosen to fight?" the woman asks.

I glance back toward the main hallway for any sign of help.

"Not today." Daesen moves to my side.

Rexar thrusts her middle finger upward and strides past.

"But soon enough," Daesen mutters, so only I can hear.

"She reminds me of a watchman." One in particular. I wrap one hand around my wrist.

"If you mean pompous and resentful, agreed."

"Why does she hate you?"

"I wondered if you knew what the finger meant."

"My sister loves to make it at the watchmen." I don't mention I did it myself just yesterday at Lidja. Is *he* where Soli learned that gesture? "I know what it means well enough."

"Rexar and I want different things for Memoria. We are bound to different roles. I am the baya's shield, not one of her legion. But mostly, she hates not being able to order me around. As the baya's shield, I don't answer to her."

"But she said Vis left her in charge."

"He did. Even still, I do not answer to her." His tone shifts, cautious, careful. "The shield and sorceress of the triad—me and Lid—we answer only to Vis. And as ruthless as Vis must act to keep our realm safe, I've never known him to make a mistake."

"Keep that to yourself, bam. Vis's ego needs no further stroking." Lidja, with that blade of a voice, slithers from around a shadowed corner. "Be careful with Rexar, Dae, or you'll be facing a war on two fronts."

"Like I said, the best of moods. Good luck, needle." And Daesen is gone.

Lidja glares from a darkened doorframe.

I glare back. "How do I find a key-gate?"

"Have you found your word of power?"

"No."

"Then why are you asking for my help again?"

"You're the only high sorceress I know, unfortunately."

"The feeling is mutual."

Dae may be a friend, but this woman…"*Why* do you hate me?"

"Why do you think that I have any feelings about you at all?"

The cut stings.

Lidja closes the distance between us, her eyes nearly glowing. "High sorceresses are strong, Alathea. We stand second only to the baya in our realm. We command magic to our will. The louder we call the magic, the stronger our power."

A fingernail taps the hollow at the base of my neck and trails upward along my throat. My neck has never felt more fragile, more exposed. The daggers in her bandolier nearly touch my chest with each breath, and another finger runs down the column of my throat.

My knees knock, my tongue ties, but I do not back away.

"That's right. We do not bow," Lidja whispers. "Not even to the baya. So if my tongue cows you, how will you stand against Orkayha?"

"Your tongue isn't my problem."

Lidja snatches her finger back, as if burned. "I hate you because the high sorceress of Denrathri died and I can't figure out why she named *you* as her successor. The magic of the triads follows our bloodlines, unless there is none to follow and someone close by is named, as it was with the first baya of Memoria. As it is with you and your sister, which means *you shouldn't be here.*"

"On that, we agree," I say. "And yet here I am, doing as *you* all need."

"What *I* need is the last high sorceress of Denrathri back. Every spell I learned came from a book she inked, from before the gate to Denrathri was locked and all routes in and out lost. She crafted me into the high sorceress I am. I *thrived* because of her." Lidja stabs a finger into the center of my chest. "I hate you, because when I look at you, I see what should have been and now will *never* be. I was going to meet her. As soon the gate opened, I would finally have met her. But instead, it's you. You're here, and it's her memories you hold in that thick, fearful head of yours and you don't *deserve* them. It *hurts.*"

Her fury hovers between us in the dark.

"If it makes you feel any better," I say, pulse racing, "I don't want to be near you either."

"It helps." Lidja sniffs. "But less than I would like. Follow me."

We stride farther into the shadowed hallway, the temperature dropping as light dims. Soon, only the flicker of fireflies offers fleeting glimpses of the doors at our sides.

"You think the gate is this way?" I stare at a dark opening in the hallway where we've stopped.

"Not there. That leads down to the cages. There." She points across the hall, to an opening just as black. "The bayas craft the key-gates to be hidden with ease. But like any idiot trying to be clever, they create them small and common. Then they carve the memory of its very shape from their own mind for safety—which makes key-gates rare, and very difficult to find. It could be anything. Down there, you won't find a gate unless your last baya created one as a scrape of dust."

"Then why should I go down there?"

"Because in our memory room, you have a chance of finding an object of significance to you. Like your weapon, but more personal." Her voice lowers, slows. Wild clover and citrus encircle me, the warmth of her too close once again. "That's how the gate will feel, Alathea, when you find it. Alive. Like it's a part of your own skin."

She splays a palm to my abdomen, and heat spirals through me. I tilt closer, into that palm, straining for the next words from her lips.

"It will feel like it's been waiting just for you. Like you will never have enough."

I shudder in a breath as she draws away, sudden and cold.

Lidja whispers, "Flame," and with a flick of her wrist, a silver light graces her palm. She slips ahead into the darkened doorframe.

I rub my cheeks, willing the strange writhing in my veins to dissipate, and follow her. Down the winding stairs, a glow grows with each step. Soft at first, then bright and brighter. We step into a room that holds the flicker of thousands of fireflies. Millions.

The memory room.

"Find a memory that calls to you. If it's tied to you, your magic will allow you in. If not, it will blast you away like the curtain."

And low in my gut comes a tug.

Forward, I step into the millions of blinking fireflies as voices stream around me. I pad among them as the tug grows stronger, until I stop in front of a cluster of fireflies where the tug persists, like an unending pull forward. Like a part of me is right there, waiting. "Now what?"

"Touch it. Ask the carrier to reveal its secrets."

I reach for the firefly. Tiny pricks of wings flutter against my palm. "What are you carrying, little one?"

The golden light on its back deepens, denser and finer at once, as if a thousand threads make up the light on the back of the beetle. With a pulse, the light expands to the size of my head, then exponentially. A doorway burns just beyond my fingertips, large enough for me to walk through.

Heart pounding, I step through, and inside.

The bright sun of midday beats down on a village of reed shacks that dot sandy earth in a circle. In the center of the sand, a man in a clay-colored shirt and breeches swings a blade in each hand, wild-eyed and shouting.

A watchman.

Heaving, eyes wild, the watchman whirls toward a woman, only the back of her heavy cloak visible.

"There are monsters everywhere," the watchman shouts.

He lashes forward, fast and sharp, toward the cloaked woman. Screams rise as blood erupts, staining the ground before the woman's cloaked feet, pooling beneath a severed hand.

The watchman lunges forward again, and a blade flashes upward from the woman's cloak—

I fling myself backward, out of the memory's doorway, flailing until cool fingers wrap around my arm. Who was that woman? Do I know her? I sink to the floor, marble soothing against my palms, the fiery doorway gone. No more than Lidja and blinking fireflies remain in the room.

"That was..." Unbearable. Someone's *memory*. "Tell me that's not how the gate will feel."

"I cannot tell you that. I told you, Ala—magic is *cruel*. It will find the gaps in your bones, in your heart, and it will pry at those frayed edges until you ache, until you *beg* to be released. It will keep from you what you most love, if that's what it wants. We may use it, but we do not rule magic—that is the Fates' role. For us, there is always a cost. But we are high sorceresses, and we have the strength to face it."

"I didn't ask for this."

"None of us did. We were born to it."

"Except me. Except Soli."

"Like I said, unlucky. Extremely so."

And suddenly, I hate her—the dead high sorceress who choose me for her magic, for this fate. "I can't search this whole isle in three days for a pinch of dust or a crumbled leaf." *Especially* if the magic feels like this every time I'm wrong.

"I don't think you need to search the whole isle."

I'll hate Lidja, too, if she's been hiding the easy way from me. "Do you know where the key-gate is?"

"I don't. It's the gate to your realm, not mine. But think of it, Alathea. Where would you hide an object, if you were a baya and needed to hide a key-gate well, but not so impossibly that it would never be found?"

The game I played with Mama all those years ago comes back again. Her dare, to hide an object of Mother's in a place Lady Jayton pointed me to—the place Mother most feared to go.

In which case...I'm already here. There is nowhere in this realm I fear more than this palace, where commanders roam the halls and this sorceress waits in the shadows for prey.

Watching for my answer, Lidja trails her fingers along the wall.

Those fingers that I saw crack a man's neck.

Magic is cruel.

Magic is death.

What if not all the truths in Elektos are actually lies? What if this sorceress *enjoys* being cruel, pointing me into a violent memory for no more than her own pleasure?

"I'm going to search the palace," I say, "by myself."

"Ala..."

But I'm already gone, stalking for the end of the dark hall, away from the high sorceress before she can try to set me on another cruel memory.

I turn to the right, to the left, again and again, until I spill through a doorway.

Above, bright sun streaks through a cupola of stained red glass, spilling to the marble floor like blood. The chamber itself contains six walls, each with a darkened doorway, one of which I've just arrived through.

Everywhere, fireflies flicker. Like the earlier memory room, low voices murmur. One voice, I know like my own. "Soli?"

Cautiously, I step onto the blood-red floor and stiffen, pulse skittering, as I hear another sound.

The twinkling of a laugh, a chime in the summer wind.

A laugh so rare, I'd know it anywhere.

Not Soli.

Mother.

CHAPTER 16

*A*nother tinkle of laughter echoes in the domed chamber. No shadows move from beyond the six dark passages, but I'm certain of what I heard.

Mother's laugh.

It's been two years since I last heard her voice the night she left. But that's not the memory that rises within me right now.

This memory is older—the waver of a curtain, Mother's taunting voice. *I could disappear.*

Could she...did she...is she *here*? Is *this* where our mothers abandoned us for?

"Mother!" I dash across the blood-red chamber to the nearest passage and plunge into the corridor. I keep my palm to the wall as I race inside, along twists and turns of the hallway, but no matter how far I run, only darkness stretches ahead.

Chest tight, I backtrack to the main chamber and try the next corridor. "Mother?"

Again, no one answers.

Again, I return to the stained chamber, sprinting as her laughter rings—

And I stare up, near the peak of the red dome, to where a pair of fireflies oscillate, unsteady, wrong.

Her laugh…is coming from a firefly.

It's not her.

She's not here, with me.

A heaviness sinks through my bones as I raise my hand toward the blinking light. "Please. Show me my mother."

The light pauses, flashes, and then sinks, dropping into my palm.

A fiery door expands, so bright and wide it nearly blinds me.

I step through.

Sage and lavender and thyme wrap around me from a garden.

Our garden.

Home.

But not as it was yesterday. Here, our yard is greener, our garden overgrown with tomatoes and basil. The sun hovers low, nearing sunset, as the two full moons stand sentinel.

And there, tucked between a row of greens and vegetables behind our log home, is Mother.

Mother, twelve years ago. Her dark hair flows unbound and wild. A yellow dress fitted to her wiry frame.

At her shins are two young girls. One digs in the mud of the garden, the other draws under a tree.

Us, twelve years ago.

Four-year-old Soli draws on slate, stubby clay sprawled around her. At five, I pick through the sweet peas, plucking weeds. A gentle breeze teases our long hair in the sweating afternoon of summer.

From the front of our log home comes a knock. Mother drops a kiss to the crown of little Ala's head, then Soli's. "I'll be right back, loves."

The back door thuds behind her.

"Ala, I dreamt."

"No, you didn't," young Ala says, still buried in the garden. Her thin elbow jerks back, tossing a beetle over her bony shoulder.

"I'm drawing it," Soli says, unperturbed. "I'm drawing where we go."

Young Ala continues to ignore her.

"There!" Soli points to the Scorched Mountains. "The moon!"

Young Ala smacks the dirt with her trowel. "No, Soli. That's not the moon. Don't say that."

"I can say it."

"No, you can't," Ala says, calm and matter-of-fact, and turns back to the peas.

Soli sniffs. "Bad, Ala. You're bad."

Ala hunches her shoulders forward and digs deeper into the dirt, hands trembling.

"I want to draw."

"No." But this time, young Ala's voice shakes.

Soli scrambles to her feet, slate in hand, and approaches. "Look!" Soli shoves the slate in Ala's face. A giant white circle shines amid the gray stone. "Sun for Soli!"

With a grunt, Ala strips the slate from Soli's hand and hurls it to the shed behind her.

The slate cleaves in two.

Soli squeals.

"I told you," Ala says. "No drawing, Soli. No suns. The watchmen wouldn't like it."

Soli stomps to collect the halves. "I draw. Mother said so."

At the name, the two turn toward the back of the log home, where Mother went.

There, through the window, stands our Mother. Back to us, her hands are on Mama's broader face. Mama's healer hands tangle in Mother's dark hair.

Mama's head tilts, like the twitch of a curious spring robin.

No. Not Mama.

Long eyelashes, a smooth complexion. Short brown hair, two shades lighter than Mama's. The woman leans into Mother's ear, her lips moving with a single word, a whispered endearment.

The stranger slides away, gone, and from the front of our home, mules whinny, a wagon creaks.

A watchmen's wagon.

Mother appears at the back door, her cheeks red, hair ruffled. "Time to come inside, little fireflies."

I hurl myself backward, my boots once again on the stained marble. The clamor of voices expands in the chamber, in my head.

I no longer stand on the soft earth of our garden.

Mother no longer yells for my sister and me.

She no longer calls us that word.

Fireflies.

Under my skin, my magic expands. Sharp and hard, until it quivers. Taut, like a gathering storm.

How could I have forgotten? When we were young, a whispered, infrequent endearment.

"Beautiful little lights I saw once," she told us when Soli asked. "Maybe one day, you'll see them, too."

The chamber fades as the magic builds in my blood. Roils, stirs, pounds.

Mother *knew*. She *knew* about this place. She knew about *magic*. And yet, when the magic in my veins escaped that night two years ago, when I caused the slit at her wrist, her blood to pool to the floor, she packed a burlap sack and ran.

She ran from her *own daughters*.

She ran from me.

Lightning erupts from my skin, and red glass rains from the sky.

CHAPTER 17

"*A*la!" Daesen rams the bedchamber door from outside.

His bedchamber door, where I've locked myself inside, the only place I knew to run and hide after the memory cleaved apart, after I brought the glass dome down with my magic.

"For Fates sake, Ala. That lash pulsed across the entire realm. Open my damn door and tell me what you did!"

What *I* did?

I fling the door open. "I was doing what *you* told me to! What you dragged me from Elektos to do!"

I smack the door shut, but he's faster, his boot wedging in the frame. I push on the door, throwing my weight into it.

He doesn't budge. "This is *my* room."

I rise to my toes and point into the hall. "Oh look, a prettier boy."

Daesen glances over his shoulder, boots shifting—

I slam and bolt the door hard enough to jar my bones.

"Ala!" He pounds the wood again from the other side, and I sink to the bed, cataloging my cuts. Sliced breeches and sleeves. Bright streaks of blood shine through cuts in the ruined fabric.

The pounding halts. Footsteps stomp away.

I slump to the floor, and my chest caves inward.

Mother.

Lie upon lie.

I once thought I knew her—both her and Mama. Before they left, before they abandoned us to fend for ourselves, perhaps I *did* know them.

But this woman—the one who would betray her union with her children mere paces away—her, I don't know at all.

Now I know Mother less even than I might know my own sister. My sister, who dreamt of the sun, who knows this realm so well... We said we would protect each other, but just how long has Soli kept secrets from me? How many?

"You are right to distrust him."

I jump, whirling to the window.

Braced outside, on Daesen's windowsill, is the commander. Towering clouds of the afternoon sky reflect on the blade at her back, and the keys at her waist chime in the wind.

I lunge for the door handle.

"Wait."

The command in that voice, so like a watchman's, leads my muscles to obey. Rexar hoists herself to the wide sill, over the hooked notch that's threaded with thick rope. Inside the room, she's massive enough to nearly block the whole window. My muscles unlock as panic shoots through my veins, and I pivot again for the door—

"Truth Six. Obey orders, always."

I halt at that truth, one I carved with my own hands. Heart in my throat, I can't manage to whisper more than, "How do you know that?"

"You're not the only one who knows the truths, Alathea of Elektos."

Swallowing, slowly I turn toward the commander, eyes to the floor, chin down. "You shouldn't be here."

115

"You've been trailed by that dog and sorceress every step in this realm. How else am I to warn you about the shield?"

I've seen enough of the danger of Daesen myself. "You've wasted your time climbing. You should leave, before he returns."

"And here I thought you were a child of the truths. Do not let them go, girl, even now that you're here—*especially* now that you're here. The truths have kept me safe in this realm, for all the long years since I crossed the silver blade and became the commander."

"You..." I press into the wall for support. "You're from Elektos."

"You and I have more in common than you imagine. If you are going to play their games, you should know what you're facing. The risks."

"I am not playing anyone's games."

"Are you not?" The commander points her dagger to the cuts on my arms, the streaks of blood. "Magic is cruel. You could use an ally in this realm."

"I have allies already." Like Daesen, who is something close to a friend. As for Lidja...she is something, too.

"You need allies who understand what it is to be from Elektos and to survive here. The dog and sorceress will keep you so occupied that you will not even speak to the army and meet the others from Elektos. We are the ones who know what it is to be born without magic, to learn to navigate this realm without any power but our own strength and wits. We know who will be weakest when the baya of Nightmares arrives. Do you truly believe you will be any better off than the rest of us when she does, with the new magic in your veins?" Rexar points to the rolling hills, to the sea beyond. "Orkayha *will* find a weakness in the triad's protection magic, and I would wager that with who you are—a girl from Elektos who stumbled into magic—you'll be the first to die when the battle arrives."

"The Realm of Memoria is not at war," I say, repeating

Daesen's words, even as the old man's warning from the death wagon rolls through me again. "It's only the triads that Orkayha hunts."

"The triads of which you are a part, weak and new as you are. Do you not want a way to keep yourself safe...or your sister?"

My pulse trips over itself. *Of course* I want that, but...my scarred palm pulses with the promise I made to Lidja to restore the Realm of Dreams.

Eyes hooded, Rexar watches me, the tattoos on her arms gleaming. Even in Elektos, a watchman would not offer a reward without something in return.

"What do you want?" I ask.

"I want the same as you. I want you to leave this realm and never return—you *and* your sister. In return, I will show you a gate home."

Home.

For a heartbeat, the scent of sage and lavender and thyme encircles me, the dirt of the garden in my nails, the sound of Soli's laughter. Even with the watchmen knowing what I am, I ache to be inside those four walls, just for a moment.

"There is a grounded gate." Rexar presses forward when I remain silent. "With no arch on the Elektos side, you would never notice it, unless you knew just where to look."

I hesitate even as the question burns on my tongue—"And where precisely would one need to look?"

"In the ruined stone wall on the southernmost corner of the burned wheat field."

I saw that ruined, knee-high wall every day from the window of the assembly house. If we could return to Elektos, even if home isn't an option...we could look for our mothers, *and* be far from the danger here.

But..."How do I know you're telling the truth?"

A knock comes from the bedroom door. "Ala, are you there?"

My sister's voice, loud and suspicious. "Is someone in there with you?"

With a single vault, Rexar returns to the windowsill and grips the rope. "Find me at the moons temple by mid-afternoon, and I will show you the proof of it."

Another knock, more urgent. "Ala?"

"I will think on it." *Is* there is way I could do this—fulfill the promise I made, and bring us home? If I can find the key-gate today or tomorrow, Soli and I could return before any attack on Memoria.

"Don't think too long, girl. I'm not known for patience. Meet me at the moons temple or you'll understand well where weakness leads."

With that, the commander leaps from the window. Moments later, the rope zips through the windowsill notch, all trace of her visit gone.

Only her offer-threat taps within me, within that hollow in my chest.

A way home.

CHAPTER 18

a chill breeze winds through Daesen's bedchamber as I swing open the door to my sister. "Rexar was here."

"The *commander*?" Soli marches into the room, a small purse clutched in her left hand. "Are you certain?"

"I am not the one of us who lies."

For a heartbeat, the accusation suspends between us.

"You are *not* the one to lecture on lies, truth-carver."

The jab lands, sharp and hard. "Why didn't you tell me about this place?"

"I tried. A hundred times. A thousand. But you never wanted to listen, and after a while, it was easier to stop trying."

If that's true, if she truly gave up on me...I swallow. "How long have you been coming here?"

"Since the day after our mothers left." The bed slopes as Soli sits at my side. "I was wandering the ravine behind our home, furious, looking for a fight. A boy stepped out of the woods. He was tall and strange, and I knocked him to the dirt, but instead of fighting back, he started telling me stories—stories that sounded just like the ones Mother used to tell us at night. He offered to show me, and I...I went with him."

"This boy—was it Daesen?"

Soli nods. "It was."

"What about the song of the girl with raven hair?"

"Oh, that's over." A broad smile spreads across my sister's face. "We decided we're better as friends. But Dae, he's been teaching me to fight ever since that day two years ago."

I want to smile back, but instead, my lips curl downward. Two years. My sister has been coming to this realm for *two years*. "You've known what you are for that long? What I am?"

"No. Dae only taught me to fight because I begged him. He said he was unbeatable, and, well..." She shrugs. "It took me seven seasons to win a sparring match, and the way that win felt —to be that strong, to beat one of the strongest beings in a magic realm, it's like nothing else, Ala. So I thought, maybe one day I'd ask Rexar to be in her army, or Dae himself...if he ever accepts Vis's offer to take over command."

She glances toward the door and continues. "But yesterday on my food route—I was actually doing what I was supposed to in the morning, dearest sister—something felt *wrong*. In my gut. A pull, in a way I've never felt before. Like something was coming. When I arrived at my friends' home after I saw you in the lane, they handed me a note from Vis. It wasn't until I was here, and the shield's memories came for me, that I understood who I was truly meant to be. That I realized who you might be, too."

Gently, Soli scoops her scarred palm beneath mine. "Even knowing Orkayha hunts us, I'm happy here, Ala. I feel...lighter. Stronger. I feel like, even with monsters hunting us and Orkayha wanting to throw us in pits—I feel *hope*. I feel like that when I'm with my friends, or with Daesen. It feels like winning a fight against someone who should easily beat you. I want to feel like that when I'm here with you now."

And as if spoken into existence, I feel it, too.

That spark in my chest. Light. Possibility.

"If we do this, Ala, imagine what Elektos will be." She rests her head on my shoulder, and her voice quiets to no more than a whisper. "Maybe if we do this, if we open the gates and set the baya to their throne, maybe that will even be enough for our mothers to come back."

Our mothers, who left because of me. I peel my sister upward, searching her for any signs of new injuries from the lash I caused in the red-stained chamber. I find none, which means if it was indeed a lash of magic as Daesen said, I've yet to find the cost.

My gaze lands on the old scar of my sister's that stretches from the base of her neck across her collarbone.

The memory from the stained chamber rises within me, little Soli's words. *Bad. You're bad, Ala.*

Was little Soli so wrong?

I point to my sister's scar. "Do you remember how you got this?"

"I've always had it." She frowns, tracing a fingertip across the puckered skin. "Right?"

"I…" *Hide and hide and hide.* For all the millions of times I've wanted to tell my sister what I did, how I hurt her…I can't risk losing her for knowing this. For knowing I'm the reason our mothers left. At least with this scar, Soli was too young to recall. "I don't know either."

"Come on, then. Let's make sure you don't get any of your own." From a small purse, she draws a vial of liquid and clean cloth. Gently, she dabs each cut on my arms, my neck, my legs. Just like Mama would have, if we'd been home. Nodding, Soli rocks to her heels. "You need new clothes. Preferably less dull ones."

I catch her hand. "If you'd been there—if anyone had been there when I shattered that glass…"

"I wasn't there. No one was but you. You can't let fear of what *might* happen stop you from finding that key-gate so we can open it."

"What if I destroy the gate? What if I hurt whoever is at my side?" But it's not *whoever*. It's Soli. It has to be her. Together will be the only way to open the gate.

"You won't destroy it. You will find it, and we will open it. Because I know you, Alathea, and you are stubborn enough to carve one hundred and five lies into stone when you believe them."

"One hundred and seven," I grumble.

Soli's lips twitch. "See?"

But it's Rexar's offer-threat that I recall again now. *A way home.* I have to find the key-gate and open it with Soli. I will—*we* will—but after that is done, perhaps, just maybe, I could convince my sister to leave this realm with me and search for our mothers far from the hunting baya of Mizura.

Which means I need to keep searching, and make sure I don't misuse magic again in the meantime. "I need to learn how to control my magic."

"I know just the someone who can help with that."

"I am certain that Lidja doesn't want to spend more time with me today."

"Interesting." Soli's smile is back, sly. "But I wasn't talking about Lidja. I was talking about Dae."

I fight the urge to duck under the blanket.

"Things are different here, Ala. No one is going to care who you like, or who you kiss. You don't have to hide how you feel about someone."

"Who says I'm feeling anything for anyone?"

Soli's grin grows. "Daesen says Lidja is all blade and bite, like the edge of autumn as it cuts into winter."

"And Dae himself?"

"Lidja says he's butter and corn. Like the steamiest, hottest day of summer."

A laugh slips from my lips, surprising us both.

Soli folds her leg beneath her, eyes sparkling. "Do you like one of them? It's all right if you do."

"Lidja hates me. Dae…" I pick at the bedsheet. "Dae flirts with rocks."

"And they probably flirt right back. But how do *you* feel?"

"I don't know."

She tugs me upward, away from the bed, toward the wardrobe. Shirts and breeches fly from her fingers to the floor. Daesen's clothes, although some are clearly too narrow and short for his broad, tall frame. Why are there such small clothes in his room?

Soli picks up a black blouse from the back with matching black breeches and holds the color against me. "Very Lidja. Do you think it suits you?"

"*Soli.*"

My sister shrugs, all innocence. "I'm just saying. You might want to figure out how you feel. Maybe working on control with butter and corn is an opportunity to figure it out."

I pinch my nose and inhale deeply. "I'm trying."

"I know. I see it."

"Then—" I swallow past a sudden rock in my throat. "Then I'm asking you for no more lies between us. For a promise of our own."

Soli stills. "What kind of promise?"

"After we do this, after we open the gate and place the baya on the throne"—saying it sounds impossible still—"we will go find our mothers. Together."

"That, dearest sister, I will promise with pleasure."

* * *

THE LUSH JUNGLE ends at the edge of the sea. A ring of smooth stones stretches along the shore to tall outcrops of red rocks. Twenty paces from Daesen, I watch as a shower of gray coats the late afternoon horizon, studded by streaks of lightning. No silver curtain shimmers between us and the storm, a different part of the isle than he brought me before.

"Isn't it dangerous to be on a shore with a storm coming?" This time, without the dizzying journey of a quick-portal in my blood, I can't help but notice how *much* water there is, far more than the lake where I sank in the wagon. "What if Orkayha's underlings attack here?"

"They wouldn't. Not here. Not yet anyway. The protection we cast with Vis is solid. There's a weakness in it, as with all magic, but Orkayha's beasts haven't found it yet." He strolls to a tall rock that juts into the sea and climbs, hand over hand, spear strapped to his back. "Plenty of time for a lesson in control."

"This might be a bad idea."

"Breaking more of Vis's prized ceilings would be a worse one." Daesen crests the rock. "But short of learning to control your magic from birth, this is what you've got. I helped your sister learn control before she even had magic. I can help you."

"Remains to be seen," I mutter.

Daesen's dimples flash. "It's going to be fun, needle. I promise."

"I think we have very different understandings of that word."

"Let's find out." He peels the spear from his back, the metal and strap across his chest thunking to the rock. His boots flop to the stone. His fingers reach for the tie of his breeches—

"What are you *doing*?" My voice comes out an octave higher than I mean it to.

"I don't usually swim with my clothes on." His shirt rises, exposing a sculpted abdomen of muscle and warm brown skin. Nothing like the glimpses I saw of boys in Elektos. The whorls of blue and black ink on his neck stretch from his shoulders, around his chest, down to his waist, down…

I slap my palm over my eyes.

Things are different here.

"This is *not* how Soli said you helped her learn control."

"We fought," my sister had said, when I asked back in the bedchamber. "Harder than I've ever battled in my life, we fought, and it taught me what I needed to know—how to focus and contain the power I hold, magic or no, until just the right moment."

"That is correct," Dae says now. Cloth wisps to the rock. "*This* is much more fun. What better way to test a pine needle than with a prick?"

I can't decide if I want to laugh or swear. "You're—you're a cocky mule."

"I'll take that as a compliment."

"I didn't mean it as one."

"Truly? We have mules in this realm, too. Have you seen the size of their—"

"Stop!"

His chuckle arcs, and a splash sounds from the water. I crack open my fingers.

Submerged to his neck, water dripping from his short curls into his eyes, Daesen hovers in the sea twenty paces from shore. His spear glints at his side, reflecting the blue-gray of the approaching storm.

"You're coiled tight as a thread spool, Ala, but that's not control." He crooks a finger. "Come in, and I'll show you what you need to learn."

"I can't go in there." My pulse races at the memory of the lake, the water clawing at my throat, sinking. "I can't swim. Not in a lake."

"That's fine, because this is the sea."

"Water all the same."

"Aren't you tired of being afraid?"

"You wouldn't understand. I suppose you're not afraid of anything."

"You would suppose wrong." Slow, lazy, like he's crawling, Daesen swims for the tall rock. "Snakes, for example."

"Snakes?" This warrior-mage is afraid of *snakes—that's* why Lidja spun the creatures from sticks. "We have those at home. They're nothing to be afraid of."

Daesen shivers as he climbs the rock. As I keep my eyes on the sea. "I can't stand them. Lidja, on the other hand, as you've seen, loves them. She used to spend whole days searching for them to hide in my bed."

What kind of bed games do they play in this realm? "And you…liked that?"

"I tied her up and left her in the afternoon rains every time."

Very strange, indeed. "In Elektos, you'd be sent to a re-education square for that kind of perversion."

"Perver—" He barks a laugh. "No, Ala, it's not like that. Lidja is practically my sister."

"I didn't ask."

"But you wanted to know. It's all over your face, needle. So I'll make you a bargain."

He waits until I meet his gaze. *Only* his gaze.

"I'll let you hide something in my bed. And I promise you'll enjoy being tied up in the rain." Daesen runs and leaps.

I hate every drop on his handsome face when he surfaces. "That's *not* a game I'd play."

"That's fine. Let's play another one. You try to keep your control, and I'll try to break it." Swimming toward shore, he waggles his fingers. "Come on in."

Try.

But my feet won't budge, the memory of the icy water from the lake in Elektos holding me to the stone shore.

"Elektos is surrounded by water. How do you not know how to swim?"

"We aren't taught how."

"Why do you think that is?" Closer, he swims toward the shore.

"To keep us from drowning."

"I'd say it's to prevent you from escaping."

I keep my gaze up. Nowhere, *nowhere* below that chest. Not a peep. "We're not prisoners." Or at least, I never used to think we were.

"Except for when they put you in that wagon. Except for every day they kept you from leaving. Don't you want to show them, Ala? Show them they don't own you, or your choices?"

"I don't want to hurt anyone."

"Of course you don't, you're not a monster. But control isn't about what you *don't* want. The root of control—the root of *magic*—is knowing yourself. It's about focus. About what you *do* want. So, what do you want, Ala?"

Back in my room, when Rexar made her offer, I wanted home. I wanted to take Soli and find our mothers. But now, here, faced with the sea and that naked chest, all I can think of is what I *don't* want.

I don't want to think about Mother lying to me for so long.

I don't want Soli to find out I'm the reason our mothers left, or the reason for her scar.

I don't want to fail at this task, and risk losing my sister, too.

"I don't know what I want."

"All right. I'll lend you one this time. But the next will be yours in truth." He thrusts his spear downward, until it stays upright in the gentle waves at his side. "Let's say you want to take my spear away from me. Come and retrieve it. I'll try to prevent you."

"I can't swim."

"It's not so deep here that you can't walk. That's not what this is about, in any case. It's about your attention. Channel your magic by intention, instead of reflex."

"My sister would just fight you for that weapon."

"True." Those damned dimples return. "But there are much more interesting obstacles I'm planning for you."

My stomach tilts. "I just focus on the spear?"

"Focus on it with every breath and take it. Right now, it's what you want. The *only* thing you want—no matter what distraction I put in your way."

I hover at the edge of the jungle and stare at the twenty paces from the shore to the spear.

It took so few breaths to sink in the lake.

"*Bawk.*" Daesen grins. "We have chickens here, too."

I consider hurling one of my precious stakes. "Turn around."

His chuckle drifts, but Daesen obliges. I duck behind a fringed palm's trunk for good measure and shuck my bandolier, followed by the soft breeches and blouse, leaving on my borrowed undergarments.

I toe toward the sea, step by step, until my feet touch the water. Surprisingly, it's warm and tinged clear gray-blue. "Daesen?"

When no one answers, I glance upward and find the sea but for the standing spear. I stride into the water, up to my ankles. Did he drown? Did a monster under the water take him? "Daesen!"

Ten paces from me, the water pops, and Daesen bounces upward, grinning, chest glittering with drops. A single rivulet darts down the center of his chest. Down, toward his—

"Stop!" I fan my palm outward, blocking the view. "You truly have awful timing."

"I'd do anything to make you smile, needle."

"Don't." I glare, even as my lips feel like doing just that. "I'm getting in—to my waist only."

He flicks at a gentle wave, smiling, and sinks back, waiting.

And waiting.

"Focus."

Inhaling deeply, I take another step toward that spear, deeper. My bare sole lands on something jagged and I stumble forward, flailing—

Daesen's hands grip my arms, holding me upright. "Steady."

My eyes squeeze tight.

"I've got you."

Fluttering open, I pin my gaze upward.

Only up.

"I won't let you drown. Much."

Without thinking, I punch his arm, quick, as hard as I can.

Daesen blinks once, twice.

I shake my stinging hand, horrified. "I—I—I *hurt* you."

"Baby fish nip harder than that, Ala." Against my arms, his thumbs trace a short, comforting circle. "Although you did surprise me. You keep surprising me." The warm water laps at my lower ribs, at his hips. "Even if you could hurt me, I would never, ever hurt you for it. In my home, *that* would be the perversion."

His thumbs circle the skin of my forearms again, just inside the crook of my elbow.

"What are you doing?"

"You've conquered the first distraction." His gaze falls to my lips. "I'm moving on to the next."

My breath shallows. "What is the next?"

"Focus, needle."

Right. I refocus behind him, ten paces from where we stand in the sea. "The spear."

"It's what you want, isn't it?"

In my blood, heat gathers, low and steady.

"I'll be by your side the whole way."

The distraction. *This* is the game.

"My little chicken."

I step deeper into the water.

"Very good." At my side, his hand on my arm, Daesen's voice is smooth, like the silk of his bed, beneath the blankets. "Out of curiosity, did your sister tell you about Mirthraya?"

"It's hard to focus when you're yammering." I consider punching him again as dimples flash. Instead, I step again toward the spear. The sea creeps up my torso. But still…Mirthraya. Another thing my sister knows but hasn't told me. "What is it?"

"It's our most sacred night in Memoria. To celebrate the turning of the season, to create new memories of our own." Sage and salt wrap around me, a warm breath at the crest of my ear. "On Mirthraya, we light fires and make love under the moons."

Waves lap at the lowest rung of my ribs as images flare behind my eyes.

Of glistening skin beside burning pyres.

Of Daesen, shirt off as it is now, in someone's arms.

Of his tattoos writhing as his hair gleams in the firelight. Of—

"Focus on the spear, Ala."

I swipe for his naked chest and miss, splashing sea water across his shaking shoulders instead. "You lie."

"About Mirthraya? Never." Daesen's amusement fades. "If Orkayha wasn't about to wreck our shores, you'd see it yourself four days from now—pyres and the fate-stars and the moons. Even you could participate, if you wanted."

"I couldn't." I couldn't be outside, naked, under the three stars and moons with a boy or girl of my choosing, with no fear of being caught. "That's not how it's done in Elektos."

"I know it's different." His eyes trace my cheeks. My brows. My lips. There, his gaze pins. "Here, we don't hide, not even from the moons. Would you like it, needle, to be naked outside with a lover, for all the moons and fate-stars to see?"

Slowly, slowly, Daesen's hands move from my arms to my waist, to the wet undergarment painted to my skin.

My breath turns shallow, tight, and I lick my lips. "I…"

"What do you *want*, Ala?"

I want the water to be darker. I want to be under it, to hide from the heat in his gaze. I want relief from the strange buzzing that threads through me, unlike the rustle of magic. Unlike, and similar, all at once.

"I want a moment of silence." Lie. Such a lie. But now that he's talking, and my body is humming, my lips seem to have disconnected from my brain. This must be magic, but I—I can't seem to break from it.

I'm not certain I want to.

"Ah, Ala." He pulls me closer, closer, until I'm on my tiptoes and the warmth of his chest brushes my skin, his mouth a breath from mine. "I don't think you want me to keep my mouth shut, not really."

The waves lap, and I lift my chin, mesmerized by the vibration that hums from my lips to my toes and back. I slide my hands from his shoulders to the top of his chest.

For stability.

He whispers, "I can do truly amazing magic with this mouth."

I gasp, my feet no longer touching at all, and just to my right is a flash. Lightning beats over the water, far away, and—the spear.

It's here, right within reach.

Dae lifts my right hand from his chest. His thumb caresses the mark of the circle and slash, following their shape.

"What do you want, Alathea?"

I extract my hand from his and reach for the spear, victory in reach—

And pause.

What do I want?

Not this spear.

Not really.

That was *his* want, for this game.

What do I want?

"Tell me." His lips nearly touch my ear.

Mouth dry, I return my scarred palm to his shoulder. My thumb rests at the edge of swirling ink at his neck.

As dangerous, as forward as this boy is, even if it means nothing...

"I want a kiss." A kiss I don't have to hide, not from the Sancta or the watchmen. Not from anyone.

Dae stills. "You want a kiss...from me?"

"Maybe. I'm not certain."

"Needle is the right name for you. Ouch." He rubs his chest.

"Wasn't that the goal? For me to say what I want? To *know* what I want?"

"I mean, a kiss from me *specifically* was *my* goal, but I'll take this as a step in the right direction."

"You're incorrigible."

"Call me more impossible words, needle, and I'll search the whole of Fides for the keys to your heart."

A laugh escapes me, breathless, wavering. "If you find those, I'll let you have it."

"In that case, I'm off to—" Daesen glances over my shoulder to the shore and rips the spear from the sea in a single sweep. His arm bands around my torso like iron, all traces of amusement wiped from his face.

"What..." But my question dies as I follow his gaze to the shallows, where bright red trails over the blue sea.

Where a man floats, unmoving.

"Drowned." I dig my fingers into Daesen's shoulder.

"No." Daesen points to the sky. In the south, a new column of smoke spikes from the jungle. "Orkayha found our weakness."

CHAPTER 19

*L*idja crouches at the body's side on the stone shore.

When we found the dead man in the sea, Daesen carried him to land with infinite care. By the time we donned our clothes, Lidja had arrived, axe in hand. With a nod to the sorceress, Dae disappeared toward the plume of ever-rising smoke in the south, leaving me here, alone with her once again.

"You charm faster than the rocks," Lidja says now.

I wrap my arms around my chest, the wet of my undergarments seeping through my blouse. "He was helping me with control. With focus."

Lidja glances my way, a quick up and down, before turning back to the dead man. "So I can see."

I bite my tongue to keep from sticking it out at her back. "Who is he?"

"One of Rexar's soldiers. Charlas was his name." Gently, the sorceress touches his lids, drawing them shut over unseeing eyes. She places a kiss on his brow and whispers as she draws a dagger from her bandolier.

Panic sears through me. What kind of awful ritual is she about to perform? "Don't—"

But Lidja simply lays the dagger on the center of the dead man's chest, blade pointed downward. "We give the dead knives to bid them a safe crossing through the spirit field of Ahnaysa." The sorceress rises and turns toward me, one less blade in her bandolier. "You might need your own before this is over. We all may."

Her gaze shifts to the smoke, a gray plume rising against the still-darkening clouds. "I'm surprised you noticed Charlas at all with Dae *helping* you."

"Nothing happened."

"Did you hear me asking?"

My finger itches to flick upward...not that she's completely wrong.

I want a kiss.

Never in my life have I been so forward. Even my very first kiss was a quiet affair in the shadows of a secret room.

You want a kiss...from me?

What would have happened if I'd said yes?

And deep in my chest, a spark ignites. As if I've wedged my chisel inside the hollow there and pried it open, just the slightest breath.

"If you don't stop blushing, I might ask anyway. It's etched across your face."

"And what if something did happen? Would you care?"

"Obviously, I wouldn't. I didn't come here to listen to you moon over the bam. Let's go. Back to the palace, to do what you're supposed to be doing."

I grind my boots into the stones. "Why are you here? How did you know where I was?"

Quick as the serpent she conjured, Lidja grabs my scarred hand. "When you made that promise, it tethered you to me. I will always know where you are, Alathea, no matter what foolish endeavor you're pursing. The Fates know I wish otherwise, but there was no other way I would have brought you into my home."

I *knew* she didn't trust me. "And now? Do you trust me now?"

"Should I? Do *you* trust me now?"

"No." I lean into her hand, my wet skin dripping on her pristine boots. "I didn't think it possible, but in truth, I like you even less."

"Then the feeling is mutual."

I wrench my hand back. "You should have told me what the promise meant."

"Would you have made that vow if we had? Stop stalling. You need to return to searching, now that you have half a chance of not destroying the key-gate."

Before, at home, I would have followed such a command without question. But now, here... "No. Take me to the southern shore."

"Do you think you can command me?"

"I'm a high sorceress, too." I will my knees to hold, and keep my chin high. "It's what I want."

"Can you not bear to be separated from him for a few moments now? Is that what this is?"

"This is me caring about my sister. If there is an attack, Soli will be there." I have no doubt in any grain of my bones. "And if she's there, I need to be, too."

"Your sister can beat almost anyone in this realm into the ground. If it's one of Orkayha's underlings, they've likely already tasted her blade."

"You and Daesen *barely* beat the mawlyr in Elektos."

"Our realm magic is dampened and unreliable across the silver curtain—dangerous, unless you're certain of its cost. Here, against our realm magic at full force, her underlings have no chance."

"And if it's not her underlings?"

"If that's Orkayha's second line, if that's her monster of a shield, you being there is an even worse idea. Daesen and Soliana will handle it."

A boom thunders overhead, and a second plume of smoke bolts upward.

Lidja unsheathes her axe. "But perhaps I should go. Just in case."

"I'm going, too."

"You will only be in the way."

"There must be something I can do to help."

"Yes. There is. Go find that gate."

"If my sister is in trouble, if she's hurt, I won't be able to open the gate at all."

Lidja hesitates.

"And if we don't open the gate," I press, "what does that mean for *your* home?"

A third plume rises, this boom strong enough to rock the stones beneath us.

I'm done waiting. I stride forward for the jungle, to the south. "After this, I'll search the palace," I say, as Lidja remains in place, knuckles pale on her axe. "But right now, I'm a sister first, and if you won't lead me there, I'll find the source myself."

Within a breath, the ferns shush behind me. "Fine." The sorceress whispers a foreign word, and we're running, faster than I've ever run before. My thighs burn, the ferns nearly flying by as we speed through the jungle.

"Can't you travel like Dae?"

"*We* cannot." Lidja shudders. "Thankfully, our magic is less nauseating than the shield's."

Through the canopy, the smoke widens, three trails combining into one massive, low gray cloud.

Ahead, a grove of palms shivers.

Lidja presses a dagger into my palm. "If I say run, you run." She raises a blade in each hand as we speed toward the quaking leaves—

An ox-like beast with massive triangular horns ambles from the emerald green, lugging its giant body out of the way.

Oxsail. The word rises from deep within me as Lidja and I shift wide around the animal. This is the creature that both Daesen and Lidja have called me. "I don't move that slowly."

"Not now, anyway."

"Would it kill you to try to be kind?"

"It might." The jungle swishes by as we sprint faster still. "Here—black doesn't look awful on you."

"That was more than kind. That was almost a compliment."

"Then I take it back."

But as we rush through the ferns, as the smoke grows even thicker, I can't help but feel that hollow in my chest crack open, just a bit wider.

Because I like how I look in black, too, far from the dull grays that match the assembly house halls. I like this feeling of almost flying, of running so fast nothing can stop me. I like the feel of a cold stake in my hand, of the solid metal that I can hold and throw and control. "Will you teach me to throw blades like you do?"

"Maybe someday, if you're fortunate and I'm bored."

"You know, this may be why some call you a witch."

"Those that do no longer have heads."

I try again. "I want you to teach me to throw."

Lidja slows, and the magic wisps from my legs quick as it came. "It is true that knowing what you want will help you draw from your magic and find the gate much faster, if you can focus. But as high sorceress, your mind is the better blade—it will grow more precise the sharper you hone it."

"Is that a yes, you'll teach me?"

"It's an acknowledgement that you still have much to learn. It's a *I will consider it.*"

"I can wait," I say, and we enter thick smoke.

Around us, the palms shudder.

Straight ahead, a single scream curls.

I stumble over an unseen root and grip the stake in my hand harder.

"What the bam didn't teach you, Alathea," Lidja says as we creep forward, "is that we seldom get precisely what we want."

* * *

THE TUMBLE of stones beneath my boots is the only way I know we're on a shore once again, this time at the southern edge of the isle. Paces away, the sea laps louder with each wave. The storm, unseen through the smoke, rumbles with thunder as evening approaches. Lidja and I crouch low, straining for sight of the village she said rests at this end of Memoria.

Or once rested.

Now only cries and moans curl from where the village must be.

Lidja's axe glints as a burst of lightning cuts through the smoke. "Stay low. Be careful."

But a scream tears from ahead and I charge forward, where my sister might be even now. "Soli!"

"Ala?" My sister's shout stretches through the smoke over the screams as I fumble forward. "You're here? Where are you? Where—"

I crash forward and arms encircle me, warm and fierce. I hold my sister, ignoring the tap of her armored plate at my back and hard metal of her jillbracer at my front. She draws back, spear in her other hand. "We arrived too late."

The smoke thins. Over Soli's shoulder, I spot Daesen, hand on a sobbing man's shoulder. Behind them, flames tear through wood and straw, what must have once been a home.

"We've sent for the wraiths," Daesen says, drawing the man into his chest. Over the man's shoulder, Daesen meets my eyes, his expression grim. Lidja strides to him, and the two converse, terse and low.

"What happened?" I ask my sister.

"Orkayha's monsters." She tugs me away from Daesen and Lidja and the crying man. I follow her around the side of a burning home, a fine layer of gray ashes coating the ground, littering the air. "A whole group of them."

Around the corner, she points to a mound of burning scales.

Mawlyrs. At least five are entangled, unmoving, and oozing pink.

I sway, the ooze meshing with the gray in my vision. "You did that?"

"Rexar's soldiers did most of it. Dae and I helped with the last two, but—" She points toward the jungle, where three more half-homes burn. "It was too late."

My earlier meal rises from my stomach, and I stumble to the base of a palm. My sister follows. "This is what she'll do, Ala. If we don't place the baya of Dreams on the throne, there will be no reason left to hope."

I glance at those homes, at that steaming pile of dead monsters, and heave. Soli soothes a hand over my back as I retch onto the ground.

Magic is death.

The Sancta wasn't wrong about everything.

"The key-gate is inside the palace. I think I can find it now." I will my stomach to calm. "I know I can."

Soli helps me stand, and we walk deeper into the palms until we find a small clearing free of palms and ferns and smoke-filled air, away from the burning homes and dead monsters. "Then you should go. I don't want you here if we missed any of her under-lings, or if her second wave arrives. Take Lidja and—"

Boom.

The very isle shudders, hurling me to the ground.

Sulfur hooks into my nose.

All around is snow.

Gray, fluttering flakes.

My head rings as I try to make sense of it. It's not winter, not yet.

Three paces from me, a hand lies palm up on the ground. From the collar of a blouse, an old scar is flecked with gray snow.

No, not snow.

Ashes.

Ashes that flake across a scarred cheek, wide amber eyes pinned to mine.

Soli.

Grunting, I roll upward.

My sister does the same, but faster, all stealth and intent as she snatches up her spear and faces the jungle on the other side of me. "Get. Out."

The falling ash halts mid-fall, suspended.

With a snap, the gray flecks disappear, swept clean.

Two feet leave the forest behind and enter our clearing.

Not feet.

Claws.

I turn to face a new monster of nightmares.

From its wide back rise talon-tipped, feathered wings, powerful as a night-raptor but seven times the size. Dark hair covers his head, tucked at the tips of pointed ears. A shirt and breeches made of black leather cover a powerful body that ends in those horrible clawed feet.

"What a lovely surprise." A voice like newly carved marble, smooth and hard and cold. Lightning slashes through the canopy, another roll of thunder. "I expected only one. But here you are, two." He glances between Soli and me as we edge closer to each other, until her armored plate stands between us and the monster. "Intriguing."

I have to get Soli out of here. Us *both* out of here. Where is that damned bond to Lidja when I need it? "Soli, get ready to run."

"Sister," Soli hisses. "Do you know who that is?"

"I'm not certain what I'm more delighted by." The monster's black eyes sparkle. "Sisters, that charming threat, or that my reputation remains intact. It's been an age since I've graced this miserable swamp."

"If you don't leave now, you never will again, Tzen." Lidja emerges from the palms at our right, axe in hand, without a glance in our direction. "I see you've grown another claw or two since we last met."

"Run," I whisper to Soli.

"*You* run. This is what *I* do, Ala."

"Ala. What a curious name." With a single leap, the monster bounds directly in front of us, his angled face no more than a pace from ours. His attention pins to Soli. "And what might your name be, sister of Ala?"

"Stay away from her," I say.

"That's not a name."

From behind him, an axe swings for the monster's wings.

Tzen whirls, clawed hand gripping Lidja's arm. "Now, now, love. I believe you have forgotten how our last encounter ended."

He hurls the sorceress into the air, Lidja rolling as she hits the dirt.

The ground quakes, and Tzen marches, clawed palms to the sky, toward the high sorceress of Memoria.

"Go!" Soli shoves the flat of her shield into my arm, pushing me toward the edge of the clearing. *"Run."*

"Not without you!"

The quake strengthens, rocking us both—

And a wall of iron punches into the clearing as Tzen raises his fists high. Tall, taller, the wall rises until it towers over us, the jungle no longer visible, cutting us off from Lidja.

The ground stills.

On the other side of the iron wall, a hard *clank*.

And Tzen turns toward us.

"What a lovely party trick—the sorceress and shield of

Denrathri here, too. Does this mean you've located your wayward baya as well?"

"Don't say anything," Soli breathes.

Another *clank* on the other side of the wall, joined by a *thud*.

Tzen stalks for us. "Are you why those two fools from Memoria were on the other side of the curtain? They were very cruel to Orkayha's darling."

"Not one step closer, monster," my sister says.

Clank. Thud. Clank. Thud. The whole of the iron wall shudders.

"Such big threats for such little girls." Tzen holds up a single taloned finger. "Trust me when I say you do not want to try my patience. I haven't heard a name from your lips. What is the name of Ala's sister?"

"It's *stay away*," I snarl.

The monster's fist punches outward and wraps into the collar of Soli's blouse. With a boom of wings, Tzen launches upward, my sister in hand.

"Soli!" I jump, grasping for her feet, but already, she's too high.

"There. Was that so difficult? Now which one of you expelled that lovely magic lash earlier?" He shakes my sister. "Was it you?"

Clank-thud-clank-thud.

"Let me go, you wartpig." My sister writhes in the monster's grasp, swiping with the rod of her spear.

I search for a way up, for any weapon to hurl at the monster—

Soli smashes her spear into Tzen, and in my veins, my magic flares. The monster only rises higher, and this time, when I jump for my sister, wind rises around me.

"You, then," he says.

"Yes, it was me!" I shout as Soli fights, twisting. I will the sparks to calm, to rise, to do something, *anything* helpful. *Focus. Control.* I want Soli down here. Safe. With me. I want—

"What do you think, Ala? Will your sister break from this height?"

I still, the sparks gone in a heartbeat. "What do you want? Anything. I'll do anything. Just promise to not hurt her."

"I begin to understand why Orkayha is so fond of others running her errands. Cooperation is simple, when you find the right vein to press." Tzen's razor teeth flash in the smoky light. "Give me your surname, and I will return her to your side."

Golden light leaks from the other side of the wall. *Clank-thud-clank-thud—*

Soli slices at the monster's neck. "Don't do it, Ala!"

The monster's claw screeches along the metal of Soli's jill-bracer until it pierces her gut where it ends. Soli gasps, dropping her spear, pushing her fist into the flow of blood.

"Soli!"

Tzen rises higher still, my sister dangling from his grip twenty, thirty paces in the air. "Tell me, little monster. What is your surname?"

Clank-thud-clank-thud—

"Don't Ala," Soli whispers, and then she goes slack in the beast's grip.

"Tell me," Tzen growls, "or I will rip out her throat."

"Thymisius," I breathe. "Let her go."

"Thymisius." His mouth twists around the name, like a rotten fruit. The monster flaps, his giant wings booming in time with a roll of thunder. "Tell your baya, Alathea Thymisius, they can hide no longer. Tell them that my queen is through with the pits. In five days, her army will come for Memoria, and this time, there will be no next triads."

"Bring her here!" I stretch for Soli as blood drops like rain and the iron wall shudders around us. "You promised."

"So I did." Tzen opens his clawed fist.

The wall splinters open in a spray of golden light.

My sister tumbles to the ground.

CHAPTER 20

"*S*oli!" I hurl myself forward, bracing my legs wide, arms out as she falls fast, too fast—

A heartbeat before she crashes into me, her plummet slows.

We thud into the ground as one.

Thunder rolls, Tzen disappears, and the skies unload. Two sets of boots pound toward us, Lidja and Daesen hurtling from the wall they destroyed a moment ago.

"Soli?" I slide from under her, everything aching, and wipe soaked hair from her face. Blood leaks from low in her torso, her leg bent at a sickening angle.

She doesn't answer. She doesn't *move*.

Daesen kneels at my sister's side. "The wraiths are on their way."

"I need a cloth."

Without hesitation, Dae strips off his shirt. I stuff it against my sister's bleeding wound. "I need—"

"Here." Lidja's empty bandolier strap dangles in my face. Her own face is streaked with pink ooze and mud. "A few mawlyrs got in the way of my blades before we could take that damned wall down."

"It's not your fault," I say as Daesen lifts Soli. We strap his soaked shirt to my sister. Even in the rain, the red seeps through in moments.

From all around the clearing, wraiths materialize, burgundy cloaks unaffected by the deluge, Lucius leading the group. *"Her heart beats strong, Alathea. Soliana has no need of a passage blade yet. She will survive."*

"I'll go with her," Daesen says. "No doubt she'll want to revisit every move as soon as she awakes—and I need to talk with Vis. We need to adjust our plan now for Orkayha's coming assault."

Daesen murmurs to Lidja as Tzen's warning echoes again among us.

In five days, her army will come for Memoria. And this time, there will be no next triads.

Daesen and the wraiths lift my sister with the greatest care, her body raised on a wooden board. Only Lidja remains, rain bouncing from her heaving shoulders.

As the group reaches the edge of the clearing, Lucius hesitates. He twists to face me, eyes bright under the hood of his cloak. *"Long have the wraiths planned for the day on which we will greet our brethren in Denrathri once again, but with Vis gone, I answer to the commander."*

I frown. What could Rexar possibly matter when my sister was nearly just killed?

"Hear me, Alathea. I cannot act against the commander's will, but I will push every limit to embrace my brethren."

I wait for more, but Lucius simply nods as if that was sufficient and follows the others into the jungle.

Why would Lucius wish to act against the commander's will unless...

The baya of Nightmares will find the weakness in the triad's protection over the realm. Have no doubt. Rexar's own words, before she offered me that gate home and threatened me.

There is always a weakness, Daesen said.

But this weakness wasn't in the protective layer that still shimmers over the isle, or from a rogue guard.

This was someone else completely.

I rock to my feet, open my mouth to the pouring sky, and scream.

I scream until my throat is raw and my lungs burn and I am empty of everything but roiling fury. It tears through my veins, swirling like a tornado that would rip the very palm trees from this soil.

No, not fury.

Vengeance.

Lidja trudges through the bloodied mud to my side. "Scream your word of your power like that, and you will cast magic strong enough to shudder the whole of Fides to its knees."

"There is only one person I want to bring to their knees right now."

"Do I want to know?"

"You'll know anyway." I hold my scarred palm to her, the promise between us humming. "Where is the Fates-damned moons temple?"

* * *

DUSK CHASES the last of the storm away as Lidja and I huddle in the jungle at the crest of a hill. Below, tucked into the cleft of this hill and the next, a temple glows with fireflies and candlelight. At the base of its steps rests a short stone with an arch through its center, shimmering faintly gray-blue.

A grounded gate.

The grounded gate.

On the other side of that shimmer…Elektos.

But instead of aching for my home on the other side, the center of the temple holds my attention. There, in the shadows, rope and chains and keys at her waist, Rexar sharpens a sword.

Lidja rocks to her heels. "I wondered when this day would come." She glances at me from the corner of her eyes. "If you want my advice, I recommend a disguise. I can spell you to look like a watchman. You can get away with a lot when others believe you're someone else."

But I shake my head, my magic mixing with fury to pour plans forward.

Threaten her. Press a hot band into her wrist. Nail her to the marble.

All of which would make me no better than a watchman. "I'm going to make her confess. Then you can bring her to the cages in your palace."

"That is...reasonable," Lidja says. "Are you certain you want to be reasonable, if she did what you suspect?"

No. I'm not certain at all.

It's not so difficult to understand, truly, what we would do for those we love—for our own family, if they asked it of us, if they said they were wronged. Vis's statement, when I first arrived here. Is this what the baya of nightmare feels? This all-consuming fury that burns like a summer bonfire?

But—"I won't become like her." Not Rexar, not Orkayha.

"She won't make it easy."

My lip ticks with a side-glance at the sorceress. "Who here does? Besides—she and I have more in common than you think. Wait until I call for you."

Lidja's voice drops, low and sharp as her blades. "Are you ordering me?"

"I'm trusting you."

"That could be a mistake."

"I know. We'll find out soon enough." I slip down the wet hill to face the commander.

As I emerge from the jungle to flat, muddy ground around the temple, Rexar nods once with smug satisfaction and then tenses, her narrowed gaze on the palm trees behind me. "Where is the dog?"

"I am alone." The lie tastes like ash, especially when I've just trusted Lidja of all beings to stay put. "Everyone else is still at the village the monsters attacked."

Rexar spits. "Don't lie to me, truth-follower. You expect me to believe the dog didn't follow you here? He follows you everywhere, like a buck in heat." She strides to the edge of the mud, peering into the rain-logged palms.

It takes every pore of control in my body to keep my stakes in my bandolier, to keep from shouting and charging at her through the mud. Does she truly not know what happened at that village, how her own people have been hurt? Or does she not care?

"Orkayha's underlings attacked one of *your* villages. He's helping them recover." *He's watching over* my *sister who* you *hurt.* My magic sparks in my veins. *Focus. Make her confess.* "Why weren't you there fighting the mawlyrs, too?"

"I pick my fights, girl. That one wasn't mine." This time, Rexar shouts into the jungle, "Where are you, dog?"

"He was injured," I lie, unable to stop from unsheathing a stake this time, watching her carefully for any sign of gloating. "That's why he's not here."

Rexar snorts. "You expect me to believe he'd let a helpless girl meet me alone?"

I frown as my magic slides pieces into place. "You...you asked me here—you offered me a way home—to lure *Daesen* here with me?"

And finally, the commander turns from the jungle to face me. "I knew if my *offer* wasn't enough, this message would be."

The moons temple by mid-afternoon or you'll understand well where weakness leads.

My magic whirs. The mawlyrs, Tzen, her demanded to meet her earlier today or else...her message was Tzen.

I was right. Somehow, she let Tzen in. *She's* the reason my sister bled.

Magic and fury smash together in my veins and pop. I thrust my stake at Rexar as she stalks for me. "You should be *protecting* this realm—protecting its people."

"I am protecting *our* home, girl." Rexar's eyes glint. "The difference is that I know what the right opportunity looks like, when it appears."

She lunges, knocking my stake away and binding a rope around my arms and torso in a single move.

I rip away, stumbling in the mud. I flick my wrist and whisper, "*Release.*"

Nothing happens.

"Cast all the magic you want, girl. That rope is spelled against it. Another gift from my friend, who knows exactly what monsters live in this realm."

Rexar reaches for me, and I lunge to run—

She yanks the rope at my back, and I fall to the mud, face-first.

Flipping to my back, I kick hard, but she steps on my calf hard enough that stars burst behind my eyes.

From the jungle, silver glints, not ten paces away. *Wait until I call.*

I want one more confession from Rexar, loud enough for Lidja to hear.

"If you call Tzen your friend," I say, gritting my teeth as Rexar leans over me, "that makes *you* the monster."

"I wouldn't call that disgusting beast *friend*. My true friend sees this unjust world for what it is. My real friend grants me gifts." Rexar unhooks the silver keys from her waist and drops them with a whisper. *"The pits of Mizura."*

From the mud, a silver-blue curtain punches upward with a snap. Beyond the shimmer, black mist swirls and screams zing. An onyx walkway stretches into the horizon, cold and brutal.

My heart skips.

She has a key-gate—and beyond it, the Realm of Mizura.

Rexar grinds her foot into my calf. "All the dog needed to do —all he's *ever* needed to do—is name me, and that power of the shield would be mine. Instead, he's hoarded it for himself." She hauls me upward by the binding of the rope. "He does not *deserve* such power. Daesen bears the sins of his father. I haven't forgotten, even if Vis has. I should have cut his toes from his foot and buried them among the gifts in the baya's room long ago. I should have—"

"You should have moved much faster." Lidja's axe flies from the jungle.

Rexar drops me to the mud, the axe barely missing her head as she leaps backward.

I scoop the keys from the mud.

In my hand, the key-gate glows.

A gift.

A gift that is easily hidden in plain sight at one's waist...

Or in the room of a squirrel-hoarder of a baya.

I toss the keys to the jungle.

"No!" Rexar roars, lunging after her gift from Orkayha.

But Lidja already has them in her hands, nose wrinkling at the mud as she flicks her wrist and whispers, "*Destroy.*"

The keys burst into ashes.

Rexar stops short, sword out, breathing hard. For a heartbeat, she and Lidja assess each other through narrowed eyes, both calculating.

Until I say, "Lidja—now."

With a smirk, Lidja leaps for Rexar, but the commander is already running, disappearing into the jungle, far from us both.

Citrus and wild clover cut through my mud-coated nose as the sorceress circles me. "There is literally one clean spot on your whole body." A wisp of a touch skims the back of my neck. "Right here."

I inhale sharply, my pulse still racing. "You half-waited for my call."

"Perhaps I prefer you less than half-dead after all." Lidja slicks a finger across my cheekbone. "Was that the vengeance you wanted?"

"Better, actually." Because even though we've let her run, alongside her confession, Rexar gave me something else.

A gift, she said. The key-gate is a gift.

And there is one place where the baya of Memoria hoards all their gifts, in the last place I would ever want to explore in this whole realm. *He's worse than a hoarder-squirrel,* my own sister said, when I first stood in the palace. *His chamber is so cluttered, even a new gift would go unnoticed.*

Shaking my mud-coated body, I don't bother to hide my smile as a streak of dirt lands on Lidja.

"I know where to find the key-gate."

CHAPTER 21

*L*idja and I stride up the steps to the palace of Memoria as the sun sinks toward evening. The mud on my body has caked thick, like a second and third layer of clothes. Outside the palace doors, the guards' eyes widen at me but shift when Lidja stops to confer with them, passing on the message to keep Rexar and anyone who now follows her out, no doubt. I move ahead, through the doors.

Daesen peels from the side of a column.

"I cannot *believe* you went to see Rexar without me," he says.

A burgundy cloak flutters from behind a column and away. Lucius must have given Daesen the same cryptic message as me.

I widen my stance and wish the mud was viscous enough to flick on the shield's stubborn face. "Did you know she's from Elektos?"

Daesen frowns. "What difference does it make if I did?"

He knew. The understanding pins me to the marble floor. He knew and didn't tell me. "It matters. How am I supposed to trust you if you don't trust me?"

"I do."

Lies. My arms nearly tremble with it. "Where is the baya's chamber?"

"At the end of the great hallway, to the left, last door. See? *I* trust *you.*"

"Just not to speak with Rexar."

He shifts. "Your head is full enough of lies already."

It's a punch, low in my gut. I turn on my heel and march away, ignoring the tap of boots behind me, and head to the end of the great hallway, to the left, to the final, gilded door, which I push open.

And I enter the baya's room.

A seating chamber greets me and behind—

The door shushes shut.

I spin to face the shield. "What do *you* want, Daesen? To dictate who I speak to? To fight my battles for me?"

"Any battle you think you have with Rexar cannot be yours alone." Daesen dumps his shield and spear inside the door. "She's my problem, not yours."

"She's the one who told Tzen where to attack! She's responsible for hurting my sister. That makes her my battle, too."

Frowning, Daesen shakes his head, his answer slow, deliberate. "No. Vis placed in her charge, and he's never wrong. That can't be right. *You* can't be right."

"Why can't I? Because you didn't figure it out first?" I stalk through the seating room to the double doors, leaving a trail of mud clumps in my wake. I throw open the doors into Vis's bedchamber. Inside, a giant bed dominates, and every single wall is lined with shelves. Shelves stuffed with piles of *things.* Boxes, vases, figurines. Just inside the door, a turquoise-and-emerald vest is pinned with needles to a raised sewing structure, as if Vis was in the middle of assembling the cloth.

"Don't let pride color what you're seeing, Ala. Rexar is awful, and she and I clash, but she wouldn't let in our enemy. She wouldn't betray Vis. She's only focused on me."

"You think that's what this is? This is about *you*? My sister is *hurt*. She could have *died*."

"Your sister is not Rexar's goal. She is not worth the risk."

Blindly, I reach to the shelves for something, anything. "Just because we weren't born in this realm, just because we weren't born with glowing sticks in our hands, just because—" My palm closes around a glass sphere in the shape of an apple just like the fruit he threw at me in the forest. "My sister is worth *every* risk. She's worth ten of you. More—one hundred. One *thousand*."

"You misunderstand. You twist everything to mean the worst, Ala."

"Because you *are* the worst!" And I hurl the sphere at his face.

Glass shatters beside him.

We both freeze, our shallow breaths the only sound in the baya's room.

"Are you ready for hard truths, friend?" Daesen prowls toward me, halting a breath from my face. Hands framed on either side of my shoulders, he leans into the shelves. Into me.

I notch my chin higher.

"In addition to having a horrible aim, the *worst* is what you've lived with your whole life. With your every movement controlled, with your choices made for you, with even your *bedmate* decided for you. They fed you lie upon lie until you believed nothing else, even when it was staring you in the face."

Air. I need air.

"There is only one evil greater than what exists on your side of the curtain, Ala."

"You have no right to talk about my home."

"Your *home* is a wasteland of mind-scrubbed people barely surviving under a brutal leader."

I smack my palms to his chest and push. Hard. Flakes of mud fall to the floor. "That's *exactly* how I would describe yours."

Instead of away, he presses closer, as if I'm nothing, as if my shove is no more than the bump of a firefly. His gaze drops to my lips, his own curling at the corner.

My breath stutters out.

His pupils flare.

The air shifts, warms.

Closer. "Do you want that kiss now?"

I lean in, until there is no more than a breath between us. "I want you to leave."

For a moment, neither of us moves. Neither of us breathes. "*Now.*"

Daesen pushes off from the shelves, and I gulp in air.

"Whatever else you believe, Ala, I am your friend."

"A friend would believe me when I say that Rexar is the one who let in Tzen."

"I was born here, Ala. I know these people like you don't."

I know what it is to scrape by. "And I was born in Elektos. I know what it takes to survive."

Daesen strides back toward the seating room, passing the needle-pinned vest. "Whoever let Tzen in, I will find them, and they will meet death. You have to trust me. To keep my realm safe, to fulfill my duty, I will do *anything.*"

"Do you know what it is to have a sister? I would do anything for *her.*" Perhaps I'm not so different from Orkayha after all. "To see her home safely—whether that is Elektos, or Dreams, or some other isle—I would destroy this whole realm, if that's what it took."

"Careful, Ala." From the corner of my eye, a silver-blue light pulses from the door.

I freeze, heart thudding as I wait for a monster to crash through the door, for a creature to rise behind me at that warning glow from his spear.

But there's nothing. No heavy, awful breath. No scales, no claws.

There's only me.

Me, making that spear in the corner glow in warning.

Me, a threat.

I want to be exactly that—enough of a threat to send him out of this room. Out of my *sight*.

"*Fly*," I breathe, and the needle-pins obey.

With a burst of cold wind, the pinned vest drops in pieces to the floor and needles fly toward me, halt, a breath from my chest. With a flick of my wrist, they pivot, prick-point outward. I aim the line of needles right for Daesen's chest.

Daesen's gaze narrows. "You think a prick of a needle will make me leave?"

"I think you should stop assuming you know better than me. Stop telling me what to do. Maybe—maybe if this is the kind of place that thinks it's so much better, that hoards its advantages and leaves everyone else to suffer and die, maybe it *deserves* to burn."

Smoke curls through the mud on my hand to the needles. I focus and focus and focus and will the silver shards to shift, to obey me, until the needles coalesce into one, into a spear. The tip trembles and reforms into a serpent's head—and snaps.

Daesen jolts backward a single step.

For a moment, we both stare at that serpent, at the magic I've woven.

I drop the magic spear with a clatter, needle-pins splitting apart and littering the floor.

Daesen inhales sharply as a fine scratch appears on his cheek.

Fates. The lash of misused magic—*my* misused magic.

"I'm not the one you should be threatening, Alathea." Dae's voice is low, taut. "Not me, not my realm."

The storm rushes my bones and I swipe a palm-sized vase from the shelf and hurl it.

The vase crashes a hands-breadth from his head.

"Then *leave*."

"With pleasure." He flings open the door and points the

teardrop tip of his spear at my chest. "And you and me, Ala—I was wrong. I was a fool to think we could be friends."

The door slams shut, and it reverberates in my chest, hard and sharp, like a chisel's edge.

"Good," I say, loud enough for him to hear through the crack. "If this is what having friends is like, I didn't want you anyway."

* * *

I CRUNCH over shattered glass with slippered feet as dawn lightens the hills of Memoria outside Vis's bedchamber. I yank a furred blanket from the giant bed and wrap it around my shoulders. After Daesen left last night, I bathed in Vis's massive marble basin, and then padded to look again at Vis's shelf upon shelf stuffed with things. One moment, I'd been building a strategy for the fastest way to search, and the next, I'd awoken to this dawn.

Now, fresh from sleep and a breakfast of breads and cheeses someone left in the sitting chamber, I take stock of Vis's room again, of where the key-gate to Denrathri must be hidden.

Two fireflies flicker in the room, escaped from the vessels I smashed last night—the vessels that unfortunately missed the shield's thick head.

He's right. I need to improve my aim.

But also…I thought we shared something in common, Daesen and me. The roles we've been forced to take up. The way he sees me, when I'm so accustomed to the shadows. That with him, I can say what comes to my tongue, and all will be fine.

Instead, that glowing spear is proof—he sees me as no different than the commander. Or worse—one of Orkayha's monsters.

Beneath the blanket, in my chest, magic thumps once, twice, hard.

Is Daesen so wrong?

I was so angry last night I didn't even think to check on Soli, to see how she was healing from Tzen's attack.

I need to find which one of these boxes or figurines or oddities is the key-gate. That's how I'll make it up to her.

I shed the blanket and stalk toward the nearest row of shelves, the thousands of boxes and vases that line them. Nowhere is there a blue-silver glow of a gate nor a tug like that of a memory connected to me. I curl my scarred palm around a red glass box.

What if I'm wrong? What if the key-gate isn't in Vis's room, and I've failed not only my sister, but this whole Fates-damned realm?

I drop the glass box to the floor.

Crash.

I don't want to be wrong. Not this time.

I pick up two more, one in each hand—

Crash.

I *hate* it here. Perhaps I should destroy every one of the vile boxes. Perhaps I should wreck this whole room, just to prove Daesen right.

"Are you trying to wake the spirits?"

Lidja stands in the doorway to the bedchamber, arms crossed, axe at her side.

Lidja, who has never pretended that we are anything other than enemies.

"Just because you know where I am doesn't mean you're invited."

The high sorceress takes in the shattered glass. "You're frustrated that you haven't found it yet."

I drop another box to the floor, the glass shattering. While Dae sees me, this high sorceress...she sees *through* me. I hate that, too. "No. That's not it at all."

Smash.

Lidja hums.

"*Fine.* Yes, it would be helpful if the Denrathri key-gate was as obvious as the one to Mizura." I *had* searched the room for any shimmering keys, just in case.

"The baya of Mizura has never been known for her subtlety. In the memories of my predecessors, her very skin flashes with bright scales." Lidja prowls forward, until she's close enough to snatch my hand. Her palm wraps around mine, the promise between us flaring sharp, and extracts the vessel from my grasp. "Perhaps if you stop crashing the vases you'll actually hear the key-gate's call."

My heart trips as she replaces it on the shelf, her warmth gone.

"Or perhaps it has no call," I say, "because it's stuffed under all these layers. I've seen hoarder-squirrel nests with fewer trinkets than your baya."

"We all have our faults. Shall I lock you in here until you find it? Or do you have more personal vendettas to run down?"

I notch my chin upward. "Did you find Rexar yet?"

"She's gone into hiding, but we've found soldiers we can trust who are searching now. They'll secure the palace until we find her."

"I suppose Daesen believed you when you told him." I trace the cool lines of a figurine. "He didn't believe me."

"Ah. That explains all the glass. A broken gift for each curse upon his name, I suppose?" Shards crunch as the sorceress circles the room, not bothering to note my scowl. "It's not about you, Alathea. For all their feuding, Rexar taught Daesen to fight when he was young. He doesn't want to believe the worst of her, not truly."

At that, my anger calms, shifts into something less jagged. "But you believed me, that I was possibly right, when I wanted to find Rexar."

"I always believe the worst of people."

"Including me."

"*Especially* you. You're the one who locked your own sister

159

away. The one currently bent on destroying our baya's bedroom despite what's in here."

And for a heartbeat, staring at this sorceress who won't stop prodding and pushing me, I miss Elektos. I miss knowing everyone's place. *My* place. What to do and who to trust. I miss being told where I should be, and knowing what the watchmen expected, what the Sancta wanted. Here, it's all disorder and chaos and this high sorceress who won't let me hide.

"Did you come just to torment me?"

"I came to tell you that your sister is healed, faster than anyone expected. She's wandering the palace for food. Something about crow stew." With a delicate shudder, she flicks a piece of dust from her sleeve.

"We have been *hungry* across the mountains. We make do with what we have. You wouldn't have any idea what that's like." The opulence of this room is proof. "That stew may not be good enough for you, but it is for me. It's *ours*."

"Rest assured, you can keep it. Orkayha won't bother prying that from your hands."

I clutch the figurine in my hand tight, tighter. "I truly don't like you. At all. Not even one bit."

"Good. That will make it easier when I do something you really don't like." In a single breath, Lidja closes the space between us and catches my hand into hers once again. She pries open my fingers and sets the figurine aside. The promise ricochets between our scarred palms, like a current of magic pulled taut. "Find the gate, Ala, and we can channel this fury somewhere useful. Unlike us, Orkayha has worn her splintered crown since Fides was born. We will have to face her together, or we will all die alone."

"I'd prefer not to die at all."

"Even better—that means you'll fight hard. Maybe even hard enough. Although I'd wager my bedchamber that you still haven't found the word for your power."

I shoot my free hand out, a heavy box flying into my hand from the shelf. With a flick of my wrist, I transform it into a spiked ball. I shove it toward Lidja's gut. "I have been practicing."

"That's something, at least." Lidja drops my scarred palm and the current between us severs, leaving me with a strange tingling in my limbs. "But only a small something. Find your word, and we will have a chance." She strides back to the seating chamber, to the main doors. "And for Fates' sake, stop smashing Vis's memory containers. They were *all* gifts to the baya, and I, for one, would strongly dislike spending the rest of my life listening to him moan about which memories he misses most." She meets my eyes one last time. "I might even say that I would hate it, very much."

With that, she's gone, as silent as she entered.

Memories.

That's it. It must be.

What could a baya—could *anyone*—value more than a memory?

A memory must be the key-gate.

Inside one of these vessels, carried by a firefly—that's where the memory will be, in this too-cluttered room.

I'm certain of it. As certain as I am that in this room of strange trinkets, in a realm far from my home, a high sorceress of Memoria is beginning to make *hate* feel like something else entirely.

CHAPTER 22

The pale blue of yet another morning in Vis's bedchamber does nothing to lighten my mood.

All yesterday, I searched through oddities in this room. I walked in and out of memories that allowed me in until I tumbled to sleep once again. When I awoke, I donned dark blue breeches and a blue blouse, set my heavy bandolier of stakes next to Vis's bed, and wove my hair into a braid.

Now I've started again.

This evening—this very sunset—Vis will arrive with the baya of Denrathri, and still I haven't found the key-gate.

No silver-blue light blinks from a firefly in any of the containers, and most of the room remains left to search.

This baya…I don't have the words to describe what I've found in the boxes, from tiny glass snakes and winged lizards and fish tucked in layers of fabric to precious jewels that glitter.

Was I wrong? Is the key-gate not in this room?

My gaze skips to the red orb I held yesterday, when Lidja snuck in. I had placed it down, unable to unlock the orb, and moved on.

But now, as sunrise brightens the shelf, I return to it, palming the glass once again.

I flick at the tiny silver clasp, but it does not open. Frowning, I bring it closer to my face, searching, and lay my palm against the lid.

Click.

The top flips open. Inside, a firefly pulses with a memory. Voices flow outward and wrap around my skin. It must be connected to me in some way, then, like Lidja showed me days ago.

A door burns hot and bright, and I step inside.

Candlelight casts pools of butter across a room. A discarded black robe lays on the floor. The scent of sweat and skin fill the air. A young man with cool beige skin and black hair sits at the edge of a bed while a young woman, naked, remains within it.

Long lashes flutter over the woman's silver eyes. "That was exactly as I imagined." Her voice is as silky as the sheet she draws her palm across. "Better."

The young man pulls a tunic over his head and doesn't answer. His hair shadows his high cheekbones in the candlelight.

"Maybe you could stay," the woman says. "I have need of a consort, and you have need of an ally, Kaiden. There is no need for this to last only one night."

The last of Kaiden's smile fades. "I cannot, Melestra. You know that. I could be no more consort to you than a sea faerie to a walrune."

"If you cannot stay," Melestra says, "I could come with you, to Memoria. We could have our pleasure, and peace. Would you not enjoy waking next to me in the golden realm?"

"You know I cannot let you into Memoria. Our secrets are ours, as yours remain here in Mizura." Kaiden tucks a silver-blond hair behind the woman's ear, as if to soften the rejection. "This was the magic of Mirthraya, no more. Fates know, I shouldn't have come here."

The woman's white skin pales further, as if she could wisp into the shadows. "One day I will craft a spell so powerful that even the Fates can't stop us."

"Until then..." Kaiden runs a thumb over Melestra's cheek. "The prophesy was yours as much as mine, and neither of us will be spared if it comes to pass. We may have brought it closer with this mistake, if your womb quickens after last night."

Melestra scoffs, but Kaiden snatches her wrist, holding tight. "Did you hear that?"

Both stare at the wooden door to the room, straining. Another creak of the floor, a whisk of a shadow moving away.

With a heavy sigh, Kaiden releases Melestra's wrist, kisses it. "Are you certain your brother will keep our secret?"

"He will. He understands the cost of not doing so."

For a moment, the two only stare at each other, a thousand words passed in silence.

"Perhaps so. But I was never going to choose her. For me, there was only ever you."

Their lips meet, hungry and desperate.

Kaiden breaks away first. "Prepare a tincture, Melestra. We should not have done this." Kaiden's eyes darken in the candlelight, until they are no more than two pools of deepest black. "We must keep the prophesy from coming to pass, no matter what that costs."

"And yet you snuck through the grounded gate anyway." In the woman's palm, a red-hilted dagger appears, reflecting the candle's glow. "Do not utter a single word more unless it is the truth. The truth you whispered in my ear last night."

In the baya's hand, an answering sword materializes, heavy and sharp and ready. "Do not make a mistake you cannot retract."

"Like this one? Perhaps my sister was right." She flips the blade, once, twice, and plunges it forward.

I wrench backward, out of the memory, landing hard on the marble floor of the baya's room.

"What did you see?"

At Daesen's cautious question, I scramble to my feet, that

flip and thrust of a sword still fading in the corner of my eye. Behind Daesen, his shield and spear are dull silver at his back.

"What do you care? I thought we weren't friends."

"Do fights last forever in Elektos? Don't be an oxsail."

"Call me that again and we'll see."

He stalks halfway to me and halts, breathing deep and long. "As much as I'd love to, I promised Lid I wouldn't let you get under my skin this time. Your sister, too." A warm breeze curls into the bedroom, and his gray eyes narrow. "Despite what you may think of me, needle, I do keep my promises. So, for fun, let's pretend we trust one another."

"But we don't."

"Play with me, for the single flash of a fate-star."

Danger. I cross my arms.

"Pretend I was your match, picked by your precious Sancta. Would you trust me then? If we shared a log home and a straw bed, would you tell me then what you saw?"

My cheeks warm, and my gaze drops to the orb in my hand. *Consort*, the woman in the memory said. Perhaps not so unlike a match in Elektos.

"What was in the memory?"

I close my eyes to recall it again, the young man who looked vaguely familiar, and the young woman with fire in her eyes. "There was a bed, someone named Kaiden, and a young woman —Melestra. The two of them were *in* the bed."

And behind that door in the memory, lurking...Could this be it? The secret kept at the root of Orkayha's vengeance?

Slowly, Daesen rakes the V of his broad hand down the column of his throat to rest at his collarbone. "Are you lying to me, needle?"

How can that touch, not even on my own skin, have set my pulse speeding? "I thought we were playing at trust."

"So now you like the game?"

"This is not a game." I strip my eyes away from him to the shelves. Anywhere but him. "I'm searching for the gate."

Boots close the space between us. "How can I help?"

I raise the memory-holding orb to his gaze. A ray of sunshine splashes across the glass, glinting. I frown, peering closer. A filigree etching glints over the surface of the orb, tiny triangles carved at random angles. I shift the orb out of the sun, and the etching disappears.

"Do you recognize the pattern?"

"Probably a hoarder-squirrel script," he says.

Of all the containers so far, this is the only one that's opened like this, that's been locked. "Help me look for others like it."

"You're asking a not-friend for help?"

"I thought we were still pretending."

"Lidja is waiting for me." A single dimple flashes. "But nothing makes her angrier than waiting, so the game must go on."

Together, we search the room, angling orbs and boxes into the sunlight, searching for more of the finely etched sides. The sun slides across the room, warming the air. The morning swings by. Breads and cheeses and nuts appear without my noticing, and the warmth shifts to the humidity of mid-afternoon.

"Ala." Dae rolls his shoulders, stepping from the shelves. "Perhaps we should—"

"Here." I inhale sharply as the sun illuminates a small crystal box in my hand, one I found buried two layers deep, on a shelf near the floor. On it, invisible until I brought it to the window, a delicate pattern of triangles winds through the heavy glass. Triangles and tiny swirls and lines are etched into a single, intricate forked scale.

A tail.

"The red orb. Where is it?"

Daesen hands the red sphere to me, and I hold it next to the crystal.

It is not a script at all.

They are scales...on a body.

Gently, Daesen flicks the latch of the crystal box, but it remains locked.

I lower my palm over the top, and it slides open. A pulsing memory awaits, sliding up and outward, nearly engulfing me before I can even step inward.

This time, it is Vis himself, missing only the white streak in his hair. He stands on the steps of the palace, that same heavy sword in hand as the other baya. A crown of golden lights weighs upon his head, but he wears all black, from tunic to scabbard, to match the sky.

On his knees in front of Vis, a man bows. Dark hair falls around his neck, his whorl of black tattoos swirling on his arms, up to his neck. Beside the man rests a spear and armored plate, both split in two.

Not ten paces from Vis and the man, a young boy stands with his hand buried in the sleeve of a woman's robe. Her long black hair, strong high cheekbones and turbulent gray eyes are proud, her jaw tight.

"Alisander dies for what he let into our realm," Vis calls, loud enough that it echoes across the green hills. "Stay vigilant, and we will slay the beast yet."

Vis faces the woman, his voice now soft. "The boy is too young to witness justice wrought like this." Although the boy's lips tremble, he does not glance from Vis's sword, nor from the man on his knees. "You should have him look away from his father's shame."

"He will better remember if he watches," the woman says, her hand curling into the boy's hair. "I brought him to witness. To make him stronger. To make certain he does not commit the mistakes of his father."

With a nod, Vis raises the blade.

The young boy averts his gaze.

Sinew and bone split, and a head rolls onto the cold marble.

I hurtle back to the burning door, dragging myself from the memory. Back to Vis's room, to the cool of the marble floor. I push up to find stormy eyes crouched at my side, gray swirling.

"What did you see?"

You.

Daesen, as a child, watching his father beheaded.

The sins of the father, Rexar had said.

And his mother, at his side, made him watch—his mother who he said had been killed by a monster.

Fates. Did his father let in the beast that slayed his mother?

Daesen rubs his high cheekbones, so alike his mother's. "What's wrong?" he asks, catching my gaze.

"I…" I search those worried eyes. Those kind, gray eyes, that looked away when he lost one of his parents. So young, so brutal.

Elektos may be a wasteland, but this realm is not always better.

On instinct, I lean forward and kiss the shield's cheek. Soft, brief, gentle.

"Oh. I. Huh. Well."

I catch Daesen's hand. "Did you love your parents, even when they were wrong?"

The gray melts, yearning. "Every day. Even now. Always."

"I'm sorry you lost them."

"You have nothing to be sorry for. Me, on the other hand…" Daesen pulls me upward. "That's what I came here to tell you. I was going to tell you right away, but then you said…and I—well." He glances toward the door, two dimple flashing. "The truth is, I find it hard to resist rattling you, needle. It's become one of my favorite parts of the day. Maybe even the best part."

This time, I'm the one who's speechless.

"But you were right. Lidja found me, and she told me what happened and…you were right about Rexar. I was wrong. The guards found her. Lidja and I are heading out as soon as they return to fetch her to the cage below the palace." From outside the door, a hard thunk. "And that probably means I've kept her waiting long enough." Quickly, he drops a kiss to the crown of my head. "You'll find it. I know you will. I trust you."

And then he's gone, leaving me alone in the baya's room, holding a new throbbing thing in that hollow in my chest.

One that's not pretend at all.

I turn toward the shelves, and pace the length of the room, searching for the last piece of the scaled body.

So close. Now I *can* hear it. I can *feel* it, the *tug, tug, tug*. A firefly, a memory, calls me in this mess of a room, wishing to be reunited with the other two pieces. I work through shelf after shelf, layer upon layer, quicker now that I have an idea where the tug must be coming from, until—

There.

A low pyramid with a wide base. I bring it into the last rays of fading sunlight, and the filigree etching gleams. A monster's triangular head, matched perfectly to the body and tail. Side by side, they almost seem to glow: pyramid, sphere, cube.

But unlike the others, this one speaks directly into my veins.

Come, it sings, no more than a whisper. *Come and see, Alathea Thymisius.*

Goose bumps flare on my arms.

Come now. Closer.

I palm the smooth surface.

The top slides open, a slim rectangle of space. I expect the memory inside to jump out, larger even than the last, but—

Nothing.

Frowning, I peer into the top of the pyramid, and my breath hitches, razor-edged against my ribs.

There is no pulsing firefly inside this vessel.

Instead, there is only a small sheath of rolled linen paper, with the faintest silver-blue sheen.

The key-gate. Not a firefly after all, but a sheet of linen. It must be.

Hand shaking, I extract the sheet, and it unravels.

Come. Quiet.

The page is blank, except for one word in the very center, inked in tight, black script. Swooping script I could never carve into stone.

A name I haven't heard in years.

Two years, to be exact.

Ever since I forbade it, when Soli and I came home with wrists burned and bruised. A name whispered at a window, by a lover who should not have existed.

But I say it now, the single word on the shimmering linen, my voice a drop in the shadows of the baya's room.

"Talia."

The name of my mother.

CHAPTER 23

I whirl a stolen black cloak from Vis's chamber over my shoulders as I race out and into the palace hallway in search of my sister. The dark of the cloak bleeds into the night shadows.

In my hand, I clutch the shimmering linen.

Can a paper shatter bones?

Talia.

Everywhere Mother shouldn't be, she is. Her name in the baya's bedroom, on a key-gate. Slinking at the corners of a memory with *not* Mama. What was she to Vis? What was this realm to Mother? And most of all, how could she hide it from Soli and me?

I dart down a hallway to a splash of light. Perhaps Soli is here, storing up on food, making ready for when we open the gate and go in search of Mother.

If we do find her, if she is still alive, I'm going to wring her neck myself.

From a closed door, a pair of armed guards march outward. I paste myself to the wall as they hurry past. Two of Rexar's soldiers. Perhaps they now answer to Daesen, if he and Lidja did as planned, and Rexar is locked in the cage below the palace.

I plunge ahead, down the narrowing corridor—and find my sister slumped at the base of a doorframe. Golden light streams from the room behind her.

I drop to my knees at her side. "What's wrong?"

"Everything."

I search her for signs of injury, for opened stitches at her side, but find none. "I thought you were healed."

"I am." But her voice—I've never heard my sister's voice like this. Wooden. Hollow.

"Then what's wrong?"

Still, no response.

I take Soli's hand, and squeeze. "Soli. I found it."

My sister says nothing. Does nothing. No reaction at all.

"The key-gate to Denrathri, Soli. I found it. We can open it now."

Amber eyes meet my own. Not the calm of glass, not the cool of autumn leaves. This, in my sister's gaze, is fire. "I found something, too."

I glance over her shoulder, into the room beyond the threshold. Inside, millions of tiny glass balls line the floors, the walls, stacked in invisible towers. Devoid of fireflies, the room pulses with soft gold just the same.

"What is it?"

Like my voice shifts the air, the vibration slides, changes. No longer low, the hum comes in waves, higher and lower and layered all at once. Voices. Thousands and millions of voices. These are not the dimmed hum of a memory but clear, like the chime of a newly forged bell.

Soli unlocks her clenched palm. "A new memory."

In the center of her scar, a glass orb no larger than the tip of a chisel flashes.

"A new—" But my voice dies as I reach for her palm, as the voices in her palm separate, until only one stands out.

A voice full of light and promise and lies.

Mother.

"A new memory," I repeat. *"New."*

"I was looking for you, and then I heard something in this hallway, and I found this room, and I heard her voice. It opened to me, and…Ala, she's alive."

Alive. And in this new memory, which means…we could find her.

My fingers itch, and I'm not certain if I ache for Mother's arms or to slap them away. "Let me see."

I tuck the linen key-gate in the hidden purse beneath my blouse. As I clasp the glass orb in my fingers, a white light expands, and I step through.

Mother flits around our faded table in our home. Her cheekbones are high, but thin, like hunger lives within her now. She is as beautiful as the day she left us with her full lips and dark amber eyes. She wears faded, dirt-stained breeches, and a threadbare brown jacket, the color of cracked mud.

Steps from Mother, in the shadowed corner near the front door, is Vis.

"It has to be here somewhere." Talia's black hair gleams in the glow of a single candle on the floor away from the front window.

"This was an unwise idea when you first conceived it. It's worse every moment we stay." Vis peeks out the window. "We should go before your Sancta realizes you've returned, or before Orkayha's monsters start lurking about."

"That is exactly why I left, Vis." The cupboards under the water basin squeak as she searches and shoves them closed. "So my daughters wouldn't grow up being told what to do."

"So you let them grow in a place that taught them to fear their own shadows, instead?"

"Elektos wasn't always like this. It shouldn't be like this now."

"If you'd been where you should have, it wouldn't be."

From outside, wheels creak.

"We have to go." Vis glances outside again, quicker. *"I didn't search for you this long to lose you now. They're expecting us. I promised."*

"They'll wait. They won't have a choice." She glares at the faded curtain that divides our home. *"It has to be—"*

From outside the front door, a splash of mud. A scrape across the wood.

"Did you hear that?" Vis whispers.

Talia raises a hand to her lips, otherwise still as a doe.

Another scrape from outside.

Vis's nostrils flare.

Mother whispers, "They're here."

I leap out from the new memory and land at my sister's side. Soli pushes to her feet, spear and armored plate now in hand.

Home. Mother is at our *home.*

But even worse...

"She is..." I can't. The depth of Mother's lies rises like a wave, cresting.

The magic of the triads follows our bloodlines, Lidja said.

And just now, Vis's words. *I didn't search for you this long to lose you now. They're expecting us.*

I try again, past the shredding in the hollow in my chest. "She is..."

"In danger," Soli says, face grim. "Right now, she's in danger, and outside our home is Tzen."

My sister is right.

Mother is home.

Tzen is outside.

Tzen, the monster who dropped my sister from the sky, who promised it's not the pits of Mizura that Orkayha plans for us anymore.

Tzen, who I led right to our door when I gave him our family's name.

174

CHAPTER 24

*T*ogether, Soli and I dash from the new memory room through the corridor, to the main hallway, and out the palace doors into the night. Down the steps, we plunge into the darkened jungle. Palms and ferns tug at my cloak. The linen key-gate in the purse at my neck thumps against my breastbone. Fire-flies hum as we run by, the two moons and three fate-stars bright.

Neither of us speak of the truth we saw in that new memory.

Of Mother.

The baya of Dreams.

"Faster," I breathe, longing for Lidja's speed-spell. "Faster, *faster.*"

Home. The warmth of our hearth. Mother's hair tickling my cheek. Her smell of pine and dirt.

Through the jungle, we run up and down hills, legs and lungs burning.

"There." Breathing hard, I point to the moons temple at the cleft in the hills. The arched stone glows at the steps of the temple. "That's the gate to Elektos."

"I know. That's the one I have always taken to go home."

Right. My sister already knows this realm far better than I ever will.

"It lets out in the ravine," Soli says. "Didn't you come through it with Dae and Lidja?"

From the darkened jungle, the hoot of a palm owl grates against my skin. I could tell my sister that I didn't. That I ran from Daesen not once, but twice. That Rexar told me this gate went elsewhere, and I nearly believed her.

But we don't have time for her to tell me I'm wrong again.

Instead, I charge from the palm trees for the grounded gate, Soli on my heels.

"Touch the rock and give me your hand!" Our palms connect and our fingers brush the stone arch—

Glittering drops of silver-blue erupt, stretching upward into an arch and down like a fine curtain.

Together, we dive through.

Dead leaves crunch beneath our boots on the other side of the gate. The evergreen brambles of the ravine are thick, even as hearth smoke slips through the trees. The dark of night is absolute, the moons covered by thick clouds, no bleating warmth of fireflies or magic here.

Home.

We scramble up the bramble-coated slope and pause at the top edge of the ravine. A scrape from the front of our home cuts the heavy silence of night.

"Tzen is mine," Soli whispers, unsheathing her spear. "Get Mother to the shed. I'll meet you there."

And my sister is gone, slipping out of the shadows and running through the mud for the front of our home before I can argue.

Quiet, quick, I sprint for the back door of our home and slide inside.

Darkness greets me, whole and silent. My boots scuff against warped wood flooring.

Wood flooring I was born to.

Faint light huddles in a corner across the room. Mother's candle. It flickers against a new slab of wood in the charred frame of our front door.

Home.

But as I survey our one room...

No Mother emerges from behind the curtain. No Vis.

From behind the wool curtain, there is only a scratch.

"Mother?"

A hard scrape.

"Talia?"

Why isn't she answering?

My vision narrows as I reach for the curtain.

Scrape.

I brush the wool to the side.

"Moth—"

Looming over our straw beds, back to me, are a pair of wings that stretch from floor to roof.

Every muscle in my body locks.

Tzen.

"Get. *Out.*"

"Tell me, Alathea," Tzen says, ignoring my order, "did your sister bleed out slowly? Do you mourn her still?"

My magic rustles, flares. He doesn't know. He doesn't know my sister lives, the one advantage I have in this tiny room. I clench my scarred palm and wish for my bandolier, forgotten in Vis's chamber. For my stakes. For—

My chisel. I glance at the straw of my thin mattress, where the chisel from the assembly house hides. If I can reach it, if I can save my sister from ever facing this beast again..."Don't say her name. Not now. Not ever."

"*Sol-ee-ah-na.*" Tzen surveys the dust-coated log walls, the ratty curtain. "It could be a song, were it not so vile."

"You're the vile thing here." I slide toward the straw, the wool sheet scraping at my back. Five steps to my hidden chisel, no more.

"Do you believe you can hide again, little monster?"

Four steps. "I'm not the monster."

"Is that so?" Calloused hands wrap around my arms and I'm hauled toward a broad chest. A row of razor teeth flash too close to my face, claws gripping my forearm. "The truth is that we're all monsters underneath."

Talons sink into my forearm.

Black spots fill my vision and coat the log walls of my home.

Beyond these walls, somewhere, is Mother. Mother and Soli and Vis. I have to keep Tzen here, away from them. My tongue feels like weighted iron as I spit in his face. "If Vis finds you here, he will rip your wings off."

"That would not be the first time someone tries and fails. But I think you already know…Visander is not here for me. Nor for you." Tzen slides his claw from my arm.

The floor rushes upward as I meet it. Blood spills from my arm, across my hand, to the wood. I stretch with my good arm for my chisel. For the door. For Mother, wherever she is.

Crouching, Tzen brings a razor-sharp talon to a vein on his neck and slices the vein open.

Out spills a black mass of quivering hard-bodied, crawling creatures.

Mother. I need you.

"Spider-ants," Tzen murmurs, stroking my hair. "My creation. Not as overbearing as the mawlyrs your ancestor created, but lovely nonetheless, don't you think? Darlings, like us all."

The creatures flow from his vein to the floor. Onto my hands.

I wrench back, away, but the creatures flood over me. My ankles, my legs. Up my torso they crawl, onto my arms, my neck, my nose. Everywhere. They are everywhere and I can't stop them and—

"Ah, there it is. Now you can tell your baya I found it." A

clawed foot taps in the corner of my vision as Tzen lifts a piece of cloth above his shoulder.

No. Not a cloth. A sketch. The same sketch Minteph found the night he threw me in the death wagon.

Tzen traces the faces. Mine, Soli's, Mother's. At Mama's face, Tzen halts, his face paling. "Goodbye, little monster."

A claw pierces my foot. Bone and muscle split apart.

I scream, a thousand shards of glass in my veins, as the sketch drifts to the floor. Black swamps my vision, the spider-ants everywhere. I swat to knock them off, but my movements are slow, my home fading, and I whisper, "Mother."

Darkness swallows me.

Sweet, charcoal darkness embraces me, like when Soli and I would curl together at the hearth's belly on the longest nights of winter, a cocoon of two against the cold.

In the darkness, in that cocoon, the spider-ants fade, scurrying away. The pain in my foot subsides until it is only an echo, vague and far away. The warmth intensifies. It flutters against me, licking hotter and hotter.

My lids flicker open.

Fire.

I cough. Above presses a thick layer of dark gray smoke.

My home is on fire with no trace of spider-ants.

"Ala!" From somewhere far away, a voice calls, breaking through the pain, the smoke.

Move.

But—my foot, my arm.

Blood leaks from my wounds.

Ala, love. Not Mother's voice, but Mama's. Practical, warm. From a memory born long ago, within these same walls. *First, we stop the bleeding, love.* Her gentle words to Soli, for endless scrapes. *Wrap it high and press it hard. Stop the bleeding, then the rest.*

Mama. I wish I could climb into her arms and sleep.

From outside, a shout, a scream.

Soli. She's *outside* these walls. Soli, and please, Fates willing, Mother, too.

With gritted teeth, I rip the end of my cloak and wrap it hard above the puncture wound in my forearm. My foot...I fight a wave of swimming black as I wrap a second strip around the mangled mess.

Smoke fills my lungs.

The rest.

Outside.

Soli. Mother. Vis.

Crawling, tears coating my cheeks, I drag myself forward, first to the smoking straw bed, and tuck my chisel into the leather pouch at my waist. Toward the smoldering curtain, I crawl, stuffing the sketch of my family into the pouch as well. One hand, one knee, then the other. Again and again. Forward, toward my front door that's open to the night, thick smoke billowing.

Five paces.

Out. Out for air and to find my sister.

Three paces.

Why haven't they come for me?

Two.

My forearm burns, lungs fogged. What will the watchmen do when they see me?

One.

I drag myself over the doorframe. Through the heavy smoke. Outward, into the night and air.

Into chaos.

A nightmare. It must be.

Because every home on my lane burns. Flames crackle and pop from thatched roofs and wooden beams crash.

Across the mud, a woman flees, her shriek melding with so many others. "Where are the watchmen? Where is Emon?"

The screams are split by a roar, and then restart with fresh panic. Two burning homes from mine, a mawlyr rises. It roars again and reels its claw-hands through the night. A woman's head splatters into the mud.

Silver-blue light spears over the dead woman and through the monster. The beast shudders to the ground.

"Ala!" Soli shouts.

My sister punches her spear forward again, keeping two mawlyrs at bay even as Vis whirls ten paces beyond her, surrounded by even more of the monsters, his sword swinging. Tzen is nowhere to be found.

I should run for Soli. For Vis. I need to help them. I know I do.

But I can only clutch my punctured arm to my chest and look where, next to Soli, a woman stands.

A woman who, for once, only has eyes for me.

Through the flames and smoke and suspended flakes of straw, Mother and I stare at each other, until her lips move with a single word.

"Ala."

And then Mother is running, wide and away from the monsters keeping us apart and I'm limping, both of us toward each other, around burning homes and through lunging monsters.

Mother's arms crash around me.

I bury my face in smoky hair, in trembling arms. The crush of my wounded arm between us is nothing compared to the burning in my chest.

"Mother."

She pulls back, tears cutting through soot-coated cheeks, and gently chucks my chin. "My baby. My first baby."

"Why?" The question rips from my very soul. "Why did you run when we're *this*? When you're *you*?"

"For you. It was all for you." Mother glances to the middle of the lane, where Soli and Vis battle a cluster of mawlyrs. "You have it, don't you? The key-gate?"

"Yes, but"—I catch her soot-coated blouse and hold her in place—"how was this for *me*?"

"To protect you. To protect you and Soli both." Amber eyes just like mine blaze. "I've been searching for a way out of our fates, for us all, for a way for us to live free of this burden that none of us chose—that no one would *ever* choose. Didn't Bex tell you?"

Wood pops and another home on our lane collapses. "We thought Mama was with you."

"No. *No*, Bex isn't with me. She was supposed to tell you. She was supposed to *stay* with you and your sister," Mother says. "When you used your magic that night, I knew they would come for you. I didn't run from you—I ran to keep their eyes on me and *away* from you."

A mawlyr escapes Soli and Vis and charges for us. I drag Mother behind me, even as I say, "What could you possibly have thought you were protecting us from by being *gone* rather than being at our side?"

Vis slams his swords through the mawlyr from behind and the monster sprays into the mud. "Talia," Vis says, eyes nearly black, chest heaving. "She's coming."

Boom.

A blast smashes us to the ground. Mud envelops my aching bones, and a high-pitched ring fills my ears.

Mother plucks me upward as Soli and Vis rise, shaking from the blast. The mawlyrs bay, their focus no longer on us, but on the far end of my burning lane, where a woman appears amidst the flames.

Mother whispers, "I was protecting you from her."

Like she commands the very air, silence ripples from the woman. From her feet upward, she sparkles like one of the fate-stars, every pore of her body covered in shimmering onyx and indigo scales. At a chain around her waist hangs a stump of carved wood that pulses silver-blue. Icy eyes shimmer beneath sweeps of black paint. Atop her white-blond hair, a splintered crown sparks.

Orkayha.

At my side, someone tugs at my tattered cloak. A girl, no more than seven.

"Is she the Sancta?" the child asks, sniffling. "Is she here to save us?"

I shove the girl behind me, and push. *"Run."*

The girl flees, into the flame-rich night.

"That's right." Orkayha's voice slides, like honey poured through wine. "Run. Run and hide, triads."

Vis raises his sword as Orkayha strides toward us. The mawlyrs close in, herding us into a circle. "Open the key-gate, Alathea," Vis says. "Open it *now*."

I pluck the key-gate from my hidden purse and reach for Soli—

With a magic-infused boom, Orkayha commands, "Stop them."

The ground shudders as a mawlyr slams between my sister and me. Soli's armored plate rings with blocked claws.

Boom. Boom. Boom.

Again, I'm hurled flat into the mud, head ringing. I push to my knees as Vis stalks toward Orkayha, razor-thin cuts bleeding across his cheeks and neck.

"Ala." From behind me, Mother's voice is dull. I spin to find her still in the mud, a shard of wood jutting from her thigh. "Help me."

She passes out.

Gritting my teeth, I unclasp what's left of my cloak, grab the splinter of wood and yank it from her leg. Mother jerks but does not wake. I smash the cloak over the open wound and press hard, shaking her bleeding leg. "Wake *up*, Mother. Wake—"

I duck as a funnel of gray smoke streaks over Mother and me, wincing at the shrieks within the swirling darkness. The funnel hits a mawlyr and the monster screams, twisting its body inward into a ball. From down the mud lane, Orkayha raises her palms, another gray funnel building.

"Stop, Orkayha!" Vis's voice cracks across the lane. "All of this —for centuries, you have been pursuing a lie."

"You know not of which you speak, Visander." The smoke in Orkayha's palms pulses. "You were not there. You could not know."

"I know your sister lied. I have *seen* it, in a memory in my realm. I have seen Melestra plotting to deceive you. I know their daughter was killed on accident, that it was not Kaiden who killed the child."

"Lies." Orkayha slams a gray funnel for Vis.

I grasp Mother's shoulder and shake. "Mother, *wake up.*"

Vis dodges the funnel, and it burrows into a smoldering home, shrieks rising. "You can be free of this false memory, Orkayha," Vis says. "I can carve it from you. *Let* me carve it from you, and be free."

Flames crack and yet another home caves inward.

"You think it is a *memory* that consumes me?" Orkayha says. "It is the *Fates* that hold me to this path, along with the rest of Fides. One memory does not change who I am. I am Orkayha, the liberator. What are nightmares, if not the truth that we fear most? Gift me your realms, and the Fates will fear *us.*"

Vis's fury vibrates the very ground. "You ask me to deliver the whole of Fides into nightmares?"

"Not just you." Orkayha gazes beyond Vis, until she finds us. "And it is not a request."

"Mother!"

Amber eyes beat open and relief shoots through me. "Don't move," I order.

I push to my good foot and limp for Soli where she battles

mawlyr after mawlyr. Mud and ooze fly as the beast in front of her crumbles.

"Soli, now!" I limp and limp and she runs for me and I draw the key-gate from my hidden purse and—

Her palm folds around mine and I whisper, *"Denrathri."*

From between our palms, the key-gate to Denrathri bursts open.

On the other side of the shimmering arch, muted red sands rise and fall, and cliffs loom far in the distance.

Behind us, Mother releases a bloodcurdling scream.

"The curse." Vis runs for us, abandoning his standoff with Orkayha. "She needs to touch the throne. Carry her through *now.*"

Soli slides an arm under me and we limp forward—

A mawlyr slams into her armored plate and I drop to the mud at Mother's side, the key-gate still open and wavering in my hand.

Mother's body writhes, her shriek unending. I push at her body, trying to roll her for the open gate, but my own shredded arm and foot scream. I can't do this alone. From the leather pouch at my waist, I palm the chisel from my room and slap the sketch of our family into Mother's fist.

"Don't forget about us this time," I say, and push to my good foot.

Vis dives into the mud at Talia's side, his hands already beneath her, shifting for the gate—

And I limp in front of Orkayha.

Too-heavy jasmine melds with smoke and blood, her scales shining like flame and moon combined.

"Out of my path, girl."

"No." I drop to my knees and stab her foot with my chisel as Vis hoists Mother through the gate.

Orkayha yanks the chisel free as I limp backward. With a snap of her wrist, she captures my punctured arm and plunges the chisel through my bandaged wound.

Black spots bash through my vision as Soli shouts.

"I was wrong," Orkayha says. "You're not a girl. Without power, without strength, you're no more than a spirit of a wraith." She pries open my hand and pinches the key-gate between her fingers. "You aren't enough to exist at all."

With my key-gate in her hand, Orkayha shoves me to the mud, and she steps through to Denrathri.

The silver-blue of the gate falters—

And from the other side, Orkayha rips the sketch in two.

The gate pops shut.

Gone.

Another mawlyr thuds to the mud, and my sister slops to my side. Blood and mud and soot coat every piece of her.

My knees tremble, then quake.

I collapse to the mud. Everything around us burns.

Soli's hand intertwines with mine as flames surround our lane. Across the line of fire, through the thick smoke, a woman watches us, unmoving, three wavering stars on her sleeve.

We all watch as our home burns to ashes.

$\mathcal{S}$oli and I limp through the grounded gate in the ravine behind our destroyed home into the moons temple of Memoria once more. The cool of Memoria pre-dawn kisses my soot-coated cheeks. My lungs drag in fresh, smokeless air.

"Don't move," Soli says, and lays me on the marble floor.

Pain knifes through me from arm to foot, my vision still on the other side of that gate and the death and ruin of my home. On Orkayha, leaping after Mother through our key-gate—and destroying it.

Vaguely, I'm aware of the shush of a heavy cloak against the marble. Chilled, bony hands fall to my torn breeches, to the dirt-coated wrap around my mangled foot. *"I had a feeling you would need me."*

Gently, Soli draws my head onto her thigh. "We opened the gate, Lucius. The routes to Denrathri are open again, but Tzen got to Ala first."

"The shield of Mizura coats his claws with poison, as does his baya. Too long unattended, the injury draws one unconscious into the fields near Ahnaysa." A blaze of yellow meets my eyes in the dark. *"Hold on."*

I scream as my own fine chisel is removed from the puncture wound in my forearm. Lucius places his hands on the weeping holes on my body. Like a cork removed from the bottom of a rain barrel, the pain consolidates and builds, overwhelming—and then sloshes away. My lungs clear, and the ripped skin of my arm closes, smooth and tight again.

I wish the screams of our people, the image of the woman's head, and the feel of spider-ants crawling on my skin would disappear as easily. "Our home is gone," I whisper, my voice a rasp.

Soli tucks a hair behind my ears. "The floor needed to be replaced anyway."

A half-laugh, half-panic bubbles in my lungs. "That's not how I want to remember it."

"Vis could carve the memory of this day from you, if you asked it of him."

As the pain in my foot lessens, as Vis's protective layer shimmers across the sky over the isle, I consider it.

Do I want to be relieved of the memory of what happened in Elektos? To forget the reek of charred flesh, the crack of a neck, the sinking of claw through sinew and muscle? Do I want to ignore that Elektos was helpless in the face of the monsters, with no watchmen, no Emon anywhere to be seen?

There was only the Sancta, watching it all burn.

I could be like Daesen, removing the memory of his mother's death.

But unlike Daesen's mother...ours lives.

I ran to protect you.

I grasp for Soli's hands and meet her gaze. "We have to find her." Mother's scream rips through me again just like it did when we opened the key-gate—the curse of the baya, just as Vis warned.

At my sister's silence, I try again. "Soli. We need to help Mother reach the throne." Only one plan for reaching Denrathri without a gate unfolds inside me, clear as the coming morning. "We need a ship to cross the sea."

Soli stares into the green of the palms, as if she can glare across the entirety of Memoria into Denrathri. "Maybe she's already reached it."

"We would hear her commands if she had."

We both glance at Soli's spear, dull silver against the ivory of the temple. Nothing. No commands rise from within, ordering us to action.

Soli sighs. "If she's not already on the throne, and she's not in imminent danger…"

"She's running. Again." Mother *and* Vis, this time. "We have to help her."

"Do we? She's with Vis. She's a baya herself."

Just as loud, I hear what my sister doesn't say. *She didn't help us.*

"This isn't about us, not really—not as her daughters, at least." I squeeze Soli's hand, hoping that is at least mostly true. "Vis said she needs to touch the throne."

"Then she should do it herself." Soli rips her hand free and paces the marble base of the temple. "I hate that we are tied to her like this. I hate that I will be her weapon. I hate *her.*"

"I know. But…she's ours." Despite the lies, despite everything, she is our mother. She is our baya, and we are bound together now whether we want to be or not.

"Would you believe anything she said?" Soli asks.

All around the temple, insects buzz louder as dawn encroaches. "No. No, I would not."

Because my sister is right. Our whole lives, she's lied to us.

I ran to protect you.

But she didn't run to protect me. Not really. If she wanted to protect me, to protect Soli, she would have stayed.

I itch for my chisel, to pierce it into the marble of this temple and carve the truth right into the braided columns that surround us.

Mother ran to protect herself.

"It is healed, Alathea. You are Fates-blessed. The poison from Tzen's claws will do no further harm."

I twist my foot, examining a patchwork of scars across the top of my arch. But aside from the skin, it feels whole and new.

I wipe blood from my chisel and tuck it in the hidden pouch beneath my tattered blouse, pushing to my feet. I wobble, and step. Instead of searing pain, my foot zings, as if it's simply been asleep as dawn breaks through the palms. Gingerly, I move toward my sister, heavy, slow. Steady.

"You're right. She would lie." I grip Soli's arm. "I want to find her not to ask her questions, but so I can tell her. I want to tell her how it felt that she abandoned us. I want to tell her that what she did to us left more than grooves on our skin. She needs to understand how all of Elektos has suffered because she's been too afraid. We have to find her so I can look her in the eye, as the high sorceress of Denrathri, and—and—"

"Wring her neck yourself?"

"No." Maybe. The cool of dawn fades, replaced by the weight of another humid day. "I want to tell her she was wrong. I want to tell her everything is like you've always told me. You were right."

For a moment, Soli just stares at me.

"Better late than never, dearest sister," Soli whispers.

My heart thumps. "I can't be the dearest if I'm the only."

"That's exactly why you're the dearest." And Soli wraps me in her arms, soft and fierce and *together*. "Even with your oxsail-stubborn head, I'd pick you as my sister a thousand times over Orkayha."

I can only shake my head, my lips curling upward despite myself. "You know I only love you sometimes."

Soli chucks me under the chin, smiling, too. "I know."

A faint tug around my midsection draws me away from my sister and down the temple's steps to peer into the jungle. "Where are Daesen and Lidja?"

They should have already been able to find me by now, with that promise I made to the high sorceress. Between the four of us, we'll find a way across the sea to Denrathri to help Mother and Vis.

On a rush of cold wind, the jungle quivers, and then quiets. The caws and chirps halt. Even the palms hold still, as if waiting.

Soli grips my hand.

And across the morning sky, the blue shimmer of Vis's protection cracks like glass.

We pull each other and Lucius back under the marble temple, shards of shimmer falling like crystal rain, piercing the jungle's canopy.

Within a breath, it's over, leaving only us and Memoria and silence in its wake.

"My friend," Soli whispers. "Her village—it's on the far west of the isle. They'll be the first to be attacked. I have to go. Will you be all right without me?"

I nod. "Meet me at the eastern shore. We'll be there, with a way to Denrathri."

Soli doesn't wait any longer, sprinting down the steps and into the jungle.

I stalk to the edge of the jungle and root for sticks among the dead leaves. The rustle of magic returns to my veins, unlike the strange off-ness of it in Elektos. With a flick of my wrist and a whisper, I create a new bandolier and two stakes.

Still, there is no trace of Daesen or Lidja arriving.

"Lucius, where are they?"

The wraith ducks behind a pillar of the moons temple. "*I would have told you sooner...*"

Sweat breaks across my brow. "Told me what sooner?"

"You understand, Alathea, that with Commander Rexar in charge, I cannot countermand her wishes."

Rexar should no longer be in command at all. "Why are you still calling her that? What happened when Daesen and Lidja found Rexar?"

"Things did not go as planned."

"Lucius!"

"They are being held, Alathea. They are in Rexar's village now."

"Rexar isn't strong enough to hold those two. A whole village wouldn't be strong enough to hold them." I search the palm trees for any sign of my sister, but she's long gone.

"No one has to be strong enough when the shield and high sorceress have been poisoned."

CHAPTER 26

*O*ith a bony squeeze to my shoulder, Lucius fades back into the jungle. As I crouch at the edge of a village deep in the lush hills of Memoria, the incessant tug in my gut continues. Daesen and Lidja are here, her trick of a promise proving useful after all.

The low buzz of insects melds with the laughter of children. A trio no older than seven races from the palm trees near where I hide. Barefoot on the red earth, shouting high and bright, they chase each other into the village between circular huts made of bamboo reeds and grass roofs. Fruit trees wind around and between the huts, the scent of sweet melon heavy in the sluggish air.

Gaze on their friends, one of the trio runs smack into a man's legs and plops to the dirt, bottom first. The child looks up, blinking, stunned, and the man peers down his nose. I've passed him in the palace, one of Rexar's army.

For a moment, the girl in Elektos flashes before me, on our burning, death-soaked lane. *Is she the Sancta? Is she here to save us?*

I unsheathe one of the stakes from my bandolier. Unlike the Sancta, I will not stand by and watch while this soldier—

The man swoops the child into his arms and up, tossing them high with a sunbeam of a smile. The child laughs and cuddles into the man.

My heart thumps. Aches.

This.

This is what the girl in Elektos should have. This is what Soli and I should have experienced, when we were young. This...*this* is what I'm fighting for.

The man kisses the child's cheek and ducks into the darkened doorway of a hut, the other two children scampering deeper into the village.

Somewhere, in one of these huts, Lidja and Daesen are waiting, poisoned.

I stick to the edge of the jungle and circle the village behind a line of palm trees, drawing upon every lesson from them both. *Focus. Control.* Where would Rexar hide them best?

In my gut, a tug draws me forward.

I slip from the shade into the exposed path. Pressing to the side of a bamboo hut, I circle inward, swift, dipping behind circular corners at every pad of soft ground nearby. Soft songs flow from inside the homes, and roasting meats set my mouth to watering. The heat of the morning presses into my bones, insects buzzing louder and louder, and—

There. A hut three times as large as the others stands right in the center of them all, with a lone guard outside a door of bamboo slats.

Tug.

Beyond that bamboo wall are Daesen and Lidja. I'm certain of it.

The guard surveys the village, and I drop farther behind the hut.

Soli would know what to do. She's the one who would be brave enough to charge forward, to confront the guard, and strong enough to help Daesen and Lidja out.

But Soli is not here.

The sun beats down, ever harder, and even the guard fidgets, tucking farther into the shade of the grass roof. From the jungle, a sudden, sharp *hoot* makes him jump.

As if he's not quite used to this place.

As if, just maybe, he wasn't born here either.

Lie and cheat and kill. That's what Vis told me he would do for his triad, for Daesen and Lidja.

And without Vis here either...I roll my shoulders back, gather every false bit of confidence from the hollow deep in my chest, and I stride forward, toward the guard, out of the shadows.

The man stiffens as I approach, his hand dropping to a dagger at his waist. Bright blue eyes scour me, taking in my shredded clothes, the stake in my hand and bandolier across my chest, the smoke that lingers still, magnified by the heat.

I pause five paces away. "Rexar sent me. She said she didn't want her guards to fall in the heat. Why don't you get some water?"

The guard lifts the leather pouch at his waist, water inside sloshing. "I've prepared ahead this time. Is she having doubts about me again?" His speech is flat like mine, and even though he wears the clothes of Rexar's guard, his cheeks carry a hollow I've only seen in Elektos. His eyes narrow; his jaw hardens. "Is that why you're really here?"

Lie. The strategy blooms inside me, inside a single breath, rapid, sharp. Say yes. Lie, gain entrance—

"No," I breathe. "Vis sent me."

The guard rocks to his heels, eyes wide, and tugs me forward, under the thatched awning. This time, his voice is no more than a whisper. "I knew it. I knew the baya wouldn't send his shield and high sorceress here. I knew Rexar was lying."

"Then let me in so I can get them out."

Two voices float from between huts ahead, and we both dip farther into the shadow.

"You're going to have to drag them out," the man whispers as he hands me a dagger from his belt. "The poison has them both unconscious."

"And yet they're enough of a threat to guard, even drugged."

From the jungle comes another sharp hoot.

"No." The man's eyes dart toward the bamboo door at our side, to the chain looped through an iron bolt. "With the protective layer gone, Orkayha's creatures could arrive any moment. That's why I'm here. The monsters—some are afraid of flame. Enough that we have a guard here to light the arrows and protect our village when they come through."

"Come through what?"

"The grounded gate to Mizura. It's inside."

I'm already reaching for the bamboo door, for the chain that binds it shut. "All the more reason to unlock this and let me in. When Rexar finds they're gone, tell her that Orkayha came for them."

For a breath, the guard simply stares at me, bright blue eyes wide. But then—he removes a key from a smaller pouch at his waist, sliding it into the bolt at the chain. "I have a daughter in Elektos. Once, I dreamt she would come to live here with me. I tried to convince her and her mother to cross the silver curtain with me, but...her mother refused." The lock clicks, opens. "It was just a dream."

"Once the baya sits on the throne of Denrathri, maybe you should try again." I touch a hand to the crook of his elbow.

The guard nods. "She's just like you, you know. My daughter. I used to sing to her at night when the nightmares crept in. But she never needed the songs, not really. She has always been like you—just as brave."

Brave.

Brave...that is the right word for the young girl with a yellow string in the death wagon. The right word for Tenion, who was searching for her father on this side of the silver curtain, who perhaps was looking for not just any key when I first met her in the assembly house...but a key-gate.

I hesitate at the door for a precious moment and whisper-sing, "*In spite of the sprite's spurious lies...*"

A fist to his heart, the man gasps. "*...go bam! your little baby bones.*" He searches my face. "Is she well?"

"Last I saw her—" I swallow, recalling the bob of her head upward from the black lake, saved from a sinking wagon by Daesen, my friend who lies within this hut ahead, poisoned. "She was being brave then, too. She was well."

"Then there is hope yet." The guard nudges me forward, to the crack of the bamboo door opening. "Be quick, brave one. I'll listen for your whisper to let you out."

I slip inside the hut, and behind me, a chain rattles back into place, locking me in the dark.

* * *

BRAVE, the guard said. Out of all the odds...Tenion was right. Her father is here, on this side of the silver curtain.

There is hope yet.

But as I peer into the black silence of the interior of the hut, I can't locate a single lick of the *brave* he saw.

"Lidja?" I whisper, pulse racing. "Daesen?"

No response arrives in the dark. The air is thick and unmoving with disused earth, and not a single strip of sunlight ekes through the bamboo walls or grass roof of the hut. The walls must be reinforced with something more than the thin stalks.

Something far more, to keep the monsters in.

I swallow. A grounded gate to Mizura. Here, inside, unseen.

I tuck the borrowed dagger into my bandolier, and with a flick of my wrist, I whisper a flame into my left palm, like Lidja did in the palace. The gold light barely reaches beyond my fingertips.

I slide my free hand along the uneven wall, invisible grooves scratching my calloused fingertips. Slowly, I make my way forward. From outside the hut, voices in the village are muffled, the constant buzz of insects no more than a distant hum. Inside, the hut remains unmoving. Still.

Too still.

"Lidja?" I try again. "Are you—*oof.*"

I trip over something, and my flame sputters out. When nothing more moves, I crouch to the dirt, gingerly feeling for what I stepped on.

"Dae!" In the dark, just barely visible as my eyes adjust, lies the shield. Unmoving, his lips are open. I press my fingers under his jaw, relief threading through me at the steady pulse there. "What have they done to you?"

"I was wondering when you'd notice what was right before your eyes."

I whirl, straightening, stretching a new flame outward for that blade of a voice. Carefully, I step over Dae, tracing the curve of the clay wall forward. "You couldn't have answered earlier?"

"And missed you stumbling about like an oxsail? I thought you knew me better."

Halfway around the hut, I find Lidja and drop to my knees in the dirt. Like Dae, she's unmoving, laid out on the dirt floor.

"What happened?"

"Untie me first, stories later. I *hate* being in the soil."

My knuckles brush against her boot, to the rope around her ankles. I tug at the binding, but it does not give. "Weren't you poisoned, too?" Dagger in hand, I feel for a loose strand to slice at the rope.

"I was. But I knew the spell to stop the draught from working."

"You couldn't have used it on Dae, too?"

"And be stuck in here with a chatty bam? No thank you. He'll wake soon enough."

"You really can be a snake."

"If I was a snake, I'd already have struck you, pretty little high sorceress. Perhaps I like hard things." Wild clover and citrus wash over me as I pick the dagger into the twine. "Have you considered that perhaps this is the kind of game I enjoy?"

I glance toward where her face must be, against the dirt, in the dark. I know she's only toying me with me, striking back for calling her a snake. But my cheeks heat nonetheless, even as I sheath the dagger and trace my palm up the line of her boot, the outside of her thigh, her waist and up, up until—

"What are you doing?" Lidja's voice hitches.

"Trying to discover why you're lying."

"I'm not—"

"Lying down, I mean, of course," I whisper, my lips at her ear.

She inhales sharply as I slide my hands around her waist, to her back. There, I find her wrists bound with a length of rope. I follow the twine outward, to where it's secured through a rock with a hole in it, directly behind her.

I slice the extended stretch of rope and drag her upward to sit. No more than a handbreadth separates our faces.

In the dark, her breath is soft, warm. "The bam used to tie me up."

"So he told me."

"He didn't know I liked it."

My pulse halts, restarts. "You want me to leave you bound?"

"Not here. Not now. Not with these spelled ropes that Orkayha left to Rexar." Closer, her breath fans my face, until clover and citrus bleat against my lips. "But ask me again another time, when the bam isn't so near."

Pulse racing, I follow the shape of the rope around her wrists, searching for a loose strand. "You were born in the wrong realm."

"Perhaps. Since you're along should I assume you forgot my baya, along with your manners?"

"The baya of Mizura was in Elektos. She—" The screams and

smoke and terror fills me, and for a moment, I simply gulp in air. A bump of a knee against my hip returns me to the dark hut, to the high sorceress in front of me. "Now she's pursuing them in Denrathri."

"Then to Denrathri we go, as soon as you get me out of this rope. We can drag the bam through the key-gate together."

The key-gate that Orkayha destroyed. "Tell me about the sea route."

"The sea—" Soft hair swishes against my lips. "You lost it."

It's not a question, so I don't answer, focusing instead on the spelled rope at her wrists for any give in the twine, any place I can safely cut the rope away.

"Even when the sea routes were open before, few ventured that path to Denrathri. A league of vicious sea faeries guards the crossing beneath the waves. Few in their right mind would want to contend with that danger."

I shudder. "I seem to have lost my right mind anyway, ever since you lied to get me through that grounded gate."

I abandon the rope around her wrists. There is no give. Even the light from my flame will be of no help. I can't risk using the dagger without cutting her skin, let alone my stakes.

"Do it," Lidja says. "Use the knife."

"I can't."

"Why not?"

"Because I'll cut you."

"Perhaps. But I heal."

Still, I hesitate, biting my lip, testing the weight of the blade. A simple wrong slice and her veins—

"Ala." This time, her knees poke hard into my back. "Tell me. What are you so afraid of now?"

And here, in the dark, with citrus and clover and the muffled buzz of the outside world far away...the truth I haven't told my own sister leaves my lips. "Two years ago, I slit Mother's wrist with my magic. That's why Mother left. Not to protect me, or Soli. She ran to protect herself."

Dirt scratches as Lidja's bound legs stretch long once again.

"What I know of you, Alathea, is that you do nothing without a reason. What was your reason that night? What drew the Fates' lash?"

"Soli made Mother angry." Like a gate has opened, the words come quicker. "I'd never seen Mother like that, furious, charging like a watchman. She was going to punish Soli, and I couldn't let that happen." Magic rushes in my veins at the memory even now, the buzz inky and sharp and righteous. "The magic inside me escaped. It leapt from my hand and slashed my mother's wrist, deep. They left that same night, both of them, Mother and Mama. That was two years ago." I meet the outline of Lidja's gaze in the dark. "Some days, it feels like yesterday."

"For some memories," she says, "two years isn't enough. A lifetime isn't enough for memories that burrow under your skin until you can't separate whether they happened to you or to someone else. They curl into your marrow and sink and you ache until you want or hurt or rage as much as the other person wanted. Maybe it doesn't matter, really, if it feels the same, if it was you or the you before, if the memory bends your bones the same either way."

At her words, I feel it. My bones bend and ache toward Mother and Mama, toward my sister. I have always bent toward Soli, and always will.

But...it's not Soli that Lidja is speaking of. This is a sorrow of her own. "Who was she?"

For a moment, there is only the stillness of the hut and the cool air between us.

"Ages ago, when the Fates birthed our world, the first high sorceress of Memoria loved a woman. She was fierce and brilliant and shined brighter than any star." From somewhere outside the hut, a single, muffled shout. "*Shayna*. My word."

Shayna. This is the word I've heard Lidja whisper, before our bursts of magic speed in the jungle.

"How could someone you've never even met be your word?" And could mine be the same?

"Even though it's a memory—not even *my* memory—since the high sorceress's memories settled into me, I have *hurt*. My chest has *ached* like it was me, and her, and it was yesterday. When I accepted the power of the high sorceress and searched for my word of power, this is the one I heard, deep within me. Over and over. Her name is my word because I could not use anything else. This is the memory that has shaped me into who I have become, into what I do, the one that is carved into my skin as a scar." She shrugs her right shoulder, as if the scar weighs her even now. "I considered asking Vis for release, like Dae did with the death of his mother, but one day…I decided instead that I needed to move on. That I can be strong, too."

I don't know anyone stronger than this sorceress, except maybe my sister.

"So that's what I did—that's what *we* do, as high sorceresses. We adjust; we forge ahead and win. Always. That's when I learned to fight. Rexar taught me, originally, until she grew bitter as Daesen grew powerful, and saw how her soldiers naturally flocked to him and away from her."

Warrior-sorceress, indeed. I slide my fingers into her palm, dagger in hand, and carefully, so carefully, I begin to cut into the rope.

"More importantly, Ala, I let go—as much as it hurt. As much as it still hurts, even some days now."

A single strand of the rope snaps free.

"Sometimes the stories we tell ourselves are just that," Lidja continues. "Stories. And sometimes we have to accept our memories and live with them, as much as they will hurt us all the way to the next plane."

My mothers left because of me. Soli was hurt because of me.

This has been my story for so long now, how could any other story be right?

"Without your word," Lidja says, "you'll not have even half the power you need to face Orkayha."

"That's why we'll have you."

"I'm not Daesen. You can't distract me. You can't hide. I see your fear, so I will tell you this, the same that I tell all the spell-weavers when they take their rites. You alone know your power. Do not fear it." Closer, her breath fans my face, until flecks of gold and green flare in the dark. "Wield it. Wield your power like the weapon it is."

In the gloss of her eyes, I see my own reflection. Amber eyes that have survived—survived and grown stronger.

I see a refection of someone who *should* be seen.

Determined, careful, I saw at the rope. "Tell me the truth. Why are you still in this hut? Even with the spelled rope, could you truly not escape?"

Lidja shifts on the ground. "I have no interest in slaying my own people, as much as I prefer silence when I'm around them."

"You really can be a snake." Carefully, I continue at the rope. "You do know there are other ways to stop people from talking than killing them."

"There may be, but none are quite as satisfying." At my ear, a warm breath, her voice low and soft. "What method would you choose, Ala, to keep someone quiet?"

Another strand of the rope snaps, and I tilt my chin ever so slightly toward her. Her lips are no more than a breath from mine, our noses nearly touching.

"Not a blade," I whisper, pulse racing. "A rope, if I could find a teacher."

"Daesen," Lidja whispers back. "He could teach you."

"Perhaps. Or perhaps he'd be too easy on me."

Her eyes spark. "You think you're so brave now, just because you've managed to find us and scheme your way in here? You can't fool me. I see you trembling. I love the dark, while you—you still want a way out of all this, to return to Elektos, to hide in the shadows. You would abandon all of this in a heartbeat if given the choice."

I pierce the rope and the final strand snaps, her hands popping free. Heart thundering, I drop the dagger in the dirt.

"Even now, I see you," she whispers. "I see you want to—"

I slide my hands into Lidja's silky hair, and I kiss her.

CHAPTER 27

*L*idja's lips are soft and warm. Her breath halts, no doubt wondering what madness has overcome me to kiss her in this dark hut that holds a grounded gate to our enemy and Daesen poisoned thirty paces away.

Wild fields and autumn storms and sweet fruit fills my senses. She kisses me back.

Her lips slant over mine, and I press into her, her hair tangled in my fingers. *Her.* All I know is her, and our lips and—

Chains jangle outside the hut, splitting us apart by two breaths.

Where did all the air go from my lungs? "Soli was wrong."

"Wrong?" Lidja's voice is wobbly, like a blade that's been bent.

"She said you were blade and bite." Somehow, my lips return to just before Lidja's. "You're more like our spring syrup—all frost and thaw."

"You *have* you lost your right mind if you believe that, oxsail." Lidja nips at my lips, as if in warning. "But perhaps I've lost mine, too."

A shaft of light erupts, and I twirl around and up. Something heavy plops to the dirt of the hut, the bamboo door shutting as quickly as it opened.

Lidja pushes up and around me, to the object lying inside the door. "A jillbracer. Either someone is coming for us, or the guard must have thought you could use something more than rags." She tosses the armored vest my way. "Tell me, Ala." Her blade of a voice returns, sharp and wicked. "Did you kiss him to keep quiet, too?"

I thrust my middle finger upward, right at her beautiful face, and hiss, "Snake."

White teeth beam in the dark. "You know I don't hate that name at all."

With a humph, I cross the hut to Daesen. He may tease me relentlessly, but at least *he* has never been anything other than easy to know.

I drop to his side. "Dae." Through his shirt, I pinch the skin of his shoulder, hard.

He groans, head flopping to the side, but remains unconscious.

"Daesen." Again, I pinch, harder this time, on both shoulders.

"Needle. If you missed me, just say it."

Relief courses through me as I find the spelled rope at his wrists, far looser than the coils that bound Lidja. "Why didn't they tie you like Lidja?"

A silver flare cuts through the dark above us, black boots at my side. "Because the poison is enough to keep him useless for a day."

Daesen grins as I help him sit up against the wall. He yanks hard at my wrists, and I plop into his lap.

"What are you doing?" I squeak, squirming away. "We have to get out of here."

But he only buries his face into the crook of my neck and breathes deeply. "I do love lavender. I have an idea, needle." Sage and salt wrap around me. "What if we picked an apple and went into the sea, and we took off all our clothes—"

I shove away, scrambling upward. "What's *wrong* with you?"

Dae shuffles to his feet, slow but chuckling.

"Like I said—useless. It's the second wave of the draught." Lidja's voice fades as she strides away from us. "Definitely the worse part."

I hold my palm to Dae's chest as he steps toe-to-toe. "It can't be worse than unconscious."

Dae's hand slips onto the back of my neck. "Would you mind if I start purring?"

Smacking his hand away, I set him in the center of the hut. *"Don't move."* I stalk to Lidja.

"Did you come to tell me I'm right?" she murmurs.

"Absolutely not." Even if she is. How are we going to accomplish anything with Daesen in this state?

Crouching, Lidja presses the silver flame in her palm forward until it illuminates the rock where she'd been tied. The stone has not a hole through the center, like I'd assumed, but an arch.

The grounded gate to Mizura.

"If we don't want to wait for Orkayha's underlings to cross through here, we need to move him either way." She shifts, examining the rock. In the shuffle of her light, behind her, silver glints. "We should—"

"What is that?" I race to the flare of silver, drawing Lidja and her flame with me.

My pulse bumps as the silver form takes shape. A long silver-black shaft of iron angled upward rests within an arched half-circle of iron. A strip of leather is taut between the open ends.

Soli's voice finds me, from back when we first saw this weapon in the muddied lanes of Elektos. *That must be what they're calling the monster-killer.*

At the base of the metal rod lie three long arrows, their tips wrapped with cloth.

Outside the hut, someone shouts, clearer than before. Boots shuffle outside the bamboo door.

"We should go," Lidja says. "We can carve an exit out the stone and bamboo on this side. It's our best escape."

But I can't stop staring at the monster-killer. "Can you wield that?" I ask Dae. "In another realm?"

Boots thud through the dirt, heavy, dragging, until Daesen halts at my side and tugs at my braid, dimples deep. "I can wield anything you want me to, needle. Just point the way, and I will see it done. With pleasure."

"That." I turn his chin away from me and to the weapon. "I am pointing that way."

"This little thing?" With a wink, he releases me and hefts the massive bow onto his shoulder. "No trouble at all. Just tell me where to point and off I'll go. I know I said little, but in truth, do you know what this reminds me of? It looks an awful lot like my—"

This time, I smash my palm to his mouth. To Lidja, I whisper, "How long will this worse part last?"

A tongue drags against my fingers, and I snatch my hand back, glaring.

Dae simply smiles. "I can last all night and day and night and—"

Lidja says, "I told you poisoned was better."

"How long?"

"I don't know! I've never seen them give anyone that much of the draught before." Worry flashes across her face—and there, past the blade of her tongue, is the truth of why she didn't escape. That she couldn't physically drag Daesen from the hut, even with magic, not without putting him at risk.

You will find no one more loyal, Vis had said about the sorceress.

Even though she could have, she didn't leave her friend behind.

"I'll carve the way out." Lidja crosses to the bamboo wall, her silver flame gone.

From the outside of the hut, a new voice floats, hard, demanding.

"Or..." I shrug on the jillbracer and leave it open over my bandolier as a plan unfolds in my mind. "If Orkayha is in Denrathri chasing my mother, that means her realm is baya-less. Her army is there, just waiting."

"Her army of monsters," Dae says with a lopsided smile, "and possibly Tzen."

But if we can draw Orkayha away, out of my realm... Mother will have the opening she needs to reach the throne.

Lidja groans, even as the bamboo door shudders. "If you're thinking what I think you may be thinking, this is a very difficult, very bad plan."

"I thought you liked hard things," I say.

"Do you know what's really hard?" Dae says, dimples back. "When I'm in my bed and—"

I shove Daesen forward and slap his palm to the grounded gate.

Chuckling, he extends a hand for Lidja as the bamboo of the entire hut rattles.

"Fine." Lidja laces one hand with Daesen and places the other on the rock.

A gate bursts forth, up and bright, obliterating the dark of the hut.

"But this is because I want to, not because you asked," Lidja says, eyes bright. From the dirt, she gathers the discarded pieces of rope and tucks a length of it at her waist. Another strand, she whips until it shifts shape, into her axe. "It's been far too long since I've been actually challenged anyway."

And as I leap through the shimmering gate after Lidja and Daesen, I can't help but think...perhaps I like hard things, too.

CHAPTER 28

The Realm of Nightmares.

Even as my boots land on hard rock, screams fill my ears. Shrieks of pain, of bone-grinding agony. They slice through the dim light of Mizura as if night has already fallen, when it should be only midday. Even the two moons are dimmed, no more than a quarter of their usual brightness.

Where we exited the grounded gate, an elevated obsidian walkway stretches beyond the horizon in one tight, unforgiving line of black. On either side are plunging, dark pits. Far below, in each, a swirling gray funnel rises. We just need to choose where the diversion will best draw Orkayha back here, to her realm, and away from Denrathri.

A cold, dry wind blows, unrelenting. Beneath the shrieks, somewhere on the black horizon, the thunderous beat of drums pounds in time with my heart.

"Orkayha's army," Lidja says at my ear. "Monsters and filth, awaiting her command."

"Waiting to rip our hearts right out," Dae says, a grin wide across his face despite the gruesome words. He shifts the monster-killer on his back as we start to move forward, careful of the narrow walkway, the looming pits. "Unless we take their heads first."

"If our bam is good at anything," Lidja says, "it is weapons."

"Then this will work," I say. It has to. Mother is too good at hiding, too good at keeping herself far from any risk. If Orkayha is chasing her, blocking her from the throne, Mother will not chance charging forward, not until it is safe.

"If the Fates believe this idea is bound to their will, then yes, it will work." Lidja frowns as smoke from the nearest pit curls toward us, prodding. "If not, we'll just have to hope the cost is one we can bear."

I slip around the creeping smoke, clutching the unlaced jill-bracer over my bandolier as wind pushes into the slashes in my breeches and blouse, chilling me to the bone. Ahead, through the smoky columns on either side of the narrow walkway, a palace of onyx emerges.

The palace of Mizura.

"There." The plan etches inside me, clear as a carved wall. "We fire the weapon there."

"That would require us to cross this entire labyrinth." Dae's voice rumbles at my back, mirth dimmed. "And unless we want to actually fight our way across Orkayha's realm, we might want to choose somewhere easier. Closer."

Lidja and I both stare at the shield.

"That's the first reasonable thing you've said since you awoke, bam," Lidja says.

Daesen frowns. "That explains why it sounded so awful."

Far ahead, a monstrous bulk threads in and out of the smoke stacks.

He's right. If we head for the palace, we'll have to face Orkayha's underlings. But if we don't, if we fire the weapon from this walkway, with the thick stacks of smoke and pits where people scream…I say, "We can't chance hurting anyone in the pits by mistake."

Orkayha's face flashes before me, her triumphant expression, her sparkling scales and glittering crown as she destroyed the key-gate to my new home, after she had already destroyed the one I loved.

I point to the palace. "We'll fire it in the palace, right into her throne."

Carefully, we shuffle forward along the onyx path in a single file, shuddering at the cries and snarls rising from the pits. The bray of the monsters grows closer, louder.

Below the raised walkway to our right, two wraiths with skin the color of ash unravel throbbing purple lines from their arms. Their eyes, usually so wide and bright, are missing altogether, empty sockets in their place. Over pale lips, a line of crisscrossed wires form a brutal lattice.

My stomach roils.

Nightmares are real, girl.

In the pit on our left, a young man collapses in an explosion of glass. His scream digs into my skin, buzzing like the air before a lightning strike.

At my back, Lidja whispers, "This was a mistake, for us all to come here. I should have stayed behind."

"You could go back now," I say. "Dae and I will follow as soon as it's done."

"And leave this bam all the glory of a victory?" She hesitates, glancing behind at the smoke, below at the yawning pits, back to me. "I think not."

A wisp of song winds its way from the pits, thin and interspersed with sobs.

Go bam*! your little baby bones...*

Lidja shivers. "If they're singing about bams, that means Orkayha's keeping them for pets. Nasty creatures. Great for insults, bad for everything else—especially your extremities. Watch your feet."

"One more reason I hate this place," Dae says. "My feet are some of my best parts."

I narrow my eyes at the shield as his dimples flash.

"Do you know what my other best parts are, Ala?"

"You'll soon be without it if you keep jabbering, bam," Lidja says.

Daesen grins, but zips his mouth shut.

If the Fates approve our plan, then I really, really hope they help this poison wear off faster.

We draw forward, quick and quiet through the smoke, the palace looming larger. A splintered scream ascends from the pit directly ahead.

"If we don't succeed," Lidja whispers, "this is what Memoria will look like before long."

I tear my gaze from the walkway to the smokestacks, to the palace and around, to a soaring black wall behind us. The wall curls to the west and east, beyond our sight. In the light of the moons, it looks like a snake. Like a strange mountain. Like—

A towering black mountain above moonlit lakes. For a heartbeat, I'm there again, outside the death wagon, staring up at the sheer mountain in the distance. "This is already happening to my home."

This is where they were taking me and Tenion and Hook and the others in that death wagon. Not to a re-education center, but to Mizura, to be thrown in an endless nightmare.

To the east, a furious bray rends the air.

"Faster," Lidja whispers. "We need to move much faster."

We break into a run—

A claw punches onto the black walkway from inside a pit.

Dae slams his armored plate upward, Lidja and I halting at his back.

A creature rises from the pit, made of smoke and wings. In its monstrous head, two line-thin eyes pinch above a razor of a beak, two hollows for its nostrils. A broad torso gives way to stalks of legs that end in talons. Its wings flare wide, black and broad and feathered—wings that from far below would appear like no more than a massive night-raptor.

These are the winged beasts I saw from below that day in Elektos. Not night-raptors, but winged monsters of smoke and terror.

The flying monster screeches, and we all slip backward, clinging to the center of the narrow walkway.

"Nothing like terror to punch the poison out," Dae whispers. "I can't risk losing this weapon into these pits."

"Then watch my back." Lidja pushes to the front of us and hurls a dagger at the vulture-monster. One after the other, silver glints and flies into its torso and wings and—

The creature lifts from the walkway with a hard pulse of its wings and swoops for us.

"Run!" I shout.

We tear backward, away from the palace and onto an offshoot.

"Fates," Lidja breathes. "No one fall. I am *not* retrieving you from one of these pits."

The vulture-monster dives.

Dae flips the monster-killer above us, as if it's his armored plate. The beast's claws ting against the metal, and it screeches back into the air.

"Next time it dives, keep running. I'll load the weapon—"

"There's too much smoke." I watch as the flying monster circles. "Orkayha won't see it."

"And we won't see Memoria again if that monster knocks us into a pit," Lidja says.

The monsters—some are afraid of flame, the guard said outside the hut.

I pop a flame into my palm. "Then aim it high."

Lidja's flame joins mine, twice as strong, burning hot.

Together, we light the cloth at the arrow's tip as Dae hefts the monster-killer bow to his shoulder and aims. "I do like when you command me, needle."

The winged beast shrieks and drops for us again.

"Now!"

The flame arrow streaks toward the beast, lighting the dark of the realm like a star streaking for the dimmed moons.

The creature screams, beak open wide as the arrow hurtles for its chest—

The winged monster swallows the arrow whole and keeps diving for us.

"*Run!*" I say again.

We tear across the narrowing walkway, scurrying like the mice of Elektos at dusk. Faster, narrower, faster, pebbles skipping from the path into the pits on either side, the monster's shriek growing and wings thrumming—

A cold wind blasts across the walkway, catching my unlaced jillbracer and dragging me to the very edge.

Lidja snatches me, jerking me onto firm footing. "I *said* no falling in." Her eyes burn into mine. "Don't make me do that again."

"I won't." The monster pursues again, and I shrug off the jillbracer. I'm the one who has always made sure my family survived. "Get your ropes ready."

The monster plunges forward—

I hurl the jillbracer at the monster's head. "Now!"

The metal vest clinks against the monster's head. In that breath of distraction, Lidja flings her ropes over the monster's shoulder. I dive under its wing, catch the loose end and jerk it over the wings, hard, pinning the rope to the stone walkway with a stake.

The monster howls, thrashing against the rope, and we run.

"Leave or palace?" Lidja says.

"Palace," I breathe. "The entrance. We'll fire it at the front doors and go back."

Past the smoke and pits we sprint, legs aching, feet pounding, past shrieks and soft, defiant voices—

"Wait!" I skid to a stop.

Dae nearly topples into me from behind.

Lidja paces backward. "What could possibly be worth stopping?"

The grains of gray smoke part in the pit to my right, enough for me to glimpse the source of that voice, to catch a flash of yellow string in dark hair. "Her."

From below, the girl looks upward.

Tenion.

Another roar of a monster, this one closer still.

Dae crouches, reloading the monster-killer on his shoulder. "Two winged monsters incoming."

"We have to get her out."

Tenion runs for the edge of the pit, scraping at the sides, jumping.

"Who is she?" Lidja unravels a rope from her belt, looping it around her waist, and hurling the free end into the pit.

"She's Soli's friend." My scarred hand pulses as I brace behind Lidja, my hand through the rope at her back. "She's *my* friend. They must have caught her again after we escaped the wagon."

"Another one," Dae says. "Three now. We're not going to make it to the palace."

"Then we'll adjust." The words leave both Lidja and me at the same time, and for a heartbeat, our gazes catch and then the rope tugs far below, and Tenion is climbing.

"Faster," Dae says. "Faster, faster, *faster.*"

Monsters roar; wings pulse.

A cloud shadows Tenion's face as she rises from the pit, as I slip to my stomach and grab Tenion's arm, Lidja and I hoisting her up onto the walkway—

Smoke explodes across the pit in a glittering pulse.

Orkayha stands between me and my friends.

* * *

ORKAYHA'S SCALES glisten like the fate-stars, her splintered crown a promise of slow pain. From the air and pits and palace in the Realm of Mizura, monsters scream, as if they know their queen has returned.

Orkayha's gaze slides over Daesen and Lidja, Tenion tucked behind them, and all three of them separated from me.

We did it. My friends and I distracted Orkayha from Denrathri. And if we could do that...we can find a way around the baya and out of Mizura for all of us.

Plans unfold in my mind, but in every one of them, one of us is left behind. I shove them aside.

"When my sister warned an intruder had breached my realm, I did not believe her," Orkayha says. "Who would be so foolish? Who would dare to invade my home?" Her eyes glint as she turns to me. "I should have expected it was a wisp of a girl who no one sees at all."

Orkayha lifts her arms, a terrible funnel of smoke howling upward from the pit—

"Daesen!" I point at the cloud. "Put a shield in place!"

"Ala, no," Daesen chokes, but Lidja whispers, "*Shayna.*"

Magic pulses and a silver-blue shimmer just like the one that once protected Memoria rises up and around the three, separating them from Orkayha and me.

The smoke blasts around the trio, smashing into the shield, but my three friends remain unaffected.

"You think that will stop me?" Orkayha snaps. "A brittle film of magic? I recall the time before the moons graced the sky. I create magic all my own. A single tap from one of my darlings and their magic will shatter into nothing, just like your home."

"Then let them go." I meet Lidja's eyes behind that shield, willing her to understand at least part of the plan. *Take Tenion back through the gate now.* In less than a heartbeat, Daesen and

Tenion turn and race for the still-open gate that shimmers faintly from where we entered.

Arms crossed, Lidja remains, as if daring me to argue.

To Orkayha, I say, "We have done *nothing* to you."

"The baya of Memoria is a liar and a snake," Orkayha says. "He is just like the first baya of that realm, that worm Kaiden, who slithered his way into my sister's heart."

"Vis said—"

Orkayha waves a hand and an icy wind slashes across the walkway. I crouch low to keep from flying into a pit.

"Visander *lies*! Just like Kaiden! Kaiden, who got my sister with child, and then killed their babe. I should have killed him. I should have pushed him from these very walls when he snuck in to see my sister. Every fiber of my being screamed at me to do. If I had only pushed, Melestra's child would have lived." Smoke rises from Orkayha's skin. "Do you know what it is to hold a babe, spirit-wraith? To love someone more than your heart should be capable of feeling? When she was in my arms, I knew this. I understood why submitting to the Fates' demands was worth it—everything was worth it, all so I could love that little one, so I could hold her in my arms and know what it was to love." Icy eyes meet mine. "Do you know what it was to lose her?"

"Then let Vis carve it from you," I say, even as a piece of my own heart cracks at the loss in her voice. "Let him release those memories."

"My memories are what keep my sister and I safe. How will she ever bear another child and not worry that she will suffer the same fate?"

"We would not harm a child. None of the triads of Memoria or Denrathri would."

Orkayha blinks up at the muted sky. "He truly hasn't told you, then. As Kaiden rotted in my pits, he finally admitted the truth— the baya of Denrathri helped him, too. Every one of the triads of Memoria and Denrathri played a part in killing the child."

This. This must be the untrue memory that Orkayha has bound herself to. "You cannot believe that, not truly."

"I *lived* it, girl." For a heartbeat, her voice cracks. "I wish it was untrue. I have wished that for every one of the years I've hunted the triads to pay for what they did." Smoke licks upward from either side of walkway. "This is where the last high sorceress of Denrathri spent the final days of her life, as did the one before her, and the one before her. She remained in my pit, alone, until she perished. This is where you will remain life after life, little wraith, until the day I end your line. I should be grateful you saved me one trip."

With a flash of smoke, Orkayha closes the distance between us and kicks.

I thud flat against the onyx, skidding to the very edge of the rock. I rake my nails into the onyx as she advances, smoke gathering in her palms.

Several walkways beyond her, with a faint pulse of silver-blue, Tenion disappears through the gate, followed by Daesen.

Closer, the protective shield pops and collapses, freeing Lidja to race toward us.

I slap my hands to the stone, holding Orkayha's attention on me. "I did not accept my power to remain trapped in your realm."

The gathering smoke halts.

"Accept?" Orkayha says. "What do you mean, accept?"

From behind the baya, an axe severs the smoke—

And connects with Orkayha's side, just a whisper of a cut, before Orkayha leaps away, right into a pit with a *whoosh.*

Lidja darts toward me, leading me up the walkway and forward. We race for the grounded gate.

"Just to be clear," Lidja says, "I was right—this was an awful plan."

The walkway shudders as a smoke monster lands on the stone ahead of us, cutting us off from reaching the gate and Daesen, who has returned with Tenion safely on the other side, the monster-killer gleaming on his shoulder.

Wings thrum above, descending fast.

"It's about to get worse," I say.

We turn to run the opposite direction, but Orkayha thunders to the walkway, wings tucking into her back.

"Answer me now, girl." Smoke and flames burn in the baya's hands, screams building within those depths as she prowls for us. "What do you mean *accept* the power?"

"Fates," Lidja whispers.

As we press closer together, back-to-back in between Orkayha and a smoke monster, I whisper Mama's long-ago swear words.

Orkayha doesn't know.

I cannot let you into Memoria. Sudden, sharp, a piece of the memory in Vis's room floods though me. *Our secrets are ours, as yours remain here.*

Orkayha, along with her sorceress and shield, has lived since the birth of Fides. None of her triad has never experienced or even witnessed the loss and flow of power out of her pits, not once.

She doesn't know that memories flow from life to life. She doesn't know that we accept our powers.

And she doesn't know that our powers can be rejected, as Mother did, leaving the realms to fall entirely...

Leaving Orkayha a way to stop the triads from ever rising again.

"If you must accept," Orkayha says, eyes shining, "that means it can be rejected. If it can be rejected, then no one else could follow. That means—"

Orkayha launches forward and grabs Lidja by the throat, swinging the sorceress to dangle her feet over the edge of a pit.

"Tell me, girl, or I'll end this one's life right now and find out for myself. How does it work?"

Lidja scrapes at the hand on her neck. "*Don't*, Ala. Nothing. Tell her nothing."

A flash rolls through me of Tzen holding my sister in the air, of her broken, bleeding body after the fall.

I won't make that mistake again.

From the grounded gate, the monster-killer flashes.

I open my mouth—

"Ala, *no!*"

—"Lidja, *now.*"

Lidja whispers, "*Shayna.*"

The monster-killer explodes.

The onyx walkway shudders, knocking me to my stomach. I grip the rock as it sways, as smoke billows and rocks clack and crack as they tumble.

Section by section, the smoke parts to reveal a rent in the walkway—and Lidja on the other side of a yawning hole, clinging to the stone.

My stomach jolts and I scramble for a way to reach her, for any path possible, but she's on an island of rock.

"She's coming," Dae calls, pointing to the sky.

"I—" I swallow, reaching through my magic for a plan. Any plan. "Lidja."

The sorceress glances from the sky to me, her eyes hooded. "Ala, we need to keep her distracted. I have a plan." Her eyes dart to Dae behind me, and she nods. "Remember what I said, bam."

A warm hand falls to my shoulder and tugs me backward toward the gate.

"No." I wrench from Daesen and stretch from the very edge of the walkway for Lidja. "Reach for me. Do it. Use your magic." Above, wings thrum. "Please. *Now*. You have to."

"I could." Lidja's gaze returns to the dimmed sky. "But this plan is better."

Wings beat and beat and beat—

"*Lidja.*" I stretch and stretch and stretch. "Please, take my hand."

"I told you, oxsail." Lidja smiles, all teeth. "We don't always get what we want. *Shayna.*"

A burst of magic rocks me and Daesen through the grounded gate as Lidja drops into the pit.

CHAPTER 29

*D*aesen and I fall through the grounded gate back to Memoria. Before I can even shift in the dirt of the hut or locate Tenion on this side, Dae rears his spear over the stone gate and splits it with a single strike.

"No!" I scramble for the fragments of stone. "We can't leave Lidja there!"

"You heard her command." Daesen's shoulders rise and fall rapidly, all traces of the poison long gone from his voice. "I had no choice."

Shouts rise from outside the hut. "Then get us out of here," I command, reaching for his arms.

He curls Tenion and me into his chest, spinning us into a quick-portal. Insects buzz loud and hard as we tumble onto clacking stones. The sea punches into the shore of Memoria, air thick with the coming afternoon storm. Even though the sky is shaded the soft blue of dusk, the brightness causes me to wince, far removed from the dark of Mizura and that hut.

That hut, which now holds only a destroyed gate back to Lidja.

Dae scans the horizon of the sea. "You heard what Lidja said.

She's giving us time. Giving Talia and Vis time. Exactly what we went there to do, right?"

"Not like that."

I walk for the edge of the water, the scent of salt and fish ahead, the click of insects in the jungle at my back.

For several breaths, all I see is Lidja ordering us to leave.

A small hand slips into mine. "You've made friends."

I shudder in a deep breath and curl Tenion into my arms, a spark of light piercing the darkness in my chest. "You were right. About everything."

"I know."

"I should have believed you sooner."

For a moment, we simply hold each other, amidst the chirping crickets and shush of the palms.

I pull her back, cataloging each shallow cut on her face, the bright blue of her eyes. *"Lucius, I need you,"* I call silently, and then, to Tenion, "I think I found someone you know."

Her eyes widen, hope sparking. The shush and chirps and caws of the jungle shift, ever so slightly.

Lucius emerges, burgundy robe bright against the deep green of the palm trees. Behind him trails my sister.

"Soli!" Tenion dives into my sister's arms, and the two speak, low and soft.

I meet Lucius's steady gaze. "Her father is here, in Rexar's village."

Lucius glances at Tenion and nods. *"I believe you are correct."* He offers Tenion a skeletal hand.

Daesen steps forward. "I'll quick-portal her there."

I frown, the memory of him unconscious in that hut raking through me. "We can't risk losing you again. Not now."

"If the guard who helped you spread word that we've been devoured by Mizura, that Rexar lied about Vis's command, she's the one at risk now, not me." Quicker than my next breath, Dae ducks to my ear and whispers, "Besides, you won't be rid of me that easily, needle. Not now, not ever."

I blink as wide as an owl as sage and salt withdraw from me, as his dimples flash and my pulse skips.

Tenion takes Daesen in one hand and Lucius in the other. She pauses at the line of palm trees. "There is one thing you can do for me, Ala," Tenion says, glancing back in my direction.

"Anything."

Bright blue eyes meet mine. "You can do better."

The three disappear into the jungle, leaving Soli and I alone, Tenion's words a direct punch to my gut.

Do better.

"She's right," I whisper. I have to do better. Much, much better.

For a moment, Soli simply looks at me, head cocked, arms crossed. "Do you know where I was when Lucius found me, Ala? I was waiting on this shore, just north of here, like we agreed. I was pacing the stones like an idiot, wondering what went wrong and where you were in this realm and how to find you. And then Lucius told me you'd *left*."

A heated wind strikes through the palms. The sea laps harder at the shore. "I—We needed to. We had to try."

"Without me? Without even letting me know?"

"I…" I hadn't even thought of it. And if I had…"I didn't want to drag you into danger. If we both were lost, then what? Then who would help Mother claim the throne? I had to do this."

"Exactly. *You.* This is all about *you.* You didn't even think of *me*, of how I might feel to hear my sister, my only real family, abandoned me for the Realm of Nightmares!"

"I'm here now. I came back." Thunder rolls above, faint, far away.

"But you might not have. You might have been trapped there, or lost, and it was all because you didn't tell me. Because you thought it was better to leave me out of it."

"I'm trying to protect you."

"We agreed, remember? Protect each other. You can memorize one hundred-some idiot lies, but you can't bring yourself to remember the one thing we agreed to. Or you don't want to remember it. Or you never intended to. Or you *lied*." Soli yanks the collar of her blouse away from her neck. "How did I get this scar, Ala?"

The words roll to my tongue, and stick. "I...I don't know."

"You're no better than Mother."

This time, thunder stretches across the entire sea, rolling toward us.

"You've been lying to me my whole life." Solis's voice breaks. "Is that all we are to each other, sister? No more than two girls born in the same home, under the same crumbling roof?" Her nails dig into my arm. "Why haven't you trusted me? Why won't you trust me even now?"

A bolt of lightning flashes, silencing the insects, as I swallow past a rock in my throat. "If you knew what I've done, you would leave me, too."

"Ala...if you don't trust me, if I don't trust you, I might as well leave now."

The words hover between us like a double-tipped spear.

"I hurt Mother. That's why she left."

"I'm certain I hurt her a thousand times with things I said—"

"No. I mean with *magic*. I sliced her wrist, deeply, with magic."

Soli stills, a statue in the swaying of the jungle. "You knew you possessed magic."

"Yes," I whisper.

"You knew, and you told me to stay away. That it was death."

"Yes."

"You carved those lies for the Sancta, and you repeated them. You made me think you *believed* them."

"I *did* believe them, Soli. They weren't wrong. Magic is death."

"Magic isn't why Lidja remained in the Realm of Mizura, sister. That's all you."

Lightning pulses the jungle white-blue. "I tried to reach her. I tried to get her to use her magic to leap."

"*You* should have used your magic! *You* should have leapt to *her!*"

My knees buckle, and I sink onto the stones.

"You're still hiding. You're still afraid." Stones clap under her boots as she crouches in front of me. "How are we supposed to do this together when you're trying your hardest not to change a thing?"

I meet my sister's eyes as thunder shudders the palms. Then the sea calms, the wind dies, the insects quiet, and everything around us stills.

"You're right. I know you're right."

Why *didn't* I try to use my magic? Why *haven't* I found my word?

You aren't enough to exist at all. Orkayha's words slice through my gut all over again.

"I'm going to do better. I'm going to help Mother—with you, at your side. With Dae."

Soli's lips flatten as lightning cracks, a roll of thunder chasing the light into silence. "You're willing to do that? To cross the sea to find her?"

I don't mention it's the one way across now, with no gate.

"It can't be worse than Mizura." I take my sister's scarred hand, the one that matches mine. "I'll do anything. Please."

"You know, Ala, I do believe you'll do anything. I'm just not certain that *anything* will be the *right* thing."

"I'm doing it to keep you safe. To protect you."

This time, I hear it.

Mother's words, from my tongue.

At my sister's silence, I try again. "To protect each other, I mean. Like we promised. Please, Soli. I need you."

"For what do you need me, Ala?"

The space widens between us again, sharp and double-edged. I search for the right answer. For the true one. "Once we land in Dreams, we need your power to quick-portal us to Mother. To the palace."

"You know, once, that's all I wanted to hear. That you understood that we were needed here." She stares over my shoulder. The waves return, crashing now, with the approaching storm. "But the thing is, Ala, I was wrong. I'm needed at home in Elektos. My friend is there now, helping my other friends, while I've been here chasing nothing. Being left behind."

"I haven't—" I reach for my sister but she winces away. "You're the shield of Dreams, Soli. You were right. Both of us are needed here, for all of Fides."

"My friend says to protect the ones we love, we fight at their side. We don't hide them away."

"That's not what I'm doing. I'm not hiding you away."

"Aren't you? When the time comes and we face Orkayha together, you and me and Mother, will you be like her? Will you lie? Will you shove me in a shed again? Will you head into battle without me?"

"You're my sister. My little sister." I resist the urge to look at that scar on her collarbone. "I'm trying. I'll do better."

"Even your voice sounds like hers." Soli kisses my cheek. "After we get into Denrathri, and I portal us to Mother, I'm going back to Elektos. To stand with my real friends."

The sky unleashes as Soli disappears into the jungle, leaving me utterly alone.

* * *

WIND LICKS my braided hair as our ship speeds across the waves. The two moons shine on giant ocean horses with webbed hooves and flowing manes as they drag us through the sea. Dae, Lucius, and my sister stand at the helm next to a woman who hasn't stopped whispering to the horses in a foreign tongue, guiding them toward the Realm of Dreams.

When we stood on the shore of Memoria, a massive ship before us, I gaped at the ocean horses as they pawed at the surf, but it was the ship's captain, with her warm brown skin and cascades of curly hair, her easy command of the prancing creatures, who I was unable to look away from. At her wrists, bracelets of shells clink, not unlike the circlet of seeds I strung for Mama all those years ago.

"How will she avoid the sea faeries?" I wondered aloud.

To that, Soli said nothing at all, only stared past me, the thread of our earlier argument taut and brittle. *You're still afraid.*

Dae smiled, fast and bright. "Easy, as she's one herself."

I followed them aboard and stuck to the back of the ship, far from the sea faerie captain and my stewing sister.

Now drops of sea lick my face as we race toward Denrathri.

Sage cuts through salt, and a warm, moonlit hand settles next to mine on the rail.

For a moment, I lean into Daesen's scent, into the comfort of his presence. "Is it true, what Orkayha said? She believes the first baya of Memoria killed her sister's child, and all the others helped."

Sea water sprays the deck as we crest a large wave. "It is true that the first baya of Memoria took Orkayha's sister as a lover. The Fates sent a prophesy that their child would become a monster and destroy everything that they loved—that any child of theirs would destroy our whole world. So Kaiden turned away from Melestra, because as a baya, he knew well the Fates' cruelty."

Again, the memory from Vis's room returns to me, of Kaiden and Melestra—Orkayha's sister. *The prophesy was yours as much as mine. We may have brought it closer with this mistake, if your womb quickens after last night. We must keep the prophesy from coming to pass, no matter what that costs.*

"But," Daesen continues, "it is also true that Melestra and Kaiden loved each other too much to remain apart. Again and again, he returned to Mizura under cover of darkness. Orkayha locked him from the realm, but Kaiden made a key-gate and found a way to his love. Nothing could keep them apart, not even Orkayha's warnings, not even fear of the Fates."

I watch the moonslight bounce on the waves and wonder what such a love could possibly feel like, to deny the Fates themselves.

Daesen says, "When Melestra grew with child, Orkayha helped the lovers hide her sister's belly. My own mother used to tell me stories of how when the child was born, Orkayha held the girl first, and never again has Fides shone with such love. The light of our world at that moment was matched only by the darkness that followed, when the child died in her sleep, and instead of telling the truth, Melestra falsely confessed to her sister that Kaiden had killed their daughter. This was the lie that birthed Orkayha's revenge on us all."

The ship lurches down a tall wave, taking my stomach with it. "That is…" I don't have words for what that is. "Why would Melestra have told her sister such a lie?"

"Sometimes it's easier to believe a lie than accept what's out of our control. We all believe words that are false at one time or another, Ala."

The ship heaves, and I grip the wooden railing harder. "I think I hate the sea."

"Lidja hates it, too. Except instead of huddling in the corner she'd be hurling daggers into the mast until we arrive."

You should have used your magic. "What do you think she's doing right now?"

"Most likely leading Orkayha on a chase to be remembered."

"Orkayha won't catch her again." The sight of Orkayha's

hands on Lidja's neck rips through me as my stomach rolls with a wave. "She'll adjust. She won't be caught."

"I'm telling myself the same damned thing, needle. If it's any comfort, Vis has always said our high sorceress is as slippery as a serpent and twice as mean."

My voice drops to a whisper. "I didn't mean to leave her behind."

"Of course you didn't. I didn't either. We didn't. Perhaps if I'd been able to rid my body of the poison, if I'd been faster, if, if, if." The moons and three fate-stars reflect in Dae's eyes. "I could spend my lifetime wrapped in 'what if' if I were to let myself. But I won't, and I won't let you. Lidja can take care of herself. She will bite and slash and wear Orkayha down."

"You love her."

"Of course I love her. I don't want her harmed. I don't want her in one of those pits. But I trust her. I trust her power. And I trust that we'll return for her. We did what we could, and Lidja made her own choice."

You didn't use your magic.

My gaze trails to my sister at the front of the ship, to her unbound hair wild in the sea wind. "I'm not certain that's true."

Dae's glance follows. "What is family for if not to make us miserable at least once a day? Especially when it comes to junctures they weren't present for."

"Soli is leaving." The waves rock beneath us. "After she quick-portals us to Mother, she's going to leave until we need her in Mizura."

"Your hothead of a sister is volunteering to skip a fight? I'll believe that when I see it. I'd wager ten apple carts that she will be there, leading the charge."

"You'd be devastated to lose so many apples."

The shield closes his eyes and sighs. "Perhaps."

I wait for more, for a crinkle at his eyes, for his dimples to show. "What's wrong?"

"Can't I be not fun from time to time?"

"That's not you. That's Lidja."

His lips twitch the slightest bit, and I bump my hip to his. "I'm your friend, remember? You can tell me."

"It's the tail end of the poison. The fun wore off, which has left me feeling like this. Like all that sea out there is inside me, but there's nothing in it. Just emptiness."

At the railing, I slip my smallest finger closer to his, until our knuckles touch. Dae has always, always tried to make me laugh. Now, seeing him like this...

"Your arms look good. And your—" I wave up and down. "Other parts, too."

"Are you trying to *flirt*, needle?"

I shift as the ship rocks, suddenly certain this was a bad idea—

"Don't misunderstand." His smallest finger traps mine. "I like it. Keep trying."

"That's it. I'm out of ideas."

"Then let me help you."

Dae pivots, his back to the sea, and tugs me to him, a fish on his hook. Closer, he pulls me, until my bandolier presses against his chest. Until sage and sweet salt wrap around me. Until I forget we're on a ship sailing above vicious sea faeries to a realm that Mother will reign.

Until I forget everything but him.

"Do you know what we're sailing away from?" His voice rumbles from his chest into mine. "What tonight is in my realm?"

"Another night?" A shiver strikes down my spine.

"My prickly needle." Daesen's whisper at my ear sends goose bumps down my skin. "It's Mirthraya."

And suddenly, it's not just salt and sage, but musk and cedar and sweat. The very air thickens.

"Do you recall what I told you of Mirthraya?"

"No." *Yes.* "Not at all." *Tell me again.*

"My lovely, lying pine needle." The corners of his lips curl upward. "Tonight, everyone in Memoria who is old enough will celebrate. Sheets will feel like silk. Berries will drip on your tongue. And skin…skin will sing, needle. We light fires and make love under the fate-stars. The moonslight will glow over every kiss."

As if his words are magic, the air shimmers gold and orange around us, a wall of magic flame veiling us from the rest of the ship. An image of Dae floats through me, naked, bathed in the burnt orange of a fire. He would be there, too, if he wasn't here on this ship.

Would I be with him?

"I've never kissed anyone in the open sky before." I'm not certain if it's Daesen I'm confessing to, or the sea, or the moons themselves. "My…my lover—" Even confessing this much, my tongue is stone. "We were only ever inside." In the shadows, in secret.

I consider telling him about the kiss I shared with Lidja in the dark of that hut, but my tongue sticks with the second confession.

"Your sister told me once how it is in Elektos," Dae says. "That you're not allowed lovers. How you hide any relationship beyond what the Sancta directs for you."

"That's true. But my lover and I didn't only hide because of that. She *wanted* to hide. She wanted to keep us a secret, even from our families. She wanted to hide me."

When she first said we needed to remain hidden, I didn't question it. But now, here, in the moonslight and the warm glow around me…I can't find the sense any longer.

I shake off the memory and raise my eyes to the gray so close to mine.

Our gazes hold.

Heat.

A flush drags along my skin. The caress of silk, a nip.

And I say, "Tell me what it feels like. To kiss like that."

A low rumble from Daesen's lips, shimmering against my chest through my suddenly heavy blouse.

"It feels like your magic. Like beauty and strength and wisdom, like the wilderness of the night sky and the shadows of the mountains all at once. The wind rises around you, and your skin covers in goose bumps and your very soul is quivering, focused on that one thing you want most. It feels like what you'll feel soon in Dreams, the call you'll feel of your magic in your realm." Dae rubs his jaw against the bone of my cheek, light and rough. "Ala...it will feel like *yes*."

My insides pool, like the sea is no longer only below us, but inside me as well. Not empty or calm, but roiling.

"But what if...what if I'm scared to use magic?"

"Then don't think of what you're scared of. Remember our lesson in the sea? Think of what you need instead."

Need.

Suddenly, I am nothing but need. My veins buzz, my mind cloaked in fogged moonslight. An image of him and me and nothing but our skin and the fate-stars and twined hums pulses through me.

"Think of what you want." Again, he slides the stubble of his jaw across my cheekbone. Rougher. "Think of me."

The orange-gold illusion around us wavers, leaps. "Lidja would probably say you're casting a spell on me."

"And what do you say?"

"I think...I think I like it. I—" I push back, and shrug off the bandolier, sighing as the weight leaves me. As if I'm in only my undergarments as we were in the sea, the dark liquid all that hovers between us. "I do think of you."

Gray pupils dilate and the orange flames dance. "Then what are you going to do about it?"

My skin tightens, a thousand little fires zipping. Sinking lower, liquid.

I step closer, my chest pressed to his. All around us, the

orange-golds zings. Heat simmers from inside my very veins. "This."

"What is *this*?" His gaze falls to my lips, even as his finger strokes the sensitive skin above my elbow, as if I wear no blouse at all. "*This* can mean many things, needle. Focus. What do you want?"

The *wanting*. It courses through me, wrapping its way through every nerve, splintering into so many things I want.

I want Lidja safe.

I want my sister to stay at my side.

I want Mother to understand what she did was wrong.

I want this fate-starred night to burn brighter.

"Tell me. I want you to tell me." My voice matches his, nails raked through sand. "What is tonight like—with you?"

His lids flicker shut, long eyelashes fluttering against moons-kissed cheeks.

"I want to know. Would you tell me?"

When they reopen, the gray shifts smooth and deep, like molten silver. His gaze caresses my cheekbones, my lips, my earlobes.

Each feels nearly like a kiss.

Nearly. Not enough.

"I shouldn't, Ala."

"Why not?"

His grip on my arms convulses. A shiver flies along my skin.

"Because maybe I'm no longer certain where this game is heading."

"I thought you liked a challenge."

"A challenge, yes. But this…" At the base of his neck, his pulse jumps. "What if this is something else? What if I'm the one wanting?"

My breath disappears.

Me.

He wants *me*.

"Then even more reason to tell me." I capture his wrist against the wooden railing, winding my fingers around the strong bones. "Tell me what it would it be like if you and I were under the moons together."

"I really do love when you command me." And those full lips lower toward mine.

My breath suspends.

At the last moment, he darts to my jaw, breath feathering where my neck meets bone, and my spine curves of its own accord. Closer.

"If I were to be with someone on this night, it would consume me."

His mouth trails to my ear, warm breath in a tight line at the ridge, and I sway, my eyes fluttering. Strong hands slide to both of my elbows, firm and soft.

"Not someone." My skin aches. "Me. How would it be with *me?*"

He groans, fingertips caressing my arms. Light and heat, all at once.

"If I were with you this night, all I would see is the shade of each pore on your skin."

His gaze dips to my neck, his gaze caressing as surely as if he's touched me.

Liquid warmth pools in my belly.

He moves to my ear, a nip at the lobe, and I gasp.

"The only sound, your sighs."

His sighs. I want his sighs. Heat spears through me.

"The only taste would be you on my tongue."

Liquid. My bones are liquid.

The tip of his nose dips, hovers along my collarbone. He inhales deeply. "The only smell your lavender skin."

My palms slip to his chest to keep from melting altogether.

Inhaling again, sharply, Daesen drags his fingertips up the

back of my arms to the collar of my blouse, tracing it to the back of my neck. To my skin.

My breath turns as shallow as a rock skipped on the sea. My skin is light as air, as if the wind will catch me and carry me wherever he directs.

Gray eyes locked on mine, Daesen dips his fingers under the collar and pushes the soft fabric down the spine of my neck, fingers pressing into my skin, marking me.

I arch into his touch.

He presses his fingers harder, thumbs drawing lazy circles on my upper back, dipping beneath the blouse, the heat of the magic flames and cool night air swirling on my skin.

His mouth lowers, hovers over the curve of my shoulder. "Your skin would turn to fire."

"I think...I think it might."

Lower, his lips sink. Lower. So close. I bend into him further, my chest pressing into his.

"*Think* is a mountain range from where I am right now, Ala. *Think* is for the daylight. Thinking is what leads to fear, to being afraid." His left arm curls around my waist, holding me in place. "This night is for letting go. For leaping, sight unseen."

My breath stops, his right hand twisting in my hair.

"Tonight, I would make you moan until the sunset burst inside you."

My knees give way.

Need explodes under my skin from the inside out. Desire pulses through me, demanding, burning alongside the writhing in my veins until there is no beginning or end and all I know is it will consume me.

All around us, gold and orange and silver flames dance.

"What is this illusion you've woven?" I breathe.

His lips hover a breath from mine, ready. "It's not mine, Ala. It's yours."

I feel it. The song of the wind through my bones. The restlessness of a coming storm in my veins.

Magic.

"Isn't that what you wanted? Your magic?"

Under the fate-stars and the moons, in the trail of the ocean horses and the wind over the waves and spray of the sea, where anyone could see us, I say, "Yes. But also, I want this."

I rise to my toes and kiss Daesen.

CHAPTER 30

The ocean horses haul our ship to Denrathri, to the base of looming cliffs shadowed by the blackest of night. Lucius remains aboard with the faerie captain as Daesen, Soli, and I lower to a small boat.

The boat rises and thuds on a wave as we oar forward in search of a place to land. As for the cliff...I'm not certain which will be harder—finding a route up that sheer face, or convincing my sister to remain after she quick-portals us to the palace.

I hope Daesen is right that Soli will change her mind and remain here with us for what we're about to face. I need her for this fight, but also...I ache to tell her that I kissed Daesen. After our kiss on the ship, I wanted to run up to my sister and tell her, to wonder with her what the kiss could have meant. But with her weapon-strapped back to me, gaze unmoving from the sea, I paused—perhaps it would be best if she came to me first.

Except she hasn't, even now, with every dip of our oars bringing us closer to Denrathri.

My magic curls within me, like it only awaits my command to lift and roar across the waves. Does Soli feel the same with her shield magic?

I open my mouth, ready to ask, ready to convince her to stay—

"We will be crushed if we approach here," Soli says, brittle and tight, her eyes on the razor cliff.

Daesen shoves an oar deep to turn us. "Sailor Soliana, I think you may be right."

My sister glares at Daesen. "We shouldn't be approaching this way at all."

Waves slap the boat as we struggle to cut away from the inward current.

"We'll find a way," I say. "There must be a path up, if we can get close enough."

"If we can find a ledge, you can quick-portal us from it." Daesen's smile flashes in the dark. "I promise I'll be the perfect—"

"No," Soli snaps. "I mean we shouldn't be *here*, in this boat, *at all*. If Mother hadn't run away, if she hadn't withheld us from here, we wouldn't be trying to sneak into our own *home* like thieves."

Home.

A wave smacks the boat, soaking my breeches.

She's right. Somewhere up there, Soli and I should have slept in a home and gathered next to a hearth with our mothers.

Instead, here we are, fighting to even make landfall.

The waves push us forward, toward the cliff, even as we haul away with the oars. If we continue like this, we'll be exhausted before we even reach my mother.

Grunting, we heave the boat against the waves, but the sea pushes back, ever closer to the cliff, until jagged pockmarks in the rock are visible.

"We're going to land here whether we want to or not," Daesen says, grim. "Get ready to jump."

Closer, the waves pull us, closer to the sheer rock, close enough that I release the oar and wobble to a crouch—

"*Now!*" Dae calls.

I leap forward, digging my fingers into one of the slight hollows of the cliff, scrambling to find purchase on the wet rock with my boots. Soli slaps onto the rock at my side, pasting herself to the stone, and Daesen jumps next. The three of us cling as our boat cracks against the cliff—but holds.

"I have a feeling we're going to need this again." One hand clinging to the cliff, Daesen hauls the boat half out of the waves and ties the rope at its tip to a jagged ledge.

Is that how he used to tie Lidja, after she hid a snake in his bed?

My toes curl, and I shake off the memory of the high sorceress in the dark of the hut, of the scratch of rope at her wrists, of her offer. *Ask me again another time.*

Instead, I dig my fingers into the cold rock and say to Soli, "You could quick-portal yourself to the top now. We'll meet you there."

Soli's lips flatten, and for a moment, I'm not certain she'll answer me at all. "I won't leave you behind—not yet."

We both glance at the long climb upward, from this angle so far it looks as if the cliff ascends right to the moons.

"If we make it up there," I say to my sister, "I'll help you throttle Mother for making us do this."

"Tempting," Soli says, but finally, her voice thaws. "When we make it up there, I'll consider it."

So we begin. Hand over hand, we lift and pull and reach with foot and hand from one impossible hollow to the next. In silence, the three of us climb and climb and my fingers ache and my thighs burn.

Halfway up the cliff, I'm caked in sweat and exhaustion. I cannot look down, nor up. There is only each tiny ledge of this cliff, and the very next one. Wind pushes against us, and I press my body into the rock.

"I could sing," Dae calls from a length below. "It might help."

"Or it will cause us to choose the sea," Soli calls back. "Lidja always says you're prettier with your mouth shut, remember?"

Already too hot from the climb, my face can't even warm further at the memory of that exact mouth on mine. What will Soli say, when I tell her?

Up we climb, up and up, my fingers too tired, my legs too tired, my head spinning. Up and up, I reach, I pull, I climb. Up, I reach and—

My hand finds only the absence of cliff, and slaps upon flat ground.

I release a choked sob as I claw myself up and over. I gulp in air and savor the flat of the isle and solid, sand-strewn ground. Clear, dry air scented with pine curls around me, melding with the distant caws of night birds. I blink at the bright eastern and western moon above, and flashes of red and tan sand stream through me, of tangerine and fuchsia lights. The memories of the past sorceresses of Denrathri unfold, of this isle where they lived from first breath until Orkayha dragged them away. The vision that popped when I first accepted this power rises, of hills of red-hued sands and bright bobbing lights, of whirring dreams, of sunsets that never end—all of it is here, just beyond the night.

Home.

This *will* be my new home—if we can set Mother upon the throne before Orkayha finds her first.

I help Soli as she crests the top, and when she flops to her own back, I say, "Stay." Wind pushes strands of my hair into my eyes, chilling the sweat on my neck. "Don't leave, not now, not when we've made it this far."

"I told you that I'm returning to Elektos."

"Then change what you said. Come find Mother with me."

Breathing hard, my sister wavers with the wind, and my heart leaps. *Stay. Please stay.*

She opens her mouth—

And frowns, her gaze hard over my shoulder, her hand

already reaching for the silver spear on her back. I snap my attention outward and unsheathe a stake.

In the flat darkness, a four-legged creature emerges. Two people, blended into one.

"The spear is not glowing," Daesen says, cresting the cliff at our side. "They are not enemies."

"No." Forward, the pair trudge, and I say, grim, "We've found our mother."

* * *

UNDER THE MOONSLIT NIGHT, sand sprays beneath our boots as Soli and I sprint for the two people who limp toward us. Daesen beats us to the pair and catches Vis as he collapses to the ground.

Chest heaving, knees wobbling, Mother sinks to his side.

The stakes on my bandolier clink as I hit the sand, searching for the source of blood already pooling beneath Vis. Multiple cuts leak from his face, his eyes swollen shut. His black shirt is sticky across his chest. Together, Soli and I begin to peel his shirt up—

Vis gasps, his hand slapping at mine. "*Lucius. I need Lucius.*"

"You need this wound wrapped if you're going to make it anywhere," I say. "I need a cloth."

Daesen's shirt is off before I can say another word. "If you wanted me to disrobe, needle, you only had to ask." But his face is ashen, his words flat as Soli helps me slide the shirt under Vis.

We ignore the baya's pained moan as we adjust the fabric tight around his torso.

Soli frowns at our mother. "What mistake did you make this time?"

While she's unharmed, Mother looks...off. Sickly and washed-out, her cheeks are further sunken and strangely green. "I tried to reach the throne," she says, "but I could not."

A low growl escapes from my sister.

243

I hold in my own and ask, "Cannot, or *will* not?"

The skin of Mother's cheek writhes. "I *cannot*." Her fingers dig into my arm, slowing me as I adjust Vis's makeshift bandage, as if I will be the one to convince my sister. "I told you—"

I gasp and yank my arm away. Drops of blood prick through my shirt.

Before she can run, I snatch Mother's hand. Her short, strong nails aren't what dug into me.

Mother's fingertips now end in razor-sharp claws.

Vis whispers, "The curse. It keeps her from the throne."

"The damned chair doesn't want me to touch it," Mother says, shivering as a chill wind crosses the sands. "It knows I don't want to sit there, it knows that I left this realm to avoid this very fate. It's pushing me away." Her voice trembles, whether with pain or rage, I'm uncertain. "That cold chair where my own mother ruled is rejecting me."

I tuck a final piece of fabric, but already blood is seeping through. "So you let Vis take a beating while you hid."

"No," Vis says, his voice fading. "I tried to pull her to the chair against the throne's wish. It was my choice. Tzen found me. His sister showed us the way out."

Why would Tzen's sister help? Before I can ask, Vis continues, "Tzen returned to Elektos. He will destroy what resistance remains."

My stomach tumbles. Screams and fire and chaos surround me, as if for a heartbeat, I'm once again on our burning lane.

We can't leave our people to face Tzen alone.

I meet Soli's gaze and say, "We have to split up."

"I knew we'd need that slip of a boat." Daesen mutters a curse. "I'll carry my baya down the cliff and then—"

"No." Soli squares her shoulders. "She means me. I'll quick-portal Vis as far down the cliff as I can, and I'll get him to Lucius. I can do it."

"I trust you," Vis says, barely more than a whisper, "just as I've trusted Lucius to carry my key-gate for Elektos."

A stiff wind sweeps across the sand, and my magic illuminates. A plan, sharp and clear and just as dangerous, pulses within me.

"Bring Vis to Lucius," I say, helping Dae lift Vis into my sister's strong arms, "and then quick-portal us into the palace. After that..." I hold my sister's eyes. This isn't what I wanted, but she has to do this. *We* have to do this.

"I can do it, Ala," Soli says.

"I know you can." But my pulse hammers nonetheless. "Take the key-gate to Elektos and stop Tzen."

With a determined nod, Soli and Vis disappear with a *pop*. Mother shudders, her breath short, and shirtless, Dae shivers in a gust of cold wind.

"I promise to admire you later, but for now..." I scoop up a handful of sand and whisper it into a shirt, my magic zinging with no more than a wisp of effort. I shove the newly made fabric into Dae's chest. "Remember how you offered to carry me?"

Mother frowns deeply. "This is *not* a conversation I want to hear."

Daesen tugs on the shirt, a single dimple flashing. "This is not the moment I imagined you taking me up on that offer."

"I'm not—but *she* is." I jerk my chin at Mother. "This time, we're carrying you to that damned throne."

CHAPTER 31

*S*oli quick-portals me into the palace after Daesen, gone
with a swift squeeze and a *pop*. Daesen tugs me into the
shadow of a marble column as the dizziness subsides and my
eyes adjust. Faint streams of coming dawn pierce a long hallway
studded with towering columns and dotted with darkened
doorways.

Far down the hallway, the tap of boots echoes.

"I don't suppose Lidja taught you any good-fortune spells?"
Dae whispers at my ear.

"You'd suppose right." I bury the urge to lean into his warmth.
"We'll make do without." We can. We will. We *have* to.

With another *pop*, Mother appears, Soli already gone. We pull
her into the shadow, and Mother doubles over in pain. The skin
of her neck bulges and writhes.

"Breathe," I whisper to her. To Dae, I raise a brow. "Ready?"

He nods, but Mother holds up a palm, one marked with the
same scar I now know well.

"Give me a moment," she whispers, voice strained. "I was right
to keep you far from here."

Like it has quick-portaled in behind her, fury pops in my chest. "We barely *survived* because you kept us away."

"But you *did* survive. You are *alive*. Your sister is *alive*. The only thing that awaits you here is death." Her shoulders heave. "Just like death was all there was for my mother and brother and sister."

My heart plummets to my toes. I've never once heard Mother mention a brother and sister. "You have…"

"Had." Mother's eyes meet mine, flat and brimming with fury, too. "They met the same fate as every shield and high sorceress. How else would you have their power?"

Now I'm the one who can't find my breath. *The magic of the triads follows our bloodlines,* Lidja said, *unless there is none to follow and someone close by is named.*

Soli and I weren't chosen randomly. *This* is why I've always had a drop of magic in me. This…this *is* what I was born to be.

"I didn't want you to ever know," Mother says. "I wanted my siblings to name someone else. I wanted to ensure they *never* knew about you and your sister, that neither of you would ever be hunted." Slowly, Mother unfolds, determination lining her face. "But somehow, they found out about you, and now you have their power and their burdens, and here we are. So yes, even if a life away from this palace was quieter, even if it was lived in the shadows, it was enough. It *is* enough, still."

And there, in the burning amber eyes that reflect my own, I finally see it.

"You're scared."

"*Of course* I'm scared. You're my little girl, and I wanted you to be safe, even if that meant keeping you behind the silver curtain, far from this place. We *were* safe, until that night."

The night I brought a whiplash of magic upon her.

"You're not the only one who's scared, Mother," I whisper, "but that doesn't mean we do nothing. That doesn't mean you can hide because you're afraid."

Down the hallway, boots tap, closer than before.

We fall silent, and over Mother's head, Daesen mouths, *We need to move.*

At my nod, he sweeps his arms under Mother, my silent warning quelling the protest that rises to her lips. *Later, we'll continue this.*

Later, I won't let her excuses stand—after we sit her upon the throne.

Boots tap and I lead us forward, slipping from shadow to shadow, just like I did in Elektos.

Boots *tap tap tap*—

We press into a column, barely breathing.

The boots pass by.

Again, forward, we slide column to column, heart in my throat.

Mother jerks in Daesen's arms with each step closer, but she bites her lip, and Daesen clamps his grip around her tighter.

Faster, he mouths.

To the next column, and the next, boots tapping and Mother writhing and—

There.

Between this column and the next, across the wide hallway a muffled voice rasps.

Waving at Daesen to remain in place, I dash across the wide hall and duck into a deep doorframe. A thin stream of light slices from the just-open door. Not-yet dawn light paints the sliver of a high-ceiling room in gray-blue. Massive red curtains hang from the far wall, and before them...

A marbled throne.

My heart trips.

"I thought they had fallen." Orkayha paces across the sliver of open door, and I press my back to the shadows. "Elektos must bow, or all our efforts will be for nothing. I thought he said the land was ours, the people tamed. He said—"

"He said they will be, once again," a woman answers, her voice smooth and vaguely familiar. "That's why he returned to quell what rises now."

"And yet he let Visander escape? Our brother is not usually the one who is so careless."

I lean closer to the crack. *His sister showed us the way out.*

A swath of gold fabric flutters. "If you're implying that I let our *enemy* escape…"

Closer, I lean—

The door creaks.

Before I can even turn to flee, the door rips open and Orkayha flashes before me and then behind.

She pins Daesen to the wall with a thud and clang, her hand around his throat.

I freeze, not even daring to glance into the shadows for where Mother must remain. For once, I'm thankful she's so good at hiding.

Daesen bucks and reaches for his spear.

"Move once more," Orkayha says, squeezing her hand tighter, "and I'll kill *her*." She nods at me, and two small objects at her waist shimmer silver-blue, one of which casts a further slice of gray. "Same for you, girl. Think of running, and he dies."

But running is not what thrums in my veins. Even without my word, my magic rises, easy and swift. It rustles and rises, building like a great gust of wind. Power punches through me, right to the tip of my tongue—

"If you utter one word other than in answer to my questions, his blood will stain the floor and I will make you clean it with your lips."

My magic dies as swiftly as it rose.

"That's better." The baya of Mizura's scales glint as dawn casts through windows high above the hallway. "How long until your mother comes for you, girl?"

Years. Never. Please, let her remain hidden. "She knows better than to walk into a trap."

"We both know that is untrue. If I drop you in a pit, will she come for you then?"

"Throw me in one, and we'll see." The threat is empty, but it's all I have because ...Orkayha doesn't know. She doesn't know that the throne itself is pushing Mother away.

Orkayha presses the blade harder to Daesen's neck. "Your sorceress was overconfident, too."

I stride forward before I even realize what I'm doing, a stake in each hand, my magic bursting forth, twisting the stakes longer, sharper. "If you've hurt her—"

Flames splash between us in a barrier, and Orkayha says, "I warned you."

A creature no more than ankle high and made of muscle scurries across the marble, silver glinting on its back. Daesen swears. "Whatever she asks, Ala, it won't be worth it."

The creature slips through the flames and silver flashes and Dae roars. A long, narrow spike is rammed through his boot, blood already staining the marble.

I lunge forward, but the flame barrier rises higher.

"He has a second foot still, girl, and bams hate unfinished business."

I retreat and keep my lips clamped shut, my magic surging in search of a plan.

"Tell me about the acceptance of power," Orkayha says. One of the key-gates at her waist twists, and my magic curls toward that strange slice of gray. "Tell me, and I might consider slowing the poison enough to leave him intact."

"She won't," Daesen croaks around Orkayha's hold, "Ala—"

Daesen roars as the bam smashes his second foot.

Panic swamps my magic.

"The next cut will end him," Orkayha says. "How do you accept one's power? Is it with a word, or a spell?"

I can't give her that answer. She will kill Daesen anyway. She will kill me, and then Mother and then Soli and Vis and Lidja and—

Orkayha shifts, her hand tighter around Daesen's throat and the gray slice from the key-gate broadens. I know that gray. I carved it with my own hands. This gate is already open, right into the hallway of the assembly house in Elektos.

Elektos must bow, or all our efforts will be for nothing.

And in the assembly house lives the Sancta, who has sent villager after villager to Mizura, who watched my home burn.

I will come for you. I promise.

The Sancta…who lied, over and over.

My magic pulses. I will not give Orkayha her answer, but I can give the baya of Mizura something else.

"Release him, and I'll give you something you want even more."

Orkayha snarls and Daesen's skin darkens, a blue cast on his lips. "What do you imagine I could possibly want more than this answer?"

"I will bring the Sancta to you." Daesen's eyes flutter shut, and I say, heart pounding, "And she will give you Elektos."

CHAPTER 32

I plunge through Orkayha's key-gate and land in the shadowed hallway of my own carving. The limestone walls of the assembly house are cold beneath my scarred palm. Daesen will be even colder soon, if I don't return with the Sancta as I promised.

From the windows of the hallway, clouds cast the carved truths in dusky gray. Low voices hum from behind closed doors.

At the far end of the hallway is the Sancta's chamber.

I slip a stake from my bandolier and thank the Fates that Orkayha didn't see through my lie.

Instead of heading for the Sancta's room, I sprint toward the stairs for the exit from the assembly house. Somewhere out there is my sister. I'll find her and once she realizes Daesen is in trouble, she'll return with me to Denrathri. I'll never have to confront the Sancta at all.

I round the corner to the stairs—

And hit a living wall with a single star on a clay-colored sleeve.

"I knew you would return," Minteph says.

Adrenaline pumps through me, and I dive forward.

He blocks me with that starred arm. "Do you truly think I'd let you run free again, knowing what you are?"

"What I am is no concern of yours." I dive again and stop just short of his iron rod.

"Everyone in Elektos is my concern." With the rod, he herds me back into the hallway, toward the Sancta's chamber. "Every breath of every person is my concern. Are they obeying our commands? Are they upholding the truths?"

"The truths cannot be more broken than by *you*. You throw our people in those wagons to take to the Realm of Nightmares. You've allied with a *monster*."

"I've done what I must to ensure Elektos thrives and set our people free from fear. I have been rewarded with what I deserve."

"You deserve a pit of your own." I bolt for the opposite side of the hallway—

Minteph smashes the iron rod into the wall, chipped flakes of the truth spraying us both. "You were in the wagon before I knew your true measure, before I knew the extent of filth in your blood."

The window halfway down the hall looms. Any farther and the Sancta will hear, and it will be impossible to escape and find Soli.

"I'm going to drag you out there, to the square, so everyone can see what reeks in you."

Behind me, a door creaks open.

Now. It has to be now.

"You're welcome to try." I bound toward the window.

My head yanks backward, the pull on my braid painful enough that tears spring to my eyes. I'm jerked into the wall past the window.

Pain zings through my bones as I drag my fingers across the gray limestone, across curves and lines I carved. Across the lies they made me learn and remember and tell, over and over again.

The lies they made me *believe*.

"No one will protect you this time," Minteph says. "Not even her."

"I'm not asking anyone to." With my stake, I stab for Minteph's ribs.

Minteph jumps backward, and I take that breath of space to sprint for the stairs but I'm tackled from behind, hard, my chest pushed flat against a door.

A door I know better than any other.

I buck, even as I angle the stake in my hand into the door's lock. "Get. Off. Me."

"Weak." Minteph's hand curls around my neck. "Even with that filth in you, you're nothing but a weak little girl."

"You know *nothing* of what I am," I wheeze.

"You're turning blue." He rasps at my ear. "I know that's the color of death."

My fingers slow. The stake is too straight, too long to maneuver. Where is the catch of the lock?

Harder still, he presses. "Magic is death."

Where is it where is it where—

A click.

The door bursts inward to my once-secret meeting room, and I tumble in, free.

Minteph follows, stumbling into a heavy wooden bench right inside the doorway—

I smash my stake into through back of his hand with all my strength, nailing him to the wood.

His shriek pierces my ear.

"Magic isn't death, not always, but it is cruel." I ignore his cries, and lean closer. "This is for the lies you made me tell." I twist the stake in his hand. "And this is for my sister's wrist." I twist again, harder.

Minteph pants, his face pale, his eyes glazing. "If I ever see you again, I will quarter your innards and stake your head to the scales for all to see."

"And if *I* see *you* again," I say, "I'll drive the monster-killer through your heart."

With that, I run.

Out the door, toward the stairs, sprinting past hallway doors that fling open.

To the end of the hallway, out, to find Soli.

Down the stairs, to the front door—

"Alathea."

Standing there, between me and the front door of the assembly house, is the one person I know I can't escape.

The Sancta.

CHAPTER 33

Instinctively, I slide away from the front door of the assembly house. The Sancta blocks my path outside into the morning to find Soli. A dagger and keys clink at her waist. Is there a key-gate on her chain like Tenion sought, after all?

"You've changed, Alathea."

"I have." I slide a new stake from my bandolier, willing my hand to stop trembling. "More than you can imagine."

"Have you lost your mind along with control of your tongue? Your mother should have taught you better." She catalogs the blood on my hand, my sleeve, the bandolier and stake in my hand. Shouts echo from upstairs. "When you decide to fight, you must remain vigilant. You must guard against becoming what you fought in the first place."

I should have been fighting you.

I spin and run down the hallway of the first floor for another way out. I shoulder into the third door, but it doesn't open. I race for the next door, faster, pushing.

Boots rap behind me, quick, gaining.

The next door is locked, too. The next and the next—

Above, boots pound on the wooden floor, toward the stairs.

The Sancta's hand clamps around my grooved wrist. "You will not find any unlocked doors on this floor. What did you do to him?"

Lie, lie, lie—

But I can't. Not here. Not now.

Not anymore.

"What he deserved."

"Be that as it may"—the Sancta pulls me forward, deeper into the hallway—"out there is a legion of watchmen on patrol. How do you plan to avoid them?"

"You could order them to leave me alone." I struggle against her iron grip.

"Half of them no longer listen, no matter what I say."

I yank as hard as I can, freeing my wrist. "I have to find my sister."

She unlocks a door, and shoves us both inside, locking it again from the inside. "It will be hard to find your sister with your head staked in the square." She strides to the far corner of the empty, dark room. Rugs cover the windows and walls.

"Then help me," I say. "Help me like you did that day in the forest. Point me to a way out of here."

Ignoring me, the Sancta only examines the rugs.

Boots pound through the hall, right outside the door.

I lunge for her waist and steal her dagger. "Help me, or your blood will join Minteph's on my blouse."

The Sancta holds her palms up. "I know you would do anything for her. You always have. But this…"

"Help me." I point the tip to her chest. "*Now.*"

"What else do you think I'm doing, but exactly that?" The Sancta slips away and nudges a rug on the wall aside, revealing three wooden slats. She pushes the wood inward, and a slim shaft of light cuts into the dusty darkness beyond.

"Quickly," the Sancta says. "I'll show you a way out."

257

A key rattles on the other side of the room's door—

"I don't trust you."

"I understand, Alathea," the Sancta meets my eyes, fear and something else I can't pinpoint churning in the depths. "But I know where your sister is."

For Soli, I jump through the hidden door and follow the Sancta.

e adjust; we forge ahead and win. Always. Lidja's words flow through me as the Sancta fits the wooden slats closed, locking us in with dust and darkness. We climb a ladder upward. Pressing against the wooden floor above, she opens another hidden door, and buttery candlelight spills through.

Inside the room, a bird squawks. *"Pretty. Quiet."*

The Sancta climbs through the hole and extends a hand for me.

Palms slick with sweat, I ignore her and heft myself up into the Sancta's chamber. A green bird perches in a yellow cage, shadowed in the corner of the musty room. A single ray of morning shines from a second chamber beyond this one.

"Pretty. Quiet. Danger."

Outside the door, the hallway creaks with running, shouting watchmen, all searching for me. "What have you done with my sister?"

Behind a large wooden desk, the Sancta rapidly opens and closes drawers. "She is at the rebels' house, where she has often been these last two years."

"The—" But the rest mists on my tongue.

The rebel's house.

Two years.

And the Sancta knows this. Not me.

"Where?" I grit out.

"A half day's walk, at least, at the edge of the fields with enough watchmen between here and there that you would need to go deep into the forest to avoid their patrols. If you somehow avoid the watchmen, you'll still have the loose mawlyrs to contend with." *Clink* after *clink* emits from where she searches the drawers. "And before you ask—I know this because despite what you think, despite what everyone thinks, I have been keeping the rebels alive, too. Especially now that the winged monster has returned."

Tzen.

My sister is perhaps facing him even now. Even though we agreed, the memory of him dropping her, of his claw in her side—

"Then I don't have time to waste with you." I head for the opening in the floor.

"Even when she was young, Soliana vied with you for the most headstrong."

I stop short. "You have no idea what my sister was like."

"Pretty. Quiet. Danger."

The chamber's door shudders with a knock as the Sancta slips a gray slab into her pouch. A watchman yells, "Sancta, we have urgent news."

The Sancta cocks her head to the shadowed room beyond us. "There's another way out."

I hesitate for only a heartbeat, the pounding at her door enough to send me forward.

She pulls another rug from the wall and opens another door. This one plunges downward until we're ensconced in complete, cool darkness. With a match, a single candled lantern flares.

Crouching beneath a low ceiling of a tunnel, the Sancta descends.

I chase. "Why now? Two years ago, you ordered us thrown in the cage."

"I saved you from that awful place. As soon as I heard they took you, I ordered you out."

"I was thrown in the *death wagon*."

"I came for you. I chased you to that road in the lakes, and when I saw that wrecked wagon—"

"It doesn't matter if you came—you were too late. Minteph was the one who found me. He tried to kill me. *Twice. Three* times. Just *now*, out there."

With a glance over her shoulder, green eyes blaze. "I will come for you, always."

"I don't *want* you to. It doesn't matter if you come for me if the rest of Elektos is burning." I tuck the dagger I stole from her into my bandolier even as Soli's words rise within me. *To protect the ones we love, we fight at their side. We don't hide them away.* "You cannot be for some of us and against the others. It's all of us or none."

"You sound just like her."

"That's because Soli has—"

"I don't mean your sister." The tunnel turns, and we descend deeper still. "You sound like your mother."

I itch to bury my stake in the Sancta's back. "You know nothing of my mother."

The Sancta's breath huffs silver as the temperature drops. "Do you know what your mother said when I first donned the clays and joined Emon? Talia warned me that if we went down this path, I would only bring Elektos pain. That we should fight alongside those we love to make our world better, not tuck them away."

Mother...*Mother* is the one who taught Soli those words. My stomach churns as we continue descending, cold air enveloping me. Could Mother possibly have known the Sancta? "You allied with our enemy."

"Orkayha wasn't our enemy, not always. In the beginning, Orkayha promised a way to make Elektos better and shield us from the dangers of magic. But when she burned your home"— her voice cracks—"I sent her a message that it's her turn. We won't stop hunting her beasts until every last one burns, and I've made certain the rebels are armed to do so."

"Why help them?" My question echoes in the tunnel, battering back into my skin. "Why help us?"

Why why why—

At a juncture in the tunnel, the Sancta lifts the lantern until its level with her gaze. She cocks her head again, the movement of a curious spring robin. "Because of you."

I stagger in the dark, my scarred hand landing on the cold rock of the wall. "What do you mean because of me?"

"I mean that you, Ala…you were my sunshine. When your mother ran off to her wild friends, I was the one who held you, who sang you to sleep."

My teeth chatter. My fingers, toes, heart—all of me freezes. "You're lying."

"Not about this. Think about it, Ala. How you've always been near me. I was there, that day, when everything went wrong. When the boy cried magic and he and his father were taken away. I tried to stop it, but I couldn't let them take you. Never you."

My very heart grinds to a halt, even as a long-ago memory of short hair brushing my cheek with a hush carves through me. "*Stop.*"

But she doesn't. "I've done everything I could to keep you close, even after your mother—" The Sancta glances behind us as a clang echoes from the dark of the tunnel. We begin to jog, and ever so slightly, the tunnel slants upward. "Even when I first met Talia when she was no more than fifteen, she was fierce and stubborn, like her head was made of rock and her heart of fire. We both knew that people in Elektos were suffering, that everyone deserved better, but as to how…we were on opposite sides. Even after your mother and I could no longer find a path forward together, I still cared for you. I still loved you. So I kept you near me the only way I knew how."

My teeth chatter, even as the cold of the tunnel evaporates. "You made me a truth-carver." She's the one who set me to carving those walls, right outside her door.

"You were a much more gifted carver than I would have imagined."

"Mama taught me."

"I know." She raises the lantern again at a split in the tunnel, and a small chain of beads falls from her sleeve.

No, not a chain, and not beads—a clumsy bracelet of pumpkin seeds, threaded onto faded string.

My heart stops. "Who gave that to you?"

"The same little girl who made one for Bex." Swiftly, the Sancta removes a slab of slate from her pouch, and hands it to me.

The lantern illuminates the jagged, broken piece of gray stone…

And half of a crudely drawn sun upon it.

The Sancta cocks her head again, and this time, the movement unleashes where I've seen it before, just days ago, in a memory, in my home…with my mother.

"You," I whisper. "Your hair was brown."

"I always thought it was the color of mud." Gently, the Sancta takes the slate back and places it in her pouch, as if it's precious to her. A shout barks from within the tunnel, and we're running once again. "Talia said it reminded her of the fields at the end of autumn."

Talia.

That lover's whisper of Mother's name.

Far behind us, a crack echoes.

My heart lodges in my throat and we run as the tunnel ascends and we run and—

The tunnel ends abruptly, a metal door ahead. With a twist of the Sancta's keys, the door swings open, and I survey where she's led me. Early morning light filters in from narrow windows below a high vaulted ceiling. The space within is filled with row after row of shelves of arrows and spears. They are not nearly as fine as the weapons in Memoria, but there's only one place in Elektos we could be.

The weapons shed.

"This will place you into the forest with at least a chance to escape," the Sancta says, drawing us down a row until she halts. Quickly, she extracts a box hidden beneath a layer of arrows, the bracelet at her wrist tinkling. "And there is something here that was once your mother's."

The Sancta unlocks the box, and from inside, a soft silver-blue glow pulses around a jeweled dagger.

A key-gate.

I blink, at a loss for words.

The Sancta caresses the blade, as if it's not hard metal but a soft cheek. "Your mother gave it to me, long ago. She wanted it back after we split, but I told her I destroyed it. It wasn't until this mornings that it began to glow."

This morning—after we opened the routes to Denrathri.

"*Why?* Why did you lie? Why did you keep it?"

"Because I loved your mother, Ala. I needed to keep a piece of her." Green eyes meet mine. "For all her faults, I love her still, just as I love you."

From the far side of the weapons shed, metal thuds, but it all fades as I stare at this woman.

Her.

This woman is the answer to everything—why Mother stayed in Elektos, why she left Denrathri.

Mother didn't leave to protect me, as she claimed.

She left to stay near *her*, for the love of this woman, for love of the *Sancta*.

My mother sacrificed our entire world for this woman...this woman, who loves my mother still.

Another clang rings against the metal door from the tunnel.

"Then prove it." Sluggish, faded, a plan pierces through me, and I stuff the key-gate dagger into my leather pouch, extracting the still-open key-gate from Orkayha. If Soli is truly a half-day run from here, if she's helping to battle Tzen even now, I don't have enough time to retrieve her and keep Daesen alive.

But with this woman in front of me, if she's telling the truth, if I do exactly as I promised Orkayha and bring her the Sancta, I can free Daesen...and the Sancta can be the one who draws Mother toward the throne. "Show my mother you were wrong. Help me place her upon the throne."

"You're asking me to cross the Scorched Mountains." The Sancta's face pales. "To face a being made of magic."

"I'm asking you to do what you do best," I say, and return the dagger I stole from her into her palms. "For me, for my mother, if what you claim is true...I'm asking you to lie."

CHAPTER 35

The key-gate snaps shut behind the Sancta and me as we step into a heavily curtained room in the palace of Denrathri. The high sun of midday barely seeps through the brocade.

I push the Sancta toward the curtains. "Mother is hiding in one of these rooms. Find her and carry her to the throne, no matter how she protests."

"I will." The Sancta chucks her knuckles under my chin, quick, the faintest brush. "For you, I will do this."

I resist the urge to scrub away her touch and instead dash out the small room and into the hallway of the palace. The cavernous marble hallway is deserted, only a dry breeze curling from where the palace doors stand open far down the hall.

From beyond those doors, a groan coils inward.

I sprint down the hall and right to the open silver doors.

Several wraiths tremble as I lunge through the open doorway, their horizontal slash of eyes watching me with unease. Behind the wraiths, the gray stone façade of the palace spears for the midday sun. The base of the palace is tucked within a massive gray stone itself, as if wedged right into a cliff face. I turn away from the palace, searching the stone platform for the source of that groan.

Black-and-white plumed birds squawk as they fly around the palace rock and out over striated hills. They glide past a solitary whirring cone of sand—a dream. I'm certain of it, even if it is the only one.

A dry wind blasts the platform, drawing my gaze to a narrow path that curves from the towering stone into nothing. Beyond the platform, far below, the rolling red sands of Denrathri are pockmarked by half-dug pits.

Another wind unfolds from behind me, lifting my hair, prodding me forward.

This is my home.

Even pockmarked, even with far, far too few dreams being spun...this is my home.

I couldn't stop Orkayha from burning Elektos. But here, now, with my power stirring, with the very wind drawing through my veins, I will stop her—as soon as I draw Daesen to safety.

I pace to one of the wraiths and, without uttering a word, ask, "*Where is he?*"

The wraith lifts a bony hand.

A pop of blue-silver shimmer fades around Daesen where he slumps on the platform against a wall of rock.

"*She will arrive soon, Alathea,*" the wraith says.

I don't need to ask who the wraith means.

Already, I'm at Daesen's side, sinking to my knees and tracing the blood caked at his forehead.

"We have to get you out of here," I say.

"Pfft. Nothing a kiss won't cure." But his words are slow and blurred, and his foot...the silver spike remains buried in his bones.

"This will require more than a kiss, Dae."

"Then I'll take three." Pain slashes his face. "I'm pretty much fine."

"I need you better than fine." Somehow, I'll hold Orkayha off until Soli arrives. I glance at the wraith who warned me of Orkayha's approach. "Can you help him?"

"We are Lucius's brethren, Alathea. Once the passages reopened to our realm, he told us of you. We owe him this." The wraith bends over Daesen's mangled foot. *"This will hurt, shield."*

Pain arches Dae's back as the wraith extracts the spike. I catch his head and cradle his neck, watching his foot and other wounds carefully for any improvement, but... "What's wrong?" I ask the wraith. "Why isn't he healing?"

"The poison has set. He will not run for at least a day, perhaps more."

A *day*—with Orkayha walking through that doorway any moment. I rock to my heels. "Daesen."

Dae winces. "Give me ten breaths to find my footing."

"Dae." I touch my forehead to his. "You have to leave."

"Don't send me away, Ala. Not now. I can still fight. My spear is just as strong from the ground."

"I have no doubt, but we need your spear to fight another day —tomorrow, in your realm, when Orkayha attacks Memoria, if we can't stop her before then. I can't protect you and deliver my mother to the throne. Soli should be here soon; I sent her a message. She'll help me expel Orkayha from Dreams, but you have to go back. You *must*."

"Needle, you've been ordering me around since we met in that shed."

"Good thing you like it."

"Look at you." A dimple flashes, no more than a flutter. "A regular old flirt."

"I've been learning from the best."

"You already were the best. You've just been intent on hiding it." A finger draws across my palm, across the scar that matches his. "I know you can do this. You can do anything."

"I still haven't found my word."

"You'll find it," he whispers. "You'll do that, too."

"I don't know what else it could be. It's not Soli." I've tried my sister's name a thousand times, since Lidja told me her own word.

"Maybe it's not a name at all. Maybe it's a feeling." His breath is soft and labored on my lips. "What if it's *love?*"

My heart thumps. Around us, the wind calms, quiets.

Love.

The hollow in my chest quivers. Creaks. Thumps. Wind curls around my ankles, up my spine.

So I whisper it. "Love."

"Love."

"LOVE."

For a breath, there is nothing between us but that word.

Nothing.

No magic.

But in my chest, in that hollow...a rattle. As if something is trying to escape. "I don't think it's love."

"That's all right, needle. That word can be hard when you've long been without. Love can take time." Dae raises my knuckles to his lips. Cold, much too cold. "How about hope?"

"Hope," I repeat. "Hope, I can do."

Silently, I thank the Fates that Vis kept the ship on this isle and ask the wraiths for help. Two glide forward to slide their arms around Daesen's back, lifting him to stand even as he sways.

"I'll be fine," Dae breathes, pain stark across his face. "A single shift of the sun, and I'll be ready for more fun."

"I have no doubt." I raise to my tiptoes and drop a kiss to his cheek. "I know you're the strong one."

"Truly, Ala. I'll return for you, and I'll smash Orkayha from here to Mizura. Don't you doubt it."

"I wouldn't. Not for a heartbeat."

And with that, the wraiths help Daesen to that narrow ledge

that curves down from the platform to the sands, leaving me on the slate platform in my pit-marked realm, alone.

But as I stride for the palace doors, as I fling them open and march inside, *alone* isn't what sparks in my chest.

As I run for the throne room to confront Orkayha myself, hope blooms.

CHAPTER 36

I throw open the doors to the throne room. Gray sky hovers outside the open windows that line the wall nearest me, but it's the smoke surging from the center of the room, a deep pit leaking sulfur and grime, that causes me to gag. Across the massive pit, thick curtains frame the dais upon which the marble throne rests.

But instead of Orkayha on Mother's throne, standing at its side is a woman.

Brick-red lips are framed in a heart-shaped face. Painted black lines curl from the corner of glaring silver eyes, and flowing silver-blond hair kisses her cheeks. A liquid-gold gown drapes her curves and flutters like a flame down the steps. Her dress stops in a heart line at the top of her chest, displaying a broad plane of white skin—skin I last saw wrapped in silk sheets.

Orkayha's sister, Melestra.

"Where is Orkayha?" I edge around the sulfuric pit toward the dais and refuse to ask my real question. *Did she find my mother?*

But instead of answering my question, Melestra glances at the curtains behind the throne and whispers, "Is Visander gone?"

Her voice jolts me. This is the voice I heard speaking with

Orkayha earlier. She's the one who let Vis escape—and then lied to her sister about it. *Why?* But instead, I say, "Tell me where your sister is, and I might answer yours."

"Is he safe?" Melestra's chest rises and falls with shallow breaths. "Tell me now, before my sister arrives and throws you into your nightmare."

That jolts me forward, stake in hand, right to the edge of the dais. "Why would I tell you *anything?*" Up, I stalk, until we're toe-to-toe, right next to the throne. "You're a liar. You lied about how your *own child* died."

Magic shoots from Melestra, slamming my back into the throne.

"You know nothing of what you speak," Melestra hisses, "which is the only reason I will not crush your bones right here. But I can and I will. I will lie and cheat and steal to know the truth. *Is. He. Safe?*"

Lie and cheat and steal.

Vis's words, right from Melestra's mouth.

My breath falters. Who is Vis to her? Why did she help him? "I understand," I say, slowly, grasping to put the pieces together. "I know what it is to spread lies and have them take on a life of their own."

"Then tell me," she whispers. "Please. Does he live still?"

But she doesn't deny that she's lied. She doesn't deny the lie she told that started this all.

"Vis isn't your enemy, just as Kaiden didn't kill your child," I say. "You're lying now, just like you lied then."

A small choked breath escapes Melestra, eyes wide for the slightest fraction of a heartbeat...and she doesn't deny it.

"End this," I say, low, urgent. "Tell Orkayha the truth and end this madness. End the hunt and the death and her march to Memoria. You can end this all."

"The truth does not set everyone free," Melestra says. "The

answer you seek is clear—you received Daesen because you fulfilled your promise. Orkayha has the Santa."

I brace my legs against the side of the throne to keep from swaying. If Orkayha has the Sancta...

Melestra captures my wrist and squeezes hard. *"Now tell me."*

"He's safe," I say, "because he's far from you and your sister."

"Then keep it that way." Melestra glances to the curtain again. "You don't understand, Alathea, not truly. You have no idea of the true power of *love*."

With that single word, Melestra disappears in a ball of light and magic, hurling me down the steps and to my knees. I push myself upward—

"I prefer prostrate." Orkayha throws the curtain aside, dirt and scratches across her face, a heavy chain around her waist. "I extend you my gratitude for fetching the Sancta, little wraith. She has promised me Elektos, as you said."

Orkayha yanks on the chain as she steps forward, and the Sancta staggers through the curtain, tied to the chain and wrists bound in iron links.

No one else enters behind her, which means Orkayha doesn't have Mother. Hope reignites in my chest and plans fly through me. *Attack. Run—*

The curtain twitches behind the Sancta, and a clawed hand locks on the waist of the Sancta's breeches.

Mother.

If the throne is pushing Mother away, then we'll drag her to it. My plan illuminates. *Draw Orkayha forward.*

"Your sister is a liar," I say as I back away from the dais, eyes on the baya of Nightmares.

Orkayha yanks the chain again as she steps toward me. "The only words I want to hear from your lips right now are about our powers. How do they move from one triad to the next? Tell me, and I'll grant you the same mercy I gifted to Visander and Daesen."

"You nearly left them dead." My stomach roils as I step backward again. "Do you even know the extent of the lies your sister has kept from you?"

"My sister holds *nothing* from me." Again, Orkayha yanks, down a single step. Fury illuminates her scales. "Tell me another lie yourself and my offer of mercy is no more than a memory."

Mother's whole arm is visible now, holding onto the Sancta tight. The Sancta braces, absorbing Mother's weight, and nods at me. *Faster*, she mouths.

So I say, "Kaiden never killed their child."

Orkayha bounds down the stairs, jerking the chain forward and the Sancta—and Mother—with her. "Tell me of the power!"

"They lied to you." Two yanks more, that's all I need. "They hid the truth from you."

"I will hide your tongue in that pit if you utter one more word other than the ones I want to hear."

"Your sister loves Vis." Back, I walk, drawing her forward. *One more yank.* "While you sent Tzen to torture him, she protected him. She helped him escape."

"Stop these lies—"

"She loves him," I press. "She loves him because—"

The magic of the triads follows our bloodlines.

Fates. I thought *I* was lying, but...Melestra *does* love Vis. Vis is who Kaiden reminded me of in that memory, and Melestra loves Vis. Kaiden didn't kill their child, but neither did their daughter die in her sleep, because...

"Vis is of her blood," I whisper. "Hers and Kaiden's."

With a shriek, Orkayha bursts toward me—

And Mother's clawed fingers slam into the marble throne.

CHAPTER 37

*A*t the Sancta's side, magic rushes from Mother and the throne she grips. I flatten to the marble as her power shreds through the throne room, severing the chain from Orkayha, tossing the baya of Mizura into the air and down into her own pit.

My own magic surges in response, up from my feet and into the hollow in my chest. It rages through me like a summer storm —like the storm gathering outside the palace is mine.

Like *power* is mine.

Wings rip from Mother's back, broad and shining with black and white and gray feathers. She bands the Sancta to her side.

A flutter of panic rips through my magic. I sprint up the dais and wrap my arms around her, too. "You're not leaving me behind. Not this time."

Skin glowing, Mother wraps her free arm around me. "Then hold tight, and make us a plan."

With a boom of wings, we're flying into the smoke over the pit from which Orkayha's wings flare far below. Out the windows, we fly into the coming storm. Lightning severs the horizon over the sea.

Only a single plan rises from my magic—a protective shield to lock Orkayha out.

"We need Soli," I shout against the wind. "We can't create the magic we need without her."

"Then find another plan," Mother shouts back. "One that gets the three of us out of here without Orkayha on our wings. We are ending this now."

Up and up and up we fly, to the very top of the palace.

Clay-red tiles spray as Mother lands us with a boom on the roof that spans domes and steep slants to a slight overhang. Far below, seagulls cry and the sea bashes into the isle's cliff.

Mother releases me, but her other arm… It remains around the Sancta.

The hollow in my chest shrinks. "You gave all this up for her?"

The Sancta brushes Mother's hair from her face, and Mother palms the Sancta's cheek, like they see only each other. Like they are the only two on this roof, in this whole realm, in the whole of Fides, as their lips meet in a kiss.

"I did," Mother whispers, even as she holds the Sancta's gaze. "For Jayton, I would do it all over again. I've loved her since before you were a wish in my heart."

The Sancta *tsks* my mother. "Talia—"

I cut her off. "Do you love her more than me? Than Soli? Than the whole of our world that hasn't dreamt since you abandoned this realm?"

"More is an impossible measure." Talia kisses Jayton's cheek, then glances at me, fleeting. "But for her, I would do anything, even if it means Fides is left to burn."

I stare at Mother, at this stranger who birthed me, at her power and certainty and righteousness. "Mother…it already has."

Lightning splices the darkening sky as Orkayha ascends, tiles flying with the thrust of her wings.

My magic flares as plans shuffle through me. *Attack. Distract.*

"Run," I whisper.

A blast of magic careens from Mother as she flies for Orkayha.

Jayton and I scurry from the edge toward the center of the roof. Thunder crashes and tiles slip. Jayton trips, and I catch her arm.

"Don't assume this means anything," I shout.

Jayton smiles anyway. "Never."

"Next time tell Mother to be practical and not bring us to a roof—"

Orkayha smashes to the tiles and rips me into her. My back to her scales, a blade bites at the base of my throat.

I fight, but Orkayha only presses harder, a sharp nip at my skin.

Mother lands at Jayton's side.

"What happens," Orkayha says, "when the power leaves a baya? How do you accept it?"

When Mother doesn't answer, Jayton leaps forward, reaching for me. "She's just a child—"

Orkayha punches out her other arm, a second dagger pointed to Jayton's chest.

Jayton stills, eyes on me, not stepping any closer. Flame erupts from Mother's palms. "Release her, and I'll tell you."

"Her?" Orkayha says, shaking her blade at the Sancta's heart as she presses harder on the blade at my neck. Warmth trickles from my throat to my collar. "Or your daughter?"

The blade digs farther into my skin, and I can't stop my gasp, but again, our plan illuminates.

Run. Run. Run.

Run and hide.

Mother was right all along.

It's the only way out of this.

"Mother," I gasp. But Mother doesn't even glance my way, her gaze pinned to the Sancta.

"I would require a promise." The flames sputter in Mother's

hands. "If I do this, Orkayha, you will leave Jayton alone. You will leave her and every baya of Denrathri alone, forever."

Run. Hide.

I can't bring the plan to my lips, not one word of it, as Mother's words rip the hollow in my chest in two.

My mother is choosing *her*.

"Talia," Jayton says, gaze wide. "Take Ala and *run*."

Hope flares in my chest as Mother squares her shoulders. Perhaps this was all just a ploy to force Orkayha to drop her guard. Perhaps—

To Jayton, Mother whispers, "I can't leave you."

My heart stops.

"Yes, you can," Jayton says. "You will." Her eyes find mine. "Because I choose our daughter."

With a scream that splices through the thunder, Jayton slams her body to the side, lunging for me—

Orkayha slashes downward for Jayton, and blood splatters my face.

I jerk forward but Orkayha bears down harder on my throat, my own blood slipping down my chest.

Jayton collapses, rolling. Mother leaps and grabs Jayton, halting her descent to the edge of the roof and crushing sea below.

Orkayha's blade slashes along my collarbone, and she releases me. My hidden purse snaps free and drops to the tiles. I stagger free, pressing my hand to my wound, heart racing. "Mother, watch out!"

But Orkayha is already there, right behind my mother, saying, "You've made your choice."

Orkayha plunges the blade right through Mother's back.

For a heartbeat, the thunder and lightning pause as I drop to Mother's side.

Amber eyes meet mine and in the finest whisper, no more than a wisp of a curtain, Mother whispers, "Alathea."

She crumples forward onto Jayton's chest.

And whispers no more.

With a bolt of lightning that spans the entire sky, Mother's back bows upward, as if yanked by an invisible rope. One by one, a line of blinking lights rise from her body, whirring higher and higher into a swirling funnel above.

My hands pool in blood as I stare at those lights.

At Mother's power…for which she's named me.

"*Accept*," Orkayha utters. "You have to accept. Which means…"

Orkayha jumps for the lights.

I unfreeze, bloodied palm open and reaching—

A wing punches into my side. I slam into the tiles, rolling down the slope of the roof, slipping, slipping, slipping.

Over.

I dig my fingers into the very edge of the roof, scrambling for a ledge at my feet, for anything other than air and cliff and roaring sea below.

Orkayha catches Mother's line of lights like a rope and coils them into a linen purse—*my* purse, no longer hidden under my blouse but in Orkayha's hands. Beneath my unmoving mother, Jayton reaches for me, her lips moving but silent.

Orkayha stalks to the edge. "As for you, it's time to join your sister."

Far below, the sea slams into the cliffs.

My magic flees, and what is left of my heart stops.

"You have my sister."

Orkayha lunges for me, and I—I push from the palace and fall to the sea, with only one word on my lips.

"*Soli*."

CHAPTER 38

*H*alfway down the cliff face of Denrathri as I fall, my shock disappears, replaced by panic.

I wheel my arms, scrambling for my power, for magic, for anything—

The water smacks me, hard as a slate wall, enveloping and under.

Heavy, cold, the sea pulls me down.

Down.

I kick, Daesen's instruction from days ago surging through my limbs.

But the waves pull harder, shoving from above and yanking from below. Down, I fall, the water darker and darker as I sink.

My bandolier is a rock, pulling me down.

Down,

down,

down.

The sea burrows into my nose, bleeds between my lips. My legs ache and burn, muscles screaming for air.

My lungs burn for relief.

But there is none to be found here, in the dark stillness of the deep sea.

I pause kicking, and the water embraces me, like a blanket cocoon with Soli.

Like a curtain, pulled from our home.

Like Mother's arms, warm and tight and fleeting.

Mother's blood now coats the roof of her own palace.

Soli is captive in the Realm of Nightmares.

Everyone I love is gone.

I open my mouth to the sea, and release one long scream from the depths of my soul.

The sea flows into my body, my veins throbbing, my pulse on fire, some small part of me still fighting.

There's no use. Orkayha has won.

My blood slows, icy and sluggish. Even the fire in my lungs quiets.

The watery darkness surrounds me, inside and out. All I am is this salted sea. The cold, the weight.

Deep in that torn hollow in my chest, my realm magic lives still, slowing my death, beating like a second heart. It pushes me inward, toward Denrathri, my home. Even now, my magic doesn't want to let me go.

Far ahead in the depths, a horn on a giant sea creature glimmers, a sleek gray shadow at its side. A long, mournful cry echoes through the water, and a massive amber eye gleams more luminous than the fate-stars in the darkest night.

My mother's eyes were amber.

The light from the creature's eye shines brighter—but not like a star.

Like the sun.

Soli.

My sister lives.

Together, we promised.

And so I must live, too.

I kick.

The sea pulls me down.

I kick again, harder, and harder.

My legs fall numb, and still I kick, and the sea pulls.

I shed the bandolier from my chest.

I shed my boots and my breaches and my blouse, every piece of cloth on me except for my leather pouch, and I kick.

My lungs *burn* and I kick.

I kick and kick and *kick*—

Until I breach the surface and *breathe.*

Coughing, I gulp in salted air, over and over, and still I kick.

I kick until my shins hit rocks and my hands bleed and I drag myself onto that sandy beach where Dae and I and Soli landed.

I collapse into the wet sand—heavy, bleeding, empty.

Breathing.

Waves lick my feet, and my tears feed the sea.

* * *

A COLD, slippery tap on my bare foot awakens me. Cold sand scratches against my legs. I flop to my back, and the two moons greet me. The three fate-stars shine coldly between them. Behind me, the unforgiving cliff looms upward. Mother's palace is there, somewhere, high above.

Again, the waves shush against the soles of my feet. Nearby, a pile of driftwood clinks with the rushing in and out of shallow water.

Every muscle groans as I sit, wrapping my arms around my naked shins. My leather pouch is cold and wet against my hip.

The sea shimmers, black and empty except for a speck of a silhouette where the moonslight hits the horizon. The waves roll in to the beach, in and in and—

Slippered feet and a web of black hair crest a wave.

Mother.

I run into the waves, right for her. With her wings gone, I slip one arm under her neck, the other behind her back. The sea helps me carry her into the beach, heavier with every step.

I drag her onto the sand, beyond the shore break. With the puncture from the dagger in her back, her chest untouched, she could almost be just sleeping. The moons' silver light casts hollows on her cheeks, her eyes closed.

"For once, you came back for me. Did you think it would make me forgive you?"

Only the waves answer, quiet, lapping.

"Soli wouldn't, you know. She wouldn't forgive you. Not for what you were going to do up there. Not for leaving us. She *hates—*"

A rock lodges in my chest, hard and firm. I can't tell her that. Not even now.

"Did you know that Soli has friends on this side of the curtain? She's been hiding them, just like you hid your own lover, just like I hid mine."

I glance at Mother's hand at my side, and turn it palm up.

The hollow circle and the slash through its center gleam in the moonlight.

"We all have this scar in common, you know. I wonder if you would have noticed, if you'd been there."

Waves smack the sand, and retreat.

"Do you remember that time when I came home with bleeding fingers my first day of carving? I missed the strike on my chisel over and over. I had blood all over my breeches and I was crying and when I arrived home, I just wanted you to hold me. I wanted you to wrap me in your arms and reassure me it was going to be all right. I wanted my mother.

"I came home, and there you were at our old table, sitting on the bench with a cup between your hands, and I stood there, waiting for you to look at me. To rush to me. To help me. But you didn't look until finally I said your name, and you—you did look at me then. You looked at me and said, *Go to your mama.*"

I lay my palm next to Mother's, my slash and hollow.

"Mama wasn't even home, but Soli was. She wrapped my fingers, and she held me, and my little sister told me it would be all right. She was ten, Mother. *Ten.* Did you not notice I was bleeding? Or did you just not care?

"I think that's when Soli stopped loving you."

The sea hisses onto the shore.

"What I don't understand, Mother, is *why.* I remember when I was little, and Soli was little, and you tucked us in. I remember those awful songs you sang us, about the sprites and bams, and I *hated* them because I knew they were wrong, but I loved that you were the one singing them. I loved your voice. I remember you kissing my forehead and telling me you would keep us safe, always.

"I remember you telling me to hide that day that I hurt Soli. To hide and hide and hide. That that would keep Soli safe. That that would keep *us* safe.

"But it didn't.

"It didn't, Mother, because of you. We weren't meant to be there. We were supposed to be here. *Here* is where we would have been safe."

The pile of driftwood clinks again, a larger wave disturbing its bed on the sand.

"I want to forgive you, but I don't know how.

"I want so many things.

"I want our home back. I want our notched walls and the warmth of our hearth when Elektos is coated in snow and we can't go outside. I want Mama to make that awful crow stew and you to say it tastes like pig's feet and Soli to laugh. I want to wrap my arms around your waist and my cheek to press against Soli's arms and we wait all three of us behind the curtain for Mama to come home and you jump and she screams and we all laugh and Mama shouts and she *forgives* you, because we're laughing and she loves our laugh.

"I want to curl up with my sister, for the straw to scratch our necks and you to sing us to sleep—even those awful, ridiculous songs. Baby bones and bams and sprites. Bams are awful, you know. You probably did know. You must have known.

"I want you to call me your little firefly again. Just once.

"I want you to hold me and tell me it's going to be all right. That everything, *everything* will be all right, that you love me and Soli and Mama and none of us, not one of us, has to hide anymore.

"I want you to tell me that you would never, ever hurt me."

As if in answer, a faint tug pulls me forward to the soaked leather pouch tied around Mother's waist. Gently, I pry open the pouch.

Inside, ink blurred from the sea, rests the sketch that used to be hidden in our home that I tucked into Mother's hand before she went through the key-gate. Mama sits apart, frowning, and I am frowning about all the wrong things, and Mother, she looks worried, too—probably about *her*.

"Soli says I am just like you."

And ever so faintly, so light I'm almost not certain it's true, the sketch shimmers.

I turn the sketch over and trace the hollow and line that splits it apart. The line reminds me of the trail of fireflies that rose from Mother, just like the ones that found me in those woods in Elektos.

Gently, I fold the wet sketch into my leather pouch next to the jeweled dagger key-gate from Jayton. There, together in the dark fabric, the shimmer is unmistakable.

This is one final gift from Mother, made in some half-breath between the throne and sea—a newly made key-gate.

I shudder in a deep breath. "Daesen says in the magic realms, you need a dagger to cross the spirit fields. Are you already there?

"I bet if you saw me now, on this beach, you'd tell me to stay. To wait. To hide here and wait for someone. To dig in the sand and eat fish and drink rain."

I push to my feet, and stare at the horizon.

A speck of light shines not from the moons, but from the dawn. No—from the dawn *and* a ship, its sails gleaming, as it heads this way.

I wade into the waves, but my knees wobble.

I am not swimming, then, and it's too far to shout, no matter how loud.

I don't need either.

Because this, even this edge of beach, at the bottom of this cliff, is my home. No matter what happened up there, for Soli—trapped in one of Orkayha's nightmare-pits alone—I will find a way.

I stride to the pile of driftwood and heft one of the smooth wood logs to the edge of the breaking waves.

I close my eyes and call the breeze, the wind, the magic in my veins. I pour it into the log, and it shifts and widens until it's a flat square of notched wood. It's flawed and far from perfect, but when I push it into the wave, it floats.

I tow the raft inward, half onto the sand, half into the sea, and eye the distance to the ship. It is far—very far. But I will make it.

"Lidja would tell me to abandon you here, after all you've done." I tug the wooden raft closer. "But that's not me. I need to get you a dagger, whether you deserve it or not."

I carry my mother onto the wood and tuck her wet clothes around her. Gently, I chuck her chin. "Soli was wrong. I'm not just like you. I will not waste my life waiting, no more than I already have."

With nothing but a makeshift paddle in hand and the leather

pouch at my waist, I push us into the waves and row us toward the sun, toward that ship, toward the wild manes that glitter like jewels in the dawn.

The sun breaches the horizon, and light spills across the sea.

"I'm done hiding. I have a sister to set free."

CHAPTER 39

*B*y mid-morning, the sea's waves are taller than my head and crash into our raft with nauseating consistency, keeping us from sight of Memoria's ship. With each wave, the strips of Mother's clothes strain against releasing her to the sea.

Between the lashes of sea water, my skin scorches and itches. Salt and sea is all I am, the roar of the wave and the weight of the crash.

But still, I paddle. My arms and shoulders and back ache, and I paddle. I shout. I shout and shout and shout, the promise in my palm rubbing raw.

I paddle harder and I curse the damned bam for being there on that glimpse of the ship between each wave but too far to reach. I curse and curse and curse—

A figure on the ship glimpses me, and across the waves, a roar flies. "*Alathea!*"

The sea smashes over me, and I paddle and in the next gap…

The ship veers toward us.

A sob escapes my parched lips as I paddle hard, harder,

toward that ship as ocean horses punch the waves, rushing the ship toward us.

Close, closer—

"Ala!" Five ship lengths away, Daesen leaps into the waves, like a spear into the sea.

"Daesen!" I try to stand and wave so he doesn't lose us as the waves crest and crash and crest, but I cannot. I can only grip my paddle and row harder and harder—

And he's here, hands slapping to the wood of my mess of a raft, and reaching for me, water streaming down his face, as I reach for him. His palm cups my cheek as a wave crashes over us, and we surface. His eyes blaze into mine, and he says, "I won't let you go."

A rope flies from the ship and Daesen catches it. The rope goes taut, and we're hauled toward the ship through the pounding waves.

A ladder drops and Daesen scoops me in his arms, careful of my burned skin. I moan in relief when we find the shade of the ship as we ascend.

Gently, he sets my feet to the wooden deck and turns my sunburnt back to the sea, and still, he doesn't let go. I press my face to his wet shirt and I slip my shaking arms around his waist —and I don't let go either.

Vaguely, I'm aware of the softest blanket falling over my shoulders, of bony hands at the back of my head, of a wash of relief from Lucius's healing magic.

"I saw my brethren, Alathea. Thank you," Lucius says, and then sternly, *"Let her breathe, shield."*

"I am," Dae murmurs. But he holds me tighter, and I do the same.

We hold each other like that, my naked front to his soaked clothes, until my shivers subside. Gently, he extracts one of his arms from around me, and gathers the blanket under my chin, searching my face.

A single dimple flashes. "You didn't have to get naked for me to save you, you know."

I release his back and thump a single fist to his chest and he captures it, drawing my hand behind him again, and my cheek back to his chest.

We stand like that as Mother's body is pulled aboard. Lucius drops a black blouse and breeches at my feet, a warning glance at Daesen.

A whisper of a breeze caresses the crown of my head, so soft I'm uncertain if it's the wind or Daesen.

Sage fills me as Dae ducks his lips to my ear. "I can help you get those on. Or help you keep them off, if you prefer."

I shake my head into his chest. "You are truly awful at knowing when's the right time."

But he only smiles, because I'm smiling, too.

* * *

THE OCEAN HORSES bound across sun-splashed whitecaps as we sail to Memoria. At the front of the ship, Daesen and Vis confer with the sea faerie captain. Vis leans heavily on a stout wooden rod, and long strips of cloth surround Dae's forehead and foot. After ensuring I was well enough, Lucius hasn't stopped hovering about them both.

I sip more of the water the wraith brought, and nibble on bread. I haven't moved from Mother's side since Daesen reluctantly peeled himself away and held up the blanket so I could pull on my borrowed clothes. After, I placed the blanket over Mother.

Daesen escapes Lucius and limps toward me, using the ship's railing for support. I hadn't realized how injured he still was himself, when he plucked me from the sea.

Wincing now, Daesen crouches at my side, his gaze on my mother. "I remember what it was like, the next morning, when I woke up and my mother was truly gone."

The ship rocks, fast and shushing. "I thought you were coming to tell me it will be all right."

"I won't lie to you, Ala. Not now, not ever." Carefully, slowly, like I'm made of fine glass, he wraps an arm around my back. His warmth seeps through my clothes. "With who we've lost, we will never be all right. We can only be different."

I shudder in a breath. "How did you survive losing her? Losing both your parents?"

"Some days I ask myself the same question. On those days, this helps." He folds his salt-stiff sleeves upward, revealing a scar in the shape of a flame on one forearm, a carved scar of a sword on the other.

"I didn't notice these scars that day in the sea."

"That's because your eyes were otherwise occupied, trying not to look."

My cheeks warm as the ship rises and falls. "Next time, I might."

Dae's lips twitch, and he drops a soft kiss to my brow. "Name the time and place, Alathea, and I am all yours to look at as much as you'd like."

For a moment, we remain like that, our eyes holding, the sea rocking, birds calling as the sun rises.

At the front of the ship, Vis thumps a wooden cane to the deck, loud enough to draw my attention. He limps to the ship's bow, as if he can see all the way to his isle...as if that will prevent him from looking again at Mother with deep sorrow like he had when she was lifted from the waves. Does he know that he is the descendent of Melestra and Kaiden, if I am indeed correct with what I guessed in the palace? Is this one of the secrets he closely guards?

Daesen clears his throat, pulling my focus back to the scar on his forearm.

"This is too fine for you to have carved yourself," I say.

"I am assuming that's not a dig on my carving skills, needle."

He primes his fingers to flick my nose, and I scrunch away, smiling.

"Of course not."

His amusement fades. "Grief carved them both. This one"—the sword—"was carved in the moments my father died. The flame appeared only when Vis carved the memory of my mother's death from me. In Memoria, grief shapes us, each one differently. It marks us so that we never forget."

I shrug the blanket from my shoulder and roll my sleeves back to unchanged skin. "Will I have one?"

"Perhaps you will. You can also ask Vis to carve this memory from you, if you want."

I search Mother's unmoving face. Her salt-dried hair wisps around her face in the sea wind, and I tuck it back behind her ears, but the strands escape over and over, uncontained.

"I understand why you did it, why you had the memory carved. But I need to remember this." I meet Dae's eyes. "I didn't accept Mother's memories when they came to me. I was too slow, too unprepared."

"Not even a high sorceress can prepare for a parent's death."

"She took my mother's power. She saw what happened—how our power transfers—when she killed her. She tried to catch me, to bring me to Mizura where she has Soli." I roll my shoulders back as the ship rocks. "I'm going to get Mother's memories back and give them to Soli." Mother named me, but I can name my sister. "Soli deserves to be the baya."

"Are you certain Soliana wants that?"

"She's the better of us. It has to be her. I *want* it to be her to make things right between us." She deserves the throne and the power that comes with it as payment for that scar on her neck, for me not trusting her enough. For hiding her away, for hiding myself away, when we could have been more—for all those reasons, my sister deserves better. She's always been stronger, and what stronger weapon could there be than my ferocious sister with the power of a realm at her back? "I want to stand by her side. Soli will take the throne in Mother's place."

Dae squeezes my hand. "I love how you watch out for your sister."

"She's always done the same for me, even when I didn't know."

"How can I help?"

Sea water stings as it flicks my cheeks, as the ship sails faster. Releasing Dae's hand, I press my cheek into Mother's scarred palm. "I need a dagger."

With a nod, Dae limps away and back. A heavy weight presses into my free hand—a shining silver blade with a jeweled hilt.

"Vis said it was a dagger worthy of a baya."

My throat clogs with rocks as I wrap Mother's hand around the knife and lay it on her chest. I lean to her forehead and kiss her, soft and cold and final. "May you scare the spirits as much as you did Mama."

And beneath the sleeve of my arm, quick and sharp, a new scar carves into my skin.

$\mathcal{B}$y mid-afternoon, our ship speeds into view of the green hills of Memoria. Dae has strayed from my side for no more than several leaps of the ocean horses over the waves, leaving me time for precious few words with Vis. Otherwise, the baya of Memoria has remained with Lucius and the faerie captain at the front of the ship.

With each shift of the sun, my magic illuminates a plan more precisely until it becomes crisp and sharp, like Lidja.

Like me.

Break into Mizura. Find Lidja and Soli. Retrieve my stolen purse with Mother's power. Get out.

Clouds trail across the sun, returning me to the first of three problems I need better plans for—Orkayha's army of monsters, and what we will need to face them.

Daesen stares at the green shore, brows falling with each length closer. "Rexar deserves worse than Vis's sword. The whole army does, for the damage they've done to Memoria."

He will hate one of the plans my magic has illuminated so far.

"We'll need that army well before nightfall, no matter the

mistakes they've made." I watch him for any sign of under-standing what I will ask next.

"We shouldn't wait for Orkayha's army to arrive, needle. Knowing a battle is coming but being unable to do anything but wait for it—that's where the fear grows. That's when you can defeat an army, before even arriving."

"You sound like a commander."

"That's a low blow."

"I meant it as a compliment."

"I prefer your flirtation." Daesen nods to the south, toward where the Realm of Mizura lies across the sea. "We should attack Orkayha's realm again now. Just the two of us."

"Dae..." My plan glows even brighter in my mind. "This time, we need an army. We need to bring the whole war to her."

Dae stiffens, gaze narrowing. He opens his mouth, closes it, and slips behind me with a swoop of a hum. "Have I mentioned how attractive you are when you scheme?"

A soft breath puffs at my ear.

"What *don't* you find attractive?"

"About you? Nothing."

Another breath, another caress, this time at my jaw. Teeth nip my neck, right below my ear.

I inhale sharply. "I know what you're doing."

"Oh?"

"It won't work."

"That's because I haven't started trying in earnest." Dae spins me around, and the rail of the ship digs into my back. He dips his lips toward mine, halting a breath away. "Shall I start now? Here, with everyone looking?"

"All of Memoria is welcome to watch—after we deliver Soli and Lidja back home."

Dae winces. "Another hit. Your sister would be proud."

"Don't start shying from a challenge now."

"You know I can't." His nose nuzzles under my ear. "I won't

deny you anything."

"Which is one of the reasons I know this plan will work." I push Daesen away. "This is the only way. We need the army. You *know* we need it, and *you* must lead them. It's time to take command of Vis's army as you were meant to."

"I don't want an army, Alathea. I want to rest under my apple trees, and a lazy day in the sun with you." Dae's frown deepens. "Soli has friends in Elektos—a group of rebels she told me once. We could send Tenion to find them and ask for aide."

"You'd send a girl to my home, where mawlyrs prowl the forest and watchmen crawl our lanes?"

Dae's shoulders fall. "No."

"Daesen. You *know* we need to use what we already have, as imperfect as it is."

"But half our army sided with *her*."

And there it is, the real issue—Rexar's betrayal. The commander who trained him, who he wanted to believe the best of, did this, and he can ignore it no longer.

"They will follow you, if you give them a chance."

"It took a race through half of Elektos to convince you to follow me."

I bump his hip. "That's because I'm as stubborn as an oxsail, remember?"

I expect at least one dimple, but Daesen rains silent. The ship falls upon wave after wave, until finally, he says, "The magic realms have failed everyone in Elektos for far too long. Why would anyone from there in our army ever follow me?"

"Because they are like Tenion's father," I say. "Because they have been waiting for a leader to make things right. They want what's good for all of Fides, and they are ready. They will follow you, if you lead them."

The shore of Memoria is close enough now that the palms rustle, and the insects click and clack.

"Needle." Dae weaves his fingers through my wind-strewn

hair. "Don't ask this of me. Please."

"Daesen…I'm not asking."

I watch as understanding sparks in his gaze.

From the corner of my eye, I catch Vis's nod at the front of the ship, once and firm. The few words we've spoken have been about this exact plan.

"Fates save me from conniving high sorceresses. I am tempted to like you less for this, needle."

"Perhaps that's better," I say, "for when I do something you really hate."

The ship halts, and the horses prance on the rocks of the shallows, manes shivering.

Daesen sighs. "You know this takes me further from my apple orchard."

"The apples will still be there when we return with your army."

"True. They will." He squeezes my hand. "But I have this awful feeling that you won't."

* * *

Returned to Memoria's throne room, Vis listened to Daesen and Rexar in turn before he judged Rexar guilty, stripped her of command and army, and sent her to the cage to await further judgment. Even so, Daesen didn't look relieved.

And Vis himself…Vis remains a mystery, his face a mask. Does he know whose blood he carries in his veins and has simply hidden it? Or could I be wrong, and Melestra loves him for another reason entirely?

In any case, he's the only one who can help me with the second gap in my plans—a way into Mizura. Even Mother's new key-gate won't help me arrive there, let alone without my sister to open it with me a first time.

The doors to the throne room thud behind Daesen, leaving

Vis and me alone. Mid-afternoon humidity pushes from the windows inside.

"You could stay here while Daesen leads the army to Mizura," Vis says, "if you would like."

"Your own high sorceress would threaten to cut you for a suggestion of leaving her behind."

"Would she? She stayed behind in Mizura for you." He taps a new silver cane on the throne. "What will she think of you kissing Daesen?"

"Likely no more than she's thought of our kiss." I want the words back immediately—especially as Vis leans toward me, eyes sparking.

"Intriguing indeed," he says. "What does my shield think of you kissing Lidja?"

"Probably that it's none of your concern."

A laugh huffs from Vis's lips. "You've adjusted to life in a baya's court more quickly than I imagined for being born on the other side of the curtain."

"It's not so different. Elektos's rulers hide secrets just the same."

Brown eyes flash. "Then say what you mean, Alathea. Orkay-ha's army approaches whether you speak plainly or not."

"Melestra loves you. Do you love her?" No, that's not what I meant to say. I want him to identify a route into Mizura. But now that I've said it …I need to know.

Vis raises a dark brow. "Do you love Daesen or Lidja?"

"That's none of your concern."

"He belongs here, you know. With me. At my side. As does Lidja."

"I haven't asked them to be elsewhere, not for more than this battle."

"Not yet, perhaps." Vis's cane taps the steps as he descends. "But soon, you might. When you take the throne, you'll need a high sorceress of your own."

"Soli will be the baya of Denrathri, not me." I meet him at the bottom of the steps, until we're toe-to-toe. "You still haven't answered my question."

"I do not love Melestra, no." The flat of his lips gives nothing away. "As for how she feels toward me, it seems you know more than I."

I search the lines of his face for the truth. Does he know who he is—who he might be, to her? Not the lost child herself, but one of her descendants?

"And my mother?" Another question I didn't expect to ask, but the moment it hovers between us...this answer, I need even more. "Did you know her, before?"

"Once, when I was new to this throne, the last baya of Denrathri visited us some twenty-four years ago. She came with a wild daughter in tow, who glowed like the sun and stormed like summer clouds. I was just learning what love might be in that arc of my life, and for a breath, I may have even thought...perhaps. But not since your mother abandoned her realm have I thought of her in that way. Not in the many, many years since then."

"You knew who she was," I breathe. "You knew and *hid* it from me, when I arrived."

"I knew who she was, but I didn't know you were hers. Talia left Denrathri before you were born, when I was young myself and could barely stand to sit on this cold chair. She left when her mother still ruled and hid so well neither Orkayha nor I could find her, even after her mother passed." Vis searches my face. "I see the resemblance now. In the way you lift your chin, in your eyes. But when you arrived, no, I didn't know who she was to you."

"If you'd told me her name then, it would be easier to trust you now."

"Would you have believed me? A baya, with claws?"

"I thought you had none."

"Not yet. Not today. But we all have claws sooner or later,

Alathea. We will need them soon enough, if that's what it takes to bury Orkayha in a pit of her own making."

My pulse leaps. "I thought the plan was to carve the memory from her."

"I cannot carve what she is unwilling to release."

"But…" I search Vis's face for any sign of mistaking his meaning. "You mean for us to kill her."

"Not us," Vis says. "You."

The throne behind Vis swirls in my vision. This is the third gap in my plan—what to do with Orkayha once we face her.

But to kill her myself—to grip a blade and drive it through her chest, her blood coating my hands—am I truly capable of that? Will her death make Mother's easier to bear? "I've never killed anyone before." The chisel I pierced through Minteph's hand is a far cry from what Vis suggests now.

"Orkayha has killed every sorceress before you. She has hunted me my entire life," Vis says. "She's hunted every one of the triads of your home and mine before we were born. Those of us born on this side of the silver curtain—we are all birthed wishing for her death."

My stomach tightens. "Then you should be the one to bring it about."

"I cannot leave my realm unguarded, not with my sorceress away and my shield about to follow." From beside the throne, Vis opens a box. Inside, a row of deadly iron stakes gleam. "If you strike true, she will die. She has not named her power onto anyone else, I am certain of it. With Orkayha dead, Denrathri and Memoria will reign. Our world will be filled with hope and dreams once more."

Around us, fireflies pulse. Is Vis being truthful, or simply hiding yet another secret?

And if this is what it takes to keep my sister safe—to provide all of Fides a chance for hope—does it matter if he's still hiding more?

I select two stakes and swing. They are as light as air and cut as swiftly as a winter wren. "None of this is possible if we don't have a way in."

Vis drops his gaze to the tight scar carved into the back of his hand. "There was a grounded gate, once, that the bayas of Memoria held dear, as dangerous as it was. It was well guarded in the hills of Memoria. I'm told you and my shield saw to its destruction."

"There must be another way."

"None that wouldn't require an army to launch an attack from the sea, which"—he holds up a palm before I can even ask— "we don't have time to cross. The way to Mizura across the waves is even longer than from here to Denrathri, and twice as perilous."

I stride to the windows to look at that sea for myself. Beyond the hills of Memoria, the sea sparkles in the mid-afternoon heat. A hint of silver-blue wavers to the west, the silver curtain disappearing as it ascends from sea to moons. The curtain protects the magic realms from Elektos, Dae had said.

But that curtain…somehow, the watchmen pass through it in death wagons. I rub the grooves of my wrist, and the vista from that night behind the death wagon rises in me. When I'd been let out of the covered cart, the black lakes surrounded me. The towering black mountain loomed ahead on our path…but that was not a mountain. It was the outside walls of Mizura.

Vis might be holding more secrets, but this isn't one of them.

There is another way into the Realm of Nightmares—one I was on the path to enter myself.

But it's not the memory of that wagon that rises in me now. Instead, it's Lidja's voice, the spark in her eyes. *You can get away with a lot when others believe you're someone else.*

"We need every wagon and oxen you have," I say, "and clothes dyed the color of clay."

CHAPTER 41

*T*he sun's descent is swift over the Scorched Mountains behind us, no more than a shift away from setting. Our line of false death wagons—ten, as many as we dared—grates across an obsidian bridge over a narrow stretch of raging sea into the Realm of Mizura. Deep grooves of wagon wheels and hooves are etched into the stone, evidence of too many years of my people being driven into Nightmares.

As we crest the bridge, the sea's roar fills my head and its spray flicks my skin as if to taste what it lost before, when I did not give up in the sea of Denrathri. At my waist, a watchman's rope itches. I keep my palm over my leather pouch, the interior stuffed with as many fine stakes as I could find in Memoria's weapons room. Beneath the watchman's shirt, my full bandolier over a Memoria blouse is comforting, as Dae's spear no doubt is to him, hidden at his back beside me.

Loaded with as many of Dae's new army as we could fit, oxen trudge with heavy wagons behind ours.

A wall of flat obsidian comes into view at the bridge's end, and I scoot to the very edge of the bench. At its base, a broad door is carved into the stone.

Break into Mizura. Find Lidja and Soli. Retrieve my stolen purse with Mother's power. Get out.

And if I take on Vis's ask, when I face Orkayha, I will need to kill her before she can launch her attack on Memoria. The magic shimmer around this last part of the plan...I keep telling myself it's there—that the army we've brought will be enough to approach the baya with my stakes, that I have what is needed to plunge the stake through her chest. Perhaps if I had my word of power, I wouldn't even need Daesen's soldiers, nor my stake. But without...

Down from the wagon's bench I climb, the oxen's snort huffing my braided hair. I place my scarred hands to the door and push.

The doors do not budge.

"What would a watchman do?" Daesen asks, low.

"What they do at every door." The sound I lived in terror of in Elektos pounds through me. "They would knock."

I rap my knuckles against the stone, and the door heaves.

"Weapons ready," Dae whispers to the covered wagon at his back. "On my command."

The door lurches open.

The Realm of Mizura unfolds before us.

Unlike the onyx walkways through the grounded gate, here there are no screams, no unending dark horizon. Here, a spit of red-and-gold mud oozes across the ground between hardened shards of rock. The strange mud pops and sparks, leaping for the canvas of the wagon as we draw forward. Even though the sun still hangs in the sky, the light here feels impossibly dim, as if the blackest of night already hovers.

No memories come from inside me, no words to describe this breathing landscape.

"Mother told me a story once that the Realm of Mizura breathes fire made of ice," Dae says with a shudder. "That the isle itself lives."

"Then let's hope the isle doesn't tell Orkayha we're here." A freezing, smoke-filled wind sweeps from the east. "We need every moment we can get before she knows."

The wagons grate onward. We traverse the slithering mud, every step forward colder, the smell of smoke stronger.

A few more paces, and the red-and-gold mud slopes downward with plumes of hissing steam. We creep forward, searching for what lies beyond, to the very edge of the sudden cliff.

The screams hit us first.

The steam parts, revealing pit after pit of nightmares across a narrow chasm.

From a pit one hundred paces away, a mawlyr looks up and sniffs.

"A challenge," Dae says, handing the oxen's straps to me. "This is no more than a challenge."

The wagon quivers as we cross a rickety bridge. A frozen wind spirals, and the mawlyr shifts its bulk toward us. The beast's tread rocks the bridge.

The mawlyr halts two long paces from the oxen, and we heave to a stop.

"Magic," the mawlyr rasps. "I smell it."

"We—we found them," I say, swallowing hard. "In the back."

It sniffs again. "Strong magic. I would like to taste."

"Your lady would not be pleased," Daesen growls. "Out of our way, beast."

The mawlyr clacks its claw-hands against the onyx and snaps its jaws. "A watchman does not order Orkayha's darlings."

Dae swings from the wagon to the walkway and limps forward, his gait still slow from the injuries at Orkayha's hand. "Our watchmen have spent a long day bringing these pit-dwellers to your realm. If Orkayha doesn't want them—"

"I have not seen a watchman who limps before now," the mawlyr rasps. "Why does this one?"

"A truth-breaker attacked us on the way here," I say. "Let us pass so we have time for another round to deliver yet tonight."

"The queen will be pleased indeed." Its gaze shifts toward the palace, icy eyes distant. "Pass." The mawlyr moves to the side.

At my urging, the oxen move forward once again. Dae limps at the oxen's side, my own back straight as a rod.

The mawlyr inhales deeply as we pass.

"Wait," it says.

Dae's hand creeps for the spear hidden at his back.

I meet the mawlyr's beady eyes.

"My queen says to bring the truth-breaker to her. She will spin their nightmare herself."

Throat closed, I nod.

The mawlyr stomps away.

Orkayha—if she didn't before, she knows someone is here now.

Quicker, we roll past pits of screams and pained moans. With each step, the screams delve into my skin.

I whisper to Daesen, "Not one of them deserves to be here."

"We can't help them and attack her army," Daesen whispers back. "What choice do we have?"

Overhead, smoke-monsters gather, circling. As one, they release an ear-shattering shriek and shoot for the palace of Mizura as the last rays of the sun disappear.

For a moment, Daesen and I stare at the shadowed palace, at the black façade against the dusk of night. With each breath, the air chills further.

"Hiding from what's right is always a choice." I stride to the back of the wagon and open the flap. One by one, Dae's army jumps to the walkway. "Get everyone out of these pits—whoever wants to leave. I'll find Lidja and Soli."

A hard *tug* from my midsection brings my gaze back to the palace. Lidja is there, I'm certain of it.

"I can't let you go alone. What if we..." Daesen pales as a new monster emerges far down the walkway, between us and the palace. The creature's height dwarfs that of a mawlyr; two sets of wings stretch from its side, its head hidden in the folds of a robe.

The beast angles toward us and barrels forward.

"May I suggest a new plan, needle?"

I rip open my false watchmen's blouse and slide a stake from my bandolier. "You fight, and I'll find our friends."

"Exactly."

I sprint for a walkway that stretches horizontal to the palace—

The monster leaps in front of me, landing with barely a tap of its boots. A long arm extends from the depths of its robes, and quick as a snake, the monster captures my wrist.

I yank backward, fighting, even as the tug in my gut draws me toward into the beast, and the scent not of rot but of wild clover fills me.

I stop fighting and look up.

Deep in the dark folds of the monster's hood, burgundy-brown eyes glitter.

CHAPTER 42

*L*idja's not-wings undulate from her shoulders, a length of star-pricked black fabric stretched high above her head. While from afar she blended in with the smoke and terror of the Realm of Mizura around us, up close...I've never been so relieved as I am in this moment.

Until she speaks.

"That clay makes you look like an oxsail in heat."

I yank the false watchman's blouse to the walkway, leaving me to my bandolier and black underneath. "I see your tongue has remained intact."

Faster than a blink, I'm enveloped in wisps of cloth and strong arms. "And yours is as unmannered as always. I knew you'd make it." She steps away as my heart races, and points at Daesen. "I assume you're the reason you two took so long. You look awful."

"I fought actual battles while you were playing dress-up." Dae grins. "Although I do think this is the most honest wardrobe you've ever worn."

"Cover your spear or you'll land us all in the pits. Assuming that's not your brilliant plan, bam."

"About that..." Quickly, I recount our disastrous encounter

with Orkayha in Denrathri. When I arrive to the part about Mother, I trail off. "The rest can wait."

"Fates," Lidja says, searching my face. Whatever she finds there, her jaw hardens. "This time, we'll succeed."

"Because we have you back?" I ask.

"Precisely." Lidja dips to my ear. "And if you want to avenge your mother, I will help you."

"I—" I swallow past the rock in my throat. Even Daesen doesn't know that Vis told me I will be the one to kill Orkayha. "Perhaps. But first, I need your help finding my sister."

"Then to the palace we go. I've heard her."

Heard her. I can't bring myself to ask more.

Lidja sheds her disguise, the ropes and rods collapsing like a storm cloud around her. She reaches for my waist, unknotting the rope there swiftly, her breath warm against my cheek. Then already she's away, flinging the rope downward into an empty pit and stuffing the loose end in Daesen's hands. "This way. I found a route into the palace from below."

Daesen braces as Lidja drops down the rope.

I turn to Daesen, at a loss for words, for what we're about to face—

"Go," he says, with a quick kiss to my forehead. "Good luck."

I grasp the twine and drop down into the dark.

Hand over hand, I lower myself until I touch solid ground, although nothing emerges in the black around me. Cold air whirls near, even Lidja no more than a hint of clover and citrus at my side.

"Be very, very quiet until I say otherwise," she whispers. "At the end of the tunnels, there is a door. Through it, stairs lead upward to a temple that abuts the palace. The throne room is right on the other side of the door there." She flattens my palm to a damp wall. "Whatever you do, don't remove your hand from this rock."

I follow Lidja, my palm sticking to the rock even when the

damp turns wet and the freezing ground seeps through my boots and into my bones. Drips of water ping, their echoes punctuating scattered screams from the pits.

Silent, we advance into what is no longer in a pit, but a tunnel.

Ahead, the thinnest stream of light cuts the black.

"Wait," Lidja whispers, her hand covering mine on the wall as the light grows, someone drawing near.

I hand Lidja a stake, and we crouch, ready—

A man limps into view, following a set of wraiths. Behind them, a woman, children, more people than I can count.

"Where are the wagons to leave?" One of the wraiths asks.

I point the way we came.

They hurry past us and away as my pulse lodges in my throat.

"It's a suitable plan you crafted," Lidja says, her voice thick, as she slides her hand from mine. "Mine would have been better, of course. But suitable."

"That was nearly a nice thing to say."

"You're right. I may take it back, if you don't run fast enough."

Sprinting once again, we dart through the tunnels.

"Dae worried about you," I whisper. "About what happened after we...after you..."

"Only Dae worried?"

"Others, too. Vis, for example."

A soft laugh skips from Lidja and flutters over my skin.

Just past a sharp turn in the wall, she halts abruptly.

"They weren't the only ones worried," she whispers. Her fingers curl around mine on the stone wall, impossibly warm even with the cold of the rock. "When Orkayha stopped chasing me, I thought my heart would stop I was so worried—for Daesen, of course."

"Of course," I breathe. I curl my fingers inward, around hers, even as I tuck her words into the hollow in my chest to examine later.

For a heartbeat, the promise in our palms pulse together.

Lidja brings my hand forward, my arm brushing her hip—

She wraps my palm around a cold handle.

"Your sister said you're good at locks."

I shudder in a breath and remove a thin stake from my pouch, nudging Lidja aside. With a click, the handle sinks, and I push the door open, the thinnest beam of blue light beyond.

"Perhaps Dae named you right after all."

I can't help but smile. "You should see me when I'm actually trying."

"Lock picking for knife throwing. It sounds like a fair trade."

"You're admitting something I'm better at?"

"I did no such thing." But her lips stretch and eyes spark, and together, we step through the door.

"*Liar.*" Unfolding, a mawlyr rasps from the shadows within. "I knew it was a *liar.*"

"Run!" Lidja shoves me into the wall and I duck past the monster.

The mawlyr plunges a claw-hand for Lidja, and I leap for her—

"I said, *run!*"

This time, I obey, sprinting for the stairs at the end of the tunnel. Up, I climb, toward where blue light streams from above, up and up until there are no more stairs, only a wooden panel, and I push upward and heft myself through a door—

"Hello, little monster."

Into Tzen.

CHAPTER 43

*G*ray rock floor radiates from the door through which I've climbed. While the tunnels were cold, this open-air temple imprints frost into my skin. Growls and grunts vibrate from mawlyrs and the smoke-winged monsters who line the three open sides of the temple, huddling close to burning torches for warmth.

Behind them, gray pillars rise upwards. Unlike the temples in Memoria, these columns are carved with intricate patterns and unattached to any dome. A third of the way up each column's towering height, a torch is secured, casting silver flame on the monsters below. Above the torches, the pillars spread to twice the girth of their lower sections, like massive wedges balanced on fine chisels.

Tzen opens his wings with a horrible snap, silencing the monsters in the temple. But it's behind him that catches my eye— there is a door built right into the side of the palace of Mizura.

Through that door is my sister.

"Alathea Thymisius," Tzen says. "Where did the timid little monster I first met flee to?"

"She realized she was never timid at all." I sprint for the door.

Wings boom, and I'm blocked from a single step farther.

"Close," Tzen says. "But far from close enough. Go home, little monster."

All around the room, monsters stomp and howl as I tread backward and reassess my path to the doors. There are monsters everywhere, uncountable—far too many to fight. "You think Orkayha's underlings can stop me from reaching my sister?"

"I think they will enjoy running you out of my realm." Tzen's lips part in a razor-toothed smile. "I advise you to obey their demands."

The monsters let loose a terrifying cheer, the vibration of it trembling the silver-flamed torches on the pillars, quivering the gray rock beneath my feet...

Gray rock that I know better than any other.

Gray limestone.

The Sancta's voice—Jayton's warning—flows to me from what feels like a lifetime ago, from the hallway of the assembly house. *If you strike the stone in the wrong place, it will crumble completely. Do you understand?*

I do understand.

My plan illuminates.

The monsters charge and I rush toward them—for the limestone columns behind their line.

The silver light of the torches gleams on their scales as they lunge, and I feint and dive around them, behind their bulky line, skidding to a halt right between two of the columns.

The mawlyrs snarl and twist—

And I summon my magic. From the soles of my feet, from the stone itself, magic sweeps upward, through me, around me.

A wind, a gale, a tornado.

With a flick of my wrist, my stake transforms into a spade, just like the one in our shed that I threatened Dae with when he'd first appeared.

Again, the spade shifts. The shovel's edges sharpen into a teardrop with a massive spear tip.

With another flick of my wrist, I punch fire from the end of my spear, surrounding myself with gold flames.

One of the mawlyr rasps, "Illusions. We do not fear those, girl."

"I am no girl." As the beasts advance, as my magic builds and builds and builds in my veins—"I am the Fates-damned high sorceress of Dreams."

I try a new word. *"Fides."*

The flames lick the beast's legs, harmless.

"Mama."

The mawlyr pounces and I rear my massive spade, angling it upward to strike against the grain of the limestone—

Tzen shouts, "Alathea, *don't!"*

And I drive my spade forward with every drop of strength and magic I can muster, straight through the narrow base of a column.

For a heartbeat, the impact only jars my bones. The mawlyrs close in on me, their rank and rot surrounding me—

BOOM.

The severed column collapses.

Right into the next one.

And the next.

Boom, boom, boom.

Already, I'm running back for the center of the room. I dive into the shadow of a fallen slab as each column collapses into the one next to it. Around the temple, rock crashes upon rock to the floor, and the floor itself cracks. Column after column crumbles, taking the floor with it. I curl into a tighter and tighter ball as several of the monsters scream and leap from the edge, others trapped beneath the stone.

Crash upon crash upon crash, until finally, there is only silence, and the thundering of my heart.

I unwind to a layer of gray rock dust, like the remnants of a deadly snowfall. Small fires burn among the rubble on scattered clumps of remaining floor.

I search for the door to the palace—now only reachable across a vast chasm between me and it.

A pace away, an impatient knock sounds from the wooden door to the stairs and tunnel below, the entrance covered by a cleaved rock. "Ala?"

Lidja.

I heave a stone from the door and reach for the handle—

A clawed foot lands, trapping the door closed.

"Orkayha and I have a disagreement, Alathea," Tzen says, eyes bright as he reassesses me. "She believes that hiding has made you unproven and weak. I believe it has honed you. It has carved you into something else—a weed that seeps through cracks to crumble realms. You have become a weapon yourself, like me."

"You're no weapon." I stand, chin up, and meet Tzen's eyes. "You're an overgrown *monster*."

Tzen snaps his wings shut and stalks toward me. "You are far from the first to believe so." On the remaining pieces of floor, monsters rise, shaking off the dust, growls filling the air, attention shifting to me. "But if that's what you need to believe to be afraid and flee, so be it."

I scramble backward, over the rock and spot a downed torch. The flame burns hot still—hot enough that if one of Orkayha's underlings indeed fears it, as Tenion's father told me outside that hut in Memoria, it will burn.

"You're right." I scramble faster across the wrecked rock. "I was raised to be terrified of you, of your claws, your teeth. I was terrified when you found my sister and me in Memoria. I didn't know what you could do to me—or to her. But do you know what I've learned since then, Tzen?" My hand curls around the torch. "We all have something we fear."

I whirl and thrust the silver flame into Tzen's face.

Hissing, he backs away and I herd him.

"Cruel little monster," Tzen says, backing across the collapsed pieces of columns, back toward the wooden door in the floor of the ruined temple. "Keep the flame away."

"Maybe you were right." I thrust the flame closer. "Maybe I am a little bit of one myself."

Tzen leaps backward, snarling. "A toothless monster pierces no skin."

"True." And behind Tzen, in the flicker of my silver torch, the wooden door heaves open in the center of the floor and black hair shines. "But a snake can."

Lidja closes her hands around Tzen's ankles and yanks, the monster falling face-first into the stone.

Tzen writhes, but Lidja thuds the flat of her axe into his lower back, and Tzen stills.

Monsters howl and roar, searching for a way to us.

Eyes gleaming, Lidja tosses a looped rope to me, and as she drags Tzen into the hole in the floor, I bound over and across the downed pillars, hurling the loop across the gap to the marble doors, running and—

I leap across the chasm and burst open the doors to where Orkayha holds my sister.

CHAPTER 44

The throne of Mizura dominates the room. Above, a glass ceiling reveals the black of night. On the obsidian floor, the throne glitters like the fate-stars reside within.

A door slams open from behind the throne and Orkayha strides forward, her splintered crown glowing. My purse, the one that holds Mother's stolen power, hangs from a chain around her neck.

In the center of the room is a pit, deep and dark, but unlike the one in the throne room of Denrathri, this pit holds my sister.

I fall to my knees at its edge. "Soli!"

Far below, my sister stands unmoving in the center of swirling smoke.

"She was certain you survived, you know. Certain, too, that your friends would arrive at your side. Where is Visander, little wraith, and his triad?" Orkayha glares at the open door, black paint streaking from beneath her eyes to her cheeks. "I expected you all this eve."

"You expected wrong."

I scramble into the pit.

Feet first, heart in my throat, I pick my way down the wall, digging my nails and boots into every piece of rock that protrudes from the steep sides until there is no more leverage and I skitter down the face of the pit.

I hit the bottom hard.

It's cold—so cold, and smoke encircles my sister.

From the top of the pit, white-blond hair flashes like lightning. "I found your nightmare." Orkayha hurls a smoldering orb at me—

I reach through the smoke for my sister.

On the other side of the swirling mass is not Soli.

Here, the smoke retracts and there is no pit, no stench of mold and rotting flesh.

There is only darkness.

"Nightmares are real." Orkayha's voice slides over my skin, as if she is no longer high above but at my side, her breath on my neck. "And yours is delicious."

I weave to the left, away from her touch, expecting to roll through the smoke and hit a pit wall.

But there is nothing.

Behind me, water drips. Muffled, flat.

Ping, ping, ping.

Ahead, a faint light sparks, flares, fades.

I stride for it, reaching—but I have no fingers.

No arm.

No skin, no bones.

Where my body should be, I am only shadow.

I heave in a breath, but the air floats right through me. I am nothing but smoke and darkness, blending with the pit.

In this vast empty space, I am alone and unseen.

I am nothing in nothingness.

Again, that spark flares, sudden and bright, into an arch—just like a door into a memory. Through the arch emerges a girl with red hair. She stands outside a door in the limestone walls of the assembly house, shaking her head at another girl inside the room.

A girl who looks just like me is curled inward and shaking.

"What a sad little wren," she says. "Who would ever want you?"

The girl brushes away, past me, without even a glance.

The light withers, and the shadow I am shudders.

Again, the light flares, another arch, and this time...it's Mother.

Amber eyes burn in the darkness, our wool curtain fluttering at her back. She huddles into the cloth as she stares at shadow-me, horror etched across her face as blood from her wrist drips and drips and drips to the floor. She turns and flees, bloody foot-steps in her wake.

Again, the light dies and bursts forth.

A small girl appears—a young Ala, no more than four. Ahead of her is a light-haired girl with a bouncing gait who hums a lilting song. Young Soli, no more than three.

"Stop, Soli!" young Ala shouts, ripping a spade from little Soli's hands. "I said stop!"

Young Ala raises her child hands, the wind whipping her hair up and around, rising, magic curling around her legs and arms, and young Soli screams as young Ala raises the trowel to strike—

"No!" I scream. *No no no*—

But no sound comes from me. Nothing but cold wind and shadow.

There is only young Soli, crying and bleeding from young Ala's hand, from her deadly magic, over and over again.

No no no.

I stretch for little Soli, for my crying sister, for the young Ala who will not halt even as her own body shudders and she cries and bleeds, too. "No," I whisper. "Soli—I lied. I did steal the chisel."

Little Ala stills, and little Soli sniffs.

"I lied again. I lied and lied—I was the one who hurt you. That scar on your neck—it was from me."

With shadow and mist, I stretch for little Soli's scar.

"Forgive me," I whisper.

"This is what you kept from me, sister?" At my side, the barest hint of warmth cuts through the cold, through my shadow. "This is what you've been afraid of?"

"I was supposed to keep you safe," I answer the darkness. "I failed. I failed and failed and hurt you and you bled and again, I failed. All I've ever done is hurt you."

A sob rises in my throat, but there is nowhere to hide any longer. There is nothing to hide, here in the cold dark, where Orkayha intends to kill us both. There is nothing to give but my honesty.

Through the shadow, through the mist, warm hands reach for me, and amber eyes blink in the dark.

"Ala. I don't remember this scar, because I forgave you the moment it happened."

My cheeks wet as she holds my eyes, serious and soft.

"You're not the one hurting me, Ala. Not then, not now. You're my sister, like you've always been. You're the one who would do anything for me, just as you are now."

And for just a moment, her voice carries me home. To our rough wooden floor, to the hearth, to our giggles in our straw bed. To grappling in the forest, to chasing each other through muddied lanes, and snuggling close on the coldest, darkest winter nights.

Always, always, it's been the two of us. Always, we've taken care of each other. Always, it's made us both stronger.

"You're right," I whisper.

Because that's who I am.

I am the sister of Soli.

Heat and magic and power swell from deep within the hollow in my chest. I scream and fling the smoke and shadow from my body and lunge and punch through the nightmare and I grab my sister.

The smoke splits, and in the darkness of the cold, damp pit, all I know is this hug that is my sister.

I know the warmth of her, the sweet summer scent and the laughter that lives alongside the fight, the belief in something better, even when it's hard—especially when it's hard. I know her unending clarity of the truth, no matter how buried it became.

Soli pushes away, small cuts jagged across her faded scar. "Don't stop now, sister."

I have to tell her this, too. "Mother...she's gone."

"I know." She presses her scarred palm to the center of her chest. "I felt it when she passed, like a flame went out."

"I was there, and I couldn't stop her—couldn't stop Orkayha." As for Mother's betrayal, I'll tell Soli that later, after we escape, once we're in our new home, at a new hearth, just the two of us. "When I found out she had you...I will always come find you, Soli. Always." Tears push behind my eyes. "Do you forgive me?"

"Alathea Thymisius. You're my sister. There's nothing to forgive."

This time, the tears do spill, free and light.

"I want you to be the new baya," I say, the words flowing to my tongue, unstoppable now. "You should take Mother's memories and the power and become the baya of Denrathri. You deserve it. I want to stand by your side, Soli."

She wipes fresh tears from my cheeks. "Ala...for me, it would be just another cage. Don't you know? I would follow *you* anywhere. I've always followed you everywhere."

As gentle as a summer night, my sister kisses my forehead.

My sister, the shield of Denrathri—the weapon I am to wield.

She is not a weapon of destruction.

Sun for Soli.

My sister is a weapon bright enough for all to witness—a weapon made for hope.

Warmth sews my bones into newly made things, and as my

sister holds my gaze, I see my own reflection in her eyes. A blaze reflects between us, over and over, without end.

"Last chance to run," Soli says. "We could still run and hide, if you wanted, if you asked it of me. For you, I would do it now. For me, you hung the moons. I would do the same for you, dearest sister."

My heart expands. "I can't be the dearest if I'm the only."

"That's exactly why you're the dearest." Soli beams. "It's exactly why I love you."

I kiss my sister's cheek. "I love you, too." I point upward to the top of the pit. "Now go and be who you were born to be."

Soli runs for the side of the pit and leaps onto the wall, scrambling upward, climbing where no one but her would find notches, up and up and up—

And I release my word, the hollow in my chest spilling out, who I am.

I am magic.

I am death to anyone who hurts my family.

I am me.

"ALATHEA."

CHAPTER 45

y magic bursts Soli into the weapon she's always been.

My sister, the sun.

The glass ceiling trembles and the entire pit collapses into nothing. Swearing, Orkayha tumbles forward, the splintered crown flying from her head and rolling to a stop at my feet.

This was no pit at all, but only a nightmare.

Chest barely moving, Soli lies five paces away. Orkayha kneels on the floor, shoulders wracking. Streaks of black shadow from her eyes, tracks of tears fresh through the paint, grief and rage etched across her face...tears and pain that have whipped through myself enough times in the last days to recognize as I rip a splinter free from the fallen crown.

She finally knows the truth.

"You spoke with your sister about her lie," I say, and stalk toward the baya of Mizura.

Orkayha's shoulders heave, but she doesn't deny it.

"You must have seen the truth before now. Perhaps it was just easier for you to hide behind the lie than face the truth." I halt less than a half-step from her. "The truth is that you've spent *centuries* killing the children of your own blood."

Orkayha's shoulders still, and she raises her gaze to me. Fury and pain burn in her eyes and she flicks her wrists—

I stab the splinter from her own crown through the stolen purse at her neck.

A line of flickering lights escapes. Upward, the lights soar, twirling like a rope lined in flame, up and up and up—

I leap to greet the line as they plummet for me.

Pulsing lights burst into my chest, one after the other, filling me fast and full. Memories pour into me, cleaner and brighter than any flame. They dive through my blood and pierce my marrow.

One after another, the memories flash, sunny and sweet and warm.

Mother, tucking hair behind my ear the night before she left, before everything changed. *One day, you'll understand.*

A smile on Jayton's face, a soft whisper of love.

My little fireflies.

Mama. Mother. Their arms around me, around Soli, around us both, weighted with love.

One after the other, the lights smash into me, burrowing into my skin.

Through the memories, one light shines brighter than all the rest, undeniable.

The truth.

I punch out an exhale, my heart restarting, reforming, and new words blast from my lips, loud enough to be heard in every corner of Fides.

"I am the baya of Dreams."

CHAPTER 46

The throne of Mizura cracks behind Orkayha, and the glass ceiling above the throne room heaves. Soli crawls toward me, recovering from our magic.

"The truth, new baya," Orkayha says, scales quivering, "is that I, too, have grown weary of hiding who I really am."

With a boom, Orkayha's scales writhe.

One vertebra at a time, she straightens, unbending, uncurling —and she explodes into a monster of wings and claws and spikes.

The transformation blasts through the room, hurling Soli and me backward. I slam against the obsidian floor, gasping as my bones thud. Paces away, Soli clutches her head.

Like the surface of the moonlit sea, my skin quivers, too.

Behind the broken throne, Orkayha occupies almost a quarter of the room, her tremendous body of onyx and smoke and cerulean scales flickering. Behind her heaving, massive torso, a spiked tail cracks the ground. On her reptilian head, a crown of horns gleams—a queen of monsters.

Orkayha thrusts her spiked tail through the hall with a blistering swipe.

"Move!" I shout, racing for my sister, pulling her upward and away. We sprint for the open door to the destroyed temple—

Orkayha unlocks her colossal jaw and releases a stream of fire.

I whisper my name, and with a burst of magic, my own body reshapes. I expand and burst, my skin stretching as I slam onto the hard floor, long and lean and strong.

I am the baya straining across the three vessels from Vis's room, a winged creature holding the truths and breaking them, impossible to ignore. I am the one to be feared now.

I roar, and the very walls of the palace of Mizura tremble.

Again, I roar.

Orkayha snaps, her scales convulsing.

My scales flame gold and red and burnt orange, just like the brilliant light that burst from Soli. I pound my clawed feet into the obsidian and knock Orkayha into the throne.

I roar and spit flame to the roof bright enough that every last being in Fides could see.

"Yes!" My sister thrusts her fist in the air. "Again!" She runs for me, ready for another command.

Orkayha's spiked tail smashes through the hall—

Right into my sister.

For a moment, every other sound disappears.

I thunder to my sister's side as blood streams from a hole in her jillbracer, just beneath her shoulder, and she falls to her knees.

"I may be the sun," Soli grits out, paling too fast, "but you can show her a Fates-damned storm."

"Promise me," I rasp, "you will not leave this plane."

With a pained smile, Soli meets my monster eyes and whispers, "I promise."

Her body slumps, unconscious.

I roar and roar and heave fire in an unending trail of rage and flames at Orkayha.

"To Memoria!" Orkayha screeches, and launches upward through the glass ceiling. Glass rains upon me as I block the shards from hitting my unmoving sister with a wing. Through the open roof, a flock of smoke-monsters take flight behind Orkayha.

I punch upward after her, as if I am lightning itself, and chase.

I chase for my sister, for my mother, for every being in Fides who has been taken to these pits, who has lived their life in fear.

For me.

Vis was right. The baya of Mizura must die, and it will be at *my* claw.

I tear after Orkayha through the night, under the moons, over her empty realm. I smash through lines of her flying monsters as the magic within me gathers and builds and pulses until I release it in a single burst of a screech, from my claws and wings and every scale of my monster skin.

The storm smashes into Orkayha and hurls her downward. She whirls toward me, and I meet her in midair in a clash of claws and jaws and scales.

A mess of fire and slashes, we fall downward, downward toward the edge of her realm, even as bolts of lightning erupt from my scales to tear at hers.

Down, down, we scratch and bite and fall until the wall at the edge of Mizura looms, the bridge to Elektos snaking outward from her realm to my home. I reel my magic in tighter, harder into my chest.

"They will see you," Orkayha rasps. "Everyone will see you for what you truly are." She sinks her teeth into my monster arm.

Pain rips through me and my scales waver as we plunge for the bridge—

"Let them." I will never, ever hide again.

I whisper my name and my magic smashes Orkayha down into the bridge just as I pull upward to the sky.

The bridge shatters under her weight and collapses inward and down under the waves, wind and stone and lightning pushing her ever downward, down into the black sea.

I fly up, higher and higher into the night sky, until not even the moons' shadows can touch me, bright as the sun myself.

CHAPTER 47

*B*right day blooms in Memoria. In the jungle beyond Vis's garden, birds call and insects yammer in the morning sun. Fireflies float on the late summer breeze. Inside the palace, Soli continues to heal, unconscious still. Several rows away from me in the garden, obscured by towering magenta lilies, jeweled dagger in hand, lies my mother.

Has Mama heard somehow that Mother has passed on? Was she outside that night two days ago, when I flew under our moons?

My gaze draws across the green hills of Memoria, to where the Scorched Mountains rise beyond the curtain. What do the people of Elektos think now that they must know monsters roam the sky as well as our lands?

The pebbles of the garden path crunch beneath a cocky stride.

"I'm surprised you're not at your sister's side," Daesen says.

Even without turning to face him, the heat of his gaze flits across my cheeks, my neck, as it has ever since he and Lidja dragged me back from Mizura, bleeding and naked but victorious, my unconscious sister in my arms.

"She'll wake up soon enough," I say. "She promised."

I catch a flare of Dae's dimple. "Lucius kicked you out, did he?"

I whack his arm with my fist, and his smile grows. "She'd throw me out anyway, if she knew I was hovering."

But in truth, I haven't been hovering. She promised, and this time, finally, I believe her, and that belief feels like the warmth of the sun in my chest. Every day, the rose hue grows under her skin. Any moment now, she'll awake, and together, we'll journey across the sea to Denrathri and we'll claim our pit-marked realm. We'll find Jayton and face the truth of what she is to my sister and me.

One by one, we'll build a new set of truths for our new home.

The truth is that it will be far from easy, but we'll face it together.

Truth one. I don't need to hover, not anymore.

I punch Daesen again, for good measure. "You're the one who can't seem to stop hovering."

This time, he grins, sheepish and broad, before the mirth fades from his handsome face. "That's because you're not the one who picked up the pieces of you two from that bridge." His gaze trails to the scars on my forearm.

The line rests near my wrist, the scar from Mother's death that formed on the ship to Memoria. At the end of the memory scar, where Orkayha's monster teeth splintered my own monster arm, the puckered skin looks like a sun.

Not that I needed a physical reminder of that moment, of our tumble downward, of her sinking beneath the weight of that bridge into the sea. When that moment overtakes me and darkness claws, I reach for the comforting truth that lives side by side with Orkayha's death—her power remains buried beneath the waves, nameless, her realm destroyed.

"I'm here," I say, my palm resting flat on his forearm. "Until my sister wakes, I'm here."

"I wouldn't be so certain," he says, "which is why I brought you something. An apology, for not warning you about..." He makes a claw of his fingers, a sheepish look on his face. *There are no beings with claws in our realm, Ala.* "I'm sorry that I didn't know, that I couldn't warn you what you could become."

"Do you mind that I have them?" Even now, the claws poke under my fingertips at the mere thought.

Daesen brings his hidden palm forward and tosses me a red apple.

I punch my finger into a claw, impaling the fruit on instinct.

Slowly, hesitant, Dae approaches me and removes the apple, and my claw retracts. Carefully, he raises my finger to his lips, and licks. "I think they'll prove quite useful, pine needle, for what's next."

"What's next is me being ill if you two don't stop mooning." Lidja bumps Daesen aside with her hip. "I need a moment with the newest baya."

Dae drops my finger, slowly, a brow lifted at the sorceress. "Jealous?"

Lidja whispers a single word and a flower in her hand unravels into a snake.

Dae leaps backward a step, two, into a bed of purple and orange flowers. Petals float around the shield, like a summer snow. "I'll be right over here."

Lidja's snake hisses, and Dae hustles farther away, toward the palace.

The snake slithers into the flowers, gone.

"Was that necessary?" I ask, the corners of my lips drawing upward.

"Sometimes fun is necessary," Lidja says. Her gaze remains on the shivering flowers. "I've been thinking of you."

For a moment, I am not certain I've heard correctly. "Did you hit your head in Mizura?"

Her lips tick, ever so slightly. "Possibly. Fates only know why else I feel like I can't keep this inside any longer."

My heart knocks. "What, exactly?"

"I was lying before. To myself. To you."

"That's what you do. You lie. You cheat and steal. You do what you need, to get what you want."

"No." Lidja frowns, running fingers through her hair, the swish of the strands falling perfectly about her shoulders. "I mean, yes. It is. But not about this. Not about..." she huffs out a long sigh, and finally lifts her eyes to mine. "I haven't moved on. That woman, the first baya from the memory I told you about...I love her still. That memory of her, of how the first high sorceress loved her, even though it wasn't me, even though the memory is not mine—it's what's shaped me."

"Oh." I search for another response, for something more over the hammering in my chest, for the sudden spike of anticipation in my veins. What is she telling me?

Lidja licks her lips and continues. "I believed falsehoods. Or half-truths, maybe. But it's no excuse for not seeing what was before me."

"And what, exactly, was before you?"

"You, of course. *You.* You look so much like her. Sometimes so much like her, it slays me."

"Lidja..." But I don't know what to say, or how to feel. This high sorceress, who I believed from the start was looking at me only in hate...her eyes flash, and now I see it.

Not hate. Not really.

Loss.

And I remind her of it.

A constant prickling of blinding, searing loss.

Suddenly, the constant lash of her tongue changes shape—not a lash at all, but a rope of sorrow binding her to me.

Whatever she feels for me, it isn't hate. It never was.

As for believing something untrue...

Tentative, I reach my palm to the plane of her cheek, my scar rough against her smooth skin. Our promise pulses in my hand.

331

"I'm the one who's been an oxsail, Ala." Leaning into my palm, her eyes blaze. "Not you. Never you."

We stare at each other, the silence stretching between us until she shifts her cheek against my palm so that her lips nearly touch my fingers. Slowly, slowly, she grasps my wrist and brings it away.

"Ala," she breathes. "There's more."

My heart thumps once, like it did in that dark hut, when her lips hovered near mine, and I kissed her silent. Her eyes shine, her breath warm and close.

I press a finger to her lips. They're so soft that I wonder if I'll leave a fingerprint when I pull away, if that kiss we shared in the dark of the village hut left a mark on her, as it did me. "I thought of you, too."

"I—"

A hard object bowls into my upper arm, and Lidja spins, rubbing her own. Two apples lie on the garden path at our feet.

Dae tosses another in the air, grin broad. "I thought you two might be hungry."

Hand to her hip, Lidja says, "Now who's jealous?"

"I'm not—"

"Enough," I say. Stepping between the two, I place a palm on each of their shoulders. For a heartbeat, sage and salt wraps around me, light and easy, a promise of how it would be with Daesen, if I were to tilt his way. And on my other side, wild clover and citrus drifts across my skin, the depths of the high sorceress unknown. With her, it would not be easy, but...

"I heard you have a message." Vis strides from the open balcony doors of his room across the pebble path into the garden, confident, healed with a slight limp, the silver cane his constant companion now. He stops at the three of us, a frown on his handsome face.

The last two days, Vis and I have wandered the paths of his garden. Sometimes in silence, sometimes me prying at the secrets he still holds. Even with Orkayha dead, he has not shared another word about Melestra, not if he knows whether Melestra resides in Mizura still or has fled elsewhere, nor about his own bloodline. He answers each prod of mine with a poke back. He may know that he is the line of the Fates' prophesy, proof of the bayas' defiance, or he may know where it truly resides. Either way, Vis continues to keep some secrets from me, I am certain.

What he has shared is pieces of what it means to be a baya. That the beast I became for that moment in Mizura...until I touch the throne of Denrathri as Mother did, the monster inside will try to claim me.

What message can be worse than that?

"There *is* a message," Lidja says, stepping away from us all, lips tight, all sign of that moment between us gone. "But not for you. For her."

My stomach sinks. "What message?"

"Last night, we heard a new rumor from Elektos." Lidja crosses her arms, and Dae shifts his feet, as if he'd like to be anywhere else as the sorceress continues.

I'm tempted to hit him again, harder this time. He knows what this message is and didn't tell me.

"They believe the Sancta is gone," Lidja says. "They think she was killed by the monster that filled the sky."

This is my answer, then. The people of Elektos think I'm a monster and a killer, even if they don't know it's me.

And they wouldn't be wrong—not about that part, at least.

"The Sancta lived last I saw," I say, recalling the reach of her hand as I released the roof of the palace to fall. As to whether she deserves to live after all she's done against the people of Fides, no matter her twisted version of who we were...I'm not certain.

"When has truth ever mattered to your home?" Lidja says.

With a pointed cough, Daesen glares at the high sorceress. "What Lidja is trying to say, needle, is that...well...Elektos is preparing for battle."

Vis's gaze sharpens. "Battle against who?"

But even before they answer, I know. Of course I know. I believed this enemy was mine, too.

"Here," I say. "Against the monster. They're going to attack the magic realms."

"The rumor is that they are gathering the watchmen at the base of the mountains to prepare for the assault," Lidja says, then hesitates. "Unfortunately, there's more. Worse."

"What could be worse than that?"

Daesen shifts his feet again, arms folding across his chest, still not looking at me. "Ala, I'm sorry."

"Tell me."

"The last part of the rumor…" Even Lidja looks uncomfortable as her gaze meets mine. "Your mama is leading them."

NOT READY TO LEAVE THE MAGIC REALMS?

REVIEWS MAKE ALL THE DIFFERENCE FOR NEW AUTHORS

Thank you for reading my debut book! I hope you enjoyed reading it as much as I enjoyed writing it.

If you enjoyed this book, would you consider leaving even a brief review on Amazon? Every review makes a huge difference in getting this book noticed—ultimately helping me write more books for you to read!

In the meantime…

SOMETIMES THE ONLY WAY TO
STOP A WAR BUILT ON LIES IS BY
FAKING A BETROTHAL.

Book 2 of the Realms of Magic is coming Spring 2024!

In the meantime, I love making new book friends. Feel free to drop by my website at www.siennaarcher.com for the latest on when my next books are releasing and to find me on social media.

ACKNOWLEDGMENTS

I am incredibly grateful for my sisters, both those who I grew up with and those who have joined the family through my brothers' good decisions, as well as the sisters I've found over the years in sometimes the least likely of places. Thank you for reading the many drafts of this book and the one that came before it, for your encouragement, for your hugs, for bearing with me through all the book talk, and for the many laughs and unending love and support.

Thank you to my family and friends for believing in me and encouraging me through this process.

Thank you to Marissa Graff for her incredibly thoughtful edits that changed my writing for the better forever. I really wouldn't have made it here without you. Thank you to Misty Morgan for her excellent line editing, and Misha Kydd for her superior proofreading. I am forever thankful to Seventhstar Art for creating a cover I'm completely head over heels in love with.

And, as always, I'm so grateful for Savannah Wolfe, Piper Knight, and the other Paranormal Beans without whom I would have remained no more than a floor puddle many times during the last several years. It's been a joy meeting new members of Team Archer, and to each of the kind readers who beta-read this book and made it better—thank you. Dreams can come true, when you find the right friends to cheer you along the way.